Bonjour, Sophie

ALSO BY ELIZABETH BUCHAN
FROM CLIPPER LARGE PRINT

I Can't Begin to Tell You

Bonjour, Sophie

Elizabeth Buchan

W F HOWES LTD

This large print edition published in 2024 by
W F Howes Ltd
Unit 5, St George's House, Rearsby Business Park,
Gaddesby Lane, Rearsby, Leicester LE7 4YH

1 3 5 7 9 10 8 6 4 2

First published in Great Britain in 2024 by Corvus, an
imprint of Atlantic Books Ltd.

Copyright © Elizabeth Buchan, 2024

The right of Elizabeth Buchan to be identified as
the author of this work has been asserted by her
in accordance with the Copyright, Designs and
Patents Act, 1988.

A CIP catalogue record for this book is available
from the British Library

ISBN 978 1 00415 937 6

Typeset by Palimpsest Book Production Limited,
Falkirk, Stirlingshire

Printed and bound by
T J Books Limited in the UK

For Annie, Belinda and Margot, maids of Kent

PROLOGUE

The dying Camille talked to her seven-year-old daughter.

'We had to fight but I never imagined that I would relish being a warrior. Your father was one too, and a hero. One day you will go to Paris and find out what happened to him.'

She was silent for a while. 'Fighting for your country is important. Very. I believed in it. Not everyone did. But there's something even more important.'

Sophie held hard onto Camille's hand.

'I was at liberty as a woman to risk my life for my country if I chose to do so.'

PART ONE

PART ONE

CHAPTER ONE

The times she had peered through the window of the school library at the rain lashing the trees and silvering the drive, counting the terms until she left.

'This isn't life.' Spreading her fingers across a pane, deliberately leaving smudges. 'But where do I find it?'

Life. The great enterprise as she had decided to call it. She had no idea of the answers. Had no one to consult. Or rather, no one she wished to consult.

What she did understand from her reading (and many books left her baffled) was that to be alive was complicated. Also, life was often shatteringly cruel and unfair, especially if you were female, and it almost always presented an enigma.

The years of boarding at Digbys School had been spent wrapped in perpetual cold. A chill that conquered soul and body and scythed merrily through regulation liberty bodices and navy knickers and specialised in torturing chilblains. Years of a regime driven by a belief that girls were intrinsically weak and easy to tempt. Governors and teachers were clear on this point.

Sophie was sceptical.

Why, she wished to know, was it that walking down the street in an unbuttoned coat was to invite a fate worse than death? Why would the novels of D. H. Lawrence result in abject corruption?

Years of being told that every sentence must have a subject, an object and a verb, and subordinate clauses that must agree.

Sophie was not going to obey that one. Words were for play, for tossing into the air. Words equalled liberty.

Years of a school ordinance that denied life was a gift – allied with the danger, the mortal danger, of beginning to believe in it all.

She would also contend (until Hettie, her beloved Hettie Knight, insisted it was rubbish) that most pupils left Digbys, the frightful school hats still welded to their heads, with minds as fresh and untouched as the day they'd entered the place.

'You've learnt *something*,' said Hettie. 'Be honest.'

Her final day at Digbys had dawned. *A bas les profs*. *A bas school games*. (Especially lacrosse. And gym. And cross-country running.) Sophie took refuge in the library, where Miss Chambers, head-mistress, American Civil War obsessive and doughty adversary, cornered her.

A spare figure in the dark green crêpe dress – exhumed from the wardrobe whenever she had to see parents. Glasses dangling around her neck.

4

'I wanted to have a word, Sophie Morel. You're a moody child. *Very* moody. I'm here to tell you that being moody is not at all interesting, just tedious.' She touched the hair coiled at her nape. 'There's no need to look at me like that. I've observed you often and I wanted to make sure that you understand where your duty lies.'

'Where does it lie, Miss Chambers?'

'In working hard for your adoptive father's parish. He's relying on you.'

Sophie almost choked.

'Self-indulgence is a sin.'

Her need for solitude. Anxiety about the future. Sadness that arrived at the wrong times . . . all wrapped up into an insecure bundle. It could, she supposed, be termed self-indulgence.

'A life of service . . .' Miss Chambers warmed to her theme, 'is the best we can wish for.' She gestured with both hands, revealing that the elbows of the crêpe dress had been patched. 'It is a gift not given to every girl.' The zealot's light in her eye imitated a car's headlamps. 'Our generation accepted it. So must yours.'

The school library would never be called inclusive. Yet its scope was sufficient (here Hettie was correct) for Sophie to have discovered from its volumes that there were levels of understanding of any one thing. That beauty was relative, and many perils ringed humanity.

'Perhaps,' she said.

'Not perhaps,' countered Miss Chambers.

5

Sympathy . . . well, a sliver . . . for the older woman watered down Sophie's indignation. Miss Chambers had a top tragic story. She had waved a fiancé off to the war from which he had never returned, leaving her to become another statistic. Drama. Heartbreak. Love . . . each year a new set of girls feasted on it, embellished it, including the tear-inducing (almost certainly mendacious) detail of Miss Chambers searching for his remains on an Italian battlefield. 'Obviously,' said Hettie, 'she had to find some way of making her life mean something. There's a limit as to how many times she can read the Gettysburg Address.'

Hettie was of the belief that the state of matrimony was the Alpha and Omega.

Sophie was not.

Her views on marriage derived from observing her adoptive parents, the Knoxes. 'Do husbands and wives,' she consulted Hettie, 'always sleep at opposite ends of the house? Osbert and Alice do.'

Hettie was unsure, offering up only that her father was particular in his habits and had a separate bathroom. Did that make things clear?

'All the same,' said Hettie, who, as the time to leave Digbys grew closer, was increasingly preoccupied with romantic love (the bliss) and marriage (settled status, a house, a porcelain dinner service). 'It must be awful to have no love.'

Sophie thought she would settle for someone who greeted her in the mornings.

'The Reverend Knox,' Miss Chambers was

saying, 'may not be your father but he and Mrs Knox have spared no effort and expense to give you a good, solid foundation. You will be working alongside them to help out in the parish.'

Sophie possessed no solid qualifications, partly because of the paucity of Digbys' academic ambition for its girls, partly because she had been either too angry, too sad or too contrarian to extract anything that might have been useful from the dull lessons. Yet, as she wrote in her private notebook, this did not mean she was stupid. It did not mean the emptiness she so often experienced would not be filled.

Miss Chambers was growing impatient.

Digbys had been founded with the best of intentions, which was to give girls of good families, but slender means, an education. The staff strove to provide it, and no one doubted the governors, but without a substantial endowment it was always going to be an uphill battle. Equipment and resources were limited. Many of the staff appeared to suffer from low spirits.

'We did our best for you, you know,' said Miss Chambers.

Now or never.

'But girls don't get the best. What you teach us is less . . . strong, less ambitious, than what boys are taught.'

Miss Chambers flushed painfully but did not disagree.

'What about science and logic and proper mathematics? Learning to argue.'

'Sophie Morel, you don't know what you're talking about.'

'Isn't that the point, Miss Chambers?'

'What you've had here is better than thousands of children in this country have had. You would do well to remember that.' The fob watch pinned on her bosom rose and fell. 'Time to go.' A raised, expectant eyebrow.

Rebellion now ignited.

After all, and after everything, Miss Chambers was expecting to be thanked. But six years of rage and despair had blunted finer feelings, *softer* feelings, and Sophie had no thanks to offer.

A final glance at the window where she had dreamed and yearned. For what? She was never sure.

Turning to look back at the door, she saw her ingratitude had found its mark on Miss Chambers' unpowdered, disappointed features. At the last minute, not so much pity but manners triumphed. 'Thank you, Miss Chambers.'

Hettie was waiting on the steps leading up to the school entrance when Sophie emerged through the doors, carrying her suitcase. 'You're late.'

Younger girls clattered past down the steps and ran to greet waiting parents. Dazed, perhaps, at the prospect of their adult lives now upon them, some of the leavers took the steps more slowly. Some of them, Sophie noted with incredulity, wept.

Hettie had changed into what Hettie's mother

called a costume. Light grey flannel skirt and matching jacket, the lapel of which sported Digbys' leavers badge, plus a virginally modest string of grey river pearls. Stockings and lace-up shoes replaced the regulation sandals and long socks.

But for the perm, Hettie had turned into her mother.

'You look nice,' said Sophie, adjusting to this new version of her friend.

'I'm sorry you don't have anything new.' Hettie was embarrassed. 'I wish I could buy you a frock.'

This was Hettie all over. Generous, and wishing things to be well and plentiful but without the means to achieve these goals. Neither of them had any money. The well-off Maurice Knight had promised an allowance to his daughter when she left school, but not quite yet, so there was no help there. Sophie had no money at all. *Dommage*, as she had learnt from Camille, her French mother.

'I'll send you a frock. Then a rich man will see you. Fall in love. Marry you and take you to Paris.'

Sophie was eighteen, would be nineteen in September – 'Autumn babies are the best,' said Camille. 'Harvest babies.' Hettie was about to be eighteen. Both knew they were infants in worldly experience. Talking, talking endlessly about the next big step, they had not the least idea how to take it.

Sophie made the usual answer. 'I won't be needing clothes, remember?'

The joke was that, on leaving, Sophie would join

a nunnery, thereby solving the conundrum of her future.

'Think of your knees,' said Hettie. 'All that praying will turn them into soup plates.'

The Knight parents, having greatly economised on their daughter's education, were planning to launch Hettie into the London season and to spare no expense in finding her a suitable husband. '*You* will need frocks. Lots of 'em,' said Sophie.

Hettie bit her lip. 'It's so unfair.'

Sophie would give much not to distress Hettie. 'Don't worry about me,' she said, heroically cheerful. 'I'll try and get a job. Or, I'll write poetry and develop into a mathematical genius.' She sobered. 'Don't dread the future, Het.'

'I do and I don't,' said Hettie. 'I want to get married and have children.' Uncertain note. 'It's just the process of getting there.'

This was to skirt the unmentionable subject of men and the details of what they did to you in bedrooms. However, their combined knowledge of the opposite sex barely covering a postcard, this was not going to be a productive conversation.

'We must closely observe men,' said Sophie. 'They can't be that different.'

'Yes, yes, we must. And compare notes.'

Liddy Barnes passed them with the laurelled expression of the top-form bully (worn for all her school career) still in situ on her plump, rather spiteful, features and called out, 'Byeeee.'

Sophie looked away. Once . . . no, twice . . .

she had stolen chocolate from Liddy's tuck box. Liddy, she reasoned, had an overabundance, which, as communists believed, cried out for redistribution.

She never owned up. Never admitted it to herself during the day. Only at night when the voice whispered in her inner ear: *you stole.*

'I'm not saying anything to *her*,' said Hettie.

I love you, Hettie, she thought. Always will.

After her mother, Hettie was the only person who elicited deep feelings from Sophie. And it had to be love because she very often put Hettie's happiness before her own.

Days into their first term, thunder had broken over Digbys. The rain torrented and two small, drenched figures took refuge in the chapel porch and edged together for shelter. Both were still tiny. Very thin.

They looked at each other, flinching.

'You're not wet, you're crying,' accused Hettie, hair plastered to her cheeks and her teeth, which had not yet been dealt with by the orthodontist, overbiting her soft underlip.

'So are you,' said Sophie. And the exchange communicated to each their respective sorrows. Grief (Sophie) and homesickness (Hettie).

'I won't tell.' Sophie had already worked out that to admit weakness was dangerous.

'Nor I.'

Shivering juniors, the equivalent of pond life.

11

Even though Sophie was older than most of her class, having come late because of her mother's illness, she remained 'the new girl' for a long time.

The term was yet young but Hettie's tears were already a frequent occurrence – Liddy's bullying, no doubt – and there in that wet porch they decided: *We are not afraid of the others*. They were pleased with the statement. Determined to believe in that bravely voiced myth. (Myths were supremely useful.) Hettie's brimming brown eyes had emitted a more hopeful, let's-do-it glint. As the years wore on, she got a brace on her teeth and rose effortlessly to be a school prefect. She had done well in the GCE exams and had spent a peaceable year in the lower sixth as Head Girl.

Sophie had not.

One of the tortures was the practice of the elder girls sharing dormitories with the younger ones. Hettie had been unfailingly kind and had a soothing knack and was loved by the girls who were small and frightened (much as she and Sophie had once been) but Sophie had found their tears, their despair, their homesickness too sharp a reminder of her unformed self.

The day before their farewell to Digbys, they had packed their trunks, snapped the lids shut in unison and grabbed each other's hands. *Done. All will be well.* She wrote in the notebook: *My psyche* . . . Then ground to a halt. What was the psyche, exactly? A term she had come across in a book. Anyway, whatever it was, apparently it could be pulled into order and made to cooperate. She wondered about that. Years of rigid routine, semi-hunger, chilblains and ice on the inside of the dormitory windows, spent in an institution founded on the principle of 'no', did not make for joyous-ness.

Towards the end, Sophie had grown bolder.

Miss Chambers, did you ever want to do anything else when you were younger?

When I was young, Sophie Morel, I was helping to fight a war.

Hettie was incredulous. 'Sophie, you never asked her that.'

The war was over and Hitler dead. It was early June 1959. No FANY uniforms and rationing for these leavers. Yet one or two of the younger staff clearly thought that war had shifted into another theatre. Bright, brisk Miss Leila, who had a mind of her own, had been known to declare: *I'm a feminist.* This electrified the staff room – so it was reported – and puzzled many of the girls, who wondered if feminism was a tricky disease.

Sophie heard it, though. Pondered it in her heart – as per Religious Studies. Thought: oh, yes.

'I'm sorry you don't have parents here.' Hettie gazed down the drive at the queue of cars easing out of the main gate. 'Your proper French parents, I mean.'

'I don't mind.'

'No need to lie to me, Sophs.'

'It's better to be on your own.'

13

'You're so brave,' said Hettie, deep-diving into the well of well-thumbed references. 'Like Sydney Carton giving his life for love.'

Charles Dickens' *A Tale of Two Cities* (one big plod for the fifth form) had been a rare instance of differing opinions between them. Hettie thrilled to the idea of total sacrifice for love. Sophie thought: um, would she have agreed to have her head cut off for the wet Lucie Manette?

Odd to see Hettie gussied up as her mother. Unsettling. Distancing.

Sophie picked up her suitcase. The real Hettie was in socks and Viyella school blouse with fuzzy blonde hair escaping from its hairband.

'We need to go,' said Hettie. 'If we're to catch the London train.'

Neither of them moved.

In the drive, girls swarmed around their parents, who issued orders and admonishments. Liddy and her best friend, Roz, leant on hockey and lacrosse sticks while their parents loaded school trunks into identical Ford Prefects. Roz's mother handed out sandwiches from a tin with an enamel lid and the two girls fell on them. Liddy's father strolled around the bonnet and took a snorter from a hip flask.

As Osbert Knox would preach: to those that are given, is very often given more, and that was not a good thing. 'Your parents,' said Miss Chambers, 'expect that their daughters' education at Digbys will produce girls with manners, deportment and

14

deep gratitude for what has been given to them. Manners ensure that everyone understands each other and behaves rationally,' she added. 'Provided there isn't another conflict.' Then, to hammer home the point: 'War is a terrible thing, girls.'

Sophie observed the sleek, bossy, fussing parents – the women looked older than she expected – and their excited daughters. Goslings racing for the water.

Hettie nipped Sophie's arm. 'Try to look a tiny bit tragic.'

'Why?' The future seemed far away and terrifyingly close and her bravado was thin because she was . . . she was afraid.

'You think this place was cruel . . .' Hettie summoned up wisdom for the moment. 'It wasn't. Merely unimaginative and unloving. We shouldn't mix them up.'

Still, they lingered on the steps.

'Here we are then,' said Sophie, with an unfamiliar note in her voice. 'Ready to go.'

CHAPTER TWO

From the outside, so ran the consensus, Poynsdean's rectory was perfectly lovely.

The principles of harmony and elegance had powered its construction. Very successfully too. Large sash windows and weathered stone implied that only serene and orderly spirits would inhabit it. However, if the rumours were correct, this had not been the case. During the swash and buckle of the smuggler era, or so Fred Pankridge informed Sophie, contraband had been stacked in the cellars, pistols in the storeroom and a blood-stain had disfigured the library for decades.

Facing south, it mounted vigilance over lush, sweet grass, tussocky marshland and, beyond that, the sea. (The sea that had cast her mother forth during the war.)

Trudging down Church Lane on a June day, cool and with a hint of rain, like so many summer days. *English* summer days.

Suitcase weighing her down. The future weighing her down. The Rectory up ahead.

'Hello, Miss . . .' She was passing the allotments and Fred Pankridge looked up from tying up the bean supports. Her friend? Loyal acquaintance would be more accurate. 'You've left school, I hear.'

'I have.'

'I'll be seeing you then for the vegetables.'

'You will, Fred.'

To step across the Rectory threshold was to be stripped of that initial joyous appreciation. It was to enter an arena where neglect co-existed with total apathy when it came to restoring and mending. Lintels sagged, doors were incapable of shutting, floors sloped, fresh paint was a foreign concept. So, too, was comfortable living. Chairs required repair. The kitchen was sparsely stocked and the few still-operational curtains were in shreds.

Osbert did not concern himself with household matters. Alice, who in her parish work preached cleanliness and godliness, rarely, if ever, lifted a bucket or wielded soap. Trusting, perhaps, that the Almighty would get around to scrubbing out the lavatory bowl?

The Knoxes made a virtue of their domestic disorder. Out of the decrepitude, Osbert teased out his philosophy. *It never does to be too comfortable.* Tried and tested rhetoric to cover up difficulties. *We have a roof over our heads and aren't we all jolly lucky?*

He said these things with all the authority of a man with a mission.

To be fair . . . did she wish to be fair? . . .

17

Osbert Knox's stipend could only just stretch to fuel and food and not much else, leaving only that authority, plus his convictions, on which to live. 'It's our conduct that matters,' Osbert lectured his parishioners. 'Truth. Transparency. Unforced worship. Humility in the face of the Almighty. Calm in the presence of your betters. Above all, never lie.'

In the main, his parishioners believed him. They *wanted* to believe him because he wanted the best for them. In a curious way, Sophie did too. It would make life so much more negotiable.

Stepping into the hall, she put down her case, breathing hard to counter dread.

Dust coated the hall table. The windows needed a wash. The floor tiles were chipped and grubby. The door to the sitting room (rarely used) was ajar. She knew it intimately. Inside would be: two chairs and a sofa sagging so maliciously that it was possible only to perch. A small occasional table – the showcase for Osbert's smarter, morocco-bound Bible (cheaper versions roosted elsewhere). A piano at the far end of the room, open lid exposing yellow keys like untended teeth.

Ah, the piano.

Alice Knox's heart may have been unknowable to Sophie, but, my God, she loved that piano. It was like a lover. Or the ideal husband she didn't have.

From it she drew a music, sometimes sweetly seductive, sometimes skewed by wincing anger

18

and angst, brutal and off-key, depending on her mood. 'Für Elise', a Chopin *étude*. All the obvious pieces. But above and always, Couperin's *Les Barricades Mystérieuses*.

'Listen well . . .' Sophie remembered Camille saying when Alice was disembowelling it one afternoon. Her mother, her darling mother, who was already growing short of breath. '*Les Barricades* is by a Frenchman. One of us. If you listen, he will tell you who you are. You'll begin to understand.'

She added, 'She can't be all bad, Sophie. There is so much yearning.'

Oh, *Les Barricades*. Camille died and Alice played it. Osbert raged in his den and Alice played it. Returning from her visits to Pitt House, Alice played it. At those times, magically mining its beauty and enigma. A shimmer of kaleidoscopic melody, harmony weaving and interlapping. Listening, Sophie wept. *I am French and in the wrong place. I should be in Paris.* Then she was comforted and intrigued. What were those mysterious barricades exactly? What did they shield?

The answers were not to be found in the Rectory.

Instead, she thought of her mother's love. The miracle of it.

'When your mother was alive, the house worked,' said Osbert. Often. 'We felt blessed.'

Sophie remembered the cleaning, the cooking, the laundering. Thankless and exhausting.

The Knoxes are stupid pigs was a regular internal monologue for Sophie in the early years. The

19

Rectory was a bad place. Later, she corrected herself: that was cruel to pigs, who were interesting creatures. And, yes, Osbert and Alice were horrible, but not through and through. They *tried* to be good people. They strove to keep the parish ticking along on godly lines. They put charity before their comfort. Except in Camille's case when they successfully married the two.

What Osbert said was true: while her mother oversaw the Rectory's domestic arrangements, the place had been orderly and fragrant.

'We're fortunate that, unlike the inn at Bethlehem, we have plenty of space,' Osbert said when he plucked the obviously pregnant Camille out of the group of exhausted French refugees being paraded in Winchelford's town hall, before bearing her away to Poynsdean.

'We escaped from the Nazis over the mountains. Fought for a place on the boat. Kept going. Only to be herded into a hall where people came and looked at us as if we were cattle. The English . . .' Camille paused. 'The English are bossy.'

Sophie had not understood fully her mother's reflections. Now, she inched towards understanding. The humiliation of defeat. The weariness at the prospect of having to survive.

After Camille's death, Sophie was left with memories of being held close. Of whispered words. *Sophie, I wish, I wish we were not living here.*

She looked down at her feet. School sandals rooted in the dust. Rebellion now firmly rooted.

She had a goal and a mission and would not stay here. Anyway, there were things she needed to understand. The world. How it worked. Herself, and how she worked.

The door to Osbert's study was open and the room was empty. She took a gamble and in she went.

Always she was struck by its beauty: waist-high panelling in English oak, a large paned window, gracious dimensions – an impression wrecked by Osbert's crudely built bookshelves along one wall and the chaos of books and papers.

'The Reverend Knox is an excellent scholar,' Alice maintained. 'Very respected and principled. Very deep in his thought.'

Her tone was one of perfected docility. Which, Sophie reckoned, she employed instead of a scream.

Yes, the Reverend Osbert Knox *was* a scholar. His edition of *Grimms' Fairy Tales* had academic notations, for goodness' sake. (The story of Bluebeard and his 'disobedient' wife being lengthily analysed.)

The road to spiritual erudition was long and toilsome. Osbert was only part of the way down it – or so he humbly maintained – and the temptation to swerve aside to sample other delights was sharp.

Giving in, he might cast aside a treatise on, say, the consideration of transubstantiation in relation to the Anglican faith in favour of a thumping yarn. Preferably with a love story at its heart.

21

Sited between the sections of abstruse theology and history were shelves of historical fiction that gave the Winchelford library stiff competition. 'It's as well to know what the parishioners enjoy,' he said when Sophie enquired about them. 'These books are a gateway into their minds.' He raised a finger. 'But they're not for you, Sophie.'

Osbert must have known of her book raids. The greedy reading. The stealthy replacing.

'Ask me, Het, anything you like about the madness of Valois kings.'

'For Lordy sake, why would I do that?'

'Go on. Ask me about the butchery of the Wars of the Roses, the hideous infamy of Joan of Arc, the foolishness of Mary, Queen of Scots, the brilliance of Elizabeth I and the pigheadedness of Charles 1.'

'If I must,' said Hettie, who liked to please.

Yes, that greedy reading. In bed. At the kitchen table. Even on a walk.

Sophie encountered 'whirling passions', 'helplessness in the face of overpowering feelings', 'melting desires' and the supreme joy of sacrificing your life to save the one you loved the Sydney Carton finale and the hero's option, frequently employed. For Sophie, whose own experience was limited and who was conscious of her lack of intellect, some of the more torturous entwinings of love, politics and battle could well have been written in Greek. But to be enfolded into the thrum and hum of the prose, the unpeeled emotions, offered escape. From grieving for her mother. From the push-pull, deadly tiring emotions of having to face her situation.

By her late teens, she could give Osbert a run for his money on matters textual.

(Hettie defended Osbert, arguing that he sounded rather lovely and soft-hearted. 'Perhaps,' she offered, 'he has more female in him than most men?' Sophie said she thought it might be that Osbert could only cope with love and passion in a historical context.)

'The Good Lord be thanked.'

Berengaria's Dilemma in hand, Sophie turned around. Osbert was framed in the doorway.

'You're here.'

So it began. Berengaria and her dilemma went back onto the shelf.

'When the reverend first came, we thought him an odd fish. So tall and mighty skinny and couldn't take the sun. But he meant well.' So said Fred Pankridge, loyal acquaintance and king of the allotments. (The Fred who had sheltered the small, orphaned Sophie under the wing of his tomatoes and sweet peas. Gossip and Poynsdean's history came with the service.)

At fifty-five, Osbert's skin still went raw in the sun, and he remained skeletal, but his height was telescoping. His cassock hung in folds in the wrong places. That cassock. Always flapping. It flapped in and out of Sophie's dreams in which Osbert Knox metamorphosed into a pterodactyl, a moulting, failing, winged raptor running full tilt but getting nowhere.

Osbert sat down at his desk, which was stacked with books and covered in papers, including several copies of *The Racing Times*. The mess was deceptive, as Sophie well knew. Within the chaos was encoded a paper trail which led Osbert to the exact document he wished in seconds.

'A milestone,' he said, still in Sunday sermon mode.

She took this to mean that he recognised she was no longer a schoolgirl.

'A happy milestone.' He rammed the point home.

In church, he press-ganged attention and worked to dominate his audience. His repertoire included the Dramatic Gesture, the Rhetorical Flourish, the Crackling Utterance, plus the habit of draping himself across the pulpit.

He raised a hand. 'Time to put aside childish things and to buckle down. Mrs Knox and I have need of you here.'

She glanced at the bookshelves, the key to Osbert's . . . to the thing she did not understand called the psyche?

He noted the direction of her gaze and tapped the book on his desk. '*The King Must Die*, my latest. Mary Renault. Very good, I must say. Very good.' There was a tiny, satisfied pause. 'Quite racy.'

His diary lay open on the desk. '9 a.m. prayers.

10 a.m. council meeting. Midday exorcism. 2 p.m. AGM Sunday school . . .'

In and out of the church, the hall, the Rectory and people's homes. Black-clad, bustling, raptorish . . . He and Alice were endlessly busy about God's plan for the world, determined to maintain a stranglehold on the lifestyle and conduct of the parish. Their energy for this work was phenomenal, their nose for sin unerring, their demands for repentance ceaseless.

'A big change for you,' Osbert was saying, switching to the tone he used for his confirmation classes. 'Thanks to the foresight of your parents and the money your mother managed to bring over, you've been given a proper grounding.'

She thought of Poynsdean. The village green, the doctor's surgery, Mr Seely selling groceries from the back of his wheezy van. Would it have been easier to accept living here if she had stayed in the village?

'I should have gone to the local school.'

'Maybe. But it was easier for Mrs Knox if you went away, especially when you were younger.'

So that was it. The casual cruelty of the remark took her breath away. 'But this was the only home I had.'

His spread hands emphasised the point. 'Digbys was a good school. Many will envy you. But now it's time to acknowledge your good fortune and to repay your debt.'

'My debt?' For a second, Sophie took it literally.

25

Osbert clarified: 'A roof over your head. Food. A bed. You could have ended up in an institution, you know. I'm sure you wish to repay us in kind.'

Summarising Sophie's indebtedness, his gaze travelled over the let-down hem on the school dress, her unravelling plait of hair, her slenderness. The appraisal appeared to puzzle him.

'You know, you could almost be pretty.' Pointing to the bookshelf, he added, 'Like one of those heroines who are rescued by a handsome hero.'

She wondered which one he had in mind. Edith with the flaxen plaits from *Alfred and the Maiden*, who brought a king to his knees, or Daniela in *Endless Horizon*, a waif working in a Victorian iron foundry who meets an escaped convict (imprisoned for stealing a loaf of bread), runs away with him to Australia and ends up running a stock farm.

Osbert steepled his hands. 'Sophie, if you are ever in trouble, or troubled, I hope you will confide in me. Yes?'

No.

'I have a lot of experience, you know.' Pause. 'In listening.'

Silence.

'I want to be of help. Children are different now. Less easy. It's our duty to help you into adult life and we'll do our best to understand how you feel.' He raised a whiskered, prawn-like eyebrow. 'You haven't lived here all these years without Mrs Knox and I becoming fond of you, you know.'

He picked up a copy of *Girl* magazine that was lying on his desk. 'I don't approve of these things but Mrs Mead thought you might like it. Her granddaughter left it behind.' He held it out. 'I took a look and it surprised me. It shows girls performing good, useful tasks. I recommend "Susan Cooks up a Storm".'

Osbert's right shoe was done up with string, a combination that pretty much summed up this mad household. 'I'm too old for a comic,' she said.

'We're looking forward to you taking over the running of the house. If you are anything like your dear mother, then our future together will be good. When she was in charge, all was orderly. Like God's kingdom. And fragrant. My goodness, how the Rectory smelt of polish and fresh bread. And it shall be again.' He addressed the string shoelace. 'Well, well. You're here and we'll get on famously. Go and say hello to Mrs Knox. She's waiting for you.'

CHAPTER THREE

When not consumed by her parish duties or playing the piano, Alice retreated to the command centre of her bedroom, which Osbert did not frequent. The ousting had happened early in what they persisted in terming 'their union', news of which quickly leaked into the village, providing excellent gossip. If anyone was daring enough to ask why, Alice cited a list of maladies, which included insomnia and neuralgia. Only cope-able with if she slept alone.

Osbert had never been heard to comment.

From the bedroom, Alice issued directives to do this or that but did not appear to notice – or perhaps care – if they fell on deaf ears. It was an open secret that anything achieved domestically in the Rectory happened in spite and not because of her.

The younger Sophie had thought Alice dead lazy. The older Sophie came to admire her field-craft. Alice was brilliant at doing exactly what she wished and masking it. Her inadequacies as a housekeeper were mulled over in detail in the village. *Never lifts a finger. The state of the place.*

But Alice easily ducked the critical arrows, never, ever referencing the muddle in the Rectory or her lack of culinary skill. If a cupboard door could shut on her failed attempts to keep supplies replenished, then there was nothing to discuss. As a cook who believed green vegetables should be boiled for an entire morning, there was nothing to discuss there either.

Resembling small, exhausted creatures, two scuffed, well-worn pairs of shoes had been abandoned outside Alice's bedroom, waiting for someone to deal with them. Sophie, in fact.

She knocked.

'Come.'

Reluctant, filled with dread, she obeyed.

The double bed, complete with sagging mattress, dominated the room. (In the days Osbert had been in occupation, bodies must have rolled together.) A handle on the chest of drawers was broken. Skimpy green curtains barely deflected the draughts from the sash windows.

All was as it ever was.

Except for – and this was a huge difference – a mirror. In the entire rectory there was only a single small shaving mirror in the bathroom. Alice disapproved of them. 'Vanity and worldliness, Sophie Morel. Sins that corrode.'

But now a handsome one with a gilt frame colonised the chest of drawers. Foursquare in front of it was Alice, adjusting a confection on her head resembling a dead animal.

The kinder Hettie said that Alice hated looking at her reflection because she was in despair at her lack of pretty things. Unkind Sophie said it was because Alice's skin was the colour of semolina.

Loathing someone demanded time and energy. Those were not always to hand and the younger Sophie wrote 'I hate Alice Knox' ten times on a piece of paper, cut it into strips and hid them in her clothes and her books. The exercise kept up momentum.

'You're ugly, *ugly*,' ran one of the playlets written and enacted in her head. (The playlets helped her to sleep.) This was directed at the fictional Alice, who then shed copious tears. Sophie refused to lend her a handkerchief. Victory achieved, Sophie was free to drift off.

The older, wilier, teenager fashioned sharper verbal missiles – *you're not my mother. I will never call you Mother*, designed to be spat out in a cold, cold voice. Escalation of warfare culminated in even more savage invective: *You are barren like the woman in the Bible* . . .

All unvoiced, of course.

'I thought you would never get here,' Alice was saying. 'You must be in the church by three o'clock. The six-year-olds require supervising for Bible class.' She poked at the thing on her head. 'Should I say welcome home?'

'Yes, please,' said Sophie.

Alice swung around. 'Well, here you are.'

The frown lines in the pale face had deepened

and there was a suggestion that the stick-thin Alice had put on weight around her middle. She was wearing her blue-flowered blouse, her one concession to colour and pattern, exhumed on special occasions from the chaos of her cupboard.

Sophie knew enough to realise that the blouse was not to celebrate her return to the fold. Neither was the dead animal, which turned out to be a brown felt pillbox hat.

'New hat?'

'Not exactly.' The reply was sharp.

Almost certainly this meant it came from Dilly Harlip's second-hand clothes shop in Winchelford. Poynsdean's women talked of its proprietor's taste and resourcefulness but there was an unspoken agreement never to mention that the merchandise was pre-worn.

'The reverend gave me a pound and instructed me to buy something new.'

A defensive edge.

'Ah.'

'I'm lunching at Lady Pitt's.' She waited for Sophie's response; when it did not materialise, she added, 'I'm owed a little light enjoyment, you know.'

Sophie waited for the backlash from Alice's conscience which inevitably followed.

'You think I should not take hospitality from those who live on the toil of others.'

'I don't think anything,' said Sophie.

Untrue. In a few minutes, the newly be-hatted

Alice would mount her bicycle and pedal away into a terrain that did not come under Osbert's jurisdiction, and Sophie thought the better of her for it.

The outings to Pitt House nourished Alice for months. Sometimes years. There would be wistful references to dazzling linen tablecloths, cake stands and marquetry tables, plus lengthy descriptions of the flower arrangements. All of which suggested that Alice's pursuit of spiritual strength and social equality was cast aside the second she stepped across the Pitt threshold.

Sophie puzzled it over. Was it possible that beneath the dogged egalitarianism lay an elitist? Did Alice suspect this of herself?

At the very least, to expose Enid Pitt's indirect sway over the Rectory would be pleasurable, if only to take revenge on her dictate that boiled cabbage was good for the bowels and should be eaten at least four times a week.

The less critical, kinder bit of Sophie understood. Pitt House was an escape. An elegant one with many seductions. Alice, she wrote in her notebook, was a woman whose fate was to be nailed to the door of parish duties, which meant she must never admit to the yearnings seething within her awkward bosom.

'Lady Enid was having the maids' quarters refurbished and said I should take this mirror. It was going to be thrown out, would you credit it? She believes a woman should have a good mirror.' She patted her hair. 'She also agrees that it's time you took over some of my duties.' Another pat. 'She has a saying, "start as you mean to go on".'

Sophie leant back against the door. 'If Lady Pitt says so.'

Alice sent her one of her looks. 'Did that school of yours teach you to be cheeky?'

No answer was required.

Alice's balding hairbrush rested beside the nail scissors that had been deployed against Sophie many times. Brutally.

Alice picked them up. 'Show me your hands. I don't want you going to church with those long nails of yours.'

Sophie kept her hands at her sides. The days of inspection were over. Yes, they were. Definitely. 'My nails are fine. No need.'

For once, Alice did not go into battle. 'I see.'

Sophie's mood hitched up a notch.

'Bread and Spam in the kitchen,' said Alice. 'Make yourself a sandwich and don't be late.'

She caught up a balding powder puff. Glared in the mirror. Made a pass across her nose, the resultant coating of pale orange on her pallor giving it a waxy bloom. She tilted her head to get a better look at her unfamiliar reflection and the dead animal was re-sited at the back of her head. 'You don't wish to be here, I daresay. The reverend imagines you do, but that doesn't fool me for a second.'

'I'll have to leave,' said Sophie.

'And how would you do that? Girls don't just

33

wander off. Not unless they're no better than they should be.' She blew a trail of orange powder onto the floor. 'It was your mother, I suppose. Talking about Paris.' Her gaze raked over Sophie. 'We had to remind her that where she came from was of no interest to us.'

Twenty-five years previously, Alice had been perilously close to thirty with no obvious future when Osbert rode into town and claimed her for his wife.

'This is 1959,' said Sophie. 'Things have changed. Girls can get jobs and pay rent.'

'*Respectable* girls? Sophie, sort out the wheat from the chaff in this matter. Or try to.' Soft but incisive. Intending to wound. 'Do any of your smart schoolfriends plan to live independently? No, I thought not.' Alice folded and refolded a handkerchief. 'Most of them will stay at home until they marry.'

'Aren't we free to choose what we do with our lives?'

Alice flicked a glance at the mirror.

'Don't you think, Mrs Knox? Don't you think that's right?' Sophie persisted.

'And does freedom buy bread?' Alice stowed the handkerchief up her sleeve. 'We're not free. God has a plan and it's useless to try and avoid it. And the plan is for you to help us here, in the parish. That's why we took you in.'

'But I'm not a slave. Any more than you are, Mrs Knox.'

'You're very foolish, Sophie Morel.'

And yet Sophie knew that Alice knew that, if the truth was made flesh and spoken, she would agree they occupied the same trap.

'You're not yet twenty-one and the reverend still has authority over you.'

After Camille had died, social services had arrived with papers to be signed. Sophie was seven years old – actually, nearly eight and as well versed in grief as any adult, but there hadn't been any question of objecting.

Sometimes, and as part of a mental exercise that she considered useful for sharpening her mind, Sophie urged herself to adopt a different perspective. The Knoxes *had* been kind to a grieving, pregnant refugee on the run. 'They didn't object when I told them I was having you.' Camille held Sophie close and spoke in French. 'They said if I worked at the Rectory they would keep us both. You see, they needed us. It was . . . *dégueulasse* . . . disgusting here. They wanted . . . how to say it? They yearned to be clean.'

'Why can't we be with Father?'

An ever-present grief surfaced. 'Your father is in Heaven.'

'Did he want to go to Heaven?'

'Not then. Later, when he was old maybe. But he and I and the others knew we had to fight for France.'

'Do you like living here?' she asked Camille.

'It's a place of safety. No more than that.'

35

Camille told her how every drawer and cupboard in the Rectory had been filled with discarded items when she first arrived. In the kitchen were scraps, rusting pans, broken buttons. A teapot with no lid. A cup minus a handle. It was the mess of two people who understood the spiritual life but had not got the hang of the temporal one.

'When I was growing up in Poitiers with your grandparents, we were comfortable.' Camille did not often refer to her childhood because it was upsetting. 'We had Marie, who did the cooking, and Agnes, who looked after our clothes. On Sundays Marie made me hot chocolate in a special cup and I drank it at the kitchen table with a lace napkin. I think about that chocolate a great deal. Everything was tidy and clean. But you mustn't ever say that we talk about how messy they are here. It would hurt their feelings.'

In the rare interludes when Camille felt better, she talked about Pierre. 'He was tall, like you are going to be. He had an interesting face. I teased him that his mouth was too big. He was a serious person who thought about what was going on in the world. He loved paintings. He had a temper. But I never minded. He said he was lucky to be married to someone who had turned out to be a warrior.'

She told stories of Paris. 'By the time I escaped Paris, most people knew someone who had been arrested. We lived in a city of secrets. We had to devise new routes through it. Keep to the back streets, the darkest alleys, we instructed each other. Nowhere was safe . . .' She drifted off. 'The Nazis burnt paintings. By Picasso and Ernst . . . they thought them degenerate. That made your father so angry.'

Sophie memorised the word. *Degenerate.*

Her seven-year-old imagination built a Paris of tall towers, a shining river and lots of dogs. She wanted to include magic swans and horse-drawn chariots but her mother never mentioned those.

Towards the end, Sophie clutched her mother's skeletal hand.

'Do you think Father is in Heaven?'

Longing was etched on her mother's face. 'If you believe in Heaven, he's there.'

'Did bad men kill him?'

'You must find out.'

'Where is Heaven?'

'That's for you to discover. That will be your adventure.'

'How?'

But Camille was slipping towards the perilous boundary between life and death and did not answer.

Her mother died.

Sophie had to continue breathing. She had to eat, walk, speak. Looking back, she was not sure how she managed any of those things.

Osbert and Alice informed Sophie that Time Healed. 'My dear . . .' To his credit, Osbert was

37

genuinely grieving. 'It is a great loss. But I am here to tell you the Lord ensures that we get over our losses.'

The Lord did nothing of the sort.

Her mother had been an exile. Homeless. Widowed. Struggling. Without her French family.

She had loved Sophie. 'My adorable, beautiful daughter. I must kiss you all the time.'

However, there was no denying that life did go on. Memories of sheltering against her mother's flank – Camille the warm, silky doe. Memories of her hand being held. Of the piercing cry Sophie had uttered when Alice crept into her bedroom to inform Sophie her mother had gone. These remained, but much else faded.

The missing metamorphosed into the conviction, almost religious in its intensity, that Camille was still with Sophie. Close closeted. Watchful. Loving.

At school, Sophie added what information she could glean to her scanty stock of war knowledge. France invaded. Paris occupied. Paris liberated. Why had Camille chosen to talk about hot chocolate rather than the events that had washed her up at the Rectory? Older and wiser Sophie understood that it was precisely the recollection of small, domestic details that made it possible for exiles to survive.

Camille also said, 'I fought for liberty. So must you.'

'*You* must clear up her things, you know,' said

Alice, a few weeks after Camille died, shuddering at the thought of doing anything so practical. 'My strength is limited and I have to keep what energy I possess for the parish.'

Camille's bedroom had been at the top of the stairs that led to what had been the servants' quarters and her presence lingered in it. In the folded blouse, the mended skirt on a hanger, lisle stockings rolled up into nests. Then there was the letter, containing a second letter, that she discovered in the linen nightdress case.

The first letter was to Sophie from her father, carried by Camille into exile.

You are not yet born but I think of you all the time. Who and what you are is still a mystery. But I love you and your mother, which is why I sent both of you away. This is my message to you if I do not survive.

The second was from her mother.

I had hoped that you would never read this but the time has come. My experiences have taught me that the unexpected and disastrous can happen, and they have. This is written with great love, Sophie. Always remember that.

How did we end up in Poynsdean?

I fought in the Paris streets with your father until it became too dangerous. You were on the way and he wanted me to go. I didn't. In the end, I arranged to be smuggled out of France and ended up here in Sussex.

Your father was killed when Paris was liberated.

39

He had survived the war but I will never know if it had changed him. But I imagined him thinking that we would all be together and we would be a normal family.

But I had you and I was becoming ill. I decided to stay here where I had work and a roof over our heads. I also concluded I might as well be miserable in this strange English village as in Paris. It gave you a home and I couldn't be sure of that if I returned to France.

Sophie, there is the money that I brought over with me. It was your father's — he made it selling paintings. I told the Knoxes it was to be spent on educating you.

Take what is left and use it to give yourself opportunities. You will have to be cunning because the men like to take charge, they like to dictate. But I have learnt you can depend on no one except yourself. You must be independent of spirit.

Faith, any kind of faith, has been hard to keep. Who knows what happens after death. Somehow, somehow, my beloved daughter, I know I shall be with you throughout your life. Watching over you, I suppose. When in good time you die, I will be there. Waiting. And your father, too.

I am writing in French, which means there's every chance it will remain private. The English are terrible at languages — they are islanders, and islanders are peculiar.

These letters were the most precious things Sophie possessed.

CHAPTER FOUR

Kitchens. Arenas of torment and torture. Designed to bury women.

'Don't be so extreme,' said Hettie. 'Some women love their kitchens.'

This one was in a hideous state. Smelling of mould.

Hand on hip, Sophie assessed the field of battle.

Unwashed pans in the sink. Food droppings. Drying-up cloths so stiff with dirt they begged Sophie to burn them. The walls needed washing, the chair seats were tacky and silverfish partied by the Rayburn.

After Camille's death, the Rectory's interior travelled further down the road of disgusting and continued to do so. Childhood innocence being a wonderful thing, it didn't bother Sophie – until she arrived at Digbys, a universe of clean skin, laundered clothes and shampooed hair, and learnt that dirt and neglect were the devil's work.

Sophie swept the floor, scrubbed the table and made inroads into the washing-up, shuddering as scummy suds seeped between her fingers. To escape, she would need money. Her money. But how to lay her hands on it? And how did one arrange travel? Book tickets? Find lodgings?

Clearing a space by the bread bin, she made the Spam sandwich and sat down to eat it. It was horrible. Horrible. She was almost nostalgic for the school buns (which tasted of bicarbonate of soda) and the fried bread (cooked to brittleness) that she and Hettie used to eat with marmalade.

Worse, much worse, than the state of the kitchen was the situation she faced. She had barely been back at the Rectory a few hours, and already she was enmeshed in the dissonance of Osbert and Alice's marriage.

Religion, charity, grime and prohibitions.

The Spam lingered on her tongue and, if such a thing was possible, it tasted pink and was repellingly moist.

Hettie said that she was strong and brave, a judgement based on Sophie's efficiency at fending off Liddy who didn't care who she hurt. Until Sophie tumbled to the solution. This was to point out to Liddy that her breasts were *very obviously* different sizes. How they had howled with laughter. Unkind, cleansing laughter.

The smell of mould intensified. It took a minute or two to locate its source before she ducked her head under the table. Sure enough, there was a lump of bacon so infested by spores that not even the mice would tackle it. Making a long arm, she wrapped it up in newspaper and dropped it in the dustbin.

Avoiding the coal-tar soap which made the skin on her hands crack and peel, she ran cold water into the sink and stared through the window above it. To the west, clouds hinted at rain.

What would be the best life?

'It must be filled with love,' she had told Het. Not for boys, but for living itself. Everything in life. Food, lovely clothes, painting. Wonderful people. Doughnuts.

Hettie looked as though she had been a witness to the Sermon on the Mount. 'Who do you love, Sophie?'

'You don't have to ask, Het. I love you. Very much.'

Loving deeply had to be, *must be*, a condition of existence but, at this precise moment, she was damned if she knew anyone else on whom she could lavish this bounty.

Time to leave for the church.

Grabbing the remains of the Spam and, rain threatening, her school gaberdine mac, she headed for the bird table.

This overlooked the lane leading to the church. A satisfactory siting which allowed both birds and parishioners to observe each other.

Fred had built it for ten-year-old Sophie from wood and an old tyre to withstand whatever the weather threw at it.

A temple for birds. *Her* temple. On the days when all was black and seeping in her head, she watched for the flurries of arrival and departure.

Listened to the bird gabble. Allowed the bustle of wing and feather to heal her.

In the lined notebook won at a parish tombola, she recorded closely observed bird manoeuvres. Spats and feints and retreats. *Dunnock first in,* she recorded with the stub of an HB pencil. *Coal tit hovering.*

Who got first dibs was decided by the weight of the bird. This meant the house sparrows and greenfinches won out, and the blue tits and coal tits were kept waiting in the laurel bush. The goldfinches and dunnocks provided a coalition of the middle.

There were lessons here. Fractious ones. About life, about bullies, about those to whom much had been given in the first place.

Overall, the birds appeared to thrive on the Rectory's detritus – fish pie, the remains of the oxtail stew, herring – food that can't have been good for them. It was possible (probable?) they were poisoned by it in droves and were replaced by myriad cousins. Sophie would never know.

She stood back. 'Sorry about the Spam.'

But joy . . . the birds arrowed in, tiny, bright-eyed, rapacious and noisy. *Welcome, Sophie.* And no, they weren't picky about what they ate.

The tits had taken refuge under the ugly laurel. Always protective towards them, she dribbled final crumbs within their reach.

She felt a rush of thankfulness for their existence, for their seeming trust, for their efficient hoovering up of the hateful Spam. Tiny hearts beating beneath the feathers, fragile and short-lived.

That moment, she was washed clean of troubled thought. There was nothing else but earth and sky, a hint of rain, and the interplay of wings and feathers as the hierarchies of the bird table got sorted.

Turning, she faced the sea. The afternoon light, more luminous from this direction, bleached the darker line of the horizon.

Where was she?

In a village. Of the type she had drawn and described in geography projects. Population: approximately fifteen hundred. A crossroads, around which clustered the older buildings. Houses straggling northwards towards the Downs. Begging, said Camille, to be lifted up.

Traffic was minimal – the screech of brakes, or a throttled back engine at the main crossroads could make a villager jump. The men worked in the fields or went away to work in the ports on the south coast. A scattering of the more progressive younger women took jobs in the nearby market town of Winchelford, where there was hot competition for the openings at Woolworth's. Married women stayed at home to take care of children and housework. They emerged only to do the unpaid community work that the government depended on (but never acknowledged).

Time to go.

The lane winding up to the church was potholed.

Bricks dislodged from the perimeter wall lay in wait to fell the unwary walker. Pockets of mud which the sun never reached sucked at shoes. Closer to the church, trees bent protectively over the lane.

White, green and grey moss colonised the lych-gate and traced lacy forms. As she opened the gate, it stained her fingers and she rubbed them on the grass.

The churchyard. A self-contained kingdom, populated with daisies and poppies. Framed by a yew and a cypress, both elderly, it guarded the uneven rows of the older headstones close to the church. More recent ones, which included the dead from the last war, fanned out in marshalled rows around the perimeter.

Camille was buried close to the yew tree. Grass thrust up against the small headstone, threatening to obscure it and the rosemary bush – *Rosmarinus, dew of the sea* – that she had asked Fred Pankridge to plant. *When the rosemary flourishes, the mistress rules,* said Fred.

Camille Morel, 1917–1948

A shuddery little breath.

Her bones might be under the stone, but Camille was not in this place. She was elsewhere.

Like the Rectory, the church was beautiful, built at a time when large plain windows superseded stained glass. On sunny days, light streamed into the chancel, suggesting enlightenment and kindness to all. The irony was not lost on Sophie.

Poynsdean's worshippers veered towards gloom and preferred the fire and brimstone aspects of their religion. If someone erred, and in Poynsdean it was easy to err, the parishioners applauded the idea of a sinner being cast into the burning pit.

The church door was stout and nail studded. When she pushed it open, all would begin. She wrestled grimly with the iron ring handle.

'*There* you are,' said Mrs Benyon when Sophie slipped inside. 'You're late. Thought you might have fled back to that posh school of yours.' She jabbed a finger in the direction of the pews, where a row of children sat furiously bored. 'What are you going to do with those?'

Betty Benyon was not known for the sweetness of her temper. An East Riding girl who'd married Eric the farrier, her acceptance by the village had taken years. The torrid rumour that she had once aspired to be a supervisor in a department store had not helped. She was tall and lanky and as hissing and unsettled as a snake in a box.

'Coming from Yorkshire, I speak as I find,' she was heard to say, which meant she was about to fell, or at least wound, some poor innocent with a verbal V-2. Life as a village wife bored her, but she had beaten herself into submission.

She glared at Sophie, conveying unequivocally that the supervision of a bunch of six-year-olds was a form of extreme torture.

Sophie glanced at Mickey – known as 'Trouble' – draped over the end of the pew. His response was to pull a face. 'If you do that, Mickey Hudd, the wind will change and then where will you be?' said Betty. 'Any more cheeking of me, I'm taking you right back to your dad. You know what will happen then?'

Mickey kicked 'Ratty' Ridd beside him, a paler version of himself. 'Ratty made me, miss.'

Stung, Ratty clenched his fists. 'Did not, liar!'

Ranged either side of them were the spotty, snotty figures of their classmates. A pleasurable shudder rippled through them at the thought of a fist fight.

Ratty Ridd hit Mickey back (good for him . . .) and the two boys launched into combat, skinny legs and arms windmilling. Their classmates observed with delight. They had seen it many times and it never failed to entertain them. Bob and Katey, sitting either side of the fighting bantams, did a bottom-shuffle out of missile range.

The dust danced and the sun illuminated the children's entranced faces. Sophie grinned. If God was supposed to be in this place, He had nipped out for a cup of tea.

Betty tried to say something above the hubbub, but no one heard – or they took this golden opportunity not to pay attention.

A cry from Ratty caused Katey to cry out. 'Miss, miss . . .'

Sophie stuck two fingers in her mouth and gave an intense whistle which echoed around the church. The two boys fell apart in surprise. 'Enough,' she said.

Betty Benyon's eyebrows crawled up her forehead. 'The pencils are in the vestry,' she snapped. 'Get 'em.'

On Sophie's return, Betty Benyon went in for the kill. 'That posh school your poor, deluded mother insisted that you went to?' Sophie paused in the act of handing out the pencils. 'Was it worth it?'

'Mrs Benyon, my mother was not deluded.'

'Extravagant, then.'

'She wasn't that, either. Please don't say such things.'

Betty Benyon fought for the last word. 'But she was foreign. So are you.'

The children did not quite understand the exchange, but they had cottoned on to the combat. A different kind of combat to the one they'd just witnessed.

Betty scented triumph. 'If you want to get on now you're back for good, you'll have to watch that posh accent.' She allowed a second to elapse. 'And mind that uppity tongue.' Another pause. 'Cat got it, Miss Sophie Morel? Or should I say, Madmoizelleeee?'

With enormous satisfaction, Sophie replied, 'Am I right in thinking, Mrs Benyon, you were new here once with a strange accent?'

Silence.

Sophie turned to the bookshelf beside the font

and pulled out *Children's Prayers,* which was resting beside other immortal works such as *The Baptist March in History* and *Outreach for the Unreached.*

At the end of the class, the children filed out of the church and scampered across the churchyard. Ratty Ridd hung back and Sophie asked if he wanted something. He jabbed a finger at her. 'My dad says your mum was a Froggy who ran away.'

It may have been three miles away, but the sea oscillated through Poynsdean's inner life. Walk out from the marsh border, skirt the pools and panne of the wetlands where the cattle were put out to graze in the summer and the sheep in the winter, and descend to the lower tidal flats and there it was, claiming supremacy over imagination, habit and custom.

Lapwing and redshanks staked their territory over the intervening marsh ditches and pools, over the tufts of salt hay grass, sea lavender and salt marsh aster and rushes. Their cries could be heard through the sea frets and they embellished the village stories of smugglers, ghostly happenings, drownings and shipwrecks.

Escaped from the church, Sophie shaded her eyes and looked across to the river in the distance.

My dad says your mum was a Froggy who ran away.

The wetlands had been Camille's place. The water is where I came from, Sophie, to here. And you did too, she said.

On hot days, mother and small daughter

picnicked beside the river, which edged its way through the shrubs and patches of trees. In the winter, they had to keep moving. Sometimes, they chased each other along the riverbank and Camille held on to Sophie as she threw sticks into the half-frozen shallows.

It was here, in the briny air and yielding ground underfoot, and not in the graveyard, that she conversed with her mother.

You left me.

Sophie, it was unwillingly. The hardest thing.

Camille resided in the stillness of the ash and hornbeam. In the passage of the startlingly clear water over the stones. In the tangle of spike grasses. In the summer, the shimmering air contained something of her essence, once so strong and determined to survive until her illness made it impossible. In the winter, the hoar breath drifting over leaves and frozen berries buoyed up her memory. And sometimes . . . sometimes, Sophie imagined she saw Camille gazing out to the sea from which she had come.

Where are you, my mother? Sheltering behind those *barricades mystérieuses*, safe from the ptero-dactyl and the piano player?

Enmeshed in the silence that wasn't silent, she watched for some time.

She wasn't calm, though. The black, seeping distress had returned. The distress that on one occasion had made her walk to the river with the idea of throwing herself in.

51

There, cradled by the sounds of water, the wind and the birds she loved, she felt better and changed her mind.

That was then.

Now?

Her eyes narrowed: a figure was making for the river. Male. Quite tall. Dressed in a loosely hanging army greatcoat with farm overalls underneath. He stopped, lit a cigarette, smoked a bit of it before stamping it underfoot. He shaded his eyes and kicked the turf. Shoved his hands into his pockets. He seemed troubled, irresolute, stormy. An outsider like herself? Or maybe he'd had one too many beers?

Moments later he swung around and set off in the direction from which he had come, but then, alerted, perhaps, by the sight of her motionless figure, he halted. Shaded his eyes and took a good look at Sophie. Raised a hand and waved.

She raised a hand in reply.

Then he was off again. Fresh cigarette in mouth, coat flapping.

Back in the Rectory, she set to work. Peel potatoes. Scrape carrots. Leave them to soak in an enamel bowl of water. Run cut finger under tap, which was almost impossible to turn on so dense was the limescale.

Dinner was at six thirty – Alice had set the timetable for the day. *Don't be late, mind.*

Upstairs, in the bedroom that she'd once shared with her mother, Sophie unpacked her case. 'You'll wear your school uniform for the present until we can get new clothes,' Alice had written to her at school. 'The grey skirt will do for the time being and the jumper has a good bit of wear in it yet. If you wrap a scarf around your neck, the gaberdine mac can double up as a coat for the winter. Don't forget to let it down. Folk round here don't like short hems.'

The books scattered over the bed were Sophie's now redundant text and exercise books. She sat down.

The maths primer was dog-eared and rumpled.

She rifled through. Pythagoras's theory, $a^2 b^2 = h^2$, carefully transcribed on the final page of her formal lessons. Its applications were many and undeniably fascinating but, unless she was a builder, an architect or a surveyor, tricky to apply.

History. What were the repercussions of the Revocation of the Edict of Nantes on the British?

Silk weavers?

She didn't care.

She pulled in an unsteady breath and willed the upsurge of anger – irrational but undeniable – directed at her parents for leaving her to cope alone, to subside back down through the sediment.

The chintz curtains had worn so thin there wasn't much point to them at all. She jerked them shut before returning to the virgin paper.

She searched her pencil case for her pen and wrote in her notebook: *Who are they, those who I know? Those with whom I live?*

Alice, a sponge sucking up information. Osbert, a pterodactyl with jitters. Betty Benyon, a snake who needs more to occupy her. Hettie, a wonderful, faithful, loving dog. Hettie's mother, Moira. What was she? With relish, she wrote: *Moira, the sheep.*

Taking possession of a blank page was one of the more pleasurable things in her life.

54

CHAPTER FIVE

Hettie sent a letter. 'Life's miserable. Or rather, I am. I hate the endless parties Mother has arranged. We are all so tired and eat far too much and I stick out like a sore thumb. Mother nags away. Apparently, my posture is terrible. She took me to someone who taught me how to carry my gloves and handbag and how to wear a coat! She insists I rotate my ankles for ten minutes every day to keep them slim and slap under my jaw to prevent a double chin.

'There is no time to be myself. I'm hopeless at conversation and the men seem to want blondes who laugh at their jokes. So far, I've failed at my one task, which is to find a husband. Do you think you and I are destined to be lonely? Some people are, you know. It's their karma.'

Having become intimate with its astonishing number of tricks and twists, Sophie understood about loneliness. But she also knew it was survivable. 'Hettie, darling, you'll get through. Promise. Anyway, you don't need a husband. You need a job.'

Growing up with Alice had been lonely. Bible

classes. Soup kitchens. Visiting the elderly. Always in a rush, Alice never scrupled to abandon Sophie to her own devices.

'God's work must come first.'

'God's work' included the WI meetings. Come rain or shine, Alice attended these, portering back to the Rectory a suitcase of local gossip and news of illnesses, bad behaviour and deaths, plus donations for charity that ranged from knitted squares for cot blankets to pound cakes and jams which Sophie was never allowed to touch.

Alice was insistent that Sophie accompany her to the upcoming meeting. 'Show willing to the village. I'm aware that Madam' – 'Madam' was maliciously inflected – 'is not interested in domestic matters, but there's plenty to learn that will be useful to you.'

'But you're not interested in domestic matters,' said Sophie.

'That's different,' said Alice.

'Village hall' was a grand soubriquet for a decaying wooden hut with a corrugated-iron roof. Requisitioned by the Home Guard during the war – a glorious occupation recorded in a group photograph hanging over the door – it had been Poynsdean's front line against the Nazis. Between lunch and tea, the hours they agreed it was likely Jerry would show up, the guard blocked traffic using the coast road. A plan that went smoothly until, one morning, Lady Enid drove up in her black car and demanded to be let through. A debate raged as to whether she should or shouldn't be allowed access, and she lost her temper. 'Do I look like a Nazi general?' 'Yes,' shouted someone in the group. Lady Enid never forgave them.

There had been talk of raising funds to build a smarter, sturdier hall. Everyone agreed – until asked to stump up – that it was necessary to repair the heart of the village, but wishing couldn't make it happen.

Furthermore, argued the detractors in the village, *if* there was any spare money, it should be used to spruce up the semi-derelict council houses in East Street, which *still* didn't have sanitation.

Mercifully, it being July, the hut's sole source of heating, a stove which chomped hods of coke, had not been lit, sparing the gathering the ordeal of dry throats and streaming noses from the fumes. The windows had been flung wide, and salt-scented air battled with the smell of must and carbolic from the primitive lavatory.

Hats anchored onto heads with hatpins (Alice's dead animal had resumed its perch), the women dished out opinions. (Of especial interest were the morals of the younger generation.) They played cards and reported on the competitive baking that occasionally took Poynsdean by storm. Betty Benyon gave a short lecture on the secrets to a top-class sponge cake. Susan Savage was explaining how to unblock an outside drain if your man wasn't there.

The words '. . . if you're prepared to give it a

good bit of welly, your drain will be sweet-smelling in no time' had barely left Susan's lips when the door was flung open and Betty's husband, Will Benyon, appeared in the doorway. Swaying.

Sophie may have lacked worldly experience, but it took only a glance to understand that Will Benyon had been occupying the pub for too long.

'Ladies! Which one of you would like to accompany me home?'

'Will . . .' Betty's cards scattered over the floor, exposing an ace of hearts. She rose, lanky and snaky, to her feet. 'What do you think you're playing at?'

He looked past her. 'Shut up, woman.'

Susan's daughter, Linda Savage, dropped a two of clubs onto the floor and scooped up the ace of hearts.

It was a neat, covert, professional manoeuvre.

Betty flushed a painful red. 'Go home, Will Benyon. I'll see to you later.'

Will addressed the fascinated audience. 'Well,' he said. 'I like a good proposition. Pity it's come from her.'

Susan Savage was on her feet. 'Scram.'

Alice picked up Betty's scattered cards.

'Women, eh?' said Will. 'No men dare to enter here.'

Betty took him by the shoulders, shoved him through the door and shut it behind him.

Alice held out the cards to Betty. 'You'd just won a trick,' she said.

Will roared away outside. Nobody blinked. Cards were scrutinised, knitting resumed, conversation swelled.

Fascinating, thought Sophie. Admirable. The Nazis would have thought twice if they had had any idea of this determined, hat-clad female army facing them.

The meeting over, Linda Savage sidled up to Sophie. She was wearing a boxy fake suede jacket over a tight sweater and pink pedal-pushers, and she looked great. Sophie almost hated her.

'If I hear one more reference to light-as-air sponge, I'll scream,' said Linda.

'At least your mum knows how to unblock a drain.'

'Good point.'

They looked each other over. They had known about each other, of course, but had never connected.

'I saw you snaffle a card.'

Linda grinned all over her peaches-and-cream complexion. 'All's fair in love and war. And Betty is just as much of a bully as her husband.' She touched Sophie's arm. 'I know you're a posho and all that, but why don't you join us in The Black Horse tonight? Nothing special, but we can have a natter.'

The fight with Alice (who eventually yielded) over going out was nothing in comparison to the fight Sophie had with herself because her clothes were so awful.

There were two alternatives. One to sob with frustration. The other was to roll up the sleeves of her blouse, double over the school skirt waistband, ignore the state of her shoes, which were past redemption, and tell herself that she had a good figure.

'Don't go anywhere we might disapprove of,' said Alice.

'I'm going round to the Savages for cocoa,' said Sophie.

The lie slipped silkily from her lips.

Women were only permitted to drink in the saloon. Linda bought them both a half-pint of cider – 'Gin's off-the-scale expensive' – and they settled at a table and listened to the rowdy gathering in the main bar where farm workers were downing beer and chasers.

A large woman in tweeds sipped whisky and chain-smoked at an adjacent table. A couple who couldn't keep their hands off each other occupied a second.

'Nice and cosy,' said Linda, who was wearing another tight sweater, a pencil skirt and plenty of make-up.

The cider was strong, loosening Sophie's tongue and spirits. The chatter, the smoke, the wooden chairs and tables, the bursts of noise from the bar, made her think that she *had* taken a step into the world. 'Nice of you to ask me.'

Linda widened her already large eyes. 'Why not? A cat may look at a king and, in this village,

60

everyone mucks in. I mean you may be from France, but you couldn't tell.'

'Would it matter if you could?'

Linda put her head on one side, as if giving this deep consideration. 'Well,' she said uncertainly. 'I suppose not. But you would stand out like a sore thumb, which you don't. You seem like one of us really.'

'That's a relief.'

'Did you tell Scrooge and his wife where you were going?'

'I said I was having cocoa with you.'

Linda's laughter was tinged with uneasiness. 'God, what a pair they are.'

Several mouthfuls in, and after some this-and-that chat, Sophie asked, 'Do you have a job?'

'Woolworth's in Winchelford. I work on the make-up counter.' The lowering of her eyelids revealed an impasto of green, sparkly eyeshadow in all its glory. 'Got this free.' She opened her eyes again. 'You must say if you ever want anything.'

'Do they pay you well?'

Linda lit an untipped cigarette and picked a shred of tobacco off her tongue. 'What do you think?' Puffing away at it. 'Charlie in Household Goods gets double an hour what I get.'

The discrepancies . . . 'How are you supposed to pay rent and pay for food?'

Linda seemed amazed by the idea. 'Rent? I live at home.'

'Don't you want to be independent?'

Imagine moving through quiet mornings, tranquillity, *being* oneself.

Linda enjoyed another lengthy drag. 'No point in muddying the waters. I've got it all worked out: I'll stay there until I get married, which I hope will be in the next year or two. I want a bit of fun first, but I don't fancy being an old maid.' She looked serious. 'Got my aunt's wedding dress on standby. Silk and lace. All it needs is a bit of alteration and I'll be the most glamorous bride seen in Poynsdean for decades.'

Linda was popular. Every so often, she was greeted by one of the men coming or going out of the main bar. 'That's Charlie . . .' She lowered her voice. 'Mother never married. It's been hard and Charlie hates most people . . . That's Simon, he's had polio and his legs aren't right . . . That's Ian, he works on the boats. Lydia Benyon wants to marry him but he's leading her a merry dance.'

The chat flowed on but, after a bit, Sophie realised that Linda was waiting for someone.

The outside door into the saloon opened and Linda's head whipped around. There was a tiny pause and colour sneaked into the peaches-and-cream. 'Hello, Johnno.'

Tall and Saxon fair, he slid an arm around Linda, who pretended to mind: '*Johnno* . . .'

He straightened up. 'And this is . . . ?'

Linda made the introductions: 'Sophie, this is Johnno Bryden from Home Farm. You know, the farm up by the rise. He's been in the army and

62

only just come home. For good. Johnno, this is Sophie. She lives with the Knoxes.'

She must have seen him back in the day. She must have heard of him back in the day. And he of her. *The Frenchie*. But they didn't *know* each other.

Bewildered, she looked at him and knew that she *did* know him. On some level. Some strange level.

'The Rectory girl,' he said gently. 'I remember.'

'He's been in the army,' Linda repeated, flushed, excited. Proprietorial?

Ah . . . she realised she *had* seen him recently. His had been the troubled figure who paced alongside the river. The tawny lion moving over the grasses.

'And National Service before that, but I'm back home now.' Johnno held out a hand.

Blue eyes. Very. Fair hair and skin that looked as if, at one point, it had been heavily tanned. He was not that handsome, perhaps not at all – but whether he was or not seemed irrelevant.

Linda's brother, Grahame, put his head around the door and beckoned to Linda.

Johnno sat down opposite Sophie. The noise dimmed and the room shrank. She searched for something of wit and substance to say. Curiously, after a second or two, it didn't seem to matter.

'I saw you the other day,' she said. 'Down by the river. You looked bothered.'

'The river. Ah, yes.'

In a slight panic, she gazed down at her half-drunk cider. 'Were you? Fed up?'

'Yes.' He didn't seem to mind the confession. 'That's so, and I take it you are, too, because you recognised it.'

So, he was observant. 'I'm not sure where my life is going.'

His smile was grim. 'But I do.'

Linda bid a noisy goodbye to Grahame and turned back. 'Are we going into Winchelford then, Johnno?'

'Sure,' he said easily, but did not take his eyes off Sophie. 'When do you fancy?'

'Johnno has a motorbike,' said Linda.

Johnno cocked an eyebrow. 'Ever been on one?'

'No. Never.'

'I'll give you a ride then,' he said. Then, reading Linda's expression, added: 'After Linda, of course.'

Johnno took himself off to the main bar. Linda flicked Sophie a look from under green lids. 'Don't say anything to anyone, will you? Dad thinks I could do better than a Bryden.'

'You like him?'

'I do . . .' The words sighed out. 'Oh yes.'

'He likes you?'

'He doesn't know it yet, but he does. It's getting him to the point where he sees it, then I'll net him in. He's a bit old-fashioned. Like all the blokes here. Thinks it's up to him to do the running.' She brushed a crumb from the pencil skirt. 'I read an article in a magazine about how, if a girl is clever and never lets on her real motive, she ends up getting them where she wants them.' She sent Sophie a creamy little smile, full of guile and hope.

'I had no idea it was so complicated.'

Linda flicked a half-scornful look in Sophie's direction. 'Yes you did.' She tapped her chest. 'In there. It's all in there.'

Sophie thought: oh, now I see. Yes, I see.

Or, more precisely, she saw Johnno.

At Digbys, the subject of sex had been traded in whispered exchanges as the girls tried to work out what it entailed. Most of them were aware of the broad-brush outline but none had a grasp of the finer details. During the grim expanses of Lent, Miss Chambers' sermons in chapel delved deep into the wickedness of lust, its power, and the unspeakableness of its consequences. 'Men have a Base Nature, girls.' And a Base Nature could ruin a girl's life.

In the dormitories, the older girls spoke of . . . *penis* . . . *penetration* . . . *orgasm* . . . in a frenzy of non-comprehension. (Tilly Watson said that she'd been told an orgasm was a sponge found off the island of Samoa in the South Seas . . .)

Their own bodies had undergone puzzling, sometimes painful developments which were never fully explained. (Their minds, too.)

But she hadn't spotted the central irony until now.

Yes, Digbys strove to prepare girls for their emergence into the world, and forbade them from being

65

wanton. At the same time, they were encouraged to stir up these dangerous and jeopardising passions in the male because they needed to find a husband who would *provide*.

Sophie was washing up at the sink when Osbert's hand clamped down on her arm.

Alice stood behind him.

'You were seen in The Black Horse,' he said. 'With Linda Savage and the Bryden boy.'

Alice gave a soft click of her tongue. 'You told us you would be somewhere else.'

'You must understand,' said Osbert, 'that boys like Johnno Bryden go abroad and come back with different ideas about how to behave with the opposite sex. They can be . . . how can I put it . . . quite insistent and, sometimes, wicked.'

'No need for details, Osbert dear,' said Alice.

He had been waiting for this moment, she reckoned. Hoping it would happen.

He was addressing Sophie. But he was also talking to a hot inner demon. 'You can't be too careful,' he said. 'My duty is to protect you.' He shuffled closer. His breath on her cheek.

It took an effort not to clench her fists.

'You must report to me immediately if he so much as lays a finger on you.'

'You must,' echoed Alice, wearily.

CHAPTER SIX

Each day back at the Rectory was a stone to be carried. Like Hettie, she had to survive them. More than once, she gazed so hard and long at the postcard of Paris propped up on her bedroom mantlepiece, which had belonged to her mother, that the images dissolved, rendering them as fluid and unresolved as her yearnings.

Then, over a Rectory supper of bubble and squeak and corned beef, Alice made an announcement.

Osbert had been inveighing against the programme for Austerity Britain – *so many people in need* – but applauding the still-infant National Health Service. All perfectly usual. *It is incumbent upon us to keep abreast of current affairs.* Then he switched to the topic of Rosa Luxemburg, which *was* startling.

A murdered communist and revolutionary firebrand was not the obvious supper subject, but Osbert had happened upon a newspaper article.

'She was opposed to capitalism and considered that it led to war and imperial plunder.' Sophie noted the fleck of cabbage on his sweater. 'She saw revolution as a way of life. I approve of her revolutionary fervour.' He laughed in his superior way. 'Her aim was to make society more equal.' The cabbage fleck fell to the floor. 'We need revolutionaries to drive out the old ways.'

Sophie had put too much salt into the bubble and squeak and was having trouble getting it down. Osbert and Alice did not seem to notice. They never did.

The evening light at the window struck gold and Sophie took another reluctant mouthful. She tried diversion. Would it ever be possible to go to university? What did one need? How did you apply? What would she study?

'Osbert . . .' Alice wiped her mouth with her handkerchief. 'Osbert, I believe the time has come for me to step back and for Sophie to take over my duties.'

Osbert arranged his knife and fork on the plate. Several expressions chased over his features. 'Did I hear correctly?'

Sophie's gaze veered from husband to wife. Had *she*, Sophie, heard correctly?

Alice assumed the brace position: shoulders pulled tightly back, neck sinews taut string. 'I've decided to make some changes. Now that Sophie is back for good.' She was articulating her words carefully. 'Lady Pitt . . . Enid's . . . health is not good. She requires a companion. She's asked me to fill that post and I was delighted to accept.'

68

A long silence, punctuated by the tick of the kitchen clock.

'You wish to abandon your duties?' Within the confines of the Rectory, Osbert's reserves of saintliness often ran short. 'That's outrageous.'

His wife was considering her needs above his, which was nothing short of blasphemy. 'How would the parish cope? What would the parish *think*?' He pushed the plate aside. 'It would be unaccountable, Alice. A dereliction.'

Alice's complexion turned waxen. 'Have I not served faithfully?'

'Yes, you have. More than could be expected.'

There was a hint of past tenderness and optimism – unexpected, rather painful to hear.

Sophie rose to her feet, hoping to flee. 'I think I should go.'

Alice said, 'You stay, Sophie Morel. What I wish to do involves you.'

'And . . .' Osbert searched for words – something that did not often occur. 'And you didn't think to discuss it with me before giving your answer to Lady Enid?'

'I said I would be happy to be her companion.' Sophie spotted belligerence behind the pale eyes. A first. 'I've served my sentence.'

'Sentence?' Bewildered, and deeply pained. 'But you agreed that our mission in life would be accomplished together. You made that promise when you became my wife.'

'I'm tired, Osbert.'

Sophie gathered up the plates. Bore them over to the sink. The plug was ill-fitting and required a hard push into the plug hole. She ran the water; the hot tap had a long dead leg (Camille used to curse it) and it took time before the hot water appeared. She required all those seconds to process what Alice was proposing.

Alice was proposing to take flight. Sophie bent over the sink. Be fair. Be fair. Equality of opportunity meant that Alice, too, deserved to have a say in the great enterprise, and to squeeze some joy out of her existence.

She shot a look over her shoulder.

Osbert and Alice glared at each other.

Sophie had lived with them all her life, yet she did not know them, understand them, or love them. Concealed behind the middle-aged visages, increasingly furrowed and worn, ran thoughts and desires of which she had no inkling. It had never occurred to her so forcibly – the 'otherness' of other people.

Stacking the plates on the sideboard and reaching for the drying-up towel, she groped for the answers.

On one point, she was absolutely clear. What transpired for Alice, the married woman, would be one thing. What happened to her would be another.

'Alice . . .' Osbert spoke from the peak of the moral high ground. 'This is not a moment for self-indulgence. I know you feel overwhelmed

70

from time to time. So do I, if I'm truthful. There is so much to do. I must minister to the spirit and you to the corporeal. There're so many in need and it never ends. But to abandon everything would be wicked, and a dereliction. You must tell Lady Enid it's not possible.'

'If I refuse?'

'You have no option but to obey me. Let me remind you of the promise you made to me when we married.'

Alice emitted a sound between a sob and a hiss.

'I shall explain to Lady Enid that you have duties and must not abandon them.' Alice's head drooped. 'Surely, you must see that Sophie cannot do what you do?' He gave an audible intake of breath. 'I'm afraid what I say goes, my dear.'

'I deserve better treatment from you.' In the kitchen half-light, Alice looked as though a pin had been driven hard into her flesh.

The anguish was shocking. This was a woman, bound in service to elderly parents and then to the demands of a ministry for so many years, who yearned for white linen tablecloths, elaborate flower arrangements and the luxury of looking into a mirror without guilt.

'Have I not served faithfully?'

'Are you questioning my judgement?' Osbert got to his feet.

The chair screeched.

Alice jumped. 'No, Osbert. Of course not.' She

pleated and unpleated her handkerchief with an unsteady hand.

He stood over his wife. Scrawny. Angry. He dropped a hand onto her shoulder.

She flinched.

'You won't get the vestry window mended that you wished me to mention to her, Osbert. That I can tell you.' It was the last shot she had in the armoury, uttered in a low, spiteful voice.

But the fight in her was almost extinguished.

The rebellion had been double-edged, concluded Sophie with sudden insight. Alice wanted to escape but Alice also *wanted* to be told what to do. She was used to it. She *expected* to be chastised. She *conceded* the constrictions of her existence must remain in place.

Alice was to pack her desires back into the box into which Osbert had confined them. Shockingly, it was how both parties desired it.

None of this was her business. It would never be her business.

'And you can wipe that expression off your face,' Alice hissed at Sophie.

She had read about the kitchen-sink dramas, featuring characters who tore each other apart and took to drink. On a London stage, they were thrilling. Apparently. Up close, she wasn't so sure.

A triumphant Osbert leapt metaphorically into the driving seat. 'It would have been better if this conversation had been in private.'

72

Alice flashed a look at him from under lowered lids. I see, thought Sophie. Alice had chosen her moment precisely because Sophie would be present.

'Both of you wish me to work for you,' she said. 'Do I not have a say?'

At a stroke, husband and wife united.

'No,' said Alice.

'No,' said Osbert. 'When you are twenty-one, we'll think again.'

'And what if *I* don't do as you ask?'

'What other option do you have?' Alice enquired, as evenly as someone who had just had their own wishes quashed might do.

The lingering odours of supper, the mess, the kitchen gloom cut through with the yellow electric light, the dishes in the sink . . . this scenario was Sophie's future.

Osbert cleared his throat. 'We must discuss how to tackle our tasks in the future. And Sophie, I wanted to have a word.'

'Osbert . . . ?' Alice checked herself.

Osbert said, 'After the other night, Mrs Knox and I discussed this at length. Again, we must warn you. There are young men in Poynsdean and you need to be on your guard.'

Silence.

'Do you understand, Sophie? Has anyone been . . . inappropriate? Touched an arm? A leg? Got too close?'

The tap dripped behind her back, alternating

with the tick of the clock. Tick. Drip. Tick. Drip.

'*Do* you understand, Sophie?'

'Yes.'

'Then we'll leave it at that.'

Alice directed one of her intense, pale stares at Sophie and left the kitchen. A few minutes later, the mangled bars of *Für Elise* could be heard sifting in miserably from the sitting room.

'She's watching me,' Sophie reported to Hettie down the phone.

'Sure about that?'

A stranger to the Rectory most likely would not have registered the surveillance, but Sophie knew Alice's ways.

Intercepting the elliptical glance, registering the scuffle of Alice's feet in the hall when she was summoned to Osbert's study. The sly questioning. Where have you been? Why? Who did you talk to?

Occasionally, fetching Osbert's tea tray from his study, she found Alice mounting guard in the kitchen.

'Is the reverend all right?'

Features softened, legs akimbo, Osbert had been dozing in his chair when Sophie had entered. 'I think so.'

'And in an equitable mood?'

'Yes.'

Alice gave a little sigh akin to the sound puff-

74

balls made when Sophie punctured them with a stick.

'I'm sure I don't need to tell you that the reverend is a good person,' she said.

'She likes to defend the man I'm pretty sure she hates,' Sophie said to Hettie. 'Odd, isn't it?'

On another occasion, Alice said, sounding both needy and defiant in the same breath, 'I'm sure you're wondering how not to become like me . . .'

Full marks for analysis.

Alice peered into the teapot, poured out the dregs into a cup and added milk.

Sophie almost gagged. 'I'll make you a fresh pot.'

'Mustn't do that.' Alice hugged the cup with its stewed brew to her chest. 'It would be a waste.'

'A cup of tea?'

Alice's gaze ferreted around the kitchen as if expecting listeners to be at the doors and windows. 'The reverend would consider it unnecessary.'

'But if you want one . . .'

Alice shook her head violently. 'As you heard the other day, I have to be a good wife.'

She sat down at the table and continued, 'So should you wish to be, Sophie. A good wife is given a roof over her head. I know you think I'm hopeless at keeping the house. It's true. My talents are . . . It's against . . . my nature. I have little strength, you know. But we came through a terrible war and order had to be restored.'

Evidently, the dregs of tea had not hit the spot. 'You won't understand how the war threatened everything.'

Sophie understood about the war. Or thought she did. 'The war's over.'

Alice inspected the cup and its disgusting contents. 'Wrong, Sophie. It's not over. It's changed how we think. We'll never feel safe and comfortable again.'

'Isn't that over-dramatic?'

Alice drained the cup. 'That just proves you *really* don't understand.'

A couple of days later, she ambushed Sophie cleaning shoes in the back scullery.

It had taken a bit of doing but Sophie had managed to prise open the swollen door into the back garden and the scullery smelt a lot better than usual.

She observed the procedures. A brush for black polish. Another for the brown. A rag for the final buffing. As Sophie worked through the pile of shoes, she looked up every so often to the garden path which led to the tangle of shrubbery at the end of the neglected garden. A place where she had often hidden.

Alice hovered in the doorway, pale, very pale, and spoke so softly that Sophie had to strain to hear. 'I know you don't believe me, Sophie, but I want to help you, and it's my duty to give you the advice that your mother might have done.'

76

Sophie wiped a clot of black polish off her thumb. A wave of tiredness went through her. She was eighteen and felt eighty. 'Mrs Knox, don't feel obliged.'

But Alice had girded herself to do her duty. 'I know you disagree . . . oh yes, I can read you, Sophie, whatever you may think . . . but women must keep quiet and observe.'

Sophie doubted her warrior mother, who had fought through the Parisian streets, would have ever said anything of the sort. 'Surely they have other options?' she said, yanking at the tongue of Alice's lace-up shoes.

Alice gazed at the tiny scullery window as if she was aiming to fly out of it. 'The men dispose. If they bully a little, it's because they have so many decisions to make. And it's very wearing for them, carrying these responsibilities. They're not so quick to understand feelings.' She turned back to Sophie. 'But we are.'

Sophie spat on the duster and gave the shoe a final rub. Remarks such as these proved that Alice was not borderline mad, as she had often speculated. 'You think that the only task of women is to be married and to keep house?'

'Yes. We must earn our home. A roof over our heads.'

Sophie picked up the next shoe, uncovering a headline from the newspaper spread over the table. Apparently, England and Iceland were skirmishing in a cod war. 'If we earned our own money, wouldn't it be different? Good money that allowed us to live decently and independently?'

Alice started. 'You *don't* understand, Sophie. Terrible things were done. All our houses were bombed. People were homeless.'

The old subject again.

'Yes, and my father lost his life.'

'By the end, all we wanted to do was to shut our front doors and be at home. The men, too.'

Broken lives. Broken houses. Broken society. Whatever the consequences of the war, Sophie knew one thing. Voluntary incarceration had not made Alice happy.

'I was wrong to accept the position with Lady Enid. It upset the reverend.'

'But you would have liked it, Mrs Knox.'

'Yes, I would have done, but duty brings other rewards. As you will discover.'

Falling in with this philosophy validated the wifedom. Osbert's coercion.

'Mrs Knox, why is it that half of humanity has control over the other half?'

'That's how it's always been.'

The final shoe in the pile now shone as brightly as a full moon. 'Girls don't think like that now.' She handed Osbert's shoes to Alice and bent over to pick up her own shoes from the floor. To her amazement, she felt a blow on the back of her head. She straightened up. 'What on earth?'

A pair of eyes drilled into her. 'You be careful.'

* * *

The routines were agreed and a list tacked up on the noticeboard in the kitchen.

Monday was laundry day. Hair wrapped in a scarf, Sophie plunged into the boiling, pounding and mangling, rounded off by the trudge to the washing line bent double by the weight of wet clothes. Sometimes, she sang to make the process more palatable and the sounds whipped away from her to sail over the fields.

'You have a very good voice,' Miss Chambers had said, back at Digbys. 'I hope you will put it to God's use.'

Did God use sopranos? She supposed He must do. Certainly he could do with a few who could sing in tune at the Sunday church services.

Wet laundry possessed a life of its own. In the wind, it flapped and bucked with the ferocity of a trapped animal, and wrapped itself around Sophie. In the cold spells, it froze into boards, which refused to fold for the basket. In the heat, her own sweat added to the damp.

'The washing must be pegged out on the line on Mondays,' said Alice. 'Do you understand? It sets an example to the village. Cleanliness is next to godliness.'

Tuesday mornings were for shopping, either in the village or, preferably, at the market, which was a bus ride away in Winchelford. In a rare tribute to Camille, Alice remarked, 'Your mother taught me that Tuesdays are better. The shopkeepers have had time to get in their supplies after the weekend.'

Shopping took up a lot of time. Even now, over a decade after the end of the war, there were queues at the butcher's and the baker's. 'You would have thought,' said Mrs Hicks, frequently encountered at the butcher's, 'that we'd got past all that by now.' Sophie mentioned this to Alice, who said that Mrs Hicks had got above herself ever since she had been allocated a house on the new council estate.

To return to the Rectory with full string bags was to be interrogated by Osbert. Had she got the best price for the cheese? She should not have paid 1/6d for apples. Any change would be demanded and she was made to count it into a tin with a lock.

'One must cherish every penny,' he said. '*Never let one escape.*'

Wednesday was the day for Bible classes in the church, the soup kitchen, and visits to the elderly confined to their homes.

Thursdays were free – unless Osbert required her.

Fridays were for the ironing.

A future unfolded with dismal clarity. The great enterprise was nothing more than a roster of household chores.

'What a joke it's turning out to be,' she wrote to Hettie.

From an article in the *Sussex Express* (found discarded on the Winchelford bus):

Recent studies of orphans have shown they are susceptible to greater anxiety and depression and are prone to erratic and anti-social behaviour. They are more likely to contemplate suicide, they have higher rates of drug and alcohol abuse, lower self-esteem and poorer health.

This was especially marked in post-war Europe, where losses were extreme. Families, friends, whole communities were decimated. A vital sense of order and stability vanished and changed the psychology of the continent.

Fifteen years on, the agencies who help survivors trace those who are unaccounted for are still hard at work. In Paris, the Bureau for Missing Persons (Le Bureau des Personnes Disparues), run by Denis Maurice . . .

The Rectory
1 July 1959

Darling Hettie,
Are you happy? Silly question, I know you're not. But happier? I've realised that happiness comes in different shades. Like colours.

To be truly happy must be special. I wouldn't know, and the newspaper says that orphans are often very unhappy. But, sometimes, there's a

81

flash of joy. When I'm watching the birds, or walking in the sun. Just for a moment.

Perhaps true happiness can only be when one knows oneself.

You and I must make the effort to get to know ourselves.

Could you do me a favour? Could you buy a stamp for France and post the enclosed letter? I have no money at the moment and I've stolen the stamp for this letter from Osbert's desk, which might land me in the village stocks . . . It's to help me find out about my father. I will pay you back.

With love,
Sophie

10, rue de l'Université
                              À Paris, le 10 juillet 1959
Chère Mademoiselle,
Thank you for your request. We can help you to discover more about your father, but we require more details. If you could kindly answer the following questions . . .

The fee will be . . .
Denis Maurice, Director
Bureau des Personnes Disparues

                                        The Rectory
                                        11 July
Hettie, I am sorry but I have to beg another favour. Could you buy a postal order and stick it into the enclosed envelope and send it off to Paris?

82

This stamp is also stolen, but I owe you double. Triple. I will pay you back as soon as I can . . .

PS Preparing myself for Paris, I unearthed this book on its history in Winchelford library. I had no idea that there were so many revolutions. In 1789 everyone got their heads cut off. In 1871 the communards, very poor people, rose up. They didn't stand a chance and some of them retreated to the Père Lachaise cemetery and were cut down between the tombs.

I'm haunted by a photograph in the book. It shows dead communards stuffed into coffins. They so frail-looking. So starved. When they took to the streets, they built barricades from furniture and they had no weapons. The French National Army mowed them down.

I can't stop looking at their faces. They must have known how vulnerable they were. How disposable and easily cast aside. How cheap their lives were. And it's an insult that no one appears to know their names.

London
13 July

Darling Sophie,
Have done as instructed. Don't worry about the money. Daddy has finally come good with the allowance – a jolly generous one which makes me feel a ghastly person when I think how much I hate the plans the parents have made.

Those poor, brave people. Though I can't help thinking it would have been better if they hadn't taken to the streets. Don't go thinking you should go and sacrifice yourself to some mad political idea . . . In fact, don't think about mad political ideas. It's uncomfortable-making. Sophie, we have to get along with things as they are. Somehow . . .

Written in Sophie's notebook:

Remember us, the communards instruct the onlooker from their coffins. We took action. We were bold.

They were heroes. A hero is pure. He or she can be trusted. My parents were the same.

Hettie doesn't understand – doesn't wish to understand. That's where we differ. But she is anxious about her future, and I am too. For her and for me.

84

CHAPTER SEVEN

School was out. A herd of feral children swarmed through Poynsdean, causing trouble. Driving his tractor around the green, Johnno's father, John Bryden, almost killed the Potter twins. So rattled was he, it was said, that he tacked up an announcement on the village noticeboard that the North Field at Home Farm was available on Wednesday afternoons for sports and games.

The WI heard this call to arms and leapt self-lessly into the breach to organise egg-and-spoon races, relay teams and football matches using hen coops for the goals.

Alice dispatched Sophie to help. 'I must have care of my strength, and you know all about games from school.'

'I hated games, Mrs Knox.'

Since the Lady Enid showdown, there had been an escalation in the issuing of Alice's low-voiced instructions. These were matched by intense piano-playing, and many references as to what Lady Enid might be thinking.

Heading for Home Farm, Sophie walked up the

28 NOV 2024

street. Snippets of the BBC Home Service drifted through open windows. Tins of whitewash, bicycles, wheelbarrows and compost heaps dotted the gardens.

Halfway up the rise, she stopped to look back at Poynsdean. A cluster of houses around the green. The cottages set further back. The derelict houses in East Street. The church. The green medley of the allotments.

Fields rolled out to the west and east, a mixture of cultivated and fallow and meadow. To the north were the Downs. The river and the wetlands were to the south, and beyond those was the sea, which sealed Poynsdean and adjacent villages into their own kingdom.

Its beauty was undeniable. Not that she was deluded about its picture-perfectness. Underneath it often lay penury and poverty of expectation.

A lane led up to the farm. In the field to her right were the ruins of two cottages, mainly heaps of stone. Victims of the migration to the cities during the Industrial Revolution.

The Industrial Revolution was the subject that, along with the American Civil War, Miss Chambers claimed for her own. 'Hard, hard lives, girls.' Miss Chambers knew how to bite down into a subject: the stink of towns and cities from tanneries, sewage, coal smoke, factory effluent . . . You could, she said, expect no mercy living in the streets of the industrialised city, only additional poverty, starvation, disease and early death.

'None of you girls will ever have to walk down a street piled with ordure or die of cholera on a pile of rags in a tenement. You will have every advantage of living your adult lives in the second half of this century. Never forget that, for millions of people, the world was a dark and horrible place, and their existence was a misery.'

'She's just an old, unmarried bat,' said Liddy, who apparently knew these things.

'And mad,' added Roz Green.

Another rumour had it that Miss Chambers was a dangerous communist and should be reported.

Yet, something of her teacher's advocacy seeped into Sophie's soul, and she found the descriptions of darkness and suffering stayed with her.

A dry patch had turned Poynsdean's habitual mud into cracked earth, which was now crumbling into her school sandals. But on the verges, and in the fields, bladder campion, cranesbill, ammi and fragile poppies bloomed joyously.

Here she was tramping along a dusty lane and Hettie, she imagined, was being chauffeured along Berkshire lanes to the shiny cookery school. Learning to make Windsor Soup and to fold a napkin. Having tea at the Ritz. Drinking cocktails so dry they made her wince. She would be wearing skirts that swung to the music's beat and waking up each morning to the revolutionary realisation that she could do what she wished with her day.

Three empty churns perched on the brick stand at the entrance to Home Farm, waiting for collection by the Milk Marketing Board. Dug in beside it were a pair of grubby ducks, who regarded her approach with indifference.

She stooped to inspect a cornflower. So blue. So precise in its formation. So free in its seeding.

'Nice, isn't it?' said a voice.

It was John Bryden, leaning on his stick, watching her.

Did he look like his son? Yes and no. He was tall, bulky and sixtyish, with a high colour, sideburns and a gaze that suggested he didn't miss much. 'I'm glad I caught you. I could do with some summer help on the farm,' he said. 'Do you think the reverend and the missus would allow you out for a few days in the coming weeks? I'd pay you.' His eyebrows twitched. 'You don't have to let on.'

Some money. Her own. Earned.

'I don't need paying, Mr Bryden.'

He straightened up. 'Yes, you do. And you should learn the value of possessing money. It gives you choice. Without it, you're stuck.'

'Then yes, please,' she said.

'That didn't take much.'

'I could come Thursdays. Possibly more often. If I can escape.'

'I'll have a word,' he said.

'Please don't tell them about the money.'

He looked at her long and thoughtfully. 'No.'

The dogs chivvied the ducks, who made their opposition clear. 'Trixie . . . Toby. Leave them

88

alone or it'll be you who fetches up in a pie.' He turned his attention back to Sophie. 'There's all manner of jobs that need doing, including harvesting the hay. It's late this year so I need extra hands. You're young. Strong. And, I take it, willing.'

Sophie picked a cornflower and tucked it into the buttonhole of her blouse.

'That's right,' he said, approvingly. 'Cherish it. There's no knowing what these new chemicals will do that are being sprayed all over the place. A lot of my colleagues swear by them. Not me.' He pointed to the road climbing up to the Downs. 'But the wildflowers are good up by the cross-roads.' He pronounced the 'cross' in the Sussex way, 'crass'. 'And up on the totty land beyond. Worth taking a look. They won't be spraying them there.'

She nodded.

'My Sheila says you're back for good. But I don't reckon you'll be here long.'

'Is it so obvious?'

'You've been busy with other ways. Been away like my Johnno and won't be content with us muck-shovellers.' He shifted on the stick. 'When you're done with those hellions in the field, come up and have a bit of tea with me and the wife.'

Later, an exhausted Sophie sat at a scrubbed oak table in the kitchen at Home Farm. A mug of tea felt like salvation. The slice of boiled fruit cake was heaven on earth.

It was warm. The kettle whistled. The chair she was occupying had a cushion. This was a home. A place, an idea, new to her.

'Eat as much as you like,' said Sheila Bryden as Sophie threw herself at a second slice.

'Vicar too busy with godly matters to feed you? His wife too busy buttering up the gentry at Pitt House?' asked John.

'Loose talk, John,' said his wife.

She was younger than her husband, thin and muscly from constant labour. She sat down opposite Sophie. 'I knew your mother. She was lovely. She never managed to speak English that well, but we understood each other. She told me about your father. Very romantic. He was older, I think. She always said she would take you back to Paris, but she got too ill.' She dug into the sugar bowl for a lump. 'Your mother loved you very much. You could tell.'

Sophie studied her tea.

Sheila continued, 'She was different. But you'd expect that, her being French and all that. That dress she wore on Sundays. Pink, I think. Yes, pink. Soft and flowing. Goodness knows where she got it from, but it was quite different from anything any of us wore. She lost weight at the end, but her skin was always a marvel. So clear, almost like pearls. She loved cream and it wasn't permitted in the Rectory. I thought that was mean and I used to give her some with our raspberries.'

'Mrs Bryden, did she have any friends?'

'Call me Sheila. Not so you'd know, but nobody in Poynsdean was mean to her – the opposite, in fact. They were sorry she had to live with the Knoxes, who made sure they got their pound of flesh.' Sheila stirred her tea. 'Poynsdean wasn't her place.' She glanced at Sophie. 'And you'll be wanting to go and find out where your family came from?'

John Bryden lit his pipe. 'Sheila, love, she'll be thinking you want her to leave.'

Sheila dangled a third slice of cake. 'I'm not saying anything you don't know. We're not all cut from the same cloth; that's the way the Almighty arranged things.' She thrust the slice at Sophie. 'You won't get fruit cake like this in France.'

Sophie ate up, enveloped in family and noise. A world unknown to her.

Johnno surged into the kitchen and her pulse crackled. 'Ah, the Rectory girl! Have you eaten all the cake?'

Sheila heaved herself to her feet. 'You'll be wanting your tea.'

'Finish your own tea first, Mum.' He dropped into an empty chair. 'Haven't seen you at the pub, Sophie. Linda was looking out for you.'

'Sophie probably isn't allowed out much,' said Sheila. 'Very sensible and proper.'

Sophie and Johnno's gazes clashed.

I don't think sensible has much going for it, said his.

I agree, said hers.

*   *   *

Egg collection was complicated. 'The little floozies lay all over the place,' said Shelia. 'They like a tease.'

This was true. Sophie peered under hedgerows, combed the long grass and searched abandoned tyres and under sacking.

Who knew that the clucking of hens held a music? Or that to alight on a trove of eggs – white, brown, sometimes stained, or pure pearl, sometimes with a feather stuck on the shell – could give such pleasure? Or that the brush of grass on flesh, the smell of earth, the sun on her body could induce dreaminess?

That afternoon was a warm one. Determined to ratchet up her hen craft, Sophie stalked Pearl and Biddy, last spotted by the ruined cottages.

In the lane, the bone-dry earth was threaded with runnels of chalk. An Adonis blue butterfly flew past. Jealous of its freedom, she observed it hovering over the verge. Then remembered it would probably only live for a few days.

Over by the cottages, the grass grew lush and vigorous. Delicious sun. Soft grass. Tired from bad dreams the previous night – anxiety. *What do I do?* – she dropped down to the ground, rolled over onto her back and closed her eyes.

When she opened them again, Johnno Bryden was standing above her. 'Want to see a dormouse nest?'

Sophie sat up and said crossly, 'I didn't hear you.'

He grinned, which made him look younger. 'They teach you a few things on National Service,' he said.

She extracted grass from her hair. 'Was it awful?'

He sat down. 'I was serving Queen and country by helping out in the hotspots of the empire. Private number 07939-254848.'

'That's no answer.'

He eased a sappy blade of grass from its moorings and bit into it. 'If you mind about having no privacy, stinking latrines and underwear that rubs you raw, pointless marching, stupid men bullying you, then yes. On the other hand, I was taken out of here, got to see the world. Met all sorts. Discovered I could like people other than my family.' The pause bordered on the theatrical. 'Found I could hate people other than my family. When you first pitch up at the barracks, they lock you in a hut with orders to clean night and day, directed by a bastard sergeant. The cursing is phenomenal but, by the end of two weeks, you're a team.'

'And you've come back to work with your father.' She paused. 'You can't hate *him*?'

'That's the plan. Always has been, whether I like it or not. My advice to you is never be born the eldest.'

She laughed.

'What about you?' he asked. 'What would you like to do?'

This was the first time anyone in Poynsdean had

bothered with Sophie's preferences. 'Not sure. Working it out.'

'Ah. *Allons enfants de la patrie* . . .'

She was astonished. 'You speak French?'

'No, but we learnt a few phrases overseas.' And he repeated one that was obviously filthy.

'In *that* area you know more French than I do.'

'I bet you speak it fluently. Your mother and all that . . .'

'Sort of,' she said. 'But I don't have a deep knowledge of it. Yet. Not the way you get from living in a country.'

'Yet?' he said. 'You *are* planning to go.'

'Am I?'

'It's OK to be wary.' He gazed out over the field that, one day, would be his. 'But, if it was me, that's what I'd be thinking.'

It was almost as if he had reached out a hand and touched her heart through her chest. His shoulder nudged hers and an excitement sparked that made her feel strange and unlike herself.

'Meanwhile, we'll both have to be content with our deep knowledge of Poynsdean.'

'I reckon it hasn't changed much since the Saxons,' she said. 'But that's what makes it what it is.'

'Like Egypt.'

'Really?'

'We were sent there to clear up the mess after the Suez crisis. The villages we visited were tough and traditional. Just like Poynsdean.'

94

He chucked the sucked-dry grass stem and selected a second.

'Not that I got to observe that much. Regrets there, for God knows when I'll get another chance.' Wry grin. 'But that's how it works.'

'I've seen photos of the pyramids in the *National Geographic* magazine in the school library,' she said. 'Can't work out how they were built.'

'Easy when you have extraordinary architects and don't mind sacrificing thousands.'

She thought about that.

Johnno had got up steam. 'We were busy being the boys and didn't think about much else. Drink. Eyeing up women if we got a chance. Expat wives drank like fishes and were bored out of their skulls. Happy days. Avoiding mosquitos and dysentery took up a lot of time. Training in the desert was a killer. That heat . . . it was like a hammer in the head. In the end, not being thirsty or drenched in sweat was all we cared about. Jordan was much the same: heat and dust. Singapore was different. I was a radio direction operator there.' He was silent for a moment. 'Skilled work. But not for that long.' A pause. 'I miss it.'

'Run away.'

He turned sceptical blue eyes on her. 'You think?'

'Speak to your father. Tell him what you feel.'

'My father inherited the farm from his father who inherited it from his.'

'You're lucky knowing your family, your father. I wish I did.'

He touched her arm. 'Sorry. I wasn't thinking.'

'But does it have to be like that?' She thought of the Rectory, the Knoxes, the weekly timetable. 'It could be different.'

His scepticism was obvious.

'Johnno, how can I find out about buying tickets to France?'

He grinned. 'You're the runaway.'

'Yes. Yes, I am.'

'You'll need to get to the London station that sells tickets for the boat train. I can find out which one.'

He got to his feet and held out a hand to help her up. 'Did you want to see that dormouse nest?'

She looked up at him. Johnno might be experienced in the ways of the world, and strong, but he was stretched between a rock and a hard place.

He returned the look, and her eyes widened.

This was new.

The dormouse nest was a scrabble of grass, leaves and honeysuckle bark.

Tucked into a hedgerow over by the hazelnut trees, it looked precarious and vulnerable, but it was probably perfectly fine. Dormice had had centuries to perfect their nest-building skills.

'Can I look?'

'Best not,' said Johnno. 'There's probably four or five babies in there. Might put them at risk.'

She could not have described the bits of Johnno. How his chin was shaped. Or how his hair fell.

Instead she appeared to be enveloped in a presence that felt electric, all-encompassing.

For a while they stood watching and were rewarded by the mother returning. Cautious. Dark-eyed. Long-tailed. Nut brown.

Johnno reached for Sophie's hand and held it.

CHAPTER EIGHT

As promised, John Bryden paid her. Not too much. Not too little. 'I'm very grateful,' she told him. 'You're right. I must earn money.'

'It's a powerful thing, Sophie Morel.'

She hid the money among the cleaning materials in the kitchen cupboard. Alice would never find it in a million years.

The Bryden farm might have been littered with abandoned tins of creosote, animal excrement and rusting equipment, but it was ruled with kindness. There was no sentimentality about the animals, but no cruelty either. 'The soil here is a heck of a tease,' said John. 'Up the top towards the Downs, it's lime-rich and chalky. Here by the farm, it changes, and down towards the wetlands it's acid and sandstone. So . . . I keep the Belted Galloways. Traditional hardy cows. And the saddleback pig.'

The two younger Bryden children – 'unexpected late crocuses,' said Sheila, 'and a big surprise. I thought we were done with Johnno and Clare' – scrambled over the machinery, swung from trees and splashed through puddles. 'If you're looking for Johnno,' she added, 'he's helping out on the Evans' farm. We do turn and turn about here with our neighbours.'

'Actually, I wasn't looking for him.'

'No? Oh well.' Sheila smiled.

It was time for the hay harvest.

Johnno briefed Sophie. This was the moment that the farms lent each other their tractors, and the doughty men of Poynsdean were put on red alert. The talk at mealtimes would be of nothing else but weather and tonnage.

Even Sophie knew that the hay harvest could be ruined in a day and Poynsdeaners, young and old, high or low, were trained to watch out for any shift in the clouds or wind. Out egg-hunting, Sophie came across the two younger Brydens keeping watch in the north field with homemade rock buns and a bottle of pop.

It was going to rain . . . It wasn't going to rain . . . and John Bryden ordered everyone out to the fields.

Cue frantic activity. Dawn-to-dusk toil to cut the hay and marshal it into rows. Ground-nesting birds took to the air in a wild, distressed exodus and rabbits and mice dashed for safety. More than one furry bloody corpse was scooped up and taken home for the pot.

Their screams made her wince. More than once, she had to turn away.

Johnno drove up on a borrowed tractor. Bare-chested. Sweat-lashed. Dusty. 'What's the matter?'

It was hot and the air pulsed between them.

She raised her streaked face. 'I didn't realise that the animals would suffer.'

The tractor was filthy with mud and manure – and, she suspected, the blood of the slaughtered – and the engine was so noisy it was difficult to hear his reply. She *thought* she heard him say: 'You'll get used to it.'

The hay required to be turned before being baled up and loaded onto the wagons. 'Easy work for the girls,' said John Bryden. He was joking, it turned out. Every muscle screamed and every shred of clothing was drenched. Loading the wagon was harder – but the barrel of country cider stowed under the hedgerow, to which everyone helped themselves, came to their aid.

When not on his tractor, John Bryden tramped back and forth from field to field. 'The hay should smell light and grassy,' he said. 'If it's acrid or musty it means there's mould in there.'

The hay scent, so fresh and with hints of sun and fruit, induced a rapture. Again and again, Sophie gave in to the temptation to plunge her hands down through its spiky richness and to inhale the scent of the wildflowers and grasses threading through it.

This, this was . . . ? The essence of summer, of fertility. It was to understand how sweet it was to indulge the senses. It was to understand how a handful of hay could provide nourishment for an animal in winter.

By the Saturday, the bales had been stacked in the barn. 'Thank the Lordy that John had the foresight to build the barn,' said Sheila. 'We don't want to be covering haystacks with tarps, like my ma and da had to do. They left it too late one year and Bill Yarn was killed by lightning trying to get one over the top.'

A copious lunchtime spread up at the farmhouse heralded the finale. Sophie was deputed to take around the plates of sandwiches. 'Egg, fish paste, anyone?'

Everyone was famished. Everyone could eat a horse. Everyone could sink a vat of cider.

Johnno was talking to Linda Savage's brother, Grahame.

She proffered a half-empty plate of sandwiches. 'Your mum says we can make more,' she said. She sniffed the warmth and field grime in the air. 'Dried grass, a touch of blackberry and apple, old shirts, and just a hint of soap . . . you could bottle it and sell it.' Johnno laughed and Grahame gave a tight smile.

Her forearms had caught the sun. 'You need to do something about those,' said Johnno and touched the tongue of sunburn running up her arm.

Grahame chewed fish-paste sandwich and asked pointedly, 'Are you seeing our Linda tonight?'

'Sure am,' replied Johnno after a moment.

Grahame tackled another sandwich. 'She's quite a girl, my sister. Luckily, she didn't inherit the family temper. That fell to me.' He directed the comment at Sophie. 'Since my father died, I'm in charge of the women in the family.'

Sophie moved away. When she returned with the refills, Grahame was talking to John Bryden. 'What was I being warned about, Johnno?'

His eyes were rimmed with dust. 'He protects his sister.'

'So? What am I to do with it?'

Johnno said, 'Grahame likes to think he's a man of the world. Don't get me wrong, he's a good man, but he doesn't see things as they are.'

Sophie digested this. 'I see,' she said, but she didn't.

His grin suggested experiences and worlds of which she knew nothing. 'Don't worry about it.'

The men retired to the yard to smoke. The two younger Bryden children took the opportunity to scoff the remainder of the sandwiches and cake, watched by their mother and Sophie.

'A change from all your book reading,' said Sheila, leaning back against the dresser. 'For a girl, this is more natural work. You don't want all that stuff in your head when you marry.'

'Are books and reading so bad?'

''Course not. But you'll need your energy for your family.' Sheila brushed crumbs off her sturdy apron. 'You do *want* to get married, I take it? Have babies?' She pointed to her children, who were making stupid faces at each other. 'They're the best thing, you know. Hard work, but the best. Being a spinster . . .' Clearly, she was choosing her words carefully. 'It can be thought to be . . . unfeminine.'

'But aren't there other things, too?'

After a long harvest, Sheila was tired. She snaffled the tobacco tin from the kitchen table, fashioned two rollies and offered one to Sophie. 'It's been nice having you around.' She patted Sophie's shoulder. 'I've grown fond. I'm talking out of turn, but I'm concerned for you, living at the Rectory. Such a strange set-up. Very odd.' She thought for a moment. 'It's fine if they want to do their thing in church, but I don't think it's a good thing for a young girl like you to be living with them.'

Sophie wanted to ask why. It also struck her that Sheila might possibly be able to give her useful information about sex, but Sheila's attention had been diverted by her daughter hacking at the fruit cake and she rushed over to save it.

On her return, Alice was lurking in the hall of the Rectory, dressed in her Lady Enid visitation outfit. This included the hat, which really, really looked as though it should be put out of its misery.

'Where've you been?'

'Up at Home Farm.'

'Ah. Your new friends.'

Sophie willed the coins hidden in her pocket not to clink.

'Had you forgotten you were supposed to help the reverend with his accounts?' Alice folded her arms around her newly bulky middle, as if to protect it. 'He wishes to see you. The potatoes for supper need peeling and, while you do so, you can reflect on the fun people like the Brydens will be poking at you behind your back.'

Oh Alice, she thought.

I bet you've never plunged your hands into new hay.

I bet you've never drunk cold cider in the midday sun.

You have never been smiled at by a man like Johnno Bryden.

She stood by the study door, steadying herself to step into Osbert's underworld.

Osbert told the story – a favourite one – of how he had been called to his life's mission. God's voice had sounded in his ear. The right ear, not the left – he was insistent on that point.

But had it been God?

Sophie had her theories.

In her notebook, she poked fun. *Let's put one over on the old windbag. Make him think he's working for Him upstairs but he's really working for me, Lucifer, downstairs.*

Poor Osbert.

'Come.' Osbert was folded over his desk, the household ledger open in front of him. His wrestling match with numbers was a regular feature. The fallout could be noisy.

If caught at a low ebb by one of Osbert's eruptions, Sophie dug with abandon into her reservoirs of malice. It was pleasurable, so *very* pleasurable, to list his inadequacies. A grown man, a vicar, a shepherd of souls, losing his temper in such a way demeaned him. Etc.

Removing a stack of papers from the chair seat, she sat down and scanned the room for new books. The latest was on the floor. She nudged it with her foot and read the title: *The Winthrop Woman* by Anya Seton.

Osbert did not look up. 'It's about the early settlers in Boston and a woman who defied the Puritan fathers and was persecuted.'

She considered for a moment. 'Do you mean it's a story about a woman who dared to think independently and was made to pay for it?'

'Sophie Morel, you think you have all the answers.'

The study windows had never enjoyed the benefits of curtains. Thus, Osbert could be observed at his desk by the passers-by in Church Lane – the visible toil giving him status in the village. He may not have been loved by the majority of his parishioners. *But he did his best . . . he rolled his sleeves up . . .* it was said.

Cassock hanging ever more loosely, eyes burning with frustration and bad temper, Osbert pointed to a column of figures. 'I am out by 1/6d.'

'You wish me to check it?'

He pushed the ledger over the desk in her direction. She glanced at it and, within seconds, spotted what was wrong. 'You've made a mistake in Outgoings. Here.'

'Are you sure?'

'The entry was in the wrong place.'

'Must I remind you that what God expects from us is humility?'

Most of her life at Digbys had been spent seeking out warmth and additional food. And shelter for the spirit. Life here elicited different responses. Mainly, the ambition to outwit her foster parents. To prick and unsettle them. To wrap them in sacking and dump them in the river. To run a knife through their hearts, even.

Mulling the options was always pleasurable. She sat composedly while a riot of murderous alternatives slid through her mind.

'Lots of people have difficulty with figures.'

She was rewarded by an offended frown. Osbert did not like to be reminded of his limitations.

Having stowed the ledger, Osbert stood up and went over to the window. 'Now . . .' He slotted his hands into opposing sleeves. 'Mrs Knox tells me that, since your return, you're not engaging with our purpose. That's disappointing.'

In the village, the vicar was known as kindly. Odd, but kindly. Sophie knew better. The plain fact was that dealing out chastisement agreed with him.

'She feels that going away to school has spoilt you for hard work. Would she be correct? Going away to school was Mrs Knox's wish, because she imagined you would benefit greatly, but it'll be a sorry thing if the result is disobedience and ingratitude.'

'I'll try to be grateful.'

He appeared hot with righteousness and an extra element that she did not recognise.

'It must be difficult for you, my dear.'

Astonished, she looked up. A sort of compassion. A sort of understanding. It knocked her prejudices flat.

'I want to do the best for you, Sophie. But you must be guided by me.'

'Why didn't you send me back to France after my mother died? She would have tried to contact her family.'

'Your mother was ill for a long time. Decisions were difficult for her.' A sigh. 'I believe she wrote a few letters but never got any replies.'

Sophie studied the bookshelves. She supposed he was telling the truth. 'Was it you or Mrs Knox who chose Digbys?'

'I was fortunate enough to know Miss Chambers, who has made it her life's work to help girls like you.' He returned to his chair. 'You were a gift to us, you know. From the Almighty. Mrs Knox and I were not blessed, and then along came your mother and you. We offered you shelter and the chance to live alongside the best of principles. It's not unreasonable to expect cooperation.'

'In the future . . .' began Sophie.

Osbert stared at the desk. Then the floor. Then the window. 'For the present, your future's with us.'

'I plan to go to Paris to search for my relations. For my father.'

'Good heavens. But of course. All in good time. In fact, I was going to look out your mother's papers. There are not many . . . she had so little . . . but they may give you a clue about who you are.' He sent her the *bless you, my child* look with which Poynsdean was familiar. 'I cannot imagine what it's like not knowing who you are.'

He didn't mean to be cruel, she told herself. Then, correcting herself: *he did*.

'But I'm here to help you direct your thoughts. Your worries and preoccupations. At your age, there are so many internal conflicts and many unanswered questions.'

Again, she detected genuine concern. But, accustomed to ascribing the worst to his motives, she had no idea how to handle it.

His eyes grew bright. His Adam's apple strained. 'I trust you took my advice to heart about watching your behaviour with the boys.' Silence. 'I also hope you will confide in me if you have any questions.'

Osbert, Alice, her situation, her powerlessness: all these were fetters, all to be shaken off.

'The money my mother brought with her. I would like to have it, please.'

'So you can use it to run away to Paris? My dear

girl, I don't know where the demanding tone has come from. You're still under our jurisdiction, and we make the decisions. You'll be given it at the correct time.' He levelled a not unsympathetic gaze at her. 'You're still very young, Sophie. Rest assured the money's safe in the post office. You may take charge of it when you're twenty-one.'

His crudely fashioned bookshelves housed shiny, colourful books all about love, passion, battle, upheaval, theology . . . She knew so little about them. About anything. 'I plan to get a job. Perhaps in London.'

'Of course.' Again, a flash of sympathy. 'Please don't doubt a rich, full life is what Mrs Knox and I would wish for you. In fact, I was discussing you with Mrs Thurber up at the school and we agreed an activity would be just the thing. She needs help with reading practice for the younger children, which would be easy to fit in with your duties here.'

Osbert stood behind her chair. 'You're too young to appreciate this but a parish is a precious thing, Sophie. Within it, we have care for its souls who need guidance and spiritual nourishment. It's not easily accomplished, and I, and Mrs Knox of course, need help.'

'And if I don't wish this life?'

'If you think about it, and I advise that you do, there's no alternative for the present.' He dropped his hands onto Sophie's shoulders. 'Until you're older, you belong here. With us. You have been grafted into the village.' A shiver ran deep into her body. 'But I understand you have larger ambitions. The world is tempting, but you don't understand how it works. How would you know how to survive in a snake pit' – these last two words were accorded a hissing emphasis – 'like London? You wouldn't. And that's not a happy thought.' He gave her shoulders a squeeze and stepped away.

She got to her feet. 'I would prefer that you didn't touch me.'

He didn't answer directly but pointed to the drawer containing the ledger. 'Thank you for your help. If Mrs Thurber won't do, you might consider book-keeping. To keep that mind of yours occupied.'

She exited as fast as possible from the study.

In her notebook, she wrote: *I can't decide if he is a wicked man, or a good man with weird characteristics.*

Sophie was used to queuing outside the phone box – to which she often resorted if she wished for a private conversation.

In warm weather, useful bits of information were bartered here. *Bus broken down. Apples extra cheap in Winchelford.* In cold weather, the impatient had been known to bang on the door and shout out: 'Time's up, you old bugger.' Or 'Come along, missus.'

The kiosk was sited on the village green directly in front of the Benyon house, which gave Betty

110

Benyon a prime view into the comings and goings. It had been hot since the hay harvest. Poynsdean drowsed in post-harvest torpor and the air shimmered over the lick of woodland fringing Home Farm and over the rise to the Downs.

No queue today. Only Grahame Savage conducting an animated conversation inside. He lifted a finger in acknowledgement, turned away, and presented Sophie with a ringside view of a sunburnt neck and sturdy torso.

Grahame emerged and planted himself foursquare in front of Sophie. 'Kept him waiting, then?'

Sophie spotted an opening. 'He's used to me not phoning on time,' she replied, calculating that news of 'the Frenchie's passionate love affair' would reach Linda within the hour and be all over Poynsdean by the evening.

He held the door open for her. 'An understanding bloke, then.'

'Famous for his patience.'

The phone box smelt of cold metal, fag ash and urine. Grahame had been drinking beer and donated an additional top note of hops and hot male. She held the door open with a foot, slotted in a two-shilling piece and pressed button 'A'. Hettie answered and Sophie pressed button 'B'.

'It's me,' she said. 'I would have gone mad if I couldn't speak to you.'

Holding the door open put uncomfortable traction on her toe. Removing her foot, she stared instead at a distorted village green through grubby glass, and inhaled male sweat.

Trunk calls were timed for three minutes, and the time pressure often made conversation awkward. In the past, Hettie had sometimes begun to describe an outing, realised that it was unfair on Sophie and checked herself.

'You can tell me where you've been,' said Sophie, working out what the problem might be. 'I'm not jealous.'

But she was.

'Oh, Sophie, it's so awful that you're having to work so hard.'

Getting their communications right was not as simple as it used to be. At Digbys it had been so easy. Now, not so much.

Hettie sounded breathless. 'Remember how we both thought cookery stupid? Well, it is. I've had to make an egg mousse with gelatine. Couldn't get the ingredients right and the whole thing collapsed.' There was a small silence. 'It'll be Coronation Chicken next.' Another silence. Then, as always, Hettie appeared to intuit what Sophie was thinking. 'Sophie? We must talk to each other. I can't bear it if we fall out. You're all I've got.' She gave a little wail. 'Sophs, I depend on you.'

The *cri de coeur* was the main thing; it was all that mattered. Sophie's love for Hettie did a tidal surge. 'I'm not jealous, Het. Not of stupid Coronation Chicken, but not of you either – of your life, I mean.'

'Don't be.'

'Well, maybe I am a little. A teaspoonful. I've been helping out on a local farm – I'm very tanned.'

'I'd much rather be there with you. You know how I hate parties and everything else Mother has thrown at me.'

'I helped bring in the hay,' said Sophie, thinking of the clothes, the parties, the *life* that she didn't have. 'I didn't know it would be so satisfying.'

Hettie sounded unconvinced. 'Promise me, Sophs, that if your resentment becomes too much, you'll tell. *Tell.* In return, I'll tell when the horror of trying to be nice to people who think I'm ugly and stupid threatens to put me in the loony bin.'

Sophie laughed. 'Done.' The first pips sounded and she said quickly, 'They've given me a time-table you wouldn't believe. Cleaning upstairs on Mondays, shopping on Tuesdays, and Osbert won't tell me where the post office book is with my money in it. He asks me questions about men and tries to tell me how to behave.'

'You were right. It's like Bluebeard.' Hettie was shocked but also fascinated. 'I mean, is he *safe*?'

'I *think* so.' *His hands on her shoulders.* 'No.'

'You must come and stay.'

'Your mother hates me.'

'Do I care? We're off to Argyll for a couple of weeks. After then.'

The call ended. Half choked by the hops and fag smoke, she hung onto the receiver for a bit.

113

The sun was on her back, underpinning the unavoidable fact that her Aertex shirt and serge shorts were far too hot.

What did she look like, with her battered strapped sandals, games shorts and school blouse? Frustration fizzed like the champagne she was never going to drink.

The receiver emitted a high-pitched noise.

On her way back, she dropped by the allotments. Fred would almost certainly be there. The Fred whom her mother had said possessed the soul of a romantic and the fingernails of a *clochard*, and knew about real, sensible things.

When Camille became too weak to work the Rectory garden, Fred sent up offerings of fruit and vegetables. 'I wanted to help. Her, not them.'

The deliveries became a fixed thing.

'I won't set foot in that church,' he said – which impressed Sophie hugely. 'All that praying and telling you what to do. My veg pays my dues.' It did, too: year after year, carrots, onions, cabbages, beans and soft fruit represented earth's bounty.

Fred had views. On planting. On weeding. On harvesting. These were inflicted on fellow gardeners and not always received gratefully. Ben Benyon had been known to call Fred a 'tinpot dictator' and the easily frightened Miss Ferndale scuttled away whenever she saw him.

Sophie pulled a crate into the shade and sat down.

'Hello, miss.' Rain or shine, Fred was dressed

114

in a thick shirt, corduroys and multi-pocketed waistcoat. 'You've caught me at the right time. I've been up delivering to the Bales.'

'Saint Fred,' she said.

He was. Mostly. Fred took home his produce to his wife but, alongside the Rectory's, a portion was put aside for the Bale family and anyone else in East Street who was having a rough time.

'Are things bad?'

'Drinking like fishes. Anything they can lay hands on. Turpentine, if that was on offer. The children look bad and the dog is starving.'

She got to her feet. 'Should we do something? Go to the council?'

Fred snorted. 'What do you think?'

He decanted beans, carrots, onions and mint into an empty trug. 'It's the dog I worry about. On his last legs.' He jerked a finger towards the hoe leaning against the shed. 'Can you give that patch a going-over?'

The soil was rich and black, dotted with decaying fragments of a previous cabbage harvest. She directed the hoe this way and that, while images of ill children and a hungry dog played in her head.

Marty Morrell, Mrs Tafton and her son and the Henley family came and went. Ben Benyon kept his distance. Miss Ferndale hid behind her runner beans. Fred poured out tea from his Thermos into a tin mug and offered it to Sophie and they discussed vegetables and flowers, weather and soil.

The behaviour of the judges at the vegetable and flower show was lingered over. 'My carrots . . . *third* place . . . it was a set-up. Criminal. Those responsible will never set foot in my garden while I still have breath. And I still have plenty.'

Fred's gooseberries mattered even more than the veg, if that were possible. 'And how did the gooseberries do?'

'Someone nobbled the judges there too.' Fred's vengeful side was being given a fair airing. 'Bill Mead, if I know anything. Good mind to knock him down.'

'I could open the door to his raspberry cage if you would like me to.'

'You could do. You could do.'

He unlocked his shed and beckoned Sophie inside. There was – just – space to admit two. She edged in.

A shelf racked with his seed jars ran down one length. A diagram of his year's planting was tacked up on the opposite wall, plus photographs of his previous wins and the familiar (and meticulous) listing of the competitions in which he had participated since 1932. Tapping it, he said, 'My life. All there.' He glanced at her almost shyly. 'Nothing much has changed. Not even with the war.'

'Do you think about it much?' she had once asked him.

'Why would I do that, miss?'

She thought his response strange. Then, having got to know more about what happened, she began

116

to understand there was so much of it. The battles, the bombs, the cruelties, the stories of the Home Guard, of the Dunkirk flotilla of little ships, of the Desert Rats and French Resistance, the D-Day landings, the taking of Berlin . . . so much, so jumbled . . .

She returned outside. 'Fred, your tomatoes are large enough to be weapons.'

Fred retorted that she had been reading too many books.

How lustrous the tomatoes were. A red that almost glowed. She crouched down to look, really look at them. Straightening up, her line of vision travelled towards the adjacent allotment through Fred's fretwork of sweet peas and runner beans trained up hazel supports.

A black-clad figure was standing there. Very still. His gaze focussed on Sophie.

Osbert.

CHAPTER NINE

The rooted figure, the intense stare, made her heart thump. What to do? Give in to nausea or laugh at the old dinosaur?

He called out, 'Sophie, I wish to talk to you.'

Emerging from his hut, Fred took in the scene and jerked a thumb in the opposite direction. 'Leg it and I'll give himself the veg.'

Sophie fled. Out of the allotments and up towards the wood licking around Home Farm, where the tree cover offered protection. Once there, she headed for the spring.

It was said that St Oluf's spring was possessed of healing properties. There was no evidence of this, but did it matter? Legends were big business. Stories shifted all the time. So much so, Sophie worked out that, when it came to the telling, truth was not important. Only the narrators.

Yet even the sceptical agreed the water from St Oluf's was special. A clear, strong water. Iron workers had used it during the medieval period, the fleeing Empress Matilda had stopped to bathe her face in it, and smugglers had survived on it when in hiding from excise men.

A raised flat stone flanked the spring, a useful platform for those wanting an excuse to sit close together. Many did.

Sophie sank down and dropped her head into her hands. In his black cassocked menace, Osbert manifested behind her lids.

She looked up. A bee was pollen-shopping on a patch of rosebay willowherb, and she watched its migration from flower to flower.

What did Osbert crave?

Her body? Her mind? Her youth?

Back went her head into her hands.

'That bad?'

The voice was familiar and she raised her head. Johnno Bryden.

He was observing Sophie from the tree cover, a replica of his father in a checked shirt and serviceable dungarees.

As he moved towards her, the sun turned his fair hair into shades of gold.

Notebook: *A lion, moving over the savannah.*

'I didn't see you.'

'If you had, it would suggest I'm losing my fieldcraft skills.'

'Meaning?'

'Blending in with your surroundings in order to surprise the enemy.'

'I wish you would surprise Osbert Knox. Give him a nasty fright.'

She spoke heatedly and Johnno frowned. 'What's that old bugger been up to?'

'I'm not sure,' she said, rattled and uncertain. 'He looks at me.' She fumbled her way through a tide of embarrassment. 'In a way that bothers me. I don't know what to think.' She shook her head. 'I shouldn't be telling you this. I'm imagining things.'

He dropped down beside her on the stone. 'You're upset. As your sergeant, I order you to watch the spring for a minute in silence.'

Obediently, the water rose up from its source, flowered over the stones and flowed onwards.

'I envy it,' she said at last. 'It goes somewhere.'

Johnno did not look at her but said in a low voice, 'You can buy a ticket for the boat train at Victoria station. Cheapest is to sit up all night. It will be uncomfortable, but it doesn't last that long.'

Impulsively, she reached out with her hand. To her delight, he took it in his. For a second, their fingers twined around the other's. Letting go almost immediately, he reached over and dabbled his hand in the water.

'I'm not sure I like to think of you going, Sophie Morel.'

His touch triggered the electric sensation that did its best to prevent Sophie breathing naturally. To counteract the violence of her reaction, she dug her fingernail into the fleshy part of her thumb. 'Come too,' she said. 'See Paris.'

'I like your jokes,' he said.

'Poynsdean isn't a prison.'

His laugh held some bitterness. 'Yes and no.'

Again, she thought of the lion padding over the grasslands and, since the subject of the future obviously troubled him, she changed it.

'Do you come down here when you need time off from the farm?'

'Yup.'

She looked around. Ivy crawled octopoidally up a tree whose leaf canopy baffled the sun. 'Thank you for being so nice.'

'I learnt a few things in the army that I had never thought about until I was locked up with the lads.' He was almost joking, but not quite. 'Human beings are like icebergs: what you see on the surface isn't what's going on underneath.' An ant ran up his arm and he shuffled it carefully onto a leaf. 'For instance, I had no idea how cruel human beings can be. Including myself.' He watched the ant's progress. 'You won't know, yet.'

She wasn't entirely sure what Johnno was driving at, only that they were skirting around an intimacy that she found thrilling.

'I also discovered men and women have appetites,' he uttered nostalgically. 'And the flesh is a bully.'

'Are you talking about women?'

'Some.'

'They must have been sad when you left.'

He sent her a look. 'These were women who you could buy for the night.'

She flushed. 'Oh. Yes, of course. I know about that. Stupid of me.'

The exchange was digested.

'That old bugger Knox,' Johnno spoke softly, 'is probably harmless. I think . . . he's been plugging away in the parish for decades with his dreary wife and nothing changes. Same old sins. Same old poverty. Same old struggle to keep the church going. Then you arrive back from school for good. Fresh and very lovely and he can't help but look at you.' He turned his head towards Sophie. 'If it was me, I would too.'

Johnno was looking at her in much the same way as Osbert had done – the difference being that she welcomed it.

'I think I understand.'

'That's lucky.' He grinned. 'I'm not quite sure what I'm saying myself.'

'You're giving Osbert Knox the benefit of the doubt. I don't, which means I've failed in the charity department.'

Johnno shrugged.

The silence between them now felt awkward and she struggled to find something interesting to say.

'But would you go away again if you could?'

'Everyone hates National Service. Until they come home and then a lot of them, like me, miss it. My mates. The adventure. I *had* to see more of the world.' He looked over to Sophie. 'There are ways of living that I had no idea about. Different thinking. Different gods. Women. That's why I signed up for a couple more years to get it out of my system. I was pretty wet behind the ears before I left. Mum and Dad didn't like the changes so much when I returned.'

On fire that he had taken her into his confidence, she pretended to be watching a woodlouse. 'Could you travel?'

'Travel costs money. None to spare on our farm.'

This sort of conversation was what she had often dreamed of at Digbys: adult and meaningful. Like biting down on fresh, chewy bread. Diffidence vanished, Sophie felt a surge of confidence and excitement. 'Should we not make our lives happen in the way we wish? Experience what we can?'

He seemed puzzled. 'Yes.'

'Don't we have a duty to live as full a life as possible? To go after those things for which we yearn?'

His smile was a touch grim. 'Unless you must run a farm or help to keep a family. That's dreamer's talk. Maybe what they teach you at a girls' school?'

Sophie never imagined she would ever defend Digbys. 'That's unfair.'

The exchange darkened the mood and Johnno was quiet for a good minute. Meanwhile, the sun filtered through the tree canopy and bathed the undergrowth in a milky light.

She had to say something. But what?

'Don't you think being among trees makes you feel better?'

He shrugged. 'Look, life deals you cards. Throws things at you. Is it worth getting angry about something that's going to happen? Isn't it better to go along and to make something of it?' He touched her forearm. 'You might not agree but I'd like you to understand my point of view.'

She felt as if she had been presented with a bouquet of flowers. All was well. He wanted her to understand him. 'Yes,' she heard herself say. Then, 'Actually, I'm going to try and change the things that I don't like.'

'A rebel,' he said easily. Affectionately, almost.

'I intend to be.'

They stood up.

Linda said Johnno liked to think he was in charge. At this moment, he was.

Feet sunk into leaf mould. Facing each other. He moved closer and she smelt tobacco and fresh male sweat. Felt the top-to-toe warmth of their bodies.

Panic flickered as she was reminded that he was older – twenty-five at least – far more experienced and would make comparisons.

Courage, Sophie.

Johnno's hands rested on her shoulders and he pulled her to him. Bending his fair head, he brushed her mouth with his. 'You're lovely,' he said. 'That old bugger has taste.'

The kiss was something that had been extensively explored in conversation at Digbys. What did it signify? What did it feel like?

124

Nice, she would tell Hettie. But not earth-shattering.

And yet, and yet, in that instant the tables switched in her favour. Johnno wanted her.

His grip slackened. 'I must go. How about a drink one evening?'

'What about Linda?'

Johnno kissed her again. 'What about her?'

'Aren't you seeing her?'

'Yes. I like her very much. Great girl.'

An unexpected, unwelcome jealousy kidnapped her body. 'I'm not sure.'

Johnno stepped away. 'Your choice.'

He moved towards the trees. Threw back over his shoulder, 'The dormouse sends her regards.'

Notebook: *The lion has several characteristics which differentiate it from other wild cats. A key one is social behaviour. Some lions are nomadic but most live within a social organisation known as a pride, where they will mate with several of the lionesses. This social organisation is unique among large cat species.*

Oh, she thought.

125

CHAPTER TEN

The windows of the Winchelford bus needed a scrub and she was having trouble seeing past the grime to view the high summer landscape.

It was Tuesday, nine o'clock and already warm. She had planned the day carefully.

On the seat beside her was her school satchel containing her hoarded and guarded savings. Her hands were clasped in her lap, tightening together every so often when she reprised her plans.

In the seats opposite, two women yattered.

The older one wrenched off her headscarf and fanned herself. The younger one spread out her left hand. 'My fingers are swollen. Going to have my ring cut off.'

The bus was elderly and the ten miles or so to Winchelford were interminable. The seats had seen much, much better days, the interior reeked of eau de tobacco and the grinding gears suggested the engine should be put on life support. Even so – small miracle that it was – the driver reached Winchelford on schedule and began the manoeuvre towards the town centre down streets clogged with market-day traffic.

Sophie alighted beside a flock of sheep being driven back out of town. The animals swerved. Bleated. Acted anxious. She didn't blame them.

Drussell Bank dominated the market square, complacent and superior. Its interior was cool, hushed and orderly, with a portrait of the young Queen in crown and sash on one wall. On another hung a large map of the world, with the remaining areas of the British Empire shaded in knicker pink. A dispirited rubber plant occupied one corner. An elephant's foot umbrella stand was placed by the entrance.

Deep breath.

The tellers were occupied at their booths, and a clerk collected up papers from out trays. A couple of farmers in trilby hats were depositing their takings. A phone rang. Then a second.

She was the only female around and she made for the nearest booth, conscious of a rustle of interest.

The youth behind the brass grille was scrubbed, shiny and busily entering numbers into a ledger. His brass name plate read: Simon Middle. He could not have been more than twenty. Twenty-one maximum.

'I would like to open a bank account,' she said. 'One that I can use here and in France.'

He looked up, every inch the bank clerk with ambition. He made a rapid assessment and into the polite expression crept wariness. 'You have the necessary papers?'

'I have the money.' Sophie placed the satchel between them, and he jerked back. 'It doesn't have a rattlesnake in it,' she informed him. 'Or a black widow spider.'

He stood upright and shot his cuffs. 'I'll have a word with Mr Willard, the manager.'

Five minutes later, she was sitting in an office listening to Mr Willard, who was deploying very simple vocabulary to explain why Sophie could not open a bank account without 'the express permission of a male relative'.

'I assume you have that permission?'

'No.'

'Then, I'm sorry . . . we must leave it at that. It's hard, and you don't understand because you are so young, but it's best to accept that's how it is. But I must say you've lightened my morning. It's not every day I get an application from a member of the fairer sex.'

Fastening her satchel with a savage yank, she said, 'Mr Willard, you're not in the least sorry, because it's the way it's always been.'

Tactical mistake. But she was way down that road. Too far to retreat. She took a strategic breath and asked in the sweetest of tones, 'Does your conscience bother you?'

Mr Willard could not have looked more startled. 'My conscience? Not at all.'

Just as sweetly, she continued, 'Could I say, Mr

128

Willard, that as a bank, you are not serving half the population.' She pointed to a second picture of the Queen above his desk. 'Society is changing and Drussell Bank is not?'

Mr Willard's avuncular attitude was tip-tupping down a slide. She could almost hear him thinking: *one of those.*

Yes, she could be counted among *one of those.*

Knees shaky, she marched back across the foyer. It was debatable if she would get to the exit in one piece. But give in to nerves she would not.

At the door, she clashed with someone entering. Dressed in an impeccably cut but worn tweed suit, a gold watch chain looping out of his waistcoat pocket.

Lord Pitt.

Over the years, she had encountered him at church fêtes and village shows, where he had to be reminded of who she was. *Our dear little refugee.* Then, as now, he tended to look at her as if she was one of the display objects in Pitt Hall.

He was all politeness. Holding the door. Standing aside to allow her out. Then, putting two and two together, he pinpointed her in Poynsdean's hier-archy. Orphan. French. A hand was thrust out. 'Miss Morel?' She nodded. 'How very odd to see you here. Is the reverend ill and you're having to do his errands?'

Generations of calculated breeding having been written into his countenance, he was not unpleasant to look at. Nor was he deliberately unkind – as far as she knew. But the man oozed a conviction that the world was constructed for his convenience.

Alice's thrilling Tales from Pitt House related how he disliked his opinions being challenged. How he disapproved of young women in principle, considering them tiresome. How angry he was about the political beliefs that tilted at landowners and their inherited wealth.

'Everyone at the Rectory is fine, thank you.'

'Visiting a bank, young lady. Very modern.'

They were at an impasse with regard to who would make the first move in or out of the doorway. She looked up. A button was missing on his waistcoat. Not so perfect after all. Not so in control. Emboldened, she said, 'Please don't let me hold you up.'

'Quite right.' He checked the watch on the substantial gold chain. 'My mother, the Dowager Lady Pitt, taught me never to keep the people who serve you waiting.'

Into the lobby he went. More than once, she had observed that those in power walked with a characteristic planting of the foot and swing of the shoulders. Lord Pitt did not disappoint.

Sophie hovered outside. She was angry but she would not be too angry. That clouded the judgement.

Mr Willard and his rules were ridiculous, the products of centuries of the patriarchy. Then she reminded herself: David beat Goliath. The tortoise beat the hare. Empress Matilda escaped from Stephen.

She squinted across the market square.

As he did most market days, Noah Crosby was playing his battered fiddle and singing. Few paid attention – he had been performing for too long and too regularly. Noah knew the score and wasn't bothered. 'Sussex music,' he said, 'mustn't die. These folk here forget too easily their history.'

She stopped to listen to the final notes of 'Turn the Cup Over'.

Noah looked out of sorts, his skin yellowish and his eyes dull. His fiddle didn't sound too good either. She asked him if he was feeling all right. 'I'm getting old, young lady.'

He launched into 'Sussex by the Sea' and she couldn't help thinking: this was music from a past that wasn't hers.

She moved off but, to salve her conscience for such treachery, she turned and waved at him.

Next stop, the library, which had been built by a nabob from the north who had made a fortune in India but chose to settle in Sussex.

Like Drussell Bank, it was a self-important building. The architect had taken his cue from the Taj Mahal, which meant it sat awkwardly in unpretentious Winchelford. But the locals defended it – 'It may be peculiar, but it's ours.' Plus, it was a useful landmark. Once, she had snaffled a copy of the *National Geographic Magazine* from a station waiting room containing pictures of the Taj Mahal.

Heat and dust. Other worlds. But, deciding there was a pleasing ambition in the fact there was a that the replica housed what literary treasure Winchelford had, she too defended it.

Chief Librarian Mrs Winsett (she always wore her badge) had taught Sophie many things. A woman who took her job seriously, she liked to wear clothing that paid tribute to a character or story. 'My little homage, and it helps to set images in the minds of the children.' On past visits, Sophie had been treated to Mrs Winsett as Jane Eyre (hair parted in the middle and a shawl) and Mrs Winsett as National Velvet (a tweed riding jacket). Today she was wearing a forestgreen twinset with jet buttons and a feathered brooch. At a guess, in homage to Robin Hood.

The library was empty. This was not unusual.

'Hello, Sophie.' Mrs Winsett was slotting library cards back into returned books, ready to stack onto the trolley. She glanced up. 'Congratulations on leaving school.'

'Mrs Winsett, may I ask some questions?'

Mrs Winsett glanced over her shoulder to check they were alone. 'Just this once. It's against the rules to hold conversations.'

Sophie took a deep breath. 'Do you have a bank account?'

'I don't need one, Sophie. My husband has the account in his name and we share everything.'

That was that.

'Mrs Winsett, have you ever been abroad?'

132

Mrs Winsett resumed her task. Card inserted into book (Domestic Science: Etiquette) book placed onto trolley. 'No, I haven't, and I'm not planning on doing so.'

'Not even to see places like . . . Rome or Greece?'

Mrs Winsett looked up. 'I can hear the yearning, Sophie. The wish to brush the dust from your feet. Get away from the country bumpkins, you're thinking. A lot of your age do.' The feathered brooch rose and fell on her compact bosom. 'It's a big step and I'm content that all the travelling I need to do is in my mind.' She tapped the final volume in the pile. 'This is by a woman philosopher. Think of that. She was the person who took a stand against Oxford University giving President Harry Truman an honorary degree. Truman had given the order for the nuclear bombs to be dropped on Nagasaki and Hiroshima. Do you know about them?'

Sophie thought that she did. Mrs Winsett said, 'Well then, I must get on.'

But the real question, the big question, came next.

'Mrs Winsett, is there a book about the facts of life?'

Mrs Winsett gave a small shriek. 'I wasn't expecting *that*.'

Sophie held her nerve. 'I'm ignorant, Mrs Winsett, and I don't want to be.'

Sophie was fully expecting to be told to take

herself off. Instead, casting a covert look around the library, Mrs Winsett lowered her voice dramatically. 'Go and sit at the table over there. Look at something else.'

Sophie made a foray into the *Encyclopaedia Britannica* and learnt that the atomic bombs on Hiroshima and Nagasaki had resulted in tens of thousands of deaths – and this was not to mention the unimaginable suffering of the survivors and the demon of radiation.

How? she thought. How could anyone invent such a thing?

She turned to an old friend, *Paris and its People* by Pierre Roc, which she considered hers.

The trolley's creaks and groans traced Mrs Winsett's progress as she patrolled the shelves.

Pierre Roc did not dwell on the war years but focussed on a Paris that looked to the future – the Paris, apparently, where Montparnasse, so deeply associated with pre-war culture, no longer reigned supreme.

'Head instead,' was the advice, 'to the cafés located around the crossroads of Saint-Germain-des-Prés, where the rue de Rennes meets the boulevard. There you can find the Café de Flore, the Café Deux Magots and the Brasserie Lipp. I found these to be where the latest philosophy was being hammered out, and the arena where nihilistic existentialism meets French ethical thought and women go to discover the new feminism for the new era.'

(She had to look up 'new feminism' and was glad that she did. "Sexual equality should not be compromised by any biological differences".)

Mrs Winsett reappeared with a volume hidden inside her cardigan. She placed it in front of Sophie. 'You have twenty minutes. I'm timing you.'

Twenty minutes of revelation.

At one minute her skin was red hot. The next, she felt the blood drain into her feet. She knew that men and women had to mate to reproduce. She also knew that the act was wreathed in significance and emotion and not a little terror. All those whispers at Digbys . . . *the sea sponge of Samoa* . . . but no one girl had held authority on the subject. There were discussions about the troubling, delicate, frequently uncomfortable, developments in their own bodies. Which didn't yield much in the way of explanation. Only that what was happening to them should be kept dark and secret.

Poynsdean boys occasionally shouted unprintable suggestions after Sophie. Once she had witnessed dogs coupling. But she was ignorant of the details, the mechanics. And what prevented that most terrible of things, the unmarried pregnancy?

Now in front of her were the medical terms and names. There were diagrams. There were apocalyptic warnings and descriptions of diseases. There was a photographic inset in blurred black and

135

white which included naked male and female torsos and a horrifying one of a woman giving birth.

Twenty minutes on the dot later, the squeak of shoes informed Sophie that Mrs Winsett was returning. Handing the book over, she said, 'You are very kind to have helped me. I'm grateful.'

'I may not go abroad,' said Mrs Winsett, 'but it does not mean I'm behind the times.'

Mid-afternoon. The market was packing up.

She was observing the activity with a new knowledge. Never again would she look at anything, think about anything, without it colouring her responses.

In the muddied, littered square, temporary pens and booths were being dismantled. Farmers loaded up pigs and sheep, their squeaks and bleats interspersed with traffic noise.

A woman with cropped grey hair packed jars of honey into the back of a Morris Minor van. She leant against the bonnet and checked the money in the pouch around her waist. A leather-waistcoated man (her husband?) bowled over and helped himself to a note from it. She tried to prevent him, but he pushed her aside and headed for The White Boar across the road. The woman got into the van and drove away.

Sophie watched it weave through the traffic out of sight and, as predicted considered the small scene she had just witnessed in relation to the diagrams. They seemed very remote from each other.

On her way to the bus stop, she bought the *Winchelford Express* and ducked into Woolworth's, past the household section with its new aluminium pans, and fetched up at the pick 'n' mix confectionery counter. She would only allow herself a few pennies to spend from her farm wages – bigger, bolder projects lay ahead. The choice therefore was humbugs, or mis-shaped chocolates being sold off cheap.

No contest. Orange cremes, coffee whips, marzipan delights . . . devouring them on the journey home, she tallied up her progress on the quest to find beauty and meaning in her life.

Cornflowers and poppies in the unsprayed fields. A hot-looking sun. Crops ripening. Her half-reflection in the grimy window.

In her notebook she would write: *Today I've taken a step forward.*

Which also committed her to contemplating subjects bigger than herself. What about the story of the woman philosopher opposing the President of the United States' decision to drop nuclear bombs on Nagasaki and Hiroshima, the President's defence being that more lives would have been lost if he had held back? The philosopher's contention? Well, yes, but the attack was still murder.

The arguments knotted themselves around her brain.

In the rue de Seine, there was a café. So her

mother had told her. Very traditional, with a wooden bar, mirrors and small tables. It was a place favoured by art dealers and gallery owners. 'You know that your father dealt in paintings. We met friends there. It was a good place to make a deal. On that day he ordered two beers and asked me to marry him.'

Was Sophie's memory of what she had been told accurate?

'Your father and I fought together . . .'

Or a figment of her imagination?

Why had Camille never returned to France before she became seriously ill? There was a boat train. They didn't have much to pack.

There was the house in Poitiers. There were those cousins. Perhaps, in the search for the story of her family, she had made them up too?

Osbert delivered an explanation with all the authority of Poynsdean's pundit. 'My dear girl, Europe was very dangerous. Swarming with refugees and everywhere in turmoil. You must remember your mother was very ill for a long time and it takes strength to travel. Mrs Knox and I felt it was our Christian duty to keep her here. We recommended that she stayed put, where you were safe. We told her that, if she wanted to repay us for keeping you both, she could continue with her household duties as long as she was able.'

His eyes burned with an emotion she could not place.

All that history. All that sadness. All those love

138

affairs. And she was only just beginning to nibble at the edges.

The bus's gears ground up and down with clicks and rasps, mimicking the staccato feint and retreat of Sophie's thoughts.

Then she thought about Johnno.

CHAPTER ELEVEN

Johnno had become an important part of the plan to further the great enterprise.

He would be blissfully unaware of his role until she managed to get hold of him. Unsure of where she would find him, she called on white witchery. Thus, if she thought about him hard enough, he would get the message.

Find Sophie Morel.

She imagined him walking towards her, the sunlight on his head.

A couple of days later, she took a chance, sneaked out of the Rectory and took herself up to the wood.

The day threatened to be hot, and the tinder-dry undergrowth crackled and rustled as she made her way along the bridle path to the spring.

There he was.

A coincidence, he said as she drew closer.

Sophie knew better but said nothing. Powers of witchery were private.

Johnno's working clothes were damp with sweat, his hands speckled with whitewash. Sophie was in her school skirt and Aertex games shirt, which needed a wash. She would have given much to strip off and plunge into the water.

Instead, they sat on the flat stone and Johnno asked her what she had been doing.

'I've been trying to open a bank account.'

'Blimey.' The surprise was genuine.

'You think that odd?'

Johnno was the first to look away. 'No.'

'You do.' He frowned slightly. 'Isn't it sensible for women to have their own bank accounts?'

In answer, he took her hand. 'Forget all that,' he said. 'For the moment.'

Looking down was to see a blur of whitewash and his strong-looking hand clasping hers. It made her feel safe – which was ridiculous.

An unfamiliar shudder of excitement and anticipation went through her.

'One of the things I learnt on service,' said Johnno eventually, 'was to shut out the outside world and to concentrate on just being. Things were sometimes too much and there was no escape from the lads, from the work, from the foreignness. I learnt to picture myself turning around so that I could peer into my own mind.' He paused and she sensed past turmoil. 'It worked.'

'But I don't want to shut out the outside world,' she said. 'I haven't seen enough of it.'

His gaze travelled thoughtfully over her – lumpy clothes, tangled hair, ghastly sandals. She had an idea that he was taking her in, thinking about what he saw, finding out things about her that she did not, as yet, know. 'You will,' he said.

She drew in an audible breath. The words contained a promise seemingly so tangible that she could reach out and grasp it.

They sat quietly, sealed into their own thoughts. Then he turned towards her and said, 'What the hell.'

Drawing her close, he kissed her. It was nicer than before, possibly because she knew more of what to expect. Possibly because she knew him a little better. Possibly that his proximity was beginning to trigger delicate and delicious feelings throughout her body.

He laid his cheek against hers and it seemed to Sophie that he smelt of sun and earth, of life and promise. Closing her eyes, she instructed herself to remember every second.

'I needed to do that.' Johnno sounded surprised.

Was she mistaken or had he betrayed a hint of vulnerability? Was he not as settled as she had imagined? The notion gave her courage.

'No one's kissed me before you,' she said.

'And?'

'It was lovely.' She took a deep breath. 'I went to the library and looked up about this . . . about sex, I suppose.'

'Blimey!' Johnno gave a crack of laughter. 'What a girl! And were you happy with what you found?'

'I'm not sure. I won't know until I know.'

His smile died. 'I'd forgotten you . . . might

be . . .' He fumbled the words. 'I don't want to ask directly.'

She could trace the sunburn running down his throat. 'If you're asking am I a virgin? Then yes, I am. The book was very helpful. I found some of the diagrams a bit . . . well, I don't know what . . . but they did simplify things.'

She heard the bus gears grinding in her head.

'Johnno, I wanted to ask you to do something for me. You might be shocked . . .'

She didn't have to spell it out further because the flash of comprehension in the blue gaze told her that he had cottoned on. A muscle flickered at the corner of his mouth but whether it was from distaste or amusement she could not make out.

'Are you asking what I think you're asking?'

They seemed to understand each other very easily.

'Yes,' she said.

'I can't take advantage of you, Sophie. I may be the bad boy come home, but there're limits.'

'That's the point.' She turned to look at him, fair and square. 'It's me that's asked you,' she said. 'I want to know what it's like. What happens.'

She witnessed a variety of expressions pass over his face, shock among them. Plus, a slight retreat.

'You're taking a risk, aren't you?'

She liked the sound of that too. 'Yes.'

'You might get pregnant.'

'The book said there were things you could do. I thought you would know.'

143

'Bloody hell.' Johnno retreated into himself and was silent for long seconds. 'But you have to like me. At least, a little. Otherwise, I can't.' He held her by the shoulders and searched her face. 'I know I said I paid for women in Egypt and elsewhere. But this would not be the same. It's not a financial thing.'

Johnno had not struck her as vain and she wondered that he should mind whether she cared for him or not.

'I do like you, Johnno.'

He breathed in sharply.

'No strings?' he said.

'That's the point,' said Sophie.

He touched her cheek. Gently. Exploratively. 'You're quite something.'

'About Linda,' she added. 'I've thought about that too. She will never know from me. She need never know from you. This is just once.' She underlined the ground rules of the bargain. 'And very private.'

'As cool as a cucumber,' said Johnno. 'Aren't you?'

'I know and I'm sorry about it. But it will be over and forgotten quickly.'

'I owe Linda,' said Johnno. 'She knew I didn't want to come home and she understood I wanted to travel. See things. Do things. She's a villager. We have that in common.'

'So am I,' Sophie was stung into saying.

'No, you're not. You might have grown up here

144

but you're not.' He touched Sophie's chin. 'She's been a good sport and she could be a good friend to you.'

A picture of Linda sitting in the pub opposite Johnno with a pint of cider, smiling at him, presented itself. To her dismay, she disliked it very much.

Johnno kissed her for a second time and those new, strong responses ran riot. Her mouth was dry with stage fright and her skin burned from his stubble.

The sun had moved and shone directly down through the clearing onto the water, which sparkled with light and dazzle. The trees stood firm and calm. Her feet sank into last year's pungent leaf mould. She might be nervous but she *was* young and strong and capable of anything.

She pulled him down – and he did not resist. 'Are you sure, Sophie?'

Are you sure?

It was painful, which took them both by surprise. 'Oh Christ,' he said.

She spoke through gritted teeth. 'Go on. Go on.'

The pain was sharp but fleeting. The discomfort lengthier but, by the end, she had a hint of the pleasure that sex might offer.

How strange and wonderful it was to be physically close to someone. Flesh on flesh. Touching an arm. Feeling the brush of fingers over her cheek. How little she had known of this kind of intimacy.

145

Afterwards, they lay on the leaf bed, their legs tangled. Sophie reflected on how she had crossed a line and how pleased she was that she had dared to do this.

Johnno turned his head towards Sophie. 'Did that hurt much?'

'It did,' she admitted and, despite her best intentions, she felt her face go red. 'But I'm glad it's done.'

He looked up at the sky. 'I don't think many girls have your courage. Or curiosity.'

She was a little offended on behalf of her sex. 'I think we do but we hide it. We're not encouraged to be curious which makes it difficult.' She had an unwelcome flashback to Osbert in his study. 'Girls have to be careful not to reveal what they're thinking.'

He propped himself up on his elbow and scrutinised her face. 'Your skin is like the alabaster I saw in Egypt. Did you know that? Do people stop you in the street to compliment you?'

She wasn't used to being praised for her looks.

'No. And I wouldn't wish them to.'

His finger hovered at the corner of her mouth. 'You're . . .' the word sounded both unused and a surprise to him '. . . unusual.'

That was new too. 'Am I?'

'I'll forgive you for not accepting my compliment because you've probably never had any.' The corners of his mouth tightened. 'Those whackos

146

in the Rectory wouldn't know what a compliment is.'

He said she had skin like Egyptian alabaster.

Did people comment on someone's skin? Yes, they did.

She scanned his face, which was close to hers. Obviously, he was still young but the set of his features suggested he had seen and done things that troubled him. The lines fanning out from the corners of his eyes also told of time spent outdoors in the sun.

'I'll say it again,' he said. 'You're lovely.'

This time, the words were uttered almost tenderly, and the floodgates opened. The only person who had been as tender had been her mother and, to Sophie's consternation, her eyes filled. 'Thank you.'

A tear slid down one cheek and Johnno wiped it away with the ball of his thumb. 'Hey. No need.'

She looked into his dark eyes – and found herself slip-sliding down a slope with no foothold, into the deepest of waters.

She was trembling and he snatched both of her hands and stilled them.

'Why are you shaking?'

She looked down at their clasped hands. 'Why are you?'

They helped each other to get dressed. She buttoned up his shirt and Johnno fastened the waistband of her school shorts, and her heartbeat in her chest was like a drum.

When they were done, she stepped back. 'Thank you,' she said. 'I won't bother you again.'

He grinned and his eyes crackled with life and irony. 'Nor I, you.'

They faced each other and the electric charges in the small space between them went back and forth.

'But I *am* going to kiss you again,' said Johnno gruffly.

When, eventually, Sophie struck out for the Rectory, she glanced back over her shoulder. Johnno was standing in the clearing with the sun striking his hair, watching her.

'Het,' she spoke in an almost whisper into the phone. 'I've done it.'

'My God,' said Hettie. 'Are you in one piece?'

The queue of three outside the phone box shifted and Sophie lowered her voice even further. 'That's the point. I'm not any more.'

'Was it . . . was it . . . nice?'

'It hurt and it's embarrassing. Then again, it isn't.'

'You'll have to give me the details before I get married. *If* I get married.' A gusty sigh wafted down the phone line. 'You're brave, Sophie.' Another little sigh. 'I mean, will you be all right?'

'I don't know. I think so. I hope so. When it came to it, I forgot about all that.'

'Sophie . . . that was *stupid*.'

Yes, it was.

Grahame tapped on the door of the telephone box and mouthed: '*Get a move on*.'

'Got to go, Het.'

She grabbed the purse that held most of her money and pushed past Grahame, who was hogging the exit.

'My sister would send her regards,' he said. 'Except she reckons you're a man-stealer.'

'And what does Linda know about it?'

He tapped his nose. 'We know.'

Sophie pushed past him. 'You don't.'

She pounded back along the lane in the direction of the Rectory and her steps beat out a point-counterpoint.

Linda didn't know anything. Grahame wouldn't know.

But there was the question of whether she had been foolish to trust Johnno and his capacity for silence.

Slap, slap went her feet. No one could possibly know about the sea change that had taken place in her mind. Or the brand-new knowledge of her body – the soreness, the splash of blood – for she barely knew it herself. Or the glimmer of insight into the relations between men and women she had gained by what had happened between her and Johnno.

She came to a halt. No need to return to the Rectory. Osbert was attending a convention with the bishop in Hastings, debating the Church's position on nuclear disarmament (cut and shut) and the upcoming relaxation of restrictions on hire-purchase agreements, which many clergy believed would encourage the poor to get into debt. (Less cut and shut. Many of the listening clergy could have done with some creature comforts.)

On hearing of the Hastings sortie, Alice had become uncharacteristically animated and announced she would be spending those nights with Lady Pitt, and Sophie was to take charge in the Rectory.

'I don't approve,' said Osbert.

Alice retired to the piano.

Sophie was almost sure she thought she overheard Alice mutter, 'What is sauce for the goose is sauce for the gander.'

Bugger the Knoxes.

Cutting down East Street, she headed for the wetlands. *Bugger them.*

The craving for solitude was strong. She needed to think. She needed to get things straight in her head.

Johnno had pointed out that she was not a villager. Not one of the Poynsdeaner born, attached to roots from earlier generations. Or, for that matter, she thought crossly, with ways of thinking that went back to the Neanderthals.

Rather, her mother and she were evidence of Poynsdean's proud war effort. *See, we opened our hearts and homes when it was needed.*

She was an outlier and deracinated. That must be accepted.

Yet she knew Poynsdean. Better than some.

Better, she reckoned, than Betty Benyon. The brown and grey of the winter fields, the green and yellow of the spring and summer. She knew in which fields the plough went fastest and where the stones choked the blades. She had watched young trees planted ten years ago grow into an obedient cluster. She had heard and witnessed the scarlet flash of the huntsmen and heard the screech of pheasant, the howl of the dogs. She knew which hedgerow the birds favoured and the bank where the best blackberries fattened in the sun.

Walking down East Street towards the run-down cottages at the end, she heard the Bales's dog before she saw it. A desolate, despairing sound.

Huddled into itself, dirty and matted, with no food or water as far as she could make out, it guarded a patch of concrete littered with faeces. As Sophie drew closer, it fell silent and watched her intently.

She walked past; halted; retraced her steps and walked up the path to the house. 'What's up?'

The gentle tone of voice may have been a novelty, for the dog managed to lift its head. Crouching down beside it, she tallied up the outrage of its condition.

Thin. So broken. Its body and its gaze fashioned by neglect and suffering. And yet, and yet, he (for it was a he) was still hungry for affection.

She stroked his battered muzzle and he whimpered. Very gently, she ran a finger over his ears and down his spine. 'What's your name, I wonder?'

151

'What the fuck are you doing?'

She swung around as Tommy Bale lurched up the path.

'Your dog, Mr Bale.' She looked up at him. 'You're not fit to own it. It's starving.'

Tommy was drunk, as he frequently was. Not good, happy drunk but bad, surly drunk. 'No point wasting food.'

'What's his name?'

'Dog. That's good enough,' he added belligerently. 'Plain English.'

Dog looked from one to the other and tried to scrabble to his feet, but sank back down onto the stained concrete.

'He's *ill*,' said Sophie. 'Don't you see that?'

'Nah.'

'And *suffering*.'

'We all suffer, lady.'

There was a flash of something in his eyes. A weariness and disappointment. At the state he was in? At his life?

'Do something.'

'What? Veterinary? It costs.'

She touched the top of Dog's head. 'He'll die.'

Tommy shrugged. 'One less dog in the village.' He glared at Sophie. 'And don't go judging me with your fancy Rectory ways.'

'I am judging you, Mr Bale. But it isn't in a fancy way but because of your cruelty to your dog.'

'Fuck off, lady.'

Dog whimpered and Tommy Bale aimed a kick at him. Just in time, Sophie interposed herself between him and Tommy. 'Give him to me.' Tommy Bale had bad teeth, which must have troubled him, and these were obvious as he stared, open-mouthed, at Sophie. 'I'll take him,' she said.

She reached out to grasp the rope tethering the dog, but the drink hadn't altogether dulled Bale's reflexes and he got there first. 'That's thieving. And what would the Rectory make of that?'

'And you,' she muttered between clenched teeth, 'can't treat an animal in this way.'

They squared up to each other.

'He's in pain because of you.'

The accusation bounced off Bale. Then it didn't and he roused himself to spit out, 'You know nothing about pain, girl. I've seen sights you've no idea about. Nasty, horrible, bloody sights.'

'The war . . . the war . . .' Miss Chambers had said. 'It brought us to the brink.'

Miss Chambers knew all about the theory and Sophie had taken it half on board. But she suspected Miss Chambers had known nothing of the Tommy Bales of this world, brutalised by fighting, killing and, yes, surviving.

'Even if you have, it doesn't mean you have to maltreat an animal.'

Bale shrugged.

'I'll pay you for Dog.'

A futile gesture? Likely as not, Bale would only procure another animal to abuse.

Not futile. It had to be possible to make a difference.

'Ten shillings.'

'Think again, lady.'

'A pound.'

He yanked at Dog's tether, which made him
whimper. 'I'm not a fool.'

'Two pounds.' That would deplete her savings.
'Final offer.'

She meant it and he knew it. The bloodshot eyes
narrowed – no doubt he was tallying how many
pints he could stand himself in The Black Bull.
This meant she had won.

Coaxing Dog back to the Rectory took some
doing. He was ill, frightened, confused and did
not yet know, nor trust, Sophie. Finally, she picked
him up and carried him towards the Rectory. He
was as light as air, smelt bad and, every so often,
yelped with pain.

In the kitchen, she eased him down into an apple
crate, fetched milk and the remains of the previous
night's supper from the larder and fed them to
him.

'You're safe, now,' she informed him. 'And I'll
give you a proper name.'

He looked up at her and he seemed to be asking
if life was worth living.

'It is,' she told him. 'It *is*.'

CHAPTER TWELVE

For the next few hours, she fed Dog not too much, not too little, which seemed to revive him. But he was jumpy and hurt and she spent a long time sitting on the floor with his head against her thigh. 'You must get used to my smell,' she instructed him.

In the hall, the telephone rang.

'I need Vicar,' said a voice. 'My husband's dying. He wants to talk to him.'

It was Mrs Forbes, and Jim had been on the brink for a long time. Many considered it a professional performance. 'I'm so sorry. Reverend Osbert is away.'

'Well, I'll just have to tell Jim to hang on, then.'

The following morning she led Dog into the garden and washed him with warm water and soap. His fur parted to reveal old and recent scars. 'Bastard,' she said furiously. 'You *bastard*.'

Dog allowed her to rub him dry and to brush his coat and she found herself talking to him. 'Oh yes,' she breathed at the transformation. 'You're a mongrel, my boy. But a good-looking one with soft fur.'

The brown eyes fixed on Sophie. Was there scepticism? Clearly, his ancestry was patchy, and neglect and suffering had been too indelibly beaten into him for him to ever shine physically.

Yes, it *was* reproach, and she laughed. 'All right, I'm lying. Nothing will make you good-looking. But I don't give two tinker's cusses.'

She led him back to the crate and hand-fed him morsels of Spam. For such a thin dog he did not seem that interested in food, but perhaps he wasn't used to eating. Afterwards, he sunk back down to the floor.

Hunkering beside him, she watched the thin flanks heave. The curve of his paw. The brown gaze. 'I promise you're safe . . .'

From her vantage point on the floor, she spotted a piece of chalk which had rolled under the sideboard. Obviously it had gathered a thick coat of dust – the dust that Alice always called the work of the Devil but never did anything about vanquishing.

'Safe. From that life. From that . . . evil. I promise.'

Dog was quiet. So was she.

Pots, pans, old gas cooker, sweating floor tiles . . . if a kitchen could be said to be depressed, this one was. How she hated it. The smells, the cold, the relentlessness of the repressed, bleached existence in the Rectory. The Knoxes deliberately cultivated discomfort, she had concluded, so there could be no question that the next life would be better than the rank muddle of the Rectory.

156

Dog twitched and whimpered in his sleep. Gently, she cupped his head and it grew heavy in her hand. If this was trust, she must not betray it.

To betray would be a sin. Not of the kind that the Knoxes preached against – those were usually, no *always*, to do with the flesh. It would be the sin of promising the beaten and dispossessed a better life, and then failing to deliver it.

Sin . . . what an interesting bully of a word. There were obvious sins. And there were secret ones.

She scrambled to her feet. In the right-hand kitchen drawer, hidden by the rolling pin, lurked a packet of Weights cigarettes. These, she had discovered, Alice indulged in. An example of a secret sin. Sophie had caught her at it, puffing away out of the back door. Nothing was said. Sophie got on with the vegetables and Alice took a last drag, threw away the butt and disappeared, leaving a small, but lethal, detonator between them.

Did Alice fear the consequences if it was pressed? Or, veteran of Rectory life, had she perfected detachment from her ruction-filled, suppressed life?

In her notebook, Sophie had once written: *Alice's yearning for Lady Enid excepted, she has hived off her needs and put them away in a box.*

She helped herself to a cigarette and lit up.

Smoke drifted above her head.

157

Dog. His life. Her commitment to it. A wrong choice? But there was no choice when an animal was being abused.

She inhaled and coughed. To be alive necessitated risk. Also, being alive, truly so, required purpose and a morality. And vision. She wasn't sure about any of these requisites.

The fag was fun to smoke but the floor was cold. Except in hot weather, the kitchen usually smelt of damp, and rain exacerbated the problem. The Rectory was nothing like the comfortable, desirable home that Hettie had as an ambition and Sophie had occasionally seen in a magazine.

Tommy Bale had accused the occupants of the Rectory of being 'fancy'. The Knoxes *said* they were egalitarians and moved around the parish clad in moral sackcloth, undeviating in their shabbiness and, apart from Osbert's dramatic sermons, modestly presented, busy with charity that tried to make things better. However, it was true that the opinions occasionally aired at gloomy kitchen suppers more than once reflected a stance of class and cultural superiority.

'Dear me, no,' Osbert would undoubtedly counter Tommy Bale. 'We're all equal before God.'

That equal? How equal was equal?

A cloud slipped moodily across the patch of sky framed in the kitchen window. In the previous few days, the mornings and evenings had contained a herald chill. Perhaps summer was on the turn?

She glanced down at sleeping Dog and her throat tightened.

'Oh, Dog,' she said. 'You and I are the same. Stuck.'

Then she thought: No, I'm not. I will not be stuck.

Mid-morning the following day, she led Dog on a rope leash, headed up to Home Farm and tapped on the kitchen door. Johnno wasn't in, but his father was.

'What have we got here?'

As always, the kitchen was untidy. Cheerfully and happily so. A pie waited to be baked on top of the range, jams and mugs cluttered the kitchen table. On the windowsill, a jam jar of pink dahlias was in need of a change of water.

How sane Home Farm was, battered with everyday living. But sane.

Big John carved a slice from the ham on the table and threw it into a frying pan with a knob of salted butter. Dog's ears pricked up. 'Looking for Johnno?' The question was slyly put.

The butter changed colour and coated the meat in a brown glaze. 'Could you do with an extra dog? He needs a good home.'

He placed the ham on a plate and halved a tomato. 'Well I'm jiggered . . . I hadn't thought of that one.'

Carrying a basket of laundry, Sheila edged into the kitchen and overheard the exchange. 'John . . .' There was a warning note. 'We've enough to deal

159

with.' She set the basket down on the table. 'Sorry, love. You'll understand.' She bent over and stroked Dog's head. 'Bit mothy, isn't he? Looks like that poor creature the Bales have. How did you get him?' Sophie explained and Sheila said, 'I see. A bit of a mess because there's not a snowflake's that the rev and that missus will take him in.'

Sophie grimaced.

John lit his pipe and a tobacco scent mingled with the smell of frying. Sophie bent down, put her arms around Dog and whispered in his ear. Sheila's stance softened. 'Put him in the barn in the south field for the moment. Providing you feed and walk him.' She glanced out of the window. 'Johnno's coming now. He'll help you. But you'll have to work out what to do with the animal.' She poked the laundry. 'He won't survive the cold weather.'

'Hello there,' said Johnno, smiling.

'Hello.'

He glanced at Dog. 'What's going on?'

Sophie explained. 'Your mother said we could put him in the south barn.'

'Well if Mother says . . .'

With Sophie's help, Johnno constructed a refuge in a corner of the barn using old bits of sheep pen.

'Hold that bit,' he said. 'And this.'

It didn't take long. Sophie was mesmerised by

160

his ease and assurance in constructing the pen. 'You make it look painless.'

'I told you I come from a long line of farmers,' he said. 'The blood runs with silage. Help me tie this up.' Sophie assisted him with the rope. He anchored a final piece around the bar and glanced over to her. 'Professionals.'

Sophie smiled.

'We'll have you lambing in the new year.' He stepped over the pen and lifted Dog onto the bed of straw. Settled him gently. 'You stay there, boy . . . did you find out his name?'

'I think his name might be Dog after all,' she said. 'I must get some food for him. And a water bowl.'

They walked down the farm lane, not saying much but occasionally exchanging glances, which made the atmosphere heat up between them.

Baffled by her emotions and at odds with herself, she wanted to say: I know a bit of you, but I don't know you. And I find myself wanting to know more. Much more.

'I hope you're not regretting what happened,' he said.

'No.'

Sounding each other out.

'We're sticking to the agreement?'

'Yes.'

'A pity.' He cocked a quizzical eyebrow.

She didn't reply. It wasn't in her power. Every so often, their hands almost met. Every so often an electric sensation sparked through her body. To ground herself, she gazed down at her feet and the sight of grubby school plimsolls reminded her of who she was, and why.

'You won't be able to leave Dog there for too long,' Johnno echoed his mother. 'Not when winter comes. He's in too bad shape.'

'I know.' She bit her lip at the thought.

'He'll tie you to Poynsdean,' said Johnno. 'You think he won't, but—'

She cut through. 'If I left, Dog could come with me.'

'He's a broken animal who's known nothing else. Think about it.'

Johnno was telling her that Dog knew only a fouled concrete path, the ring that had tethered him and the kicks and blows that had come his way. Her anger was triggered all over again.

'There are many ways of being tied to a place.' Johnno sounded bitter. 'Ask me.'

Sophie stopped dead and faced him. 'You can escape if you wish. Your father still has years ahead of him and your brother could step into your shoes when he's older.' Johnno's gaze ranged past her shoulder to the field. 'Johnno, look at me. You think I don't understand. Maybe I don't. But maybe I can tell when our minds get chained up.' Was she being as unhelpful as she sounded? 'Listen, Johnno, your mum and dad will hate it, but you could choose another life. Live somewhere else.'

'Just as you could.'

Between them, they could take on the world. Rebels on the barricades.

She closed her eyes for a second. 'Yes.' On opening them, he had moved closer. 'Johnno, please . . .'

He touched her cheek. 'Why not?'

'Because . . .'

She wanted to say that doing this invited involvement and muddle. She wanted her mind and spirit to be clean of desires and free to go where she wished.

In the distance, a car ground its way up the rise towards the Downs. A seabird cried.

'We had a pact.'

He bent over and brushed his lips against her cheek. 'But you want this.' She breathed in sharply and did not reply. 'Tell me you want this.' He searched her face. '*Tell me.*'

Oh God, she thought.

'Yes,' she said.

Dog knew her now and kept watch for her daily visits. These were made easier by the warm weather holding as summer wore to its end.

Cunning, *much* cunning was required in getting to him, and she worked out how to slip away when the Knoxes were out and about in the parish, or holed up in their respective lairs. At the first opportunity, she had read up on care for canines in the library ('What next?' said Mrs Winsett) and bought antiseptic cream for his wounds.

163

Dog listened out for the clunk of the gate. For the sound of her tread on the grass. When she came into sight, he struggled to his feet and stood quite rigid as if he feared she was a chimera.

He also learnt to wag his tail.

Dropping down beside him, she stroked his battered body and realised that the tugs at her throat and heart meant she was beginning to love him.

Oh God, she thought, learning the lesson in incremental hikes. With love comes vulnerability and pain and terror for the loved.

Sitting beside her, Dog pushed his nose onto her lap.

She took him on short walks and he began to cover the territory, doing his best to imitate a dog in fine fettle.

Often, the spectacle of him trying to be an ordinary dog made her cry.

'Dog . . . Dog . . . what shall I do with you? What shall I do with me?'

Occasionally when she talked to him about the rabbits who had a warren at the end of the field, or her plans to find him a home, he responded with a thump of his tail. When she left, she made sure that he was fed, comfortable and as warm as she could make him.

Once or twice, she realised that Johnno had been there in between her visits. The water had been changed or the hay raked over.

Johnno and Dog. Dog and Johnno.

164

Number one rule learnt early at Digbys: it is unwise to feel too much.

Feelings made you vulnerable. Weaker.

And yet, and yet.

One afternoon in late August Johnno roared down the farm lane in the dirty old farm van and leant out of the window. 'Spotted you coming up the lane. We're going to the sea,' he said, and there was no gainsaying that.

Not that Sophie wished to. It was a micro-second decision. Knoxes? Potatoes peeled? Oven cleaned?

'Only if I can bring Dog.'

'What makes you think it's your outing rather than his?'

Dog in between them on the front seat, they drove down the lane and bowled along the Eastbourne road. Sophie had her arms around Dog to keep him steady and he seemed to like it.

His breath wasn't so good but she didn't mind.

'Everyone needs a change,' said Johnno, who was driving with only one hand on the wheel, which she wondered about. 'Don't worry . . .' He read her thoughts. 'I used to drive the army truck. My reflexes are good.'

An increasingly familiar tide of excitement came running in, its searching, salty ripples flowing over her defences.

Johnno drove right onto the beach. The wheels spun and the van slithered as he parked under a sand dune. Dog eased out and shook himself. A nippy little breeze hit as Sophie bent over to slip

165

the rope over his head, and she pulled on her jumper.

'A walk along the beach and then fish and chips,' said Johnno.

The beach stretched away, with the pier in the distance. Sophie shaded her eyes. 'The pier looks like a palace.'

They walked along the promenade towards it. At this end of the beach, the tide had thrown seaweed and driftwood onto the rocks. Two small children sat stoically on a pile of them. The sun came out and Sophie took off her jumper and tied it around her waist. Without warning, Johnno reached over and took her hand and held it in his big, warm grip.

Dog was free to roam but he seemed disinclined to go far and returned frequently to Sophie's side.

'He's fond of you,' said Johnno. 'Who wouldn't be?'

They clattered down the steps onto the beach. Sophie was wearing the dreaded and useless school sandals. After a minute or so, she took them off. 'One day I'll have a set of shoes specially for the beach.'

'And dancing?'

Sandals in hand, she stood upright. 'And dancing.'

'Good, I like dancing.'

She turned away so that he could not witness her delighted grin and gazed over the water.

'And what do you see, Sophie?'

Another tease. 'The sea.'

'And how do you see the sea?'

Difficult to explain how stirring and intriguing she found it. How it formed a persistent, haunting presence in her thoughts and dreams. The sea that had cast Camille (and her) onto these shores.

'I think so many things about it.'

Shading her eyes, she gazed over in (what she trusted) was the direction of France and encountered a midday horizon illuminated with bright sun, interspersed with some nippy little clouds.

'I came from over there.'

He slipped an arm around her shoulders. 'Mum says that your mum was the talk of the village. Mrs Cabby has it that the refugees were brought over by a sea monster like in the old stories, and your mother was the best of the bunch.'

'That's so nice, Johnno. I like that.'

They ate the fish and chips sitting on the edge of the esplanade, legs dangling over the edge, with Dog's rope wrapped around Sophie's wrist. It was one of those afternoons when a preternatural calm settled over the water, a silken rolling expanse. There was an uneven strip of beach huts and, over by the pier, gaudily striped booths and shops selling sticks of rock, paper windmills, painted pebbles and Tizer.

The salt on her chips puckered her lips. 'Johnno, how come you got time off?'

'I didn't ask,' he said. 'Just like you.'

They exchanged glances. Both laughed. Looked

away. Looked back at each other. 'I should be cleaning,' she said. 'It's in the timetable.'

'Good God,' said Johnno. 'They are the limit.'

She felt a surprising, and unusual, desire to defend the setup. 'Timetables are the only way they can function. They're so odd. So ill-matched. I don't think Alice knew what she was taking on when they got married. Osbert certainly didn't.' She looked down at her hands. 'But, but . . .' And clasped them tight. 'But.'

'What?'

'I don't how to say this.'

'You do.'

'Osbert. I think he's sex-starved. He creeps around.' Pause. 'Looking at me.'

'Does that mean what I think it means?' Johnno whistled, a low, ominous sound. 'The old bugger.' He suddenly looked the soldier. Hard-edged. 'Don't go near him.'

'That's difficult.'

'If he lays a finger on you, I'll kill him.' Johnno was deadly serious. 'The minute there's any trouble, come and get me.'

His vehemence took her aback. His protectiveness sneakily enchanted her. 'Johnno, I can cope. But thank you.'

'Take it from me, men can be dangerous.' He was playing the seasoned soldier again. 'Especially if you haven't been about a bit.'

She recollected the drooping cassock on Osbert's shrinking figure. The frequently ridiculous gestures

168

accompanying his sermons. He was repellent, absurd, and, as she was beginning to think, possessed by awful snooping instincts. But when it came down to it, was he dangerous?

'I'll be fine.'

'That's what they all say.'

She considered. 'Maybe I'm reading too much into his behaviour.' She turned to look at him. 'Can I ask you something?'

'Sounds serious.'

'It's about sex again.'

He wiped his chin.

'Do men think about it a lot?'

The answer, when it arrived, seemed to be dragged out of him. 'They do. A lot.' He turned back to face Sophie. 'It's only fair to ask you if girls do.'

'They would if they knew what to think about.'

That made him shout with laughter.

He balled up the newspaper. 'The sea reminds me of how much I don't know and haven't seen. And will never know, probably.'

'Don't say that.'

He reached over and pinched the last but one of Sophie's chips.

'Thief.' She stuffed the final chip into her mouth. 'Unlike you, I want to find out what I don't know.'

Johnno dug into his pockets and produced two apples. 'Fancy an Eastbourne pippin?'

She did. 'Lovely.' Its colours rippled green to yellow to gold and its flesh was creamy.

Johnno crunched down into his. The juice on his fingers glistened and Sophie thought: I must remember this moment. Sea, sun, the breeze. Dog and a sweet apple.

Johnno was a fatalist. Johnno had a soft heart. Johnno did not wish to hurt his parents.

'Is it that you feel that because you must take on Home Farm, there's not much point learning about other things?'

He laid a hand on her thigh. 'I wouldn't put it like that.'

The newspapers at Winchelford library had continued to open up Sophie's world. She had learnt, for example, that bolstered by the success of the Sputnik project, Soviet premier Khrushchev was annoyed by the Americans locating nuclear missiles in West Germany (which was supposed to be a secret but wasn't) and was increasingly aggressive about 'the German situation' and the 'malignant canker' of Allied-occupied Berlin.

('If you ask me,' said Mrs Winsett, 'that man has problems at home that give him the pip.')

'We should know what's going on and what might happen to us. What do you think about Khrushchev?'

The question sounded pretentious. Ridiculous. She *was* ridiculous and pretentious.

But, all grace, Johnno answered, 'He's a bully. And worse. Would need to be to get where he's got to. Probably got a room stuffed with the corpses of his enemies.'

Dog was getting restless, and he pulled at the rope. 'Shouldn't we know why the East hates the West? Russia was our ally in the war.'

Johnno got to his feet and held out a hand to Sophie. 'The world is big. People not on this island see things differently to us, something we didn't clock when we set out to rule half of it.' He leant across and wiped her chin. 'You've got grease all over. *Very* attractive.'

Johnno didn't mind her challenges. Or her questions. That made it so easy between them. Whereas poor Hettie wailed that she had made the hideous error of mentioning Khrushchev at one of the torpor-inducing dinner parties (in the green dress, too, which was far too tight), only to be told by her dinner partner that birds with brains weren't allowed. In a voice loud enough for everyone to hear.

An afternoon offshore breeze had now got up, ruffling the calm. It seemed to Sophie that the blues in the water and dispersing across the sky were so radiantly celestial that they were in danger of piercing her heart. No matter that her shoes were school sandals, and her chin was slicked with grease; she, Sophie Morel, was at liberty to gaze upon these. And to read into their infinities what she wished.

The tide was coming in. Johnno pointed to the spumy water running up the beach and she caught a faint sigh. 'See that. Never still. Always on the move. As the farmer, I need to be calm and settled.

If I think about what I've seen and done and could do, then I'll be as restless as the sea.'

'You're a good person.' She didn't, *couldn't*, approve the Sydney Carton-ish willingness to sacrifice himself. Yet, his nobility moved her. 'I hope your parents know that.'

He captured her hand and gently pulled her fingers, one by one. 'Do you mean that?'

She looked up at him. His face reflected emotions she couldn't place. Anger? Despair?

'Yes, I mean it. Good is the right word. I couldn't do it.'

'If you have parents, it's easier.'

Ah.

That hurt.

'I'm not sure I have the capacity for good,' she said, feet bouncing against the stone esplanade. 'Johnno, you're not like the teachers at Digbys who felt they didn't have much choice other than to sacrifice their life to a profession that didn't suit them. Are you?'

He shrugged.

They exchanged a look – and every nerve end in her body gave voice. In the end, she was the first to look away. Johnno seemed to relax. Back came the humour and an unexpected tenderness.

'This is becoming a habit but I'm going to have to kiss you,' he said. 'Apologies in advance.'

He did so for a long, long minute and she felt his warmth and tasted salt and her mouth burned from it. This was different. A sensation embedded

172

itself in her body, so powerful that she lost breath. The realisation crept through her that what she was experiencing was desire. Eventually, he moved back.

'Apologies accepted,' she said.

Mouths smarting, occasionally laughing for no good reason, they sauntered along the esplanade in search of the ice-cream kiosk.

In the van driving back to Poynsdean, Johnno kept both hands on the wheel and eyes firmly on the road. In between them was Dog, who now had a red-and-white ribbon tied around his neck.

Without so much as a by-your-leave he had plonked his head onto her lap, and she combed her fingers through the tufty fur between his ears. Her hands, her mouth, the rope that held Dog were sticky from ice-cream melt and she didn't have a handkerchief. Her nose glowed with sunburn and sand grated between her toes. Every so often, she sneaked a glance at Johnno's profile which, she decided, was reminiscent of a Roman statue.

She had discovered that moments of happiness such as this were wonderful. Wonderful. And no one was more surprised than she was.

Johnno said, 'Any chance of a rethink?'

She didn't have to ask what about.

'What do you want, Sophie?'

What did she want? The freedom to set sail over the sea. The power accrued with being able to pay her way. To be experienced. To never again eat bubble and squeak.

She said as much and he said, 'It's easy to tell you've never had ties to a place.'

Yet it hadn't taken much – sex, ice cream and a shared dog – for Sophie to be veering wildly off course.

'Perhaps . . .'

Her heart thumped out an extra strong beat.

'Linda,' she reached for an obvious objection. 'Doesn't she have first call?'

He shifted irritably in his seat. 'Linda knows the form. I see who I wish.' He changed gear and the noise of it ground into the van's interior. 'If you had changed your mind about our arrangement. *If* . . . I was thinking we could do this again and enjoy ourselves before our real lives kick off.'

Why not? She interrogated the inner Sophie. The one who had – temporarily – fallen silent.

Little by little, she was slipping into a hotbed of feeling. A process that went contrary to *everything* she had mapped for the future.

There was something thrilling about it. Dark and possibly dangerous.

She shook her head.

'We'll keep things as they were, then,' he said.

She bent her head and flexed her sandy fingers. Then she looked directly at Johnno. 'You do see why, don't you?'

'No,' he said. 'I don't.'

A little later, he added, 'I'm not giving up.'

CHAPTER THIRTEEN

The supper of fishcakes and cabbage that evening at the Rectory was almost more than Sophie could stomach. Instead, she dined off hot, strong rebellion.

An elderly haddock had been sacrificed for the fishcakes, which were booby-trapped with bones. The cabbage was overdone. (If there was a way of cooking cabbage to make it desirable, she hadn't found it.) A trace of gas hung over the room because Sophie had accidentally left a ring on. The atmosphere was sour with overcooked food, incipient mould and – she fancied – subversive desires.

She cleared supper and eased the dishes into the sink. At one end of the table, Osbert was talking lengthily about his 'cherished friend, the bishop' and Alice sat as tight and bound up as a parcel at the other. The only comment she made was to chastise Sophie for buying corned beef rather than the cheaper Spam. After that, she relapsed into silence and, no doubt, entertained herself with images of chandeliers, silver teapots and four-poster beds.

As usual, neither of the women listened to Osbert. The paean to the bishop was paused and he picked up the accounts book, which contained the household entries going back several years. 'My dears?'

Alice produced a bus ticket and a receipt. 'Bleach, Jubilee Wax and Rinso.' She handed it over.

These were entered, in Osbert's fierce hand-writing. Sophie scraped the remains of the fish-cakes into the pig bucket.

'Sophie?'

'Cheese, 2/3d.'

There was a hesitation. 'If I'm not mistaken, that's more expensive than previously.' He ran a finger along a column. 'Yes, it is. I must ask you to be more careful.'

'I do try.'

'But not hard enough.'

Swinging around to face the Knoxes, she said, 'You won't mind, then, if we discuss plans for me to leave the Rectory.' She swallowed. 'My mother was very grateful to you for taking us in, but it's time to go.'

Husband and wife exchanged a rare look. Usually, they ignored one another.

'I notice *you* don't thank us,' said Alice.

Osbert said, 'We've explained, Sophie Morel, you do not have jurisdiction over your life until you're twenty-one. We do. You must remain here. Unless, of course, you get married, in which case your husband will take responsibility for you.'

Hatred tasted good. It tasted satisfying. And, she was beginning to realise, it was also addictive. 'I ask again. The money my mother left me. Could I have it, please?'

Osbert's head shot up.

'You said it's in a post office account?'

Osbert steepled his hands, pointed fingers imitating the brass rubbing of the bishop in the north aisle of the church. 'Correct. Under our management, until such time . . .'

Be smart. Be duplicitous. Summon an image to make herself cry, which would soften them. The worst one she could think of was her father being shot, or her mother gasping for breath.

She gave a sob.

'Oh, my dear . . .' Osbert leapt to his feet and slid an arm around her shoulders. 'You mustn't take on. It doesn't do any good.'

Her flesh prickled in protest.

'Osbert.' Alice was very sharp. 'Let go of her.'

His fingers dug into her shoulder, his breath filmed over her neck, his skinny flank pressed into hers. It was almost – the thought sharpened her disgust – as though Osbert was willing himself as close to sinning as possible, in order to claim victory when he didn't.

'*Osbert.*'

'Reverend Knox, please don't touch me.'

He stepped away, and she felt as if she had been thrown up out of murky waters and left to choke on slimed rocks.

'There's no point crying, Sophie,' he said. 'Obeying God can be hard. He demands much of us, but consider the spiritual rewards. If you bow to the inevitable then all will be well.'

'Spiritual rewards'. What were they? A vague feeling of goodness? Immunity from illness or grief? Material rewards were so much simpler to understand and *that*, she suspected, was where her post office account came in.

'There's no need for us to speak about this again,' said Osbert. He was pressed up against the table, which she had not got round to wiping.

'Reverend Knox,' she said. 'You've got haddock and breadcrumbs on your cassock.'

Notebook: *Mrs Winsett, the librarian, is a hen who has sacked the cockerel. She rules her library roost and dispenses knowledge like eggs.*

Without warning, Alice pushed into the bedroom where Sophie was sitting on the bed writing.

Sophie jumped. 'Mrs Knox . . . Do you need something?'

By this stage of the marriage, Alice's 'honeymoon' dressing-gown had been patched and darned into a different garment, so motley that it might have been rejected by the ragbag. 'You know you're not allowed a light on at this time of night, Sophie. Electricity has to be paid for. Somehow. Digbys may have been profligate with it but we aren't here.'

An army of kirby grips flattened her hair against her head.

'I think you should call me Alice.' Her shadow loomed dark and flat on the wall. 'It's time.'

Sophie stared at her. After all these years. The transition from 'Mrs Knox' to 'Alice' with nothing in between was almost shocking.

Alice fiddled with a rogue kirby grip. 'Sophie's such an inappropriate name. So frivolous. Why your mother insisted on it I've no idea. Susan or Jane would have done very well.' She eyed the notebook. 'Modest, sensible, English names.'

Like Osbert, Sophie almost said. 'I don't imagine my mother thought we . . . I . . . would still be here.' As it so often was, the notion was treacherously painful. 'She didn't expect to die.'

Alice moved on to tying and retying the rope (a replacement for the original cord) cinched around her awkward waist. 'Never once . . .' burst from her. 'Never once did you pay attention to me when you were growing up. I was owed something, you know. It was the reverend's idea to take your mother in, and I never liked it. But I put up with it. I had to. Now, the story is repeating itself.'

'I don't understand.'

Alice loomed over her. 'Your mother was a source of temptation.'

If you lived by the Bible, Sophie supposed, you judged the world through its lens. 'Like Eve and the serpent?'

'Men . . .'

179

Men?

'It makes no difference if they're dressed in a cassock or a fig leaf, men are the same. Your mother was beautiful. You'll have noticed that I am not. My choices have been few, right from the beginning. In return for being "Mrs Knox", I got a life of hard labour and religion.' She sat down on the bed beside Sophie. 'In this world, Sophie Morel, if you're female and have neither beauty nor money, your choices are few.'

Alice smelt fusty – she had lived in that bedroom for too long.

Sophie edged away.

'What about brains?'

'Not much point having brains unless you know the right people and use them. Looks get you further. Your mother had bad experiences, that I will give her. But she knew how to use her charms. Oh, yes.'

Sophie thought of Osbert. His skeletal, raptor body. The pursed lips and, what she was coming to understand, his secret desires. 'You should not accuse my mother. She would never have stepped out of line.'

Alice shrugged. Her shadow thrown onto the wall reassembled. 'She didn't have to. It was the idea in the reverend's mind. Ideas are strong. Very persistent.' There was a pause. 'You have a lot to learn.'

Sophie exclaimed, 'That's why you sent me to boarding school?'

180

'Maybe.'

'Even though I had lost my mother?'

'Your mother wished it too.'

Camille knew? Or suspected that it would be best if Sophie went away?

'That was cruel.'

'Yes. But you were not a pretty child and it also gave you an education,' Alice pointed out. 'No need to look like that. It's what's your mother planned for you.' She snatched the notebook from Sophie. Rifled through it. 'Ungrateful, I see.' A shake of the head. 'Be careful with your ingratitude.'

The blood drummed in Sophie's ears. How could her mother ever have accepted living in this . . . this place of vipers? This household seemingly so resolute in its purpose but seething with anger and resentments?

'I would have given much to have gone to a music school,' said Alice dreamily, her fingers picking out a tune on her dressing-gown-clad thigh.

So. Alice had suffered. Alice had yearned. Apart from Alice's abortive bid to escape to Lady Enid, Sophie had never caught a hint of covert desires, an inner life.

Perhaps she hadn't looked hard enough?

She observed Alice's fingers plucking out the silent tune. Discovered something else, too. Pity and empathy were tricky, slippery elements. They diluted dislike.

'My mother must have known that you didn't want her. Did she ever try to leave?'

'Leave. Stay. Choices? Poor Sophie, you've no idea about the war. Not really . . . for all that education you've had and I didn't. You've no idea how difficult survival became.'

Colour was stealing into the semolina-hued cheeks.

'The wisest clung on to anything they could, for no one knew what was coming. If you were ill . . . well, shall we say your mother recognised that our charity, however threadbare and unpalatable, was better than the alternative.'

Sophie retrieved her notebook. Closed it and held it against her chest. 'I'll be gone as soon as I can.'

'No doubt of it,' Alice replied.

'And you should go and work for Lady Enid. If that's what you wish.'

Alice ignored that. 'But, for the time being, you'll stay here and earn your keep. Like it or hate it, you've been brought up by us and I'm owed your service.'

'It's a form of slavery,' said Sophie.

'For such an *educated* girl, you talk nonsense. We have been parents to you.'

My mother . . . my father . . .

While she had known her mother, she had to rely on imagination to give her father shape and form. Tall. Handsome in a French kind of way – whatever that was. Brave. The hero patriot who had died for his country. (No matter that she was still working on what a hero was, exactly.) The father who would have loved his daughter beyond words. Who loved her mother enough to send her away to save her life.

'Here we are.' Extracting a bar of coal-tar soap out of her dressing-gown pocket, Alice laid it on the bed between them. 'A reminder that tomorrow morning, the laundry needs doing first thing.'

Pink. Desiccated. A touch of soap slime slicked onto the bedclothes.

Both stared at it.

Both resented what it represented.

Both hated its smell.

'Good night,' said Alice.

It took a minute or two for Alice to make her way down the unlit stairs. From the door of her bedroom, Sophie observed her progress.

She heard the door to Alice's bedroom at one end of the corridor shut. Snap . . . click.

A black shape peeled away from the newel post, a fluid phantom with a seeming black wingspan.

Sophie started. Despite Alice's strictures, her light was still on. Dim and inefficient, it still allowed her to make out the figure of Osbert standing at the bottom of the stairs, face upturned, hands locked around the newel post.

His stare was intense. Searching. Greedy. Desperate.

Her first instinct was to flee back into her bedroom. Her second to stand her ground and see it through. No weakness, no show of fear . . . . Osbert must not win.

After a moment, he turned away and padded off to his bedroom at the other end of the corridor.

She backed into her bedroom, slammed the door shut and collapsed onto the bed.

How laughably ignorant – dangerously so – the whispered conversations about sex at Digbys had turned out to be. Nibbling around the subject, they'd had no idea of its reach. Its power. Its Janus faces.

Johnno had shown Sophie the truth of it carefully and considerately. He taught her the lie of the body. What it was. What it did. With him it seemed natural and right, any embarrassment dulled.

She scrabbled at the bedspread and held on to it for dear life. What was driving Osbert was as horrible as hellfire; it oozed darkness and need.

Her teeth chattered.

Hettie sent her a parcel containing a book.

It's called Bonjour Tristesse *and it's all about the French and sex and is highly scandalous. Apparently, the French are very good at sex. The English aren't. Did you know that? Charlie Frant gave it to me – he pinched it from his sister. He's been pestering me to kiss him and said it would teach me a thing or two. Apparently, the worst bits have been left out for the English translation so maybe the English won't find much enlightenment.*

I've covered it in brown paper so Mr and Mrs Toad won't spot it.

Sophie read it in snatches. On the bus. Before sleep. Sitting with Dog. Subverted by the lawlessness of its heroine's behaviour, cheering on her refusal to be bourgeois, sucked into the heat of the summer blazing on the pages.

What drove her breath away was the heroine's ability not to mind what she did if it satisfied her current impulse.

Hettie was on holiday and telephoning was tricky. Letters had to be the substitute.

Blimey, Het. What a novel. It reeks of sex. Are the French (that includes me) so different? Can't get over how amoral and spoilt Cécile is. Yet you can't stop reading about her. It's a sad book, though. By making sure her father doesn't marry his new lover, she's condemned herself to . . . well, guilt for one thing. But I love that it's about sun and sand and the freedom to do what you want, how you want. The south of France sounds paradise. Did you think that? How wonderful she makes being eighteen appear. Do you feel wonderful, Het?

No, Hettie replied by return. *Charlie Frant did get up the nerve to kiss me. He smelt awful and his lips were flabby. Pity me. He reminded me of a blob-fish . . . When I told him not to do it again, he got very angry and told me in so many words that I was very lucky to be kissed by him. No one else has shown the slightest inclination to kiss me and I'm in despair. Are blobfish my fate?*

185

On her next visit to the library, Sophie looked up blobfish and discovered they lived at great depth in the oceans and didn't need bones as a result and their bodies collapsed when caught or taken into shallow water. Leaning over her shoulder, Mrs Winsett remarked, 'That's how I feel sometimes.'

Seated at the library table with the blobfish photo in front of her, Sophie wrote: *You are so kind and lovely, Het. I hope you find the right husband, not just any old one. I will picture you in the future sitting by a fireside, surrounded by children, or dining à deux in a chic black dress with a kind, clever husband.*

I'm scheming to get my mother's money. If I do, then I can scarper. I feel stronger about doing that. I know about sex now . . . Did she? . . . *and other things they never taught us.*

Being honest with Hettie was important, and glossing over the churn of her stomach whenever she thought of Johnno was not being quite straight.

Osbert's lustful upturned face rose in front of her, melding unpleasantly with thoughts of Johnno.

She frowned. No, she had not got the measure of this thing called sex.

But, she finished with, *I seem to have a dog. His name is Dog. Long story. He will have to be part of the escape plans. Wish me luck.*

A day later, she wrote: *I've done some research, Het. I will need a passport, which means I have to go to the French consulate in Cromwell Road. Do you know where that is? I've written to them asking for an appointment. Can I stay with you?*

Osbert has turned out to be a sex pest. Miss Chambers was right: men do have a Base Nature. I caught him spying on me. Thanks to Johnno, I know for sure now what he's after. His spying and slimy remarks might be interesting to log as part of life's experience, if you see what I mean, but I have decided to go now because I don't want to put up with it any more. Also, they are a bit frightening.

That was nowhere close to describing the depth and nuance of her turmoil.

I hate Poynsdean. It's nothing but gloom and hypocrisies. I have nowhere to call home. I don't belong anywhere, which means I'm free. Not like you. Don't mistake me, I'm SO GLAD you have somewhere you feel rooted and safe. But, Het, I can't stay here in Knoxdom in case it claims me. But I don't feel brave.

Het wrote, *You are the bravest person I know. Paris will love you. Do you think the Base Nature of men will be easier to deal with if they are French? I'm not brave, Sophs. I'm muddling my way through here. But I shall think of you boldly striking out to find your family.*

Mother says she will consider having you to stay. Can one divorce one's mother?

CHAPTER FOURTEEN

Sophie deposited two string bags bulging with vegetables and tins on the kitchen table. She was thinking about Mr Khrushchev and his bombs and the latest spat between him and the United States, which had not improved her mood. Human beings were so complicated. So clever. So stupid.

Osbert appeared in the doorway. 'I want to see you in my study.'

She made her way to the study, as slowly as she dared.

He was at his desk, elbows bent, hands churched, as was his wont.

In front of him was the copy of *Bonjour Tristesse* in all its brown-paper-jacketed disguise.

Sophie stood stock still. 'Where did you get that?'

Osbert's fingers uncoupled and rewove themselves into each other. 'What are you doing with this . . . disgraceful book?'

She looked past the dust and piles of papers, towards a drowsy, leafy vista of high summer. Fred and his wife, Sally, were walking up Church Lane to the graveyard. Fred helping Sally, who was clinging to his arm.

'You've been in my bedroom.'

He didn't confirm and he didn't deny. 'This is a disgusting book which should be banned. Every page from beginning to end is filth.'

'So disgusting that you've read it all.'

'It was important that I acquainted myself with the facts.'

He said Cécile's behaviour had no redeeming features. No guiding light to shape it. Nor any moral compass. 'What she does is disgraceful and obscene.' His eyes glistened, and his mouth slackened. 'She has sexual intercourse with a boy to whom she is not married.'

Sophie picked her way through the moral logic. 'Isn't it more concerning that she deliberately ruined someone's life? Someone who had been kind to her.'

'Yes, yes. Of course.' Osbert shook off the objection. 'But the sexual impropriety. I think we should discuss that.'

'I don't wish to discuss it and you were wrong to take my book. Could I have it back, please?'

His two forefingers pointed heavenwards. 'You helped yourself to my books without permission, Sophie. Don't think I didn't notice. But I was happy to let you do so. I saw them as part of your education.'

She reprised the wimpled and crinolined heroines waiting for their kings, knights, squires, cham-

189

pions to redeem, save or marry them. Not one of them would ever have the equivalent of a bank account. Which she would.

She bloody would.

'It belongs to Hettie.'

'Your friend Hettie? Goodness . . . I am surprised.' Blinking rapidly (she noted it all to record later), he declared, 'I shall think less of her.'

Was it ever thus that the young, the old and middle-aged did not have a clue about the other? Once upon a time even Osbert – *even Osbert* – must have felt the energy surging under his breast-bone and run with the baton of ideas and ambitions. *I will build Jerusalem in Poynsdean.* Somewhere along the race, the baton had slipped from his grasp. Now, it was difficult for him to understand that even shy, frustrated (beloved) Hettie wanted to find out what was powering her generation.

The cassock flapped half-heartedly as he got up from the desk, its hem in need of repair and a food stain sprouting over the black serge. He stood beside her and laid his hand on her forearm. 'I daresay you think I'm impossibly old-fashioned, but I only have your welfare at heart.

'Bringing up a little girl wasn't easy,' he continued. 'My wife and I had to guard you against the worst of the world. It was our duty. We did our best.'

Late-afternoon sun came through the window, resting on the beautiful panelling and piles of paper.

She *must* aim for fairness. Bringing her up *hadn't* been easy, and neither Alice nor Osbert were equipped for the task. Sophie's despairs, her otherness, her lack of cooperation, her obvious dislike of her foster parents, must have tested them greatly.

On the other hand, she, and her behaviour, had offered them a convenient and domestic via dolorosa down which to travel, which, she reckoned, all would-be martyrs craved. Surely they were grateful?

'It was difficult at times . . .' she began. 'I see that. I try to see . . .'

Her sentence was never finished.

Osbert's hand had travelled up her arm to rest on her breast. 'You have to be so careful,' he said. 'Always.'

She froze.

'Take your hand away.'

His fingers splayed over the soft upper breast. 'This is what I'm trying to guard you against. This is the sort of thing that can happen.'

'I'll report you.'

Osbert actually smiled. 'Who would believe you? The refugee foster child or the long-time vicar of the parish?'

She threw out her last defence. 'I'll call for Mrs Knox.'

And won.

'My dear.' In a trice, Osbert resumed his seat at his desk. 'I have just taught you a valuable

191

lesson. You must remember that.' With a finger, he edged *Bonjour Tristesse* over the desk towards her. 'Take it.'

She gazed down at him, crumpled and, yes, defensive. *I don't have to be frightened of you. I can choose not to be.*

Liberation.

She waited for a reply from the French consulate.

Occasionally, she encountered Johnno driving the tractor around the green, or piloting the battered family car with his mother and brothers as passengers. Once, she fancied she spotted Linda riding up beside him and she felt as though her heart had been put through the Rectory mangle.

When she had first met him, she had rated Johnno's looks as nothing to write home about. But, as she got to know him, subtle transformations took place. Now, he was handsome – beautiful, even. Strong, obviously. But slightly troubled and more easily wounded than he would wish the onlooker to know.

It made her feel breathless and a little faint to think she knew.

Dog was not that much stronger, she reported to the Brydens up at the farm. 'But his spirit is . . . and that's a start, isn't it?'

Sheila busied herself with the evening meal. Big John lit his pipe. 'Careful,' he said. 'They get to you, these beasts. Then you're trapped.' He twinkled at her. 'All manner of beasts.'

Fool, she told herself. Fool. It was true: Dog had limped into her heart, turning it pulpy and vulnerable.

Reason told her that Dog was frail and she would find it difficult to look after him.

Reason pointed out that to become enmeshed with Johnno was not going to help her either.

Shockingly – and this was the big discovery – reason only took you so far. Emotion had greater strength, a longer tail. But it ushered in conflict; was troubling, less easy to analyse. Why, for example, did she mind that Johnno was almost certainly seeing Linda?

October was not so far ahead. The leaves on the trees were thinking of changing. In the evenings, migrating birds massed on telegraph wires. The landscape was harvested. Golden. Relaxed and untidy from its fertile months. The year was not exactly vanishing, but it was on the turn.

She was nearly nineteen.

Het, do you think we'll be up to the freedom of being twenty-one?

I'm relying on you to tell me, Sophs. If twenty-one is awful, I'll stay at twenty.

More than once, she caught Dog shivering. On her next trip to Winchelford market, she bought a cheap tartan rug and made sure it was wrapped around him when she went to visit.

Sometimes, she was confronted by the brown dog gaze and she could swear that he was asking: why can't I be with you?

'Well you will be,' she told him. 'Promise.' She sat down beside him and settled the rug over his back. 'Dog, you and I will find somewhere to live together. We might not always be warm or well fed . . . that depends on so many things that I can't work out yet . . . but you'll have a home.'

Apart from the occasional cries of roosting birds and a car engine in the distance, she and Dog were enfolded by silence. Well, not exactly total silence for that was impossible in the countryside. But quiet.

It seeped into her consciousness, soothing and strengthening, drawing the sting out of her anxieties.

A couple of days later, she was up at the barn talking to Dog. 'Do you like your rug?' And 'Why don't we have a walk down on the wetlands?'

Johnno appeared in the opening to the barn and the tension energetically gestating in her chest exploded.

'Thought you might be here.' She smiled up at him and he dropped down beside her. 'When you look like that,' he said, 'I find it hard to keep my hands off you.'

She caught her breath, thinking I can't believe I'm behaving like a heroine in one of Osbert's novels.

'I kept away,' said Johnno. 'It seemed sensible. I don't want to press you into anything you don't want.'

Sophie plucked at a piece of straw and prevented

herself from asking: *Have you been seeing Linda?*
'We had our agreement and I'm grateful. You showed me . . .'

'I showed you this . . .' At that he pulled her to her feet.

His mouth was insistent but the hand cupping her cheek was tender and gentle.

When she got her breath back, she said, 'You were the best of teachers. I'm grateful.'

'We could continue.'

Unable to look at Johnno, she stroked Dog.

'What are you afraid of, Sophie?'

A shadow formed. Black-clad and Osbert-shaped. She thought of the task she had set herself. 'I'm not afraid, Johnno.'

He searched her face. 'Rubbish. That bugger is frightening you.'

'Yes. No. Not really. I've decided he can't frighten me.'

Johnno pulled Sophie to him. 'Has he attacked you? Done anything?' His grip was business-like. 'You've got to get out of there.'

'I'm making my plans.' The thudding in her chest was borderline painful. 'Almost there.'

He ran a finger down Dog's back. 'I spend a lot of my time not saying what I think. Pretending, perhaps. Particularly to my parents, who I don't want to hurt. But you and I should agree to be truthful with each other.'

'OK. It's a deal.'

She could see the words mustering. The tumbling

of barriers she knew now he had erected against giving confidences.

That touched her very much. Almost unbearably.

'I think about you, Sophie. Can't get you out of my head.' His smile hovered between the lustful and the rueful. 'I think . . . I suspect . . . you feel the same.'

'Yes, I do. And it's a nuisance.'

His eyes lit up. 'I like that. Lots of girls would have denied what they felt. Or been to shy to own up.'

'We've just agreed to be honest.' She pushed back the hair from her hot face. 'I've got to try. It's a good thing.'

Silence. Again.

'What we have . . .' The swashbuckling Johnno had been replaced by a serious Johnno, 'are things in common, Sophie. We should pool our worries. You're anxious about what comes next in your life. I know exactly what I'm facing but I'm unsure that I want it.' Their heads were close together. 'We could be Team Bryden.' He traced the shape of her mouth. 'The two of us.'

It was very difficult to think straight when consumed by intense feeling.

'Don't close your eyes, Sophie.'

'It's better I don't look at you while I work out what you're asking me.'

'To—'

She cut across. 'Are you asking me to be your lover? Only you're dressing it up?'

196

He gave a sharp intake of breath and muttered something to himself.

'Johnno, we are being truthful.'

'Actually, yes.'

Through the opening into the barn, Sophie was fed the vista of early autumn fields and woodland, the many shades of green progressively patched with russets and browns. Increasingly light-headed and giddy, she was riddled with lust and love. *Honestly, Het, what do I do?* The *wickedness*, she imagined Alice saying. *Fallen woman*, would be more novel-reading Osbert's tack. Then there was the village. Although under assault since the war, the manners and mores that held Poynsdean tight had not slackened that much since Queen Victoria's day.

Would taking a lover progress the grand enterprise?

Men will always try to take advantage, said Miss Chambers.

'Wouldn't that make things complicated?'

She meant Linda.

'We're adults. We should expect complications.'

'Ah.'

'We could be happy.'

The only memory she had of happiness was of being held by Camille and of her mother's voice in her ear. Did one taste happiness? Smell it? Feel it?

'But I was thinking that . . .' He was looking down at her in a way that almost stopped her breath. 'Thinking that . . . it would be more serious than that.'

'More serious than making love?'

'Yes.'

'Going steady?'

The shock was electric. Giddy-making.

Apparently this was the dream of most girls. Going steady was a stage in a girl's life, a culmination of their ambitions, as marked as any other rite of passage. Going steady was to be walked home from the cinema on a Friday or Saturday night, and to be kissed in a doorway while parents kept vigil upstairs.

It was almost, but not quite, a binding commitment. Plus, and this was hugely important, it was, for many, the pathway to the altar.

A vision of herself reigning over the kitchen at Home Farm – installing new electricity, replacing the kitchen range and polishing the floor tiles – arrived unexpectedly in her head. Startled, she dismissed it.

'Remember how good we were in the wood,' he said almost shyly. 'It made me think.'

The risks she had taken. Yet she had done it. And yes, yes, it had been a substantial experience with . . . and she swallowed hard at the thought . . . no consequences.

'Sophie, look at me.'

She did so.

He took her hands in his. Strong and determined. 'Do you want to?'

Yes, and yes. There was no denying she was alight. But the risks here were different. If she went steady, where would that leave the great enterprise? Sex was obviously a gateway into pleasure, but she wasn't easy with its consequent messy desires and yearnings. Look at you, Sophie, floating in an ocean of emotional turbulence with no means of keeping afloat.

This was not the plan. It might be Hettie's. In fact, she was sure it would be Hettie's and she was sorry it wasn't Hettie, darling Het, sitting with Johnno in a barn.

Dog whined and shifted closer to Sophie.

'It would be Friday nights, then?'

'More than that.' Johnno summoned patience. 'We get on, don't we? We could have a good life together.' He paused. 'I've seen you on the farm. I know you understand about . . .'

'The early mornings, the weather, the mud, the failed harvests and sick animals . . .'

He shrugged. 'Make fun of it all if you like, but that's how people have survived for centuries.'

'Sorry, sorry.'

She pulled Dog closer to her and buried her face in his neck. He smelt warm and reasonably clean.

'Sophie, you know how I feel about taking on the farm. My parents say they want to retire and I need someone like you . . .' She didn't like the 'someone like you' and frowned, and he cottoned on. 'I mean *you* to help me.'

Girls were taught to put everyone else first, to

defend themselves against a rubbish, predatory world and to find safe places. Oh blast, she thought, as tears edged to the surface. Don't let me cry. Johnno was thinking his own way through his predicament, of course he was, and he should do so. But was he thinking about hers?

'Johnno, I know how difficult it's been for you since leaving the army . . .'

'Yes and no.' He caught her hand. 'The farm's better than most have. It would be hard work but, in return, there would be a roof over your head. In time, you might come to love the livestock and the farmland.'

She blinked back the mist that suddenly obscured her vision. Her mouth opened and shut. 'Johnno, are you asking me to marry you?'

'You dumb cluck, yes.'

Her insides churned. 'A farmer's wife? Your wife?'

'I think it would suit you. I would make you suit it.' He pulled her close. 'Say yes,' he commanded. The sergeant ordering the men. The knight in one of Osbert's novels riding home to claim the damsel.

'Say yes.'

Johnno smelt of earth and lime. Of tobacco and straw.

'Sophie, this has happened so fast, but you've become very important to me.'

In that moment, she understood what it was to hold power.

Only for a moment. Once she gave an answer, the balance would shift in Johnno's favour.

In a rush, he said: 'I've fallen in love with you, Sophie. I hope . . . hope you feel the same.'

'I don't know.' She turned her hands palms up in his, savouring warmth and strength. 'It's so unexpected.'

'I would treat you properly.' He kissed her forehead, her cheek, her neck. 'We could be good together.'

Too far, too fast. 'Won't I be hated?'

He got the drift. 'Linda's a great girl. Special. Yes, special. But you've got in the way, Sophie. Everything was clear until I met you. Of course I knew who you were, but you rose, like a beautiful spirit, from the marsh and I could see nothing else.'

'I didn't know you were a poet.'

As far as Sophie understood, nature and nurture were not egalitarian. Never had been and never would be. A clear inner voice pointed out that, if she agreed to be with Johnno, she would be only a step along the way to his main concern: his farm, his future.

No, that was unfair.

But for her . . . what? A home, children and a husband? Which she had always said was not for her.

At Digbys, they had been taught that women who rejected the norms of household and husband were unfeminine, no better than they should be.

Unfulfilled and sexless. Or – cue for blushing, horrified whispers – attracted to their own sex. Wherever they went, wherever they settled, the brave, single, domestic-life-rejecting woman would be saddled with the stigma that no one desired them.

'Sophie . . . ?'

Love. Generosity. Being settled.

The straw rustled as Dog circled around his nest and collapsed down into it. He needed a home. She knew how to help him. She knew, too, what she should do for Johnno, because it had come to her in a flash that she *would* be good for him and the life at Home Farm would be a good one.

She couldn't stop herself. Her arms snaked up around Johnno and the wild, tumultuous feelings rocked her through and through.

"Yes . . . and yes."

CHAPTER FIFTEEN

A week . . . ten days . . . went by with no word from Johnno.

At first, she thought nothing of it. Then, she did.

He had lied to her.

No, he wouldn't do that.

Oh for Lord's sake, he might. Osbert Knox's novels were stuffed with stories of deceived women.

Johnno's silence hurt in a way that floored her. Inexperienced in the silence between lovers, it smarted, festered, made her ache. In heroine-speak this was to be 'helpless' or 'mortally wounded'.

'I hate feeling like this,' she confided to Hettie on the phone. 'I hate being . . . in thrall.'

Hettie could provide no comfort. 'I haven't been in love, so I don't know,' she said, unwilling to provide false cheer. The honesty that always made Sophie love her the more. Hettie added, 'What's it like?'

A rapid seesaw of mood swings. Melting sensations. Laughing and crying in the same breath.

Sleeplessness. No appetite and, not that she knew much about it, a longing for wine.

Hettie was awed. 'Hell,' she said. 'Is this what I'm in for when it happens to me?'

'I hope so, Het.'

Morning and evening, Sophie visited the barn and sat looking over the fields with her arms wrapped around Dog.

She found herself cleaning the grouting of the tiles in the bathroom.

She listened to Alice fumbling with *Les Barricades Mystérieuses* and tears dripped down her cheeks.

Her notebook filled up. *What is the nature of belief? Answer, the feeling of being certain that something exists or is true. Johnno exists and I believed him when he asked me to marry him.*

She peeled the potatoes and cut them into angry hunks. *How dare he do this to me?*

Is he all right? Not sad? Not in trouble?

She found herself in Osbert's study searching for a story which, in sweeping her away, could offer solace.

Many of the heroines in Osbert's novels preached patience. They sat it out in restricting gowns and corsets until the object of their affections had come to his senses, which generally took the entire novel.

No solace there.

The alternative was to dig deep into herself. What would she find in the new rawness and uncertainty?

In much the same manner as the Sussex landscape with its blue skies and knitted clouds, its wildflowers, metamorphosed from the tactile, gloriously coloured and scented celebration of late summer into a place of falling leaves and more mud than not, a shadow fell over Sophie's interior landscape. The river ran through it.

'Ratty in *The Wind in the Willows* wasn't a rat but a water vole,' Johnno had told her. 'As endangered as the hazel dormouse or the long-eared bat. Water voles have blunt noses, small ears and furry tails, and live in holes in the riverbank. You can always tell where they are because there's a nibbled "lawn" around the entrance . . .'

Notebook . . . But she couldn't write. The facility had deserted her. It had fled up to Home Farm. Leaving her empty and hot-eyed.

Her birthday came and went – Fred gave her a bunch of his dahlias but otherwise it was unremarked. The rooms in the Rectory cooled. The year *was* turning; autumn and winter were in sight and the house prepared itself for its customary transformation into an icebox.

Alice's cardigans emerged. Late September to May, Alice regularly wore two over her dress. In the past, they had been home-knitted affairs, often donated by a parishioner. Recently, she had changed her approach, buying cheap synthetic knitwear from the shop in Winchelford. 'I work so hard I have little strength left,' she said. 'I need extra protection.'

The reproof of two cardigans for a cold house

economically conveyed the message was that no one else remotely matched the sacrifices and privations she practised daily.

Notebook: *Alice is a masochist. (Can a sponge be a masochist?) Was she born with it? Or did she develop it when she realised that masochism was her only weapon as Osbert's wife?*

She bet to herself that Alice had never looked at a painting for pleasure.

Had never read one of Osbert's gloopy novels.

Had never walked the ridge along the Downs with the sun on her face and the swifts screaming wildly.

There was only one thing Alice permitted herself and that was the bittersweet pleasure of Lady Pitt's invitations.

'You think I'm a fool,' said Alice when Sophie remarked on the latest cardigan in eye-watering nylon yellow. 'You don't know the half of my life.'

But she did know. The childish lens had dropped away. The pale, suffering, put-upon would-be saint holed up at one end of the Rectory vanished. In its place was a secret, and corrupted, wielder of power.

She forgot that Alice had sharp eyes.

Alice watched Sophie put away the vegetables sent up by Fred. 'I don't know what you're up to.' She added: 'You look pale.'

'I didn't sleep well.'

'You're not feeling sick, are you?' She moved

closer. 'You haven't done anything stupid?' There was a tiny pause. 'The Bryden boy?'

The question dropped from Alice's lips with an agreeable frisson. An enjoyment almost.

'It would be very shocking . . .'

Something clicked. Of course. Of *course*. Why hadn't she spotted it? Alice *wouldn't mind* if Sophie was in trouble. In fact, it would thrill her. There would be a tremendous job to be done in the parish, soothing and explaining away the scandal. *Despite our best efforts. All our teaching. She's French, you see. Nothing to be done.*

Alice on a crusade would be a happier woman. The masterminding of outrage would shift her focus onto something other than Lady Pitt's silver epergne and flower arrangements which, thanks to Osbert, she would not be enjoying as the latter's companion. Tackling the women of Poynsdean who had manned the village trenches during the war, her anger would be cathartic and righteous.

And highly satisfactory.

'What are you suggesting?'

Alice's gaze travelled over Sophie. 'Just doing my duty. The Brydens are very respected . . .'

'Where *is* my cup of tea?' Osbert propelled himself into the kitchen and caught the end of the conversation. 'The Bryden boy. Lots of chatter about him since his return. I do hope, Sophie, you are being circumspect.'

His voice slid over 'circumspect' as if it was the

key to the intimacies into which, given the opportunity, he would plunge.

Sophie finished laying up the tea tray and presented it to Osbert. 'No comment,' she said. 'Was there anything else?'

Over supper in the kitchen, she took the plunge. Cleared her throat. Summoned all her determination.

'I have a dog. It's not very strong and I would like it to come and live in the Rectory. Would you be willing? I'll take care of him. He'll be no trouble.'

'Out of the question.' Alice laid down her knife and fork.

'Out of the question,' echoed Osbert.

'He's been so badly treated. He needs rest, warmth, food. Like any human. Like one of your parishioners.'

'It never does to conflate the needs of humans and animals,' said Osbert. 'They are quite different in God's hierarchy.'

Alice was nodding. 'During the war, all dogs were put down.' She seemed to relish the memory. 'The reverend is right. Animals . . . dogs . . . are lower forms of life.'

'You can't take on this responsibility without our help.' Osbert looked towards Alice, who nodded. 'And we're not equipped to have a dog here. You must arrange for him to be given a new home. Or . . .' He assumed his 'God is merciful' expression. 'Or, put down.'

Charity? Love for sentient beings? Sharing?

None of these figured in the responses.

'Return him to the Bales.' Alice flicked a glance at her husband.

'You knew about him, then,' said Sophie.

'My dear,' said Osbert, 'I'm a vicar in a small parish. You've been brave in taking this creature on, I'll give you that, but it won't do.'

After the meal was over, Sophie forced herself to follow Osbert into his study. 'I would like to help the dog. He's old and ill.'

Osbert slapped some papers down on his desk. 'I don't often hear you say please.'

Dog, she thought, I'm doing this for you. 'Please, Reverend Knox.'

He allowed several seconds to elapse before shaking his head.

'So you refuse to help him?'

'Have I not made myself clear?'

Luckily, Dog took up the slack in her unconscious.

She found herself dreaming about him (and not of Johnno). Dreams in which he was well, strong, young and had never felt blows on his body. In the dreams, they walked together towards the sea, his nose nudging her hand.

In life, progress was not good. Dog was weak and often listless, preferring to remain balled up on the straw. She understood. The dog brain could not develop a perspective on his future, but brutality and suffering had been beaten into his bones in the past and that is what told on him. If it killed her, she was going to make sure that he faced neither again. Plus, the nights were sharper, the days cooler, and something had to be done.

She coaxed him out for a walk down to the wetlands.

They made it down the lane, they made it across the field, they made it to the nearest part of the riverbank before Dog cried halt.

'Good boy.' She sat down beside him and rubbed his back gently, feeling the ripple of damp fur against her fingertips and the sharp outcrops of his spine. 'Do you think I've been taken for a ride?'

Confirming his superpowers, Dog looked up at Sophie. Dog knew what was what, and his expression told her how fragile promises were.

Betrayal. Pain. Stoicism.

She held his head between her hands.

You saved me, he seemed to be saying.

He subsided onto her lap and they sat for some time, his breathing heavy, then rapid and less regular.

Eventually, she checked her watch. It was getting late. 'Time to go,' she said, but Dog wouldn't, or couldn't, move and she noted with horror that the brown eyes were dulling. She tugged at the lead. No response.

She crouched protectively over him. 'Dog?'

A deep, powerful instinct told her that this was it for Dog.

Even so. 'Please, Dog,' she begged, intimations of the grief to come streaking through her veins. 'Don't. Stay with me.'

A breeze shuffled through the reeds on the bank. Beyond, patches of water gleamed in the marshes. She sensed a wildness creep into the darkening day, the savage approach of death, in the face of which she was powerless.

Gently, she cradled him. 'It's all right, my boy,' she said. 'You're not going out of this world unloved. I loved you. I loved you . . .'

He whimpered and sighed.

'You are not going out alone. I am here.'

So she sat on, the lumps of hard earth and the stones biting into her, cherishing Dog as the life ebbed out of him. 'Maybe where you're going there will be wild green space, rabbits to chase, and love and care. Which you should have had. And you never did until it was too late.'

Dog looked at Sophie one final time. Then, he was gone.

How long did she remain cradling him? Sophie didn't care. She wanted Dog's spirit to be well away by the time she left, racing up into the night sky to God knew where. She wanted to be sure he was running free and well. She wanted to give thanks that he trusted her enough to die in her presence, and to tell him he had a place in her memory for good.

She covered Dog with rushes that she managed

to tug up, and what branches she could find, and headed to Home Farm.

Sheila answered the knock. 'Sophie . . . how nice.'

'Is Johnno around?'

Sheila levelled a look at Sophie – not unsympathetic, not unfriendly but not inviting. 'I'll find him.'

She left the door open and Sophie on the doorstep. Waiting, trembling and tearful, she registered the sounds of doors opening and shutting and Johnno's younger brother shouting insults at his sister. Light spilled through the kitchen door. A smell of new bread wafted in her direction. Someone had tried to polish the red terracotta tiles in the passage and there were smears of polish by the doormat. There was a rip in the curtain that hung over the door to keep out the winter draughts.

The farmhouse and its comforts were contained within a magic circle. If she stepped into it, it would enfold her, keep her, nourish her.

'Sophie . . .' Johnno appeared from the direction of the living room.

He was in his Sunday clothes, which was odd – close shaved and his hair brushed into military neatness. He had a mug of tea in one hand, which he put down on the ledge. 'Mum didn't say it was you.'

'Why haven't you been in touch?'

He looked as though the world sat sullenly on

his shoulders. 'I don't know what to say.' He peered at her red eyes and dishevelment and his expression changed to one of alarm. 'What's happened?'

'Dog has died,' she said, her resolution not to cry broken immediately. 'I need help to bury him.'

He glanced over his shoulder to the living room. 'I'm sorry, Sophie, I can't. We have people in. A meeting I can't leave. I'll explain but not now.'

'Lend me a shovel then. I'll do it. He's by the river.'

He looked at his watch. 'Sophie, it won't be safe. There's talk of strangers near the marsh when it gets dark.'

'I can't leave Dog out for an animal to get at him.'

'OK . . .' He sounded ragged and his voice was without its usual uplift.

She knew him well enough to know something was up. 'What's happened?'

He muttered something under his breath.

'What?'

How obsessively in the past days had she tried to sum up Johnno? Several parts good humour, one part bitterness, many parts energy. Topping them all was kindness. Not today, not now on the farmhouse doorstep. He was angry. Definitely. And she was sensing shame. And sadness.

Her cheeks were now slicked with tears and Johnno hauled a handkerchief out of his pocket. 'Sophie . . .'

'Johnno!' his mother called from the kitchen and he changed tack. 'Sophie, take the shovel from the tools in the shed. Do what you can tonight and I will help you early tomorrow morning. That's the best I can think of for the moment. I'll meet you at eight.'

Sophie told him where to find Dog.

'Sophie . . .'

But she was already walking away and did not look back.

In the shed she selected a shovel. It smelt of whitewash and hay and lime and silage. And dogs. Elements of farm life of which she had imagined she would grow fond and accustomed.

214

CHAPTER SIXTEEN

She chose a place near the river where the soil would be softer. Even so, she couldn't manage to dig more than a couple of feet down.

Blisters arrived in her palm, then cramp in her hands, bringing the operation to a halt. But she was agonised that shallow meant vulnerable and animals might get at the body.

She laid Dog in the hole. Crouching down, she smoothed his fur and arranged his legs in the way he had done when alive, before scattering what rushes she could tug up over him and covering him with earth.

'Oh, Dog . . . I swear I will never walk past any abused animal. That's my promise.'

Dog had liked the river walk. As had her mother, whose essence was here too. She looked down at her handiwork. The two of them could range the spirit world together.

The sun set. With its disappearance came a chill and she buttoned up her cardigan. Johnno was right. In the gloom, she felt for the first time that the marsh and the river hinted at disturbing, inexplicable terrors.

Back at the Rectory, she ran a bowl of cold water and tipped salt into it, as much as she dared, and plunged her hands into it. It hurt, it really hurt, and that was what she craved deep down. The smart and the pain being easier, so much easier, to bear than grief for Dog.

Johnno was already waiting for her the following morning, his figure enlarging as she made her way over the tussocky grass with the shovel.

He took it from her and pointed to the grave. 'I'm sorry, Sophie.'

The nightmare scenario. During the night, an animal had been at work, and Dog's back legs protruded from the earth.

'Oh, Dog. Forgive me.'

Johnno seized the shovel and prised Dog free of his earth covering. 'Nothing to forgive.' He dug ferociously and within a short time, the grave was of a decent depth and Dog was laid back in it. Johnno heaped the earth over him, and they stamped and tamped it down until they were satisfied.

Dog now lay under a firm, compacted grave. Sophie dropped down on one knee and laid her hand on the surface. 'Goodbye.'

The sounds of the river were extra pronounced. A wisp of mist lay over the marsh. As she watched, it dissolved.

They were silent and did not touch one another.

Johnno leant on the shovel. Sophie lifted her face towards the sun.

The distance between them was one of strangers. As if their bodies had never enjoyed each other. As if words of love and longing had never been exchanged.

All that had vanished.

Bewildered, she brushed earth off her fingers and dismissed any thought of the heroines who watched and waited. Instead she thought of Cécile in *Bonjour Tristesse*. 'What are you not telling me?'

The Johnno, the lion, to whom she had grown used was not there. He had metamorphosed into someone deeply troubled.

'You haven't been in touch for over a week.'

'Unforgiveable,' he said. His eyes flew to hers. 'I should have done. But I needed to sort things out.'

Her stomach gave a lurch. 'You asked me to marry you. Or did I imagine it? You were quite clear that you thought we could make a go of life on the farm. Together.'

'Yes, I did, and I meant it.'

His mouth tightened with strain, and the knuckles on the hand that was clasping the shovel whitened. All the golden swagger had vanished. He was telling the truth, of that she was sure – which was something. 'Tell me.'

He drove the shovel into the earth with such force it must have jarred his wrists. 'We can't get married.'

There it was.

'I'm not good enough?'

'Don't be stupid.'

John and Sheila have objected? Johnno's changed his mind about marriage. He's decided to run away.

'I never wanted anything more in my life than to marry you, but it isn't possible.'

There it was. Anger turned her sharp. 'What do you mean "isn't possible"? Of course it's possible.'

He squared his shoulders in a way that meant business. In the way she imagined he must have done when going into desert skirmishes and Egyptian villages to sort out the trouble. 'I'm going to marry Linda after all.'

Would she ever forget this moment? Standing by the river, the early autumn morning sun on their faces. Dog under her feet. Her hands still earthy. Realising that if certain bridges were crossed, there was no way back.

Her first thought was of flight. To run away from the trouble and pain of this moment.

'But why?'

He grabbed her so tightly that she cried out. 'I meant it when I said I loved you. I love you more than I can say.'

She searched his face: the bitter regret in his eyes, the tightened mouth. 'Then *why*?'

He released Sophie. 'Linda is pregnant.'

Sophie sat down hard on the ground. 'You were still going with Linda.' Pulling herself together. 'But I knew that.'

He sat down beside her. 'Let's be clear. You set

the rules of what was between us. You were insistent you didn't want involvement. You wanted me to take your virginity and that to be that.' He took her hand and cherished it with a calloused hand. 'It was a very strange situation. With Linda it was more straightforward.'

She turned her head to look at him. 'I was wrong about what I felt. It changed. I don't understand how, but it did.'

He dug into his pockets. Lit a cigarette. 'She's almost five months gone. You . . . we . . . were too late.'

In previous eras, Sophie might have called him a scoundrel, a cheat, a cad or something in that vein. She would have had the option of denouncing him to the village priest (although since that was Osbert, that was never going to happen). Or she could adopt the position of the heroine of *My Heart's Desire*, who announced on the final page that she would give up her married lover for the good of everyone concerned.

Linda had wanted Johnno. Negotiating in a tight jumper through parental expectation, village life, pragmatism and her private dreams of a fair-haired hero, she had triumphantly netted in her ambition.

Sophie bowed her head. 'She'll marry you?' It was a question that didn't need asking. Of course Linda would. She had put down the marker from the moment Johnno had first marched back into Poynsdean.

'She needs to marry me. There's a baby to think

about,' said Johnno. 'Poynsdean can be unforgiving.'

Her hurt and shock made it hard to breathe.
She laid a hand on Johnno's arm. 'Then we won't
see each other again.'

'I know,' he said in an unfamiliar voice. 'No
more after this.'

She looked around at the river. The sky. 'You
. . . Linda . . . didn't consider adoption.'

Johnno got to his feet and walked over to the
riverbank. The distance between them emphasised
how far they were now apart. 'I wouldn't think of
it.' He frowned. 'I'm surprised you suggested it.'

Stand upright. Face him.

She did. 'Sorry. I was wrong. It's because it
hurts, Johnno. Very much.'

He was silent for a moment. Running a hand
through a clump of the rushes. 'I didn't know how
you would make me feel and how everything
would fall into place and make sense. How . . .'
The words arrived in a way that told her he didn't
get much practice in expressing his deepest feelings. 'How you would haunt me.'

She dug her nails into her flesh.

'It was great,' he said. 'I felt . . . I felt that you
and I understood who and what we were, and we
could make a go of it. I can't explain it, but it was
there.'

She looked down at her clenched hands. 'Me
too.'

'It was something precious,' he added.

220

It wasn't a word she would ever imagine Johnno using.

Precious.

To her eternal shame, Sophie cried, 'Are you sure it's yours?'

Johnno flinched. 'As sure as I can be.'

Sophie pressed her hands to her face to prevent the tears running down her cheeks.

'I can't abandon a woman I've got up the duff.'

Yes, you can, she wanted to throw at him. *That* had happened in a couple of Osbert's novels.

'A child, Sophie. It can't be abandoned either.'

Shocked at herself, shaking with emotion, she checked any further protest. He was right. 'You're bigger and better than me, Johnno.'

Johnno gazed longingly at her. Then he didn't. He tugged the shovel out of the ground and hoisted it over his shoulder. 'I'm sorry, Sophie. I'm sorry. I thought it was all going to be wonderful. But it isn't.'

Hettie was so taken aback she could barely utter: 'Tell me everything.' She listened to Sophie's recital, which took so long that she had to ring back from her end in London. 'You've been given the royal run-around.'

Hettie had a bundle of new phrases which, normally, Sophie would have enjoyed and demanded to know where she had picked them up. Nightclub? Cocktail party? Cinema? But while she could barely think, she didn't care.

221

How to convey the physical pain of a love affair that had turned into disaster? She never imagined that her body would ache, in the legs and stomach. In the head. All over.

Hettie cleared her throat. 'When's he getting married?'

'As soon as. She's almost five months gone. She's been living in fear and never said a word until her mother marched her to the doctor. There were big scenes at the farm.'

I have to honour her, said Johnno.

I can't abandon her.

It will kill me because it's you I want.

As the three-minute pips sounded, Hettie said, 'Come down and stay, Sophs. We can discuss it properly.'

'Your mother still hates me.'

'True. But she'll live.'

'I've heard tell,' said Osbert, a couple of days later through the open door of his study. 'I've heard tell.'

I bet you have . . . Sophie was dusting the hall. The motes danced around, eluding her like everything else.

The village would be electric with it. Sparking with gossip. Rejoicing in the upheaval and spectacle. Enjoying the view from Morality Hill. Quick to confine their daughters.

Osbert would have considered long and hard as to when he would broach the subject with Sophie. She knew the form. The pacing up and down the study, the placing of a reflective finger on a novel, preferably featuring a trapped maiden. Or the running of said finger along the edge of the panelling. Then, and only then, would he decide the optimum moment to confront her.

Unmarried mothers – and the custom when referring to them was to drop one's tone to a barely audible hush – weren't banished to the Church Home for Unmarried Mothers in Eastbourne or Bournemouth until they were six months into the pregnancy, giving everyone plenty of opportunity to clock the bulge which was the signal for the praetorian guard of older women to light the fires of Poynsdean's very own *auto-da-fé*.

For the women, there were the abundant pleasures of gossip, the indulgence in the snobbery of morality – 'My Tilly/Susan/Lizzie would have never . . .' and the joys of condemnation. Or, equally, the joys of compassion: 'We must forgive her'.

In public, Poynsdean men echoed their women. They didn't have much choice. But, covertly, secretly, they daydreamed of a young girl having taken her clothes off.

At the homes, so it was said, the baby was snatched at birth and given away to proper people, i.e. married ones.

'The study, if you would, Sophie.'

She chucked the duster into the tray of cleaning materials. Resisted the urge to kick it.

Osbert was standing by the window, a scraggy

223

black figure. He did not turn around at her entrance. 'You've been pipped at the post,' he said.

Could she, this very moment, flee the Rectory and the claustrophobic, uneasy, revolting Knox life?

'I'll be officiating at the wedding.' He cleared his throat. 'I'm afraid the bride has asked that you don't attend.' Osbert wore his top sanctimonious expression. 'Linda Savage has fallen from grace and is no better than she should be. She will be judged accordingly but we have a duty not to ignore the sinner, however much we disapprove. I'm pleased to say that Johnno Bryden has shaped up, as we knew he would, and she will be saved. A good man.'

'Wild horses wouldn't get me to their wedding.'

'Now, now,' he said. 'It never does to be a bad loser.' He fiddled with some papers on his desk. 'Linda is guilty of immorality and we are sorry for it. Boys will be boys, of course. Lucky for the pair of them that their future is in place and Home Farm will be there for them.'

A picture emerged of Linda in a white dress that was too tight across the middle, making her way up the aisle; the guests looking everywhere – the carved ceiling, the tiny ancient Lady chapel, the marble memorials on the walls – except at the bride.

'Corruption,' he was saying. 'The modern world is corrupting the young.'

224

Sophie stared at him.

'Moral corruption,' he amplified.

'Reverend Knox, they're *not* corrupt.' Defending Linda was not what she had had in mind, but here she was. 'You shouldn't be marrying them if you feel like that. Someone else should do it.'

A disturbing smile darted across his lips. 'Interesting you're defending unconscionable behaviour.'

What was the sum of herself at this point? Sick at heart. Sick to the stomach. Her gaze reached past Osbert to the window where, beyond the glistening wetlands and marsh, lay the sea. The mere thought had the power to lift her mood and, suddenly, she had escaped from the study with its scratched panels and Osbert's leer to a sailing boat skimming over the water in the sun and the wind.

'I'm sure you're upset that Johnno chose Linda. But you'll get over it.'

She bit her lip hard, which made her wince.

'And the dog?' enquired Osbert. 'What's happened there? So unwise a responsibility . . .'

'He's dead.' Afraid that she would not get the words out, she cut him short. 'His life had been too hard. I buried him by the river.'

But Dog was with her in the boat. Ears streaming in the wind. Happy and whole.

Weeping with delight, she rested her hand on his head. '*Bonjour*, Dog.'

'*Bonjour*, Sophie. Time to go.'

225

CHAPTER SEVENTEEN

D o chores. Assemble supper. Think strategy. Stoke courage.

Osbert was attending a parish meeting which, he warned Alice and Sophie, would be a long one. Serious issues would be debated. Chiefly, the question of whether alcohol – which Osbert held to be the Devil in liquid form – could be sold at the village harvest festival.

Alice was 'taking tea' at Pitt House. 'Dear Lady Enid demanded I came. "You need a treat," she told me. "Let that girl earn her keep."'

In their absence, the Rectory breathed easier.

Close eyes.

Open eyes.

Feel grief snap down like the bite of an animal. For Dog. For Johnno. Without Dog, she was drained. The humiliations of being wounded and weakened punched at odd moments. Never again, she told herself. *Never.*

She let herself into the study where, lured by the vista of a drowsy and beautiful late afternoon, she lingered by the window.

Turning away, she ran a hand over the panelling.

A master of his craft had chosen the English oak, carved it and fitted the pieces together. It was complete and unto itself. No Knox could destroy its beauty.

Everything, *everything*, in the house was better without them.

Osbert's diary was open on top of a pile of papers. Fierce HB pencil spelt out his day. 'Service'. 'Sermon'. 'Accounts'.

She paged back through the week and Osbert's world fluttered between her fingers: 'Adams funeral', 'Confirmation class', 'Bishop' and, repeated several times, a weaselly, suggestive word, 'Penance'.

For what? Hatred of Alice? Appetites raging? Religious doubt? Possibly all of them surging around the skinny frame.

The accounts book was stacked under the diary.

Pre-1947, a meticulous record of a household existing precariously on Osbert's stipend.

From then on, neatly written figures brought into focus additional funding . . . a monthly credit of £3.00 from an unnamed source. This continued for years. (After rationing was lifted in 1954, the purchase of cheese figured regularly.)

Month after month. Year after year.

She began with Osbert's desk drawers. These were stuffed with pencil stubs, pieces of string, pencil sharpeners, rubbers. Plus a bottle of Royal Blue Quink ink, a pair of leather gloves whose fingers had split, and a stone with 'Skegness' painted onto it.

A sheet of blotting paper occupied the desktop, lurid pink and almost at the end of its useful life. Blotted and re-blotted with the ghostly reverses of Osbert's sermons and correspondence including, she noted, her own name.

It was ever thus. From the moment of orphaning, Sophie's life had been turned over like a stone and poked under, beginning with the almoner at the hospital where Camille was finally admitted. Then the Knoxes. Then Digbys. Marked. Assessed. Directed.

Osbert's Bible lay on the floor and she rifled through the pages before turning her attention to the bookshelves. Dreary biographies of the saints. Nothing. Treatises on doctrinal controversies. Nothing. Doctrinal disputes in the sixteenth century (oh Lord, oh Lord . . .) Nothing.

As she worked, the suspicion hardened that the monthly £3 came from the money her mother had left.

Osbert had been taking the money.

To do so, he would have visited the post office on a regular basis.

Therefore he would keep the book somewhere where it was easy to access.

She glanced at her watch. Ran an eye over Osbert's fiction. *Desire in Italy, The White Knight, Dreaming Towers* . . .

Which one might be hiding it?

A voice said, 'I know what you're doing.'

Sophie swung around.

Alice stood foursquare in the doorway. The dead animal roosted on its perch, the flowered blouse strained over her plumped-up midriff. (The shoes were a different story and in great need of repair.)

'I know what you're doing,' repeated Alice.

Sophie considered. 'I'm looking for what's mine.'

'And what would you do with it?'

'Mrs Knox . . . Alice, that's my concern.'

Alice advanced into the room. 'What an extraordinarily ungrateful person you are.'

Compromise and negotiation were necessary when dealing with Khrushchev and Soviet Russia, or so said articles in the newspapers. She prepared to use those tactics.

'I'm grateful that you took my mother in when she was at rock bottom.' Alice clicked her tongue. 'But I don't belong here. We all know that.' There, it was said. 'Also, I realise that I no longer have to obey you.' The negotiating tone mutated into one which – she trusted – sounded tough and determined. Turning back to the bookshelf, she pulled out a book at random. It was Norah Loft's *The Lute Player*.

A photograph drifted to the floor.

Both women made a grab for it. Alice won. Peered short-sightedly at the image. 'Your mother,' she spat.

Sophie craned over Alice's shoulder.

Yes, her mother. Photographed outside the Rectory's front door. It was frosty, and Camille was wearing a coat and a knitted scarf. Unsmiling

229

and thin, her gaze directed away from whoever held the camera. But beautiful, very beautiful, thought her daughter, as grief burned through her.

Alice held the photo between finger and thumb. 'I took this. At the end of the war. After she died, Osbert said we should keep it for you. But really he wanted it for himself.' She shrugged. 'I chose not to say anything. The problem had gone away.'

'My mother was a problem?'

'I'll leave you to work that one out.' Alice sat down at the desk. 'Men are beasts. We've discussed it already. At the mercy of their organs, and everything in this life is a conspiracy to hide what they really are.' She sounded almost dreamy, 'There's so much that is only half seen, sometimes never seen. Never understood. There is only one thing that's truly known . . . men are beasts.'

Clearly, the theory of men's Base Nature was universal.

Something struck her as wrong about this, even though she had plenty to mourn. Perhaps it was the wholesale-ness of the statement. There was much beauty in the world, and a ton of people, many of them men, who did good things. There was progress, too – in which Sophie would put her faith. And the struggle for fairness and a just society.

She was tempted to remind Alice of Johnno and his honour.

Instead, countering Alice's surprising nihilism, she said, 'I can't believe you've never met a man who meant well.'

'You'll learn,' said Alice.

'Will you give me the photograph?'

Alice handed it over. 'Good riddance.' She pulled off the hat and laid it on the blotting paper, revealing crushed hair. 'I'll give you what you want, Sophie Morel, if . . . if in return you never tell anyone it was me.'

The Lute Player dropped through Sophie's fingers to the floor.

Caught between mirth and sheer astonishment, she asked, 'Do you mean I should lie?' This was the woman who had supervised her every move. Jabbed her, nagged her into the acceptance of her religion. *Obedience. Truthfulness.* 'Wouldn't that be a sin?'

'Do you think I mind about sinning?'

'I thought you minded very much, Alice.'

'Ah, the clever Sophie Morel. For all your privileged education you haven't worked out the basics. Sin was invented to keep people in order.'

All this was far, far too illogical and bewildering. 'And what about God?'

'Him too.' A pause. 'Of course.'

'But your life . . . your work?'

Alice eyeballed Sophie (who had so many questions she almost choked). The pale eyes widened. 'I'll tell you why. Once upon a time, there was a plain child, the youngest of six, in a home where there was no money and little care. It was a disgrace that this child had ever been born. The mother couldn't cope and the father drank.

Somehow, this child understood that if she showed up at the local church there was a chance she would be fed, and someone might teach her the alphabet. Which is what happened. The child was grateful and, when she grew up, she helped out on Sundays.'

'I see.'

Alice threw her one of her looks.

'One day a new curate turned up. Full of energy and youthful. But that wasn't so important. What was, was that he was looking for a wife.' Alice's gaze drifted to Osbert's paper-strewn desk. 'You only have one chance in life, don't you? Many don't even have that. I was no bargain. Very plain, poor and ill-educated. But I could be of service. The reverend, as he became, was an option which I took. You may not think my husband is much of one and . . .' a smile fought for life on the pale mouth, 'you would be correct. But he was an option.'

In a month of Sundays, Sophie would never have thought she would utter these words: 'You do yourself down. You're a figure in the parish.'

'The truth, Sophie Morel, is that I'm selfish and unforgiving and I'm not sure I can stomach watching you live a different life from mine. Maybe, if you had been my real daughter . . . Maybe then.' She fiddled with the hat, which appeared to be fighting back. 'Let's be clear about one thing. I'm sending you away *not* because my husband, my idiot husband, is taken with you . . .

232

that doesn't matter.' She picked her way over the paper-strewn room to the bookshelf by the window. 'It's because you now know what sort of person I am.'

The absurdity of these . . . revelations. The absurdity of the situation. Sophie was tempted to laugh, but an inner voice spelt out: *Alice perceives things more clearly than you have done.*

She longed to talk to Johnno. To Hettie.

If she could talk to Johnno, they would plot their way out of the Rectory and make off with her money.

Stupid. Stupid to think about Johnno.

Alice went over to the bookshelves and ran a fingernail over the spines of the books. The scrape of her nail on the bindings set Sophie's teeth on edge.

'Here we are.' She extracted *A Commentary on the Gospel of St James* from its companions. It fell open to reveal a hollow heart that had been scooped out of its pages.

'Does the reverend have it in for St James?'

Alice said, 'He wouldn't know a commentary if it sat in his lap.' She lowered her voice. 'He doesn't actually *read* these things. But he would have you believe he did.'

Nested in the hollow heart, there it was. Slim, with grey marbled floppy covers, 'Post Office Savings Bank' printed in red on its cover.

Alice clasped it tight to her chest. Sophie held out a hand. 'I want to know how much is in there.'

The answer came off pat. 'Over a thousand pounds.'

'A *thousand* pounds.' Enough to keep Sophie for several months, until she got a job.

Alice did not budge. 'I'll give it to you on condition that you leave here. And don't come back. Ever.'

How peculiar human nature was. In that moment, Sophie found herself riddled with regret that Alice and she had never had the slightest sympathy for one another. Had spent all those years in irritable, hostile proximity.

She sought a point of contact. Just one. 'Will you play the Couperin for me? To take with me as a memory.'

Without a word, Alice got up and went into the sitting room. Note by note, *Les Barricades Mystérieuses* filtered back to Sophie, gathering tempo, gathering poignancy and not a little mystery.

She stood at the door of the sitting room and watched Alice play it out.

'You know,' the words were dragged from Alice, 'I could have been a mother to you if you had let me.'

Les Barricades . . . shielding the secrets of soul and heart. The music, so poignant and yearning. The sadness of Alice's confession. The waste of the years.

The final note sounded, and Alice swivelled on the piano stool and held out the post office book.

'Your birth certificate is in here as well. You hadn't thought of that. You'll get nowhere without it. And a letter from the French consulate. It came the other day. Osbert took it.'

Adversaries? But adversaries who had, after all these years, made an accommodation with each other.

'Remember your promise.'

'How will you explain?'

'It will be the mystery that the reverend and I can mull over on winter nights. It will give us something to talk about.'

'You'll lie?'

Alice depressed the F sharp key and the note sidled into the room. 'I'll lie.'

It was said gladly. Fluently. And with the utmost relish.

'Hettie, I'm on my way.'

'What took you so long?'

'Fear.'

Down her end of the telephone, Hettie took a big breath. 'There's no need. You'll be safe with us.'

'Even with your mother?'

'She's had a new perm, which always puts her in a good mood.'

Sophie glanced over to the Benyon house. Sure enough, Betty lurked at the window.

She would soon be shot of her.

Hands trembling, she dialled Home Farm and asked to speak to Johnno.

'Yes,' he said when he came to the phone.

'Johnno . . . I wanted . . . this is goodbye.'

'Oh God.' There was a silence. 'Of course. I should have known.' She heard him light up a cigarette. 'I hate the idea of you going. But you must. I can see that. If it was me, I would.'

Just in time, she stopped herself lashing out. *Linda won't make you happy.*

How could she be so obvious? So predictable? So dog in the manger? The Modern Woman must cede no space to jealousy and possessiveness in the emotional armoury. Anyway, if Johnno was correct, Linda had been pregnant *before* Sophie offered herself on a plate to Johnno.

Yet, there they were, swooping like birds in a wind.

Jealousy and regret.

To her despair, and despite everything, despite every precept she had schooled herself in, she heard herself say, 'I hope she'll make you happy.'

Johnno's reply was savage. 'What do you bloody think?'

'Sorry, sorry.' She paused. 'I'm not going to make a scene.'

His voice came down the line, urgent and intimate, spearing into her head and heart. 'We understand each other. That won't change.'

'If you want to say goodbye, I'll be at Dog's grave early tomorrow morning.'

'Yes.' She heard him blow out smoke. 'Yes.'

*   *   *

236

'Certified copy of an entry of birth . . .'

There she was. Certified in the sub-district of Winchelford in Sussex county. Father: Pierre Augustin Morel. Mother: Camille Marie Morel, née Debord.

It validated her. She had a being. She was real.

During the afternoon, she went over her financial situation. For something that held her future, the post office savings book was mighty insubstantial. Account particulars: Bee Lane, No 2807. These, the instructions informed her, were to be quoted on every withdrawal form and any letter she sent to them, otherwise the transactions would not be authorised. It would, they said, be advisable to keep copies.

The adult life of records, papers, tallies.

In December 1945, an opening deposit of five thousand pounds had been recorded in royal blue ink.

She thought about that.

Endeavoured to piece together her mother's thinking.

Camille could have hidden this money from the Knoxes during the war, assuming that she would be returning to France. Then realised she wouldn't be doing so and deposited it instead in the post office. It was telling that the withdrawals were sporadic and tiny until her mother's death. Camille had been careful, oh so careful. But, after Sophie was sent to Digbys, fees had to be paid and then there were the regular withdrawals of £3.00 a month, continuing up to the present.

Plus, six weeks ago the huge sum of £300 had been taken out.

What had Osbert done with her money?

Maybe, like Johnno in Egypt, he had paid for a woman? (Did they cost that much?) Or maybe he was paying off a blackmailer? Maybe he liked the feel of such a large sum in his pocket. (That she understood.)

Nevertheless, he had taken it. Another notch on the tally of dislike and distrust.

Next?

Pack her things. Not that there was very much to pack, and most of what she did possess, she would gladly abandon. Her notebook, underwear, her school dress and a couple of blouses and her skirt would have to do. Into the attaché case they went, which she hid under the bed.

The great enterprise.

Next.

As dawn broke, she edged barefoot down the stairs with her case. Tiptoed into the kitchen. Osbert's margarine and Spam sandwiches for the coming day were on the table, wrapped in a damp towel. Snatching them up, she eased open the kitchen door and left it wide open.

Fresh morning air would cleanse the Augean stables.

It was too early for the birds to be feeding. But

she would not leave without saying goodbye to the creatures who had helped her, given her pleasure, repaid her care. For all these years.

Dismembering Osbert's lunch, she scattered it over the bird table.

Enjoy, my beautiful birds. My friends.

She put on her hated sandals – re-christened the Sandals of Freedom. Moving silently around the side of the house, she avoided the gravel path and walked down to the gate. Before she turned towards the marsh, she looked back in farewell to the Rectory, in all its innate beauty.

The rising sun reflected light onto the elegant, decaying windows, illuminating its slippage. Its despair . . . yes, despair at how its fabric was slipping away . . .

She froze.

A figure was watching her departure from an upper window.

Osbert.

He was stark naked, arms stretched out as if on a cross.

Apart from Johnno, statues and pictures and the like, she didn't know much about naked men. At the distance she was now from the house, the details were fuzzed. What she could read into Osbert's angularity and protuberances was, as reflected in the anguished body, a tortured spirit.

Repulsive.

Yet, and yet, it wasn't entirely so. No doubt it was a trick of the light, but the tableau had a painterly quality, the brushstrokes coaxing the fallibility and frailty of the human to the surface.

He, the Reverend Osbert Knox, the black figure from childhood, appeared so pale, weak and diminished framed in the window that a response as strong as repulsion was a waste of energy.

Sophie smiled to herself and carried on down the lane.

240

CHAPTER EIGHTEEN

Over the marsh, the dark was lessening. To the east, dusky colours streaked the horizon. The sky was huge and the shadows creeping into existence elongated. The silence was almost total.

Until the birds began.

It was the signal for the earth to shake into life. There was a rustle in the rushes, a flicker of silvered water, the smell of decay rising and mixing with the still-fresh growth.

The attaché case stashed under the hedgerow in the lane, she set off across the tussocky grass towards Dog's grave. The farewell pilgrimage, and wetlands, marsh, out-of-sight sea wrapped their soul around her, committing themselves to memory.

Behind her, Poynsdean would be waking. Village life. Hard and hardworking, settled in routine and expectation. Out over the sea, the dawn light unveiled sea and sky. It filled her vision. Over there it would be different. Nothing would be set. Nothing would be routine.

Against this grandeur, this natural panorama, her insignificance was startling. How little she mattered. The lash of a wave could bear her out to sea and push her down. A falling tree could crush her body. Human beings were in transit and soon forgotten. A phrase had tripped off Hettie's newly world-weary tongue last time they spoke: 'No one amounts to a hill of beans. Not even the Queen.' (*That* was some concession on royalist Hettie's part.)

Under the twin assaults of love for Johnno and fear for the future, the inner Sophie shivered and shrank. Take comfort from the Hill of Beans theory, she instructed herself. Nobody mattered. Nothing mattered.

So she told herself.

Dog's grave was settling, which was reassuring. Already, a suggestion of grass had crept over it and the earth had flattened.

She looked towards the river, longing to catch sight of a spectral shape. Was her mother there? But she knew in her bones that Camille had already left.

'Sleep well, my Dog,' she said, hunkering down beside him. 'I loved you too, and I won't be leaving you. You will come with me. Somehow.'

It was true. Her mother and Hettie excepted – and Johnno – her love for Dog had been as powerful as anything she had ever experienced.

'Dog . . . Dog . . . you've turned me into a crusader.' A picture of a sword-wielding knight seen in one of her childhood books sprang into her mind. So ridiculous. 'You've given me something important. Because of you, I will fight cruelty to animals.'

Always. Always.

There was a movement behind and, insanely joyful that he had come, she swung round, 'Johnno . . .'

The words were stillborn.

Materialising out of the dawn light was the black pterodactyl – the figure of derision, the subject of Het's stifled giggles but, also and horribly, the stuff of her nightmares.

He came beetling up, the nicks on his shaved chin oozing blood.

Mercifully, *mercifully*, he was dressed in the flapping cassock and the shoes tied up with string.

'You followed me.'

'Indeed so. Remember I have a duty of care.'

'I release you from it, Reverend Knox. You may let me go. I'll take charge of myself.'

Her voice was sharp and on the edge of panic.

'You're not fit to do so. Too young. Too inexperienced.'

'Reverend Knox, I've just seen you standing at a window without clothes. I would ask how fit you are to take charge of me?'

He didn't miss a beat. 'It's my daily practice,' he said. 'Being naked for a little while each day is good for the soul. Good for the body. It builds up resistance. It's a discipline.'

'Why stand at the window? It's . . .' she fumbled for the word – and the concept – which was new to her, '. . . exhibitionist. Are you hoping someone will see you?'

'It was very early,' he said. 'I wasn't expecting you to be sneaking out of the Rectory.'

'So you say.'

His motives? The impulses? She had no idea, but no one in their right mind would wish to dwell on that image to tease them out.

'Reverend Knox, I'm going now.'

Was there sufficient determination? Conviction?

A breeze had got up and a rustle of grasses and rushes accompanied its passage across the field.

He shaded his eyes and scanned the horizon. 'So, you persist in going to join your friend?'

'Yes, in London.' She glanced over to the hedge where she had left the case, calculating whether to make a run for it. 'I won't be returning.'

'Let me see. We've fed and clothed you for eighteen years. We've given you shelter and, I trust, guidance on how to live a good and moral life. Surely you owe us a goodbye?'

Astonishingly, she registered hurt behind his frown and, for a second, she held the extraordinary thought that she had Osbert all wrong.

He grabbed Sophie's arm. 'I'd like you to explain to me how I've erred in your upbringing, because I've discovered you've stolen something of mine.'

So that was it.

'The boot's on the other foot, Reverend Knox.' She pulled her arm away. 'The birth certificate and the post office book are mine. The money is mine and I know you've been taking it.'

'£3.00 a month for your upkeep is not overly generous.'

'But the £300 that you took out is.'

He ignored that one. 'How did you find it?'

'I looked through your papers and your books.'

'No, you didn't. They're untouched. Was it my wife?' The question slunk out and there was an odd, avid look on his face. Suddenly, she understood that the post office book was a component in the war being fought (mainly out of sight) between husband and wife.

'Mrs Knox? No.'

'You're lying to me. I can spot a liar at ten paces.'

It was pure exhilaration to lead Osbert down the wrong path. 'You taught me never to lie. Remember?'

'I think it was my wife.'

A vision of Alice's battered body being discovered at the bottom of the stairs. 'No. *No.*' Rooting for a footing among the tufts of grass. 'What did you do with my £300?' Osbert didn't bother to answer. 'I'll make a few suggestions. The horses? You read *The Racing Times*. Another woman for whom you're buying things? Paying her rent? Someone blackmailing you?'

'Listen to you,' he said.

Aware that she wasn't quite as on top of the situation as she would like, she pressed on. 'An alternative is drink, but that's not so likely.'

245

The jibes glanced off him. 'My dear, it never does to be too clever. Too smart. I own I took that money and gave it to the parish charity box. It was for a moral purpose.'

'And the morality of not consulting me?'

'I know best,' he replied.

She didn't believe him.

The anger, misery, frustration of the years balled up into rage. 'Reverend Knox, we haven't . . . don't . . . get on but there were times when I admired you for your work in the parish. In taking my money, you've proved yourself as shabby as a criminal.'

He dabbed at a tiny smear of blood by the corner of his mouth. 'You are very ignorant.'

True. She was ignorant, and her vocabulary of outrage was impoverished. She longed for the power that came from experience. 'You didn't give that money to charity.'

'You will never know.'

'You disgust me.'

'And it's for you to pass judgement?' He spoke so softly she was forced to edge closer to him to hear. 'It's a hard burden to take on a child. There's so much to think about. Their bodies. Their spiritual life. Their minds. The number of times I've questioned myself as to whether I was making the right decisions. And, in the end, to have no thanks . . .'

Shoulders hunched. Eyes hooded. Cassock drooping.

Sickened, she looked away.

And yet . . . buried in the declaration was a plea for fairness. Please understand what it means to reconcile a life, a faith and work with the care of a child who was not blood of my blood.

She was so used to hating him, distrusting him, deriding him, that there was little room to acknowledge that he, too, had struggled with the years of stewardship.

'No one is all bad, my dear. No one is all good.'

The cliche struck a false note – and a warning. It was time to go. To shake off the dust of this village and the discordance of her life in the Rectory.

'Oh no you don't.' Osbert calculated correctly what Sophie was thinking. He lurched forward – and she knew, she knew what was coming and swivelled sharply. Her foot caught in a tussock of grass, twisted, and pain shot through her leg.

She didn't have time to cry out before Osbert was on her, pushing her down to the ground and scrabbling beneath his cassock. 'You owe me this too,' he said.

He was naked beneath the cassock. Her frantic gaze took in the sky, a bird skimming across it, the jut of Osbert's blood-flecked jaw.

'Get off me.'

For someone so scrawny, Osbert was surprisingly strong. Pinioning her arms, he wrenched up her skirt and grunted with satisfaction.

'Where's your God?' she managed before he covered her mouth.

It was rage, not fear, that got Sophie through the following seconds as she fought him.

He grabbed a breast and she gasped with pain. Her rage intensified and she twisted to the left, rolled over and struggled to get to her feet. But he was there before her. Capturing her arms, he yanked them together.

Her rage exploded. *I will kill him.*

Just as rapidly, it died. Spreadeagled and pinioned, it was hopeless to fight and she wanted, *needed*, to survive. How? Instinct took over. If she couldn't protect her body, she could protect her mind.

She thought of Het, laughing at some joke or other. Of Johnno's warm hand holding hers. Of her mother. She thought of her unknown father, to whom she could not put a face, cradling a gun and marching towards the enemy.

She thought of Dog.

How he had turned to her and rested his muzzle on her knee. Trust that he had never known before. Or her, for that matter.

She thought of her story of them all sailing together in a boat over a perfect sea.

With a grunt, Osbert forced a leg between hers and, face almost pressed into the earth, she managed to scream.

From somewhere above came a shout and a thump.

Osbert's body sagged down over hers.

'Sophie . . . Sophie . . .'

It was Johnno. Knight extraordinary. Whom she loved.

She breathed in earth and turf and the blood beating a drum in her ears lessened. The terror subsided. What remained was shuddering disgust and shock.

Johnno yanked Osbert's inert body off Sophie, freed her hands and pulled her upright. 'Oh my God. I had no idea . . .' He nudged Osbert's prone body. '*No* idea.' He pulled her close. 'Sophie . . .'

She collapsed against him. 'Thank you, thank you . . .'

'Let's go.'

She glanced down at the ground to where Osbert lay on his back, naked legs scrambled akimbo, mouth open. 'He's alive?' She sounded panicked. 'Johnno?'

Johnno dropped down onto one knee and felt for the pulse at Osbert's neck. 'The old bugger will be fine. With a bit of luck he'll get pneumonia. Or a bird will peck out his eyes.' He got to his feet and nudged the prone body none too gently. Osbert groaned and his hands flapped. 'What a piece of . . .' He cut himself off.

Osbert's eyes opened. Johnno looked down. 'You should be in jail.'

'How dare you,' whispered Osbert.

Johnno laughed. It wasn't a good sound. 'Come on.' Wrapping his arm around Sophie, he urged her over the field towards the road.

She stumbled, cried, shook, but he held her tight

and safe. 'My suitcase,' she managed to get out. 'I'm catching the train.'

'You're in no fit state.'

'Do you imagine I'm staying here after this?'

He sighed heavily. 'I'll take you.'

He had brought the van and, legs threatening to collapse and clutching the suitcase, she climbed into the passenger seat and inhaled the familiar mix of wheat and silage. 'I almost didn't come,' he said. 'I didn't want to say goodbye.'

The clunk of a hard object against flesh and bone. The long exhale of horrible breath. The silence that followed.

'Johnno, what did you hit him with?'

'Piece of wood. I saw what was happening when I parked the van.'

Crouching in the seat, Sophie wept tears of shock and sorrow while Johnno drove her to the station. At the entrance, he handed her down and told her he would buy a platform ticket and sit with her until the train arrived.

'I have your father to thank for this.' She waved her ticket in front of him. 'I saved the money I earned at the farm.'

'He says cheap at the price – you're the best egg collector ever.'

She managed a watery laugh.

They sat on a bench on the platform for the London trains, surrounded by a constellation of cigarette butts which Johnno brushed to one side with a foot.

'How do I look?' she asked, worried that her torn skirt would be obvious.

'Beautiful.' In her clumpy shoes and school skirt this would be far from the truth. He touched her cheek. 'You look a bit blotchy on the cheeks but nothing terrible.'

Her hand flew to her face and she scrubbed at her skin, trying to rid herself of the feel and touch of Osbert. 'I'll never forgive him.'

The platform filled up. Women in headscarves, a couple of travelling salesmen with brown suitcases, a group of sixth formers who draped themselves over the adjacent bench. Touched with autumn chill, a breeze funnelled gritty air through the station.

Johnno took her hand. His thumb moved over hers.

She was too weak to resist but said, 'Someone might see us and you'll be in trouble with Linda.'

'Maybe. I'll deal with it.' A muscle tightened at his jawline. 'Sophie, take it from me. What you've just been through was bad, really bad. I'm not saying you'll forget it. You won't. But I am saying that, after a while, it will fade.' He rubbed her fingers. 'Not entirely, but it will fade. I know.'

She looked down at their entwined hands.

Finding Johnno had been one thing. Wanting to read him was another. Longing to understand what went on in the fair head she had grown to love. That was something. That was challenging.

'Something similar happened to you?'

251

'You can't avoid it in the army.' He reached over and smoothed down her hair. 'Say after me . . . to hell with that old bugger.'

'To hell with that old bugger.'

'And, he has no power over me.'

'Osbert Knox has no power over me,' she repeated, sobbing.

Johnno's mouth tightened into a hard, ugly line. 'I'll kill him for what he's done.'

They sat in silence. Eventually, he said, 'You *do* have enough money? Dad gave me a tenner to buy seed.' He got his wallet out of his pocket. 'Take it. He'll understand.'

'The best egg collector.' Lush grass. Clucking hens. Eggs streaked with dung and feathers. Sun on her back. Mud up her legs. She shook her head. 'I have my mother's money and, even if I didn't, I can't take it, Johnno.'

He didn't try to argue, shoved his wallet back into his trousers and sent her a wry smile.

Peering along the platform into the distance where the London train, a poisoned arrow wreathed in smoke, sped towards the platform, the voice became urgent. Forget your ambitions, it admonished. Forget the race for independence. Linda could have the baby and give it to Johnno. She, Sophie, would welcome it into their married home. Or, if Linda did not wish to give the baby up, they could share it. There would be no problems and it could come and go between Linda and Johnno. Easy.

'Sophie . . . I'm sorry. So sorry.' He pulled himself closer. 'This isn't the moment to kiss you, but I want to.' Instead he stroked her hair. 'I don't know . . . I don't know how . . .'

She reached up and their hands clung together.

How ignorant she was. Had been. Up till now, her experience of a moral universe had been Osbert's shouted (and ignored) admonitions from the pulpit. Half heard. Half absorbed.

Johnno's fingers gripped hers so hard it was painful. Edging closer to an understanding, she welcomed the discomfort. Osbert maintained 'being good' demanded sacrifice. Translated? She must not break down and beg Johnno to abandon Linda.

And what if it was Johnno who said: *Forget Linda, you must come with me*?

She longed for him to say it. He *ought* to say it. 'Johnno?'

But Johnno was silent.

The moment passed, leaving her bereaved of one possible future. *Dommage*, the spirit of Camille muttered in her daughter's ear. At least you know. 'Will you tell anyone about Osbert? Warn people? Johnno, you must.'

'I'll do my best.'

'Shouldn't you tell the police? He might pick on someone else who might get hurt.'

'I could, but then you wouldn't be able to leave. The police would keep you here for questioning. It's up to you.' His grip tightened on her hand.

253

'Listen. Every village has an Osbert. Trust me. It's a matter of keeping them under control. People keep an eye out and warn their daughters.'

'Nobody warned me.' She held out her wrists where bruises were forming.

'I remember Dad telling me there were rumours about a Bale daughter but she left Poynsdean and everyone went shtum. Dad did say he was a bit worried when you came back from school.'

'Right,' she said.

'I promise to go and see him, tell him that he's a monstrous old pervert and if he ever does anything like that again he'll have me to answer to.'

The thought struck her. 'Johnno, you could be up for assault.'

He shook his head. 'Too big a risk for him.'

She experimented with breathing in extra slowly. 'When are you and Linda . . . you know?'

'It was all set for two weeks' time. Special licence. But I'm not having that man marrying us. I'm going to insist on the registry office.' An eyebrow climbed. 'Wait for the drama.'

Linda squeezing into a dress (no belt). Perhaps carrying a bouquet in front of her to conceal the bulge. Linda making her vows. Linda being helped into the van. Linda in the kitchen at Home Farm. Linda tucking into the wedding breakfast with the greed of a pregnant woman.

Johnno smoking outside in the yard with his father.

With a hiss and a shriek, the train drew in.

Johnno helped her stow the case into the third-class compartment. A woman in a red hat with two small children watched him.

Sophie commandeered the window. 'Goodbye, Johnno.'

'Goodbye, Sophie.'

She wanted to instruct him to live a happy life, but the words stuck. He didn't have anything to say either.

That muscle flickered in his cheek.

Sophie's eyes filled.

She felt desperate. Shocked. Sad, so sad. Beating underneath was an angry, contrary drumbeat. Johnno had not considered the world well lost for love. He had not swept her up and away.

Yet, nor had she.

Should. Ought.

But Johnno was right. He was right. *Repeat to yourself many, many times.* Johnno's child needed its parents and a home.

A jolt. The train began to move. Within seconds, Johnno had vanished but she was damned if she would put her head out of the window. Instead, she wrestled with the leather strap, hauled up the glass and sat down.

He was gone.

The stupidity of refusing to look back at him now hit her foursquare. *Fool.* One final glimpse wouldn't have changed the outcome.

A familiar landscape slid past the window at increasing speed.

The woman in the red hat smiled at her. 'Partings are always tricky.'

'Yes.'

'Have you been sweethearts long?'

'Yes.' Too tired, shocked and sad to explain.

'Don't worry, he'll be waiting for you when you get back.'

'Yes.'

The smaller child hit the elder and a squall broke out. Automatically, and without even a glance in their direction, their mother reached out an arm and separated the pair. 'Is it serious? I mean . . . are you . . .' Her gaze dropped to Sophie's left hand.

A madness took hold of Sophie.

'Oh yes,' she said, forcing a smile. 'The wedding's in the spring.'

'Have you got the dress?'

'It's being made . . . altered . . . in London.'

The woman produced a couple of biscuits from her basket and wrapped a child's hand around each, impressing Sophie with her ability to perform these actions still without looking at the children. Settling back onto the grubby plush, she said, 'Tell me about it.'

From the depths of her confusion and anguish, Sophie summoned the materials of her lies.

'It's my aunt's dress. Lace and silk, with a train. I'm a little bigger than she is and it's being let out . . .'

In that fashion came into being: three brides-maids (in powder blue), a wedding cake with tiny, iced hayricks on the top, arrangements of lilies and roses and a bouquet of jasmine and ivy.

Also whipped into existence: tables laid up for sixty, coronation chicken and fruit salad, and a honeymoon in Dawlish.

Evidently her listener – 'please call me Jane' – found this recital profoundly satisfying, almost moving, and grew misty-eyed. 'Sounds wonderful.'

'We'll be taking Dog . . .' she burnished the lie. 'Couldn't leave him behind.'

Observing autumn fields, the weeping trees, the muddy tracks from the train window, she thought: it's true. Dog is coming with me.

PART TWO

PART TWO

CHAPTER NINETEEN

The cross-channel ferry was well under way and it was growing light. Up on deck, Sophie clutched at a railing and peered at the French coast.

What came into view was not as momentous as her imaginings.

A hazy coastline. A beach. A port with buildings which looked depressingly reminiscent of the ones in Dover. A town oozing over the land beyond.

Of course, she told herself, all these were French. They would be so much more interesting than the village halls, rectories and stifling social norms she had left behind. Over here, people had different ideas, held the secret to the art of living. The weather would be better.

A sea breeze slapped her cheek. Stiffened her spine. Its indifference importing a bracing tension into her reflections which, in turn, buffed up her courage.

Abandoning was a new process. Far more complicated than she had imagined. Throwing away an old life and her adopted country in one mighty scoop made the ground tilt, much as the deck was doing. Plus – and here was the infuriating discovery – it was possible to mourn leaving the things she thought she had hated.

Crested with foam, a wave rolled past. Out here the water was clear ice green, indifferent and cool, a more powerful animal than the skittish sea over which she had gazed at Poynsdean.

From it, she would be cast forth. Very much as her mother had been.

Jonah from the whale.

As Osbert might say.

Fingers tightening on the rail. *No.*

She would, she must, refuse oxygen to any allusion, any reminder, any reference to Osbert's teachings. His prayers. His febrile sermonising.

Has Osbert stamped himself on me, Hettie?

No, darling.

I'm frightened he has. All that lecturing about duty and sacrifice.

Well then, unstamp it. When you go to Paris you'll be thoroughly unstamped.

She caught her breath.

Who *was* she?

Like everything, bravery fluctuated.

A door from the deck opened and banged shut. A man in a trilby hat and mackintosh took shelter behind a lifeboat and tried to light a cigarette. He glanced at Sophie, gave a polite smile and moved away.

It was cold. Frighteningly cold.

From this moment on, she was alone.

Left behind was the shield of the chintzed and ruffled Knight London mansion where she had initially been permitted to stay *for one week only*. A week that, courtesy of Hettie's cajoling and her promise to dance with Lord Peregrine Lubbock, had been extended until Christmas.

Then, 'I've fed and watered your friend for many weeks, Hettie. My charity has run out,' Moira announced over the teacups in the despairing desert days between Christmas and New Year.

Yes. Time to go.

She was grateful, she told Moira. Very.

'Good. I wish you well,' replied Moira with obvious insincerity. 'As long as you haven't infected Hettie with odd ideas.' A pause. 'A wish to be independent and to have a job. That sort of thing.'

'I do have a mind of my own,' said an indignant Hettie.

The swell intensified. Spray pattered over her exposed flesh. She was being wiped clean of associations and of the darkness from which she had fled.

It felt surprisingly painful, though. Why? Why was that? She swallowed – and it was as if a tooth was being torn from her gum.

Think better. Harder. More purposefully.

She would be washed clean. Even so, as the water roared past the ship and the spray curdled into mist, the spectres of those she *had* loved rose up. Camille, Hettie and Johnno. And Dog. They were not easily discarded.

263

Osbert fulminated about the moral existence and turned out not to observe what he preached. Johnno was an apostate, a wild card. The rover returned. But it was Johnno who understood, in his bones, the hard choices and constructs of the moral.

She was frightened by what she had done, by what she was sailing towards, by the task that she had set herself.

Locate her family.

Slipstream into the great enterprise.

Find her father. The hero?

A nose nudged her leg. Her hand brushed warm, clean fur.

Dog, are you there?

Stay with me.

Please.

Sophie sat down on the bed in a cheap hotel – the cheapest she could find – close to the Gare du Nord.

The room did not smell good. The noise from outside suggested that sleeping would be impossible, and the bathroom arrangements were a little anxious-making. It was growing dark. It was chilly. The one electric bulb gave off a creepy yellow light.

She smiled at a memory.

'If you're really going to Paris,' said Hettie, 'you have to perk up your image.' She dragged a skirt and jumper out of her wardrobe and thrust them at Sophie. 'I don't need these. You do. *Vogue* says that an image is vital, particularly in Paris. You'll need these as well.'

'These' included a cone-shaped stitched bra which was designed to emulate the Hollywood girl sweater look, and a rubberised suspender belt.

Hettie said, 'Apparently underwear is key.'

'Your mother will kill me if you give these to me.'

'As she's vowed she'd rather die than set foot on the Continent, you're safe.'

Skirt, jumper, bra and suspender belt were in her suitcase.

Tears tracked down Hettie's cheeks when she heard the story of the final farewell with Johnno. 'So, so sad.' She had turned angrily red at the recital of Osbert's assault. 'How horrible.' A tiny pause. 'Peregrine Lubbock did much the same to me. After the Batewell dance.'

'*What?*'

Hettie shrugged. 'It's easier to put up with when they're young, don't you think? Horrible old bodies aren't. Peregrine didn't get what he wanted. But it wasn't nice.'

'It can be nice.'

She thought of how nice, and a pain crept around the region of her heart.

'Does thinking about . . . it . . . the awful bit . . . give you nightmares?'

'It sort of attacks me in flashes. But I'll make myself fine. It could have been much worse, but it wasn't, thanks to Johnno.'

265

Hettie reflected and said in the new, serious manner she had developed, 'He wouldn't have suited you, Sophs. You were only thinking of marrying him because you didn't know what else to do.'

Perhaps . . . Perhaps Hettie had got it right. She heaved herself to her feet, eased open the suitcase and unpacked Hettie's skirt and jumper.

She had suggested to Hettie to come with her. Escape to Paris. They had been drinking tea in the drawing room. On the mantlepiece, displayed in date order, were many invitations to dances, dinners and racing.

Hettie glanced at them.

'Can't. I have to go through the Season. The parents have spent so much money.'

Hettie had been saddened. Or was it chastened?

'Sorry, sorry, darling Het. Don't think about it. It was a stupid suggestion.'

Sophie spent her first night in Paris trying to sleep. As she suspected, the traffic noise was awful. So were her apprehensions.

If she turned her head, she could just make out the skirt hanging off the rail, its ghostly outline symbolic of how tenuous were her plans, how vague her future.

Towards dawn, she drifted into the half-world between sleep and consciousness.

Tenebrae . . . the darkness where reminiscence took hold.

The seven-year-old Sophie clambered onto the bed where her mother lay, mouth agape, twitching

266

from pain. The doctor was due with the morphine, but he was late.

Maman, tell me about your family.

Camille was too ill to speak and, never at a loss, Sophie supplied the details.

Her mother was an only child but had numerous wild cousins, including pigtailed Barbette.

Barbette lived with her brothers in a *manoir* in Poitiers, and Camille stayed there many times. In the narration, Sophie ensured that the *manoir* had a huge kitchen and rooms through which light flooded and grounds where it was possible to hide all day.

The battles the siblings and their cousins fought. (Sophie was now in full swing.)

The alliances they made.

The adventures they had.

The *tartines* they secretly consumed, talking *their* language, thinking *their* way.

'*Maman,* you and Barbette were caught stealing raisins from the kitchen. Did you remember?'

Richly coloured, lavishly detailed, every game, every den, every clandestine feast of that cousin and sibling-populated world . . . all wrestled into being with tears and smiles by Sophie sitting at the bedside.

'Did I tell you that?' her mother managed to murmur. 'I forget.'

Conjuring up the dying Camille's past. The drive that conjured the visions into a narrative had never been so strong, so clear in intent.

Hôtel du Gare
Paris 10

À Paris, le 22 janvier 1960

Dear Bureau des Personnes Disparues,

I am writing to find out if you have made any progress with finding out what happened to my father, Pierre Morel? I refer to my initial letter of June 1959.

In your reply you requested payment which I sent, via a postal order.

Since then I have heard nothing. I would appreciate a report . . .

Chère Mademoiselle,
I apologise for the lack of contact. Since you wrote, the office has been reorganised and we fell behind.

However, in case you have decided that we are either reprobate or careless of our clients, I must inform you that a letter was sent to the Rectory in Poynsdean but was returned to sender. I have noted your current address, to which I will reply unless advised otherwise.

I am returning the postal order with this letter because, I am desolated to tell you, it is not possible to use it in France. I'm afraid this is a situation I cannot do anything about. However much as I approve of operating on hope alone, I am afraid I must eat. We need, therefore, to rethink the manner of payment, which I am happy to do.

Once that is settled, I will put things in train. I must warn you, however, that it might take several months. R. Maurice

Cher Monsieur Maurice,
Thank you for your letter informing me that my postal order was invalid. I am now in Paris and would like to visit you as soon as possible.
To recap: my father's name was Pierre Augustin Morel . . .

So it began.

Cher Monsieur Maurice,

CHAPTER TWENTY

The staircase leading up to the office of the Bureau des Personnes Disparues was dusty. Very dusty.

In the office, a young woman with elaborately rolled hair and red lipstick was typing hard at a desk by the window, which overlooked the rue de l'Université.

She had an appointment with a Monsieur Maurice, Sophie informed Mademoiselle Red Lips, who replied that she was completely desolated but Sophie must wait. She sat down in the chair indicated.

If objective number one, after trudging off the boat train at the Gare du Nord, had been to find a cheap hotel, objective number two had been to make sense of the Paris geography. Where did its heart lie? Where might she feel at home?

Where might she get a job?

Certainly not in the eye-wateringly fashionable district, the roosting place of Balmain, Givenchy and Christian Dior, where she found herself on her first excursion. There, a spy learning fieldcraft, stomach growling with hunger, she lurked for some

270

time outside Dior's entrance in the avenue Montaigne, observing a procession of svelte women in toque hats and pearls stalk in and out.

The gap between these long-legged betoqued gazelles and the fascinated nineteen-year-old from a Sussex village was . . . laughable. It was not only the clothes. It was that the interior lives of these slender, wobbling women had to be qualitatively different. They served the gods of beauty and fashion and no one – no one – would accuse Sophie of being among these elect. Not even Hettie's swirling skirt and tight jumper and the resulting perked-up image could argue otherwise.

She beat a strategic retreat to the Seine for her subsequent excursion.

Barges sailed up and downstream, flying British, French and Dutch flags. Under the graffitied bridges, *clochards* had staked out kingdoms. Anglers dotted the banks. Dogs, leaving malodorous evidence of their passing, roamed where they pleased.

In this slice of Paris, cafés, theatres and music halls were plentiful and, from all sides could be heard the cheerful invitations of '*Allons, chéri, tu viens?*' from women who ranged from the startlingly gorgeous to the obviously worn out. Further north, the Bastille area and the Place des Vosges, with its seventeenth-century town houses, were dilapidated but nonetheless exuded . . . well, what?

A sense of themselves.

271

Despite her war wounds, Paris has not conceded, she wrote in her notebook.

And to Hettie. *There are SEX SHOPS with leather curtains. At least, I think that's what they are. And homeless men who sleep on the ventilation grids . . .*

Permitting herself only one meal a day, hunger was a companion. A tricky one which nipped at her sides. But it sharpened her senses, luring her into the sensory whirlpool of Parisian smells: bread, coffee, debris. A cache of perfume. Cheese and meats as she passed the fromageries and the charcuteries.

The *popotes* dish out soup to the destitute . . . This from Camille while she lived. Had she remembered correctly? She thought so. The bistros have menus with *prix fixes*. The *restaurants à nappes* specialise in the *plat du jour* and a pleasing number of the restaurants have female names . . . La Mère Marie, Chez Antoinette.

Wandering the incense-scented interior of Notre-Dame, her thoughts looped back to the Knoxes. What she would give to set them both down in one of the mysteriously shaded aisles and observe their reactions as they found themselves face to face with wicked Catholic idolatry?

Every village has an Osbert, said Johnno.

She wondered how he knew. She had not known him long enough to find out.

A familiar double-lock of choking sadness and longing caught her tight for painful minutes.

Then, it loosened. And she was fine.

At a lunch at Fortnum's in London, to which

Hettie had insisted on taking her before she left for Paris, she consulted Hettie as to whether she should write to Alice. 'To tell her I'm not dead.'

'I wouldn't bother,' said Hettie, the robustness of the answer taking Sophie by surprise. 'The Knoxes have made their own world and now you've left it. They can stew.'

She remembered putting down her coffee spoon and asking, 'What's happened to your lovely charity, Het?'

Hettie's gaze had drifted across the luxurious restaurant. There was a tight, miserable line to her mouth. 'It's being whittled away,' she said tiredly. 'By life.'

Mademoiselle Red Lips took a phone call and replaced the receiver. Again, she was cast into desolation (a word much used), but Monsieur Maurice would be a little while yet and she begged Mademoiselle Morel to be patient.

She lit a cigarette, blew a smoke ring and asked Sophie if she was American. Sophie replied that, actually, she was French.

'That's good. America is full of bloated capitalists, gangsters and lynchings. It wants to conquer us with Coca-Cola and Hollywood. And, of course, the *Reader's Digest*.'

She made a little sound between 'phtt' and a raspberry.

'Where do you live, Mademoiselle . . . .?' asked Sophie. 'I'm sorry, I don't know your name.'

273

'Mademoiselle Axel. I live on the Left Bank,' was the reluctant admission. 'Off the boul Saint-Mich.'

She had questioned too far. Mademoiselle Axel returned to her typing and Sophie to her thoughts.

Ah, the Left Bank, whose heartbeat, she had already worked out, was quite different to that of the Right Bank. Plus, she had been given to understand that it exhibited an existential soul – a term she neither understood nor could spell, but was determined to find out about.

Its buildings smaller in scale than the *grands bâtiments* over the river, the Left Bank surged with youth. There were dozens of cafés and food vendors. Small delivery vans darted around like insects. Pedestrians bunched at street corners. There was a male fashion for wearing white scarves knotted around the neck, aping '*les intellos*', as the article in a discarded newspaper in the Métro informed her.

The girls went in for full skirts and flat shoes. Dungarees and lace-up shoes. Jeans and tight jackets nipped in at the waist. In Saint-Germain-des-Prés, she spotted girls wearing skin-tight leotards and sporting ponytails, and her spirits shot up. Liberated from modesty, scornful of shackles, they looked fun. In control. Ready for the new world.

A tread sounded coming up the stairs.

'Mademoiselle Morel?' Monsieur Maurice had arrived. Finally.

274

Sophie did a double take.

He was twenty-seven, maybe twenty-eight? Possibly a little more. Mid-height. Lit cigarette in hand. An air that combined the kind and not so kind.

'You're surprised, mademoiselle?'

'I thought you'd be older.'

'Ah, you're thinking of my father, who retired last year. I'm Raphael Maurice, his oldest son. I worked with him and now I've taken over.'

He ushered her into his office with instructions to sit. She took the chair opposite him and held on tight to her bag.

His lips twitched. 'Why don't you put your bag on the floor.'

She did so. Safety net removed.

'Have you been at the agency long, Monsieur Maurice?'

From across the desk and the well-used ashtray, he appraised Sophie. 'Is my inexperience so apparent?'

'I've come from England to see you. It's entirely reasonable for me to question your credentials.'

'So it is . . . and it's entirely reasonable for me to ask if you are serious about this investigation? Or does it depend on my age?'

She could read nothing into his expression. Still, instinct told her he was skilled at exhuming the truth from the burial grounds of deception, faulty memory and desperation. 'The search is important to me. Very.'

275

'Most who come into this office feel the same. I admit a few wasted my father's time. Some will waste mine.'

'I want to find out what happened to my father.' As sometimes happened, her eyes misted over. 'He was a hero and died for France.'

He lit a cigarette. 'A hero? *Eh bien*, we should begin.'

Her letter lying between them, Sophie was subjected to a session of hard questioning by a professional interrogator. That was the not so kind aspect of Raphael Maurice. Sceptical. Unreadable. Keeping his counsel. He went after every aspect of family history that could be mustered, the circumstances of her father's death as far as she knew them, and circled obsessively around the question of why her mother had remained in Poynsdean.

The chair was uncomfortable and waged war against her . . . Maybe it was intended to.

Question: Are you sure your father wasn't deported to a camp/didn't run away to South America/didn't start a second family?

'My father fought for his country. He wouldn't have gone away.'

'But are you sure?'

'No, I can't be sure.' The same answer multiplied several times.

She was dreaming. She must be. The clack of Mademoiselle Axel's shoes on the floorboards next door. The pungent Gitanes. The garlic taste in her mouth from the very cheap stew she had just eaten. French filtering in and out of her hearing, reminding her of the struggle when she tried to keep up.

'You write here that she was always worried that he was betrayed by a fellow Frenchman. A serious accusation.'

'My mother was a good person. She wouldn't make it up.'

'Mademoiselle, I hesitate to correct your logic, but good people can be mistaken. Good people can make things up. For instance, how would she know if your father died a hero when she had had no contact with France?'

'That's what she told me.'

'Perhaps . . . perhaps, when we near the end, we reach for comforting stories? And we give them out to those we wish to console.'

She turned her head. Stared out of the window.

Had Camille told her these things?

'You tell me you were only seven when she died, which makes it doubtful your memories are absolutely accurate.' He softened. 'My condolences. So very hard for a child.'

'Let me assure you, monsieur. One remembers.'

He jotted a note down. 'So how do you think she would she have obtained this information?'

'My mother told me that my father fell out with someone before she left Paris. It was all to do with some paintings.' Pause. 'It's vague.'

His raised eyebrows underscored the point about fallible memory.

'What about any of your French relatives? Have you contacted them?'

'I know my maternal grandparents lived in Poitiers. I don't know about my father's family, except that they lived in Paris which is where my parents met. My father had a brother who died when he was a child, and I think my mother said my father's parents were also dead.'

A second cigarette was lit.

'What you're asking will be difficult. Since the bureau has been set up, hundreds of people have applied to us for help.' He pointed to the map on the wall which showed the territorial changes in Europe since 1945. 'What we do is literally to search through Europe, sometimes further. The highways and byways of human traffic. Imagine a world where everything has broken down. Communications. Banks. Libraries. Businesses. Law and order. You couldn't find an alarm clock, nappies, aspirin. Cooking pans. There were huge migrations of people who did anything they had to to survive.'

Outrage at it all was reflected in his face.

'It was a descent into anarchy. Vengeance was demanded and it was taken. That's how it was when the war ended, all over Europe. And in the chaos, thousands, millions of lost people clamouring to find their place again. He laid a careful hand on a pile of papers. 'In these documents we read through the poetry of the lost.'

The poet of lost souls.

She was almost overcome. But not entirely.

'Monsieur, *can* you help me?'

He raised an eyebrow. 'The war created many liars and many criminals. They know the system. They know how to hide.' He got up from the chair and poked his head out of the office, commanding Mademoiselle Axel to fetch file number 195.

'You're aware of what I charge?'

She thought of her stockpile of francs. Very finite. Post office book finite. One meal a day finite. 'Yes.'

'You could pay in tranches.'

It was kindly meant. But she didn't like it. 'I can pay,' she said stiffly.

He considered. 'You realise that some survivors don't wish to be found? For all sorts of reasons. Guilt. They didn't get on with their families. The desire for a new life. Or they've been so damaged mentally and physically they can't return.'

She watched cigarette smoke drift towards the window.

'*Chère mademoiselle*, what I'm saying is the answers could hurt you. You must consider that. Equally, there may be no answers at all and you must think about that too.' He arranged the file in front of him. 'Life does not tie itself up into neat parcels. Answers cannot be coaxed from the ether. Wishing and wanting cannot be turned into the solid flesh.'

The poet in full flood. The psychologist?

'Please, Monsieur Maurice.'

'Then you must give me a few weeks.'

That night in her cheap hotel in the Gare du Nord, she pondered.

Traffic noisy. Very. Mattress sagging. Suspect sheets. Stomach . . . well, empty.

Perched on the bed, she opened her notebook and tested her writing muscles. Their flexibility. Their strength. Sensing iron creeping into their composition.

Why was she writing? Something to do? A bid to understand her experiences, to make sense of what jostled within? Sadness. The fight to neutralise the grievance that she had been short-changed by her life so far and wanted – needed – to turn it around. Her determination to discover who she was. Her feelings at leaving Hettie behind. The pain of not having Johnno.

Raphael Maurice. Truffle hound. Defends his patch. He has a good nose. I think.

But given the work he does, it's curious that RM considers knowledge can be dangerous. Surely, surely you can never have too much knowledge?

She looked over to the peeling wallpaper by the window.

Oh Lord, she thought, everything is going to take its time, and I'll have to find a job.

But I am in Paris.

CHAPTER TWENTY-ONE

In the office of Madame Marie's Agence Matrimoniale in the rue des Petits Hôtels, Sophie, the newest and lowliest recruit to the staff, sifted through the incoming mail. She was barely keeping body and soul together and could have eaten her scarf, but it was a job. One which, pleasingly, she had held down for over two months.

Chère Madame Marie, I'm on leave from French West Africa and will be returning in a couple of weeks and I wish to get married before I do so. My wife must be from the upper classes, modest and with the intention of bearing children. She must be of independent means, not brainy, and be prepared to offer me unconditional loyalty . . .

. . . Could you find me a husband? He must be under fifty, Catholic and very tidy. I am forty-five and a good cook. My daubes and pâtisseries are universally admired. I do not expect grand romance or anything like that. I am not beautiful and no one is likely to fall in love with me, but I am useful. I'm sure I could make the right person comfortable . . .

. . . I've been very ill and my strength is limited but I have money. If I could find a wife who would

281

be willing to look after me, she would be repaid with financial security . . .

Precise requirements.

Financial arrangements.

Health revelations.

Very practical. Very unemotional.

'Even so, Het, I can't help feeling that the agency is drenched in yearning,' Sophie wrote. '*Drenched.*'

Hettie couldn't get enough of the details. 'Tell me, tell me everything,' she demanded in her letters. 'Who are these people?'

A *comtesse*, no less. A prince (although everyone was dubious about him). A younger daughter looking after hideously demanding parents. A cleaner who longed for a better life. Miserable and lonely men. Bakers and doctors. Farmers. A lighthouse man offering a good home in the round. Sad bachelors from former French colonies and frightful bores from the *banlieues*.

'But,' she added, 'some of them may be horrible people, some may have no money or looks, but they *have* made an effort to do something about their situation. I admire that. Even though I remain sceptical about getting married . . .'

Sophie had just read an article about Simone de Beauvoir's *The Second Sex*. It had affected her powerfully.

She managed to phone Hettie in London. 'Tell me everything, Het. Have *you* got a job? It should be easy with your good exam results.'

'I'm not going to rule the world with a GCE in

domestic science. And the parents would die a thousand deaths if I worked in a shop or something. It's miserable in London. Boys still don't rate me and the other girls talk about me. I don't fit in.' She gave a nervous little cough. 'I don't mind that much but it's awkward.'

'I'm an outsider too, Het. Maybe it's a good thing in the long run?'

'Anyway, *you* gave me an idea. I nipped in to talk to a London marriage bureau, to see if they could find me someone double quick. Like an impoverished Scottish laird, or a tea planter.'

The voice of Simone de Beauvoir was in Sophie's ear. 'Het, getting married is what men want you to do. Marriage keeps women under.'

'You've been reading that article again.'

'Simone de Beauvoir says marriage is a trap. I agree.'

'Says you who nearly did.'

'I loved Johnno.'

'Yes, but you also thought it was a way out. You'd have got a home and security.' There was a new note in Hettie's voice. Harder. More realistic. 'I know my parents are annoying and short-sighted, but live with them I must.'

'Don't do anything rash, Het. I beg . . .'

'No,' uttered Hettie – in a strange way.

This subjugation . . . yes, subjugation to the Knight *mère* and *père* was where the two of them disagreed.

'You haven't told your parents where I work?'

283

'Are you mad?'

She imagined Hettie sitting in the hallway of the Knight mansion where the telephone was sited. Umbrellas in the elephant's foot, a clothes brush on the stand, black-and-white tiles on the floor. 'You and I ought to be thinking about working for world peace. No more wars. No more bombs. We ought to be talking about Chairman Mao and Russia. And what radiation can do to children.'

'But we don't,' said Hettie. 'Talk about it. Or do anything. You rabbit on about Paris and finding your father. I just want some peace. I want my stomach to stop churning.'

'Do I rabbit on?'

'Yes.'

'Sorry.'

Sophie considered how Europe had remained fractious after the war and how Hitler's past wickedness sat like a black parrot on its shoulders. 'There're so many things to do with your life other than wielding a tartan duster for some ancient laird.'

'Actually . . .' A long, long pause. 'Actually, he's thirty-six and ex-army but has a private income. He lives near Dorking and has spent years abroad in Egypt and India. He likes traditional sports.'

'No,' said Sophie. '*No. Please* tell me you haven't—'

The new, ruthless Hettie cut across. 'His name is William. He likes dogs.'

'You've never had a dog.'

'True, but if I'm miserable, I'll have him to love. Like Jasper in *Rebecca*.'

Long silence.

'Say something, Sophs.'

She was gasping from shock. Said the first thing, the stupid thing, that came into her head. 'Aren't you supposed to marry someone with a title? Wasn't that the deal with your parents?'

'His second cousin is an Honourable. That will have to do.'

'You won't be happy,' Sophie said.

'That's cruel, Sophie.'

Sophie put down the receiver. Cried. With an ugly, screwed-up face and no handkerchief.

Since then, they had not been in touch.

Astonished at where she now found herself, Sophie looked around the office. An attic room in a dilapidated building near the Gare du Nord. There had been no repairs since before the war and the place whistled with draughts. It was now late March. All the same, all three staff worked in their overcoats. The two-bar gas heater had perfected the circus trick of eating money, and the coin jar was always empty. This was because any coins there were walked next door to the office occupied by Madame Marie, their boss, who argued that she required heat to think. Squeezed onto the landing outside the attics was a tiny water closet, the organisation of which meant that employees rapidly learnt the practicalities of tact and sensitivity.

Madame Marie had dyed blonde hair, dangling

earrings and a perpetual cigarette. 'Can you type?' she asked, at the initial interview.

'Yes.'

A lie.

'You probably can't,' said madame. 'Do you have any experience in this area?'

'I've been jilted.'

'We all have, *chère mademoiselle*. We all have. But, you can speak English. We get some English applications. It's tiresome but we have a duty to be good to our foreign friends and . . .' She scrutinised Sophie. 'It's astonishing to think employing someone English is an asset.' Ash floated off her cigarette. 'It will be a first for the agency.'

'I'm French, madame.'

'*Bof.*' A shrug. 'We'll say we are international.'

The deal was sealed.

In the freezing office, she sat next to Claudine, who had a naturally deep voice and a matter-of-fact manner. 'Men are very silly,' she whispered to Sophie on her first day. 'But we must put up with them. Manipulate them. We have to pretend they are gods.'

She did, too. If a man was due in the office, Claudine sidled into the tiny water closet and emerged with hair teased into a helmet, startling pink lipstick, her voice half an octave higher and a demeanour as compliant as a doormat.

After said man had left, inevitably she would lean over and say: '*C'est un vrai con, celui-là.*'

A similar rebellious streak ran through the

much younger, kohl-eyed and boss-hating Blanche. If Madame Marie went out, she would issue a series of pronouncements, chief among them the notion that those who are absent are always wrong. It was a useful phrase: *les absents ont toujours tort.*

Both were suspicious of Sophie until Sophie confessed one morning that her cone-shaped bra was killing her.

Cue for bonding and an almighty discussion on underwear. An oath was sworn to take Sophie shopping for a proper *soutien-gorge* as soon as payday arrived.

An envelope addressed to Sophie arrived at the Hôtel du Gare. It was the invitation to Hettie's wedding at St Margaret's, Westminster, reception at Claridge's. Et cetera.

It was no secret that the Knight parents had long planned for this day of apotheosis and they were doing everything by the book. Flowers, buffets, champagne. On the back of the invitation, Hettie had written in pencil:

I'll have a house in Dorking and a housekeeper who makes suet dumplings and mutton stew. A husband who plays golf. And a regimental brooch.

She sat for a long time with the invitation balanced on her knee.

Hettie. *Hettie.*

She never replied.

The silence between them lengthened.

The summons to the Bureau des Personnes Disparues arrived in early April.

Once again up the dusty stairs. Once again to sit in the chair bent on inflicting torture.

Opening a file, Raphael Maurice pushed three small black-and-white photographs over to Sophie. 'Take a look at these.'

Photo one: two men at the window inside a large room. One is balancing a gun on the windowsill and taking aim. The other is holding spare ammunition. Photo two: a male and a female stand behind a street barricade, each holding a petrol bomb. In the background is the distinctive outline of Notre-Dame. Photo three is a headshot of a young man with wavy hair and a squarish chin. He is wearing a grimy-looking shirt and a knitted gilet. There is a streak of blood on his left cheek.

He observed her closely.

'Do you think one of these might be your father?'

Swallowing. 'I wouldn't know. My mother didn't have any photos.'

'I've found out that your father was a member of a Resistance group called Les Loups which operated in the area called the Marais. Or the Pletzel, as it was nicknamed. The Little Place. A high-risk area in which to operate, since it had been emptied in the round-ups. The Marais had been colonised by Jewish people who'd fled pogroms in Eastern Europe, and there weren't many people left.'

She sifted through the information. 'How do you know about Les Loups?'

288

'When you do as much research as I do, you get to hear the names. And I have sources.'

She supposed that, of the strings of information stretching back into the past, some were tangled, some broken. But some were intact. The trick was to know which.

He continued, 'Les Loups dubbed themselves *résistants de la première heure*. If you like, a group who signed up early. There was often bad feeling between those groups and the *résistants de la dernière heure*, who only took up arms after the Allied landings.'

Yes, that fitted. Her father would have been the sort of person to have committed early.

'Les Loups were responsible for several notable operations and for hiding people on the run. They had to be careful, though. The reprisals could be dreadful.'

Relief. She hadn't been mistaken. 'So, he was a hero.'

'Heroism can be complicated.' A careful pronouncement. 'You tell me that your mother escaped from France in early 1942, leaving him behind. Your parents knew they were at risk and took the decision for your mother to leave.' This was accompanied by a respectful uplift of eyebrows. 'Not so many got out. Your mother must have been resourceful.'

He pushed a piece of paper over to Sophie. 'This is what I've found.'

'Camille Morel, née Debord, was a graduate in

art teaching and art. She worked as an unpaid assistant curator at the Jeu de Paume and was ordered to stay on when the Nazis took over the building. Here she secretly recorded the looting of paintings until it became too dangerous and she disappeared into the Resistance.'

Her father defended his country. A wolf. A street fighter. Her mother outwitted the occupiers. A she-wolf. The information was atavistically thrilling.

'Is something the matter, mademoiselle?'

She struggled to form the thought. 'War is horrible and wrong. But my father did the right thing by fighting and, probably, killing, and I revere him for it. How can I believe both?'

Monsieur Maurice did not react. Merely shuffled his papers.

She had said too much.

Then he said, 'Asking questions has consequences. And you're very young.'

'I'll be twenty in the autumn.'

'Precisely, mademoiselle.' His gaze travelled over her crossed feet. The hands in her lap. 'I know what I'm talking about. Forgive me, but it's unlikely you will understand yet. Later, yes. But now you can't know what you might stir up. What you might find. What the knowledge might do to you. It was a treacherous period and people betrayed each other left, right, and centre. They behaved badly.'

He offered her a cigarette and lit one for himself.

'Information is destructive as well as constructive. It can become a weapon. A fatal blow.' He was obviously concerned – but also wreathed in smoke, which lent him some glamour.

'I can't be afraid of the answers.'

'War triggers vendettas. Paris was, and is, not exempt. Asking questions exposes secrets, and some are best left hidden.'

He was suggesting that she was out of her depth.

It was Fred who had showed Sophie what lay under stones. Peering at the creatures writhing out of sight, leaving ghost-white traces over the soil.

'Aren't you talking yourself out of a job?'

'I always take care to warn my clients.'

He seemed exhausted. Weighed down, perhaps, by all that he knew.

'Where I used to live, there were novels about women who had to wait out their lives because they had no choice as the men were in charge. I don't wish to be like those women.'

Silence. Then, picking up the headshot, he said. 'So, this is Christian Martin. He fought with Les Loups from the beginning and had quite a repu-tation for violence. After the war, Martin was suspected of killing a *collabo* but it was never proved. My contact has promised me a report on Martin, which I'm waiting for. Martin will have known your father. He runs a gallery in the Place des Vosges.'

'I'll go and see him.'

'Be careful.'

291

CHAPTER TWENTY-TWO

Gallery Martin looked run-down. So did the Place des Vosges.

The war was over. The war was not over. Peeling paint. Damaged stonework. Yet, walking through the stone arcades, she was struck by the elegance imprinted on its bones. Like the Rectory. But this was a French elegance, manufactured by a French king who wanted to stamp a sizzling new architectural vision on a medieval city and make it a talking point among the envious. Later kings, of course, moved away to Versailles.

She knew this from Osbert's novels.

Those novelists had summoned the rustle of silk and the clink of swords. The thump of leather boots. The muttering of rebellion and plot. The curses of the malcontent and the scratching pen of the political philosopher – who might well have drawn the contrast between the cool beauty and symmetry of these houses and the poverty of the surrounding Marais.

She hovered under an arcade.

What else to record? The hassle and jostle of Eastern European Jews who'd fled the pogrom.

The tailors, hatters, shoemakers and rag-men who had packed into the apartments, only to be herded up and taken away.

Schoolboys in blue overalls filed into the central garden through the iron gate held open by their teacher. Sober and quiescent – until suddenly, they weren't. A starburst explosion and small, shouting, released figures pounded the paths and kicked up dust.

Pinned to the door of the Gallery Martin was a job advert for an assistant. Languages desirable. Reading through it, something shifted. Monsieur Raphael Maurice, she thought, you may be right. I might not like what I discover. Shall I run?

Seek and ye shall find. So said the Lord, as channelled by Osbert, the Lord's personal interpreter.

She took a deep, shuddery breath. There Osbert was, still lurking in her mental highways and byways. An intolerable colonisation. One day . . . one day, not so far off, she would have the strength, the worldly knowledge, to pull him up by the roots and kill him.

Pushing the gallery's glass door open took a bit of doing. It was heavy and had more than one lock to guard against a break-in.

Inside, the gallery space had an unsettled air. All four walls were bare. Paintings were stacked everywhere. Papers littered the desk.

A man emerged from a room at the back of the gallery. 'You must forgive the disorder. This is the day we are rearranging the gallery. Are you thinking to buy?'

She swung around. 'No.'

'Then how can I help?'

An Osbert novel might describe him thus: a man in his forties with a dusting of grey in his swept-back hair, immaculately dressed in a light tweed jacket and black leather shoes.

A more closely observed description might point out the hunch of his shoulders. Or that he did not look particularly heathy. Someone else might guess, from the closed expression, that he didn't like people very much. The important thing, however, was that she recognised the square jaw from the Les Loups photograph.

He took in the shabby un-chicness of her. The very un-French image.

Quite a reputation for violence.

She swallowed.

Yes, she was out of her depth but an idea seized her by the scruff. Her mouth opened and, aston-ished, she heard herself say, 'I'd like to apply for the job. I speak English very well and I'm willing to learn.' She rounded off the job application with, 'I can do anything.'

'I doubt it. But I admire the chutzpah.'

'Try me, monsieur.'

'I caught my previous assistant with his hand in the till and I need someone quickly, but you won't have the qualifications.'

'So try me.'

A reluctant softening of the mouth and a thaw. 'It might be as well to have a coffee.'

When it arrived, a biscuit sat in the saucer, a combination of wafer and a sublime praline filling. She snaffled it in one bite. He offered her a second. 'You're hungry.'

It was a statement, not a question. 'Is it so obvious?'

'Not so long ago we were all experts on signs of hunger. My guess is you have very little money and you're hoarding it and meals come second. *Alors* . . . let's find out if you do know something or nothing. Who's this painting by?'

He pointed to a canvas stacked face up beside the door. It depicted a black frame slotted inside a second, larger frame which was covered in slashes and bled paint the colour of arterial blood. The effect was violent and disconcerting. *Not* the beauty that she had vowed to seek out and to worship.

She had no knowledge on which to call, only her primary response. 'Although the paint has shock value, it's the energy and attack that make the painting.' A bit of a fumble. 'The artist is trying to do something different?'

Christian Martin nodded. 'Not bad. Josef Kurzt would appreciate your point. He wanted to be different. This was his cry for help. He killed himself in Austria after finishing it.'

'Then there's a scream buried in it.'

'Not *bad*,' he repeated.

295

'How did it come to be in Paris?'

The question appeared to drop into a darkness of post-war secrets.

'It belongs to me,' Christian Martin answered finally. 'I keep it in the gallery. My wife doesn't care for it.' Pause. 'Twentieth-century Viennese art has a particular flavour. Artists trashed the old classical rule that said the relationship between beauty and truth was the most important. Painters such as Egon Schiele argued that ugliness and the exposed body were more telling.'

'I think I see.'

Do I?

'Do you?'

What lay behind his scepticism she could not know. But he did not appear to be the sort of person who broke rules.

A blush splattered up her cheek, signalling embarrassment but also intense curiosity. 'I didn't know, but I'm willing to learn.'

He asked for her details and she had another moment to decide. Should she confess to her real motives? Carry on? *War triggers vendettas, said Raphael Maurice.*

Was she up to the challenge she had set herself to dig through the facts and to probe for the truth?

'My name is Sophie Knox,' she lied. 'My mother was French.'

'Then you must have connections in France?'

'Yes.'

'Are you in touch with them?'

'No. No, not yet.' His lack of response told her nothing. 'My mother fled from France and came to England. She died when I was seven and had been ill for some time.'

'And your father?'

'My father is dead.'

He was looking at Sophie. And he wasn't. He was looking past her into the places of which she had no knowledge.

'During the war?'

She glanced down at her hands and answered truthfully, 'Yes.'

At that moment, she felt afraid. More than a little. The adrenaline was playing out, her lies were deserting her and she was in danger of plummeting into the chasm over which she was now perched.

A sigh escaped Christian Martin, a sound she could not interpret. 'Then I salute your courage in coming to France by yourself.'

The coffee cups chattered in his grasp as he gathered them up. 'Nerve damage from the war.' He held out his left hand. 'Collateral. We who fought all have it, whether it's obvious or not.'

'I'm sorry. That must be difficult sometimes.'

He gave a nod.

Imparting this information was to tell her he had decided to employ her. For courage, she stuck a nail into the soft part of a thumb.

'You're not experienced enough to be my assistant, but if you'd like to work as a dogsbody and messenger then you may join the gallery.'

297

They agreed terms. She expressed her gratitude and he escorted her to the door. 'I'm delighted, mademoiselle.' He pushed it open. 'One thing: you never said if your father was also French.'

The hand holding open the door was clean and manicured. Civilised-looking. Yet this man had been a street fighter. His mind had been shaped by violence as surely as hers had been by bereavement and an uneven, solitary childhood.

Be careful.

'I never knew him but, yes, my father was French.'

'*Dommage*,' said Madame Marie later that afternoon, filing away at a red nail, not bothering to look at Sophie, who stood over her desk. 'You must work out your notice until the end of the week. You've found a better-paid job, I suppose.'

'Not better paid,' said Sophie. 'But I'm not sure I believe in marriage.'

Madame Marie concentrated on her nail architecture. 'Do any of us?'

When she left the office for the final time, Claudine passed her a note: *N'oublies pas le soutien-gorge . . .*

The first day.

Christian Martin showed her around. 'This is Walter Carter,' – a gangly American with excellent teeth said, 'Oh, hi' – 'and this is Emile, who does much of the heavy lifting in the gallery. We could not function without him.' Emile grinned and lit

298

a cigarette. He did not look well nourished, and his teeth were not in the same class.

Running the length of the gallery above it, a stuffy basement downstairs was painted entirely in white. 'Storage and packing,' she was informed. At one end of the corridor was an additional door. 'This room remains locked,' said Christian. 'No one enters it but me.'

Sophie's new career was inaugurated in the stuffy basement. She was to pack up sold paintings to the gallery's – rigorous – specifications, ready for delivery. Paper. Insulation. More paper. Specially adapted wooden crating. 'No wastage,' instructed Christian. 'And I check. Materials are hard to get.'

At the end of the week, Christian handed out wages in an envelope. That was a moment. At last, Sophie from Poynsdean was finally replaced by a new Sophie manufactured from Parisian soil and grit.

She slotted the francs into her wallet.

Where to live? The Hôtel du Gare was becoming a place of noisy torment and she consulted Walt Carter, who seemed approachable.

He was. More than.

'You look like a discerning kind of girl,' said Walt, grinning. (With such teeth, the urge to smile must be constant.) 'I know a place.'

He whisked her up the rue de Turenne, pushed her down a passage at number 66, past Weber Métaux metal company ('*everyone* knows Métaux'), to a large-windowed house at the end, speckled with peeling paint. 'You'll freeze in the winter but it's a roof over the head. And cheap.'

Summer was still ahead and she shivered in the unheated room, but cheap was good. Plus, the nearby café served coffee which – forget, oh please let her forget the Rectory's slops of tea – was the liquid of the gods.

She was beginning to dream in French. She loved her baguette just a shade overdone. It was growing warmer. She bought violets and daisies and stuck them in a cup in her room. She tossed a franc into a street musician's tin and ate a slice of cheese sitting beside the Seine.

This was Paris where she was free to carry out these small actions, unsupervised, unjudged.

Lowly as it was, she liked the job. It had set hours (more or less), routine (sort of), companionship, and the modest pile of franc notes left on her desk on Friday afternoons.

She couldn't fathom Christian Martin. Punctilious? Yes and no. Hardworking? Yes. Contained? She couldn't be sure – for something seethed behind the cool exterior. Which of course, in the best tradition of an Osbert novel, could be guilt.

Dangerous?

Once, he caught her looking at him.

'Do I interest you?'

'You do,' she replied. 'Very much.'

He wasn't pleased. 'I can't imagine why.'

He pronounced that he was happy with her work and her hours would be increased. Good. Yet more than once, he ordered the staff to go home after lunch. 'You must leave before the client arrives,' he said. 'Some clients prefer to be private.'

On those days, guidebook in hand, she paced out the old Paris. The Marais down to the quai des Célestins. The quai des Célestins to the Hôtel de Ville.

Paris was full of strange sensations: the slap of her feet over the cobblestones. Being hit by the smell of coffee. (In all the Poynsdean and Digbys years, she had never inhaled such richness, such promise.) The terror that occasionally pounced: *I am on my own.* The understanding that she had everything to learn.

Her hunger for new information felt physical. She craved stories History. Gossip.

In the early 1900s, the guidebook told her, *waves of Jewish immigrants fleeing Eastern Europe settled in the Marais to eke out a living. Landlords profited from the influx by sub-dividing spacious apartments . . . It was in danger of becoming a slum.*

Many of the buildings in the district have been untouched for over a hundred years and the streets are a jumble of sheds, tiny boutiques and studios, plus formerly magnificent hôtels *from the* grand siècle. *Most buildings lack running water and electricity.*

Why had Christian Martin chosen to open his gallery somewhere as run-down as the Place des Vosges?

'Easy,' said Walt. 'There's a plan to demolish

the area and replace the buildings with the new urban modernist style . . .'

'*No.*' Sophie was almost breathless at the thought. 'Surely they couldn't do that . . . ?'

Walt snipped his fingers together. 'Money.'

Notebook: *Christian Martin plans to profit from wicked destruction?*

The guidebook chatted on: *There are no wholesale changes in the streets, where most cafés and bars are pre-war and look much the same . . .*

She found herself scanning the frontages. Could my father have been in this café? Would my mother have known this house?

Did they walk down this street? Loiter at the river? Drink onion soup in *Les Halles*?

A collage of Paris was being pieced together, a construct that was both imagined and real. Assembling in her head was a map unique to Sophie, its boundaries marked by her peregrinations through Paris's arteries and veins.

The guidebook reproduced a photograph of a plaque in place de l'Odéon, put up in memory of a Resistance fighter killed on that spot: *Mort le 12 janvier 1944. Fusillé par les Allemands.*

She kept returning to the page. It had jolted her.

Checking into the Bureau des Personnes Disparues for an update, she mentioned the plaque to Raphael Maurice. 'Is it possible my father could be similarly recognised, somewhere in the city, and we don't know about it?'

He was surrounded by papers and a brimming ashtray. 'I don't think so, mademoiselle.'

She eyed him up – rooted to his chair, walled in by paper and smoke.

'Monsieur Maurice, I want you to know I disagree with you.'

'You would not be alone.'

'You tried to discourage me from questioning, I think. But questions should be asked. All the time. It's our duty to investigate dark areas.'

At that moment, it occurred to her that, if one nerved oneself to say something difficult, those nerves often made one overdo it.

He listened. 'I wanted you to understand that the answers arrive with a price, one that's hard to absorb if you're alone and unprotected.'

'I must take the risk.'

'Have you tackled Monsieur Martin?' She shook her head. 'Perhaps you don't feel up to it.' He sent her a considering look. 'I rest my case.'

She persisted with her point. 'One can't avoid the past.'

'You can. Believe me.'

Something – his expression, the way he held himself – told her that, for him, the past had not been particularly happy. Or rewarding.

'It's 1960. Standing on one's own two feet is part of the deal. But thank you for your concern.'

He drummed his fingers on the desk. 'Good. Well, since we will have quite a lot of contact, I think you should call me Raf. Everyone else does.' An almost intimacy?

She coloured. 'I nearly forgot to tell you – I'm known as Sophie Knox at the gallery, not Morel.'

'A sensible strategy if you're not willing to talk to him yet.'

'Do you know where Les Loups fought?'

Mademoiselle Axel sashayed into the office and placed a cup of coffee on Raf's desk. 'Your next appointment is waiting.'

'Monsieur Maurice?' she pressed. Then, less certainly, 'Raf?'

He pulled the coffee towards him. 'I don't, but I know someone who will.'

It wasn't all plain sailing.

Sometimes, she caught sight of herself in shop windows. *Les vitrines*, as she had learnt to call them. Disappointingly, they still reflected a thin and insignificant figure.

No image yet.

Once, as she turned away from contemplating shoes she could never possibly afford, she heard piano music drifting into the street through an open window.

Alice, she thought, a strange, unsettling feeling ripping at her. Alice.

Poynsdean – England – was a foreign country whose memory she had dropped into the waters of the Lethe. But the music . . . the music told her otherwise. Muddy, sea-fretted Poynsdean, and

304

Paris, rising like the phoenix from the ashes of war, were pulled together by a skein of notes that made her cry.

Notebook: *There is no such thing as a vacuum. We are connected wherever we are. Dog is still with me. Johnno too, perhaps. And Hettie . . . Hettie?*

She spent some of the time re-exploring loneliness, arriving at the electric conclusion that, however despised, Digbys *had* provided a shelter of sorts. At night, her dreams were often so vivid she woke. They were of marshlands and birds. Of lying down beside Johnno. Of the rush of love and desire. Of her flight from Osbert across dawn-streaked fields. From these she would awake, shaken, spitting defiance. Very often tear-stained.

Notebook: *The moral high ground is a cold and windy place. Doing the right thing is supposed to be reward sufficient unto itself.*

I hate Linda. I shouldn't but I do. I don't want what she has. Or I think I don't.

Insistence on doing the right thing is a tool designed to keep children and women in check.

The notebook balanced with difficulty on her knee, she dug her pencil into the paper, sifting through the sharp ironies. Home Farm comforts and luxuries (such as a table to eat off) were being enjoyed by Linda, who would not have wasted a single thought on Sophie.

Often towards the morning, when sleep became lighter and dream-filled, Johnno again stalked out

305

of the deeper recesses of her unconscious, and she knew that she had a way to go before she was free of him.

She was lonely, yes, but not unhappy. Easy in her own company, her perceptions sharpening. She was learning. Her diet was organised: breakfast was half a baguette; supper was frequently the other half, with shavings of cheese or ham she had bought on the way to work. Or a bowl of vegetable soup. Perfectly doable on her wages.

And there was Walter Carter. ('Call me Walt.')

His father ran a prestigious gallery in Boston and Walt was interning – *un stagiaire* – at the Gallery Martin, where he had been for six months. 'Which means,' he told Sophie, 'that I already know about Paris. Hitch your wagon to mine and we'll do fine.'

It was most charmingly uttered, and Sophie grinned.

'We're going to be pals.'

She was wrestling with a roll of brown paper on the table in the basement and getting tangled up. 'We don't know each other,' she said rather helplessly.

'How very English. We will, though. Be good friends.'

The words weaselled under her defences and settled in the space left by Hettie.

'Gosh,' she said. 'That's direct. But nice. So nice.'

'You should also know that I hate art. Or rather, it doesn't do anything for me.'

'Why are you working here then?'

He shrugged. 'When you have a father as powerful as mine, you do as you're told until such time as the cage door swings open and the little bird flies.'

Walt wasn't expected to do anything as menial as packing parcels. Of course not. 'I have cloth hands, honey.' Walt was assigned to the record-keeping, which had to be kept meticulously up to date – except that administration was not Walt's thing either. 'Help me out, Sophie. Pretty please.'

Of course she did. One, she liked him. Two, she wanted to learn.

Price bought. Price sold. Damage. Restoration. Provenance.

Ah, provenance.

'A big, big subject,' said Walt. 'You should hear my father on it. Or rather, you shouldn't. He's obsessed.'

Provenance was all – or should be – when selling paintings. Provenance told stories, some of them good, some intriguing. (This she did know, thanks to the breathless *To Save My King* on Osbert's bookshelves. After his execution, Charles I's paintings were sold for knockdown prices to butchers and bakers.) Some revealed shocking histories of theft and looting. Some provenances were forged. Who was going to own up to stealing or forgery? Gallerists took infinite trouble to trace a provenance, Walt explained, because it was the key to how a painting was treated and, thus, the key to their fortunes.

'Not always easy after the war,' he added, lowering his tone, which suggested he knew things but wouldn't be revealing them.

'Walt, can I ask you something?'

'Love it when people consult me.'

'Why the locked room down the corridor?'

He ringed her neck with his fingers. 'I take it you've heard the fairy story of Bluebeard and his chamber? *That* chamber.'

By and large, Digbys' teachings had proved not to be reliable guides to life, except for five salient precepts which she appreciated did make sense. Order, good administration, taking decisions and reliability. Regular hours. These were key, said Miss Chambers. It was the British way of doing things, which had done the empire proud.

In Paris, Sophie wasn't so sure.

The beat of the city's heart sounded through the walls of the gallery and it was impossible not to listen. A tangle of aromas – from bakeries, perfumeries, pissoirs, the river, that wonderful river and the like – drifted in through the heavy glass door.

'Walt, we should be out there.'

Spotting marigolds in window boxes, dodging war-damaged buildings, taking in the view from the Sacré-Coeur, drinking coffee on the Left Bank.

Even on short acquaintance, she would have betted he would agree.

He did. 'The office cuts a person off from important diurnal rhythms which kept one on an even

308

keel,' he said, with an intensity at odds with his easy-going exterior.

She hadn't a clue what 'diurnal rhythms' were, but they sounded as if they supported the case.

Spring had arrived. In the parks on the Île de la Cité, in Buttes-Chaumont, and the Jardin du Luxembourg the signals rippled in. Babies were being aired. Children were dusted down from winter confinement. River barges acquired a decoration of laundry pinned to their rigging. The awnings went up over cafés and restaurants. Flea markets began to hum. The rubbish in the street took on a different smell.

At les Puces de Montreuil – 'the oldest Parisian flea market' said the guidebook – Sophie made her first purchases and bore them back to number 66. A battered kettle in pale blue enamel. Two glasses engraved with a floral frieze. A couple of porcelain plates which, if she held them up to the light, were nearly transparent.

'War trophies,' said Walt. 'Markets are stuffed with stolen loot.'

'Oh Lord, I hadn't thought of that. I shouldn't have them.'

'Well,' Walt rolled out the bleeding obvious, 'they're not going back to the original owners.'

Those purchases, innocently made, had almost certainly been ripped from someone's home . . . The misgivings nipped and buzzed. Then died. She would care for these objects. Was that not something?

Hold the polished glass up and study its clarities and imperfections. Wipe the kettle clean of its former life. Plus, to eat off porcelain is much more enjoyable than eating off pottery, she informed Walt. And I tell it so every time I do . . .

Sights, smells, sensations. She was overwhelmed with sensations, with her delight in all the novelty, with the unfolding of her senses. None of it should be wasted. She *must* not waste it.

First, she must write to Hettie.

My Hettie, I will never understand you marrying this William person. But I was hasty. I didn't understand how complicated things are, or how very different responses can be to the same problem. I wasn't really listening to you. Differences in temperament matter. I see that now.

What I feel for you as my friend is impossible to describe. But when I look at a beautiful building, hear music, watch the play of light on the Seine, then I think of you.

Forgive me? she wrote. *Please.*

The reply came by return: *Nothing to forgive.*

The letters began to flow.

I sit in the sun and think about whether I can afford a slice of Camembert from the crèmerie or not. Paris has a strange, upside-down effect on one.

So does marriage, said Hettie, adding, *so does Dorking.*

CHAPTER TWENTY-THREE

Today's tasks.

Pack up two landscapes framed in unpainted wood. Record details in the log. Man the desk in the gallery when Christian Martin took his lunch break. Rearrange and catalogue the reference books.

The two landscapes were third rate. But, as luck would have it, that was their strongest selling point. They were pounced on as the 'perfect' wedding present by Madame Claude who disliked – mild description – her son's choice of bride. 'She'll have to put them up and look at them every day,' said Madame Claude. *'Ça me plaît.'*

That bride had her work cut out. *I send luck.* Sophie wrapped the first layers of packaging around them, finessing the outer wrapping. *I hope you will be happy despite these.*

Christian and Emile edged into the basement carrying a large painting between them.

Christian propped it up against the wall. 'Behold, *The Skaters.*'

Sophie blinked.

Electric colours. Blazing with energy. An obvious

intention to subvert the assumptions about figurative art and, while the painter was at it, the art of skating itself.

A male figure in the group had an arm – was it an arm? – around a female partner, from whose distorted mouth issued a scream. The remainder of the group dissolved into explosions of colour.

Christian said: 'Realism as we think of it is abandoned here. Rather, the artist and his circle were concerned with the realities of emotion. See, he's skating with his wife, girlfriend, or even his daughter . . . and all seems fine on the outside. Note the scarf and his skates, which are rendered in detail. But inside, it's turmoil. The group were called expressionists and Hitler hated them.'

'Is it . . . is it valuable?'

He was prepared to enlighten her. 'Very.'

She glanced at the stack of paintings. Some were packaged and waiting to go.

The wrappings and the crates. The hammers and nails and labels.

'There must a fortune in this room.'

'Art has always been a currency.' Christian brushed a finger across the frame of *The Skaters*. Treating it like a pet dog, she thought. 'So much better than the paper kind. Looking at this tells you something. You may not like it but, here, you can see that souls are tormented, and you have to ask yourself why. You don't get that from a franc note.'

Later, Walt took her out to lunch, which he

312

insisted was on him: *I'm rich*. She didn't protest too much as he whisked her up the rue de Turenne to a restaurant with maroon wooden shutters and a dim interior. 'You won't regret this.'

She didn't and wouldn't. The garlic soup was heavenly and the fish had just swum in from the sea. The bread was something else again and, apart from anything else, she wouldn't have to worry about eating that evening.

They ate in silence. An American habit?

Halfway through, Walt said, 'Apologies for the silence but I had to concentrate on the food.' He extracted a notebook from his pocket, the kind with an elastic band that journalists favoured, and wrote a sentence. 'It's my daily discipline.'

The relish with which they were attacking the meal did not suggest much discipline in either of them. 'Of course.'

Their acquaintance had been short, and Walt looked as though he had been fed full-fat cream from day one of his existence, and had few cares. But studying him over the lunch table, she thought this was perhaps not the full story.

'I can see that I fascinate you.' He dropped the notebook back into his pocket. 'But you fascinate me in return. So English.'

'I'm French. *Totally* French.'

His eyebrows shot up. 'OK. OK. I'll take your word for it, but if I sliced you in half, the word "England" would be there. Like in a stick of rock.'

She looked away.

313

'Hey,' he said. 'It's not so bad. Being English, I mean.'

Was it or wasn't it so bad? Was identity to do with what she felt? Or what had happened to her? 'I'm neither one nor the other.'

'OK, you're a sea nymph, swimming between the two.'

It was a pleasant semi-joke, made in oh so pleasant surroundings. Easy from the meal, they both laughed.

She edged a fishbone onto the rim of her plate. The door to the *cabinets* at the end of the room opened and shut. The waiter refilled their water jug.

In a way, she was free to be who she wished.

Later, she asked Walt, 'And what makes the cage door swing open and to where would the little bird fly?'

'Now, there's the thing.'

He shot her a look, weighing her up. Being direct and open did not guarantee he would trust her with secret or important information. He tapped his coffee cup with the spoon and she read *no, yes, no* in its tiny reverberation.

Yes. She was in.

'I want to be a cookery writer. US food is OK. Hominy grits and all that, and the states all have their specialties. But none of them have the beauty . . . yes, beauty . . . of French food. I think the US needs to know more.'

Sophie grinned. 'If I knew what hominy grits were I'm sure I'd agree.'

314

'You don't have to know. What you do have to know is that the dessert you have just eaten was made by one of the great Paris chefs. Years of experience went into that *tarte aux cerises*.'

This was startling. 'Really!' It *had* been delicious. But, 'I'm sorry,' she admitted, hating to display more ignorance, 'the eminence of the chef didn't occur to me.'

The boyish tone morphed into an older, more professional one. 'French food is made up of so much. History. Technique. Discipline. Creativity. Observing the rituals. You can't see that yet but, by the time I'm done with you, you will.' He was now very serious. 'The French have an artisanal approach to life, especially when it comes to their food. The US goes in for mass production and for profit and productivity.' He grinned. 'Are you on board, Miss Sophie?'

She wrote to Hettie, 'If only I had known what I was getting into. A wrecked liver will be the least of it. Walt says not to worry about the *crise de foie*, as everyone has them in Paris. It's a badge of honour.'

As spring unfolded in a dazzle, every week brought a new restaurant. Montmartre. The Left Bank. The Place Pigalle. Every week there were more dishes to consume, to analyse. 'Store up memories of this . . .' Walt paused in his consumption of *boeuf en daube*, 'they will help in bleak times.' He speared another piece of the beef onto his fork. 'I know.'

315

It was all so diverting. For days on end, Sophie ignored *you are here to find your father*. 'Ah yes,' she heard herself pronouncing. 'That *sole meunière* wasn't quite done.' Or, 'Those *côtelettes de veau surprise* were perfect.'

She amused herself with her own audacity, but with each forkful she learnt something.

Walt said that she was an excellent student. The best. When he consulted her opinion or spouted his own, she would analyse his expressions – so good-natured, so generous. His frequent smiles revealed those beautiful American teeth. Astonished, because she thought all that had ended with Johnno, she caught a shiver of desire. For Walt's wholesomeness. His straightforwardness.

I think it's to do with love and joy, she appended her letter to Hettie. *Am I mad? Have I gone over to the stupid side? I had no idea that food and wine could, and should, be a focus of celebration. Being with Walt is a bit like floating on calm, sunny water. It's easy and lovely. I can't help but conclude that the way food is seen in England contributes greatly to our repression* . . . (Here she crossed out 'our' and substituted 'English'.) *The French think so differently about everything, really, but most of all, they think differently about food.*

You must come, Hettie . . .

To her extreme surprise, back came a telegram. 'Arriving Thursday, 1 p.m.'

*　　*　　*

Hettie stepped down from the boat train at the Gare du Nord and Sophie observed her progress down the platform with a porter in tow.

A hand squeezed her heart. Hettie looked wrong. Very wrong. Thin and sad, the frizz of blonde hair flattened and without the inner light that, however bad times had been, had always been there.

'I've got two days,' Hettie said as they clung to each other. 'Two lovely, wonderful, special days.'

'Then we're not going to waste too much time on sightseeing. Only the basics so you can say you've been to Paris because, Het, we are going to talk and talk.'

Which they did. You? Me? How? When? What is to be done?

You were asked to bake sixty scones for a church tea? Sixty?

You're writing . . . . keeping a notebook?

William won't allow you to wear low-necked frocks?

There's a locked room in the gallery?

Seeing Paris through Hettie's eyes was useful. Of course, there was the backdrop of war damage, ruined buildings and blackened structures, but 'Paris is moving into the future,' said Sophie, milking her new role of guide and pundit. Paris was turning herself into a city of possibilities, a bandaged, but beautiful, setting for art and culture and razor-sharp modernity.

Hettie did not fall over herself to tell Sophie how impressed she was. Instead, she was quiet. Worryingly quiet. Only rousing herself to ask if it

317

was true that girls, walking the streets at night, were often kidnapped into a life of utmost sexual depravity.

However, at a meal at the Restaurant Saints Pères near the Marais, the old Hettie returned to life.

'Everything about my hotel is intriguing. Especially the plumbing.' She held up a hand on which now reposed a wedding band and a depressingly modest engagement ring.

'I wish you could stay with me. I'd have slept on the floor.'

'William made me promise I wouldn't stay with you.'

'Does he dislike the idea of me?'

'Yes. Does it matter?'

Sophie ordered white wine for them both. 'How lovely,' said Hettie. 'These days, I mostly drink sherry.' There was a tiny pause. 'Or a gin.' Another pause. 'But not too often.'

The implications sloshed around the notion of not-too-often sherry and gin. Sophie reached an arm across the table. 'Isn't he treating you well?'

Hettie's fingers closed around hers. 'Put it this way, I got what everyone wanted for me. Including me.'

'But?'

'But . . .'

Hettie watched two French women with camel skirts and artfully arranged scarves around their necks light up cigarettes and sighed, a sound

318

conveying low-level despair. 'Married life is dull. Ditchwater would be more interesting.' She ticked off the contents of her days on her fingers. One, mornings organising the marital home. Two, the flower-arranging roster at St Olave's ('far too grand for the village and so gloomy'). Three, consultations with the housekeeper, who arrived most mornings smelling of drink. Four, coffee mornings ('it's like drinking mud') with fellow wives. Five . . .

'William plays a lot of golf and lunches at the club most days.' Which left Hettie alone for most of the day. 'You know, just like Charlotte Collins in *Pride and Prejudice*.'

'Charlotte Collins couldn't bear to be in the same room as her husband.'

Silence.

'You do *like* him?'

Hettie grabbed the coffee which had just been served. 'The thing is . . .' she began. 'The thing is there won't be children.'

'Hettie!'

'A wound in the war . . . Burma.' Hettie was now bright scarlet. 'He never said.'

'And he never mentioned this to the marriage bureau?' Sophie was outraged. 'That's almost criminal. Have you had it out with him?'

'It was ghastly. I was so angry and sad, I could hardly speak. He begged forgiveness.'

'You must leave him. At once.'

A flicker of anger which Sophie knew was

directed as much at Hettie herself as at her. 'You know my set-up. What the parents would think. What would have to come out in the courts. I couldn't do that to anyone. Not even William.' She looked everywhere but at Sophie. 'It's changed how I see things.' She looked up. 'Sophs, you're the only person I've told.'

'You're stuck, then.'

Disappointment. Dullness. Confinement.

'Yes.'

Sophie thought for a moment. Hard and furious. 'Then you're bloody well going to send him a telegram now to say you will be staying on for a couple of days and we will do Paris.'

Taking charge of Hettie and sorting her out for the duration of that small escape from Dorking was a therapy of sorts.

Une leçon psychologique – as Sophie had begun to categorise the shifts in mind and behaviour. (It sounded better in French.)

'Hettie, you must think, think, *think*. You must not ruin your life.'

'And you,' said Hettie, 'better get on with finding out about your father.' She swallowed. The I'm being brave swallow. 'Do you like the gallery?'

Sophie considered. On the obvious level, it was easy. Yes, I like the gallery and the job very much. On a deeper level, the answer was less straightforward. The place gave her a nagging sense of *déjà vu*. But of what? And why? It was as if she knew it, or about it, from a long time ago. 'Am I mad?' she asked, when she explained this to Hettie.

Hettie affirmed fondly that this was the case.

'I'm known as Sophie Knox. The Morel bit is secret.'

Hettie was enchanted. 'Sort of secret service-ish?'

'Sort of.'

Christian issued invitations to them both to the next Gallery Martin show. It was to be that evening, and Sophie had been helping to prepare.

'Never expected that,' said Sophie. 'He must think you are a potential client.'

This gave them precisely zero time to panic about clothes. Sophie wore her skirt and tight jumper, Hettie a floral dress with a modest neckline.

'Do I look a hundred in this?'

She did, she did . . . but Sophie wasn't going to say.

'Never.'

The gallery was stuffed with ferociously fashionable-looking people. Chatter. Clinking glass. High heels striking the tiled floor. No cigarette smoke, for the sake of the paintings. 'Observe,' Sophie instructed Hettie. 'We must remember the details.'

Hettie tugged at her neckline.

Walt made a beeline for them. 'This must be Hettie.' The white-toothed smile was bestowed with dazzling grace. 'Am I glad to see you.'

Amused and kind, he instantly commandeered Hettie. 'I feel I know you.' A sun sailed out from behind black clouds and Hettie bestowed the first proper smile since her arrival.

'*Mesdemoiselles*, Hector de la Crochais is demanding that I introduce you.'

The two girls exchanged looks. *Predator. Base Nature.*

'However, I demand to keep Hettie to myself.' Walt led them up to an elderly, dapper Frenchman in a bow tie. 'Hector, you must amuse Sophie while I show Hettie the gallery.'

Hector said to Sophie, 'Christian mentioned you and I insisted on meeting you.'

She stifled a shudder.

Wrong. Hector turned out to be charming and full of delicious malice, and a mightily entertaining run-down of the people present rolled from his plump lips. '*Le monde,*' he said, 'is a privileged class made up of a ragbag of aristos and well-to-do bourgeoisie. Unless you understand that, you'll never understand France.' He gestured towards a fossilised, over-powdered woman fingering yellowing but substantial pearls. 'An illegitimate daughter of a count who blags her way into society on the strength of it. And that one . . .' he indicated a stooped, greying man in an equally ancient suit, '*un hobereau de province* . . . what you would call a country squire, I think. I bet you that both of them will know everything there is to know about their lineage. And anyone else's. It'll be their hobby.'

His shrewd gaze skewered her. 'And you, made-moiselle, are at the beginning of your life.' Gnomic pronouncement delivered, he moved on.

Sophie had intended to keep Hettie close and guarded, but there was no need. She and Walt were quickfire talking in front of a painting entitled *The Dawn of Civilisation* by Clément Brive.

Was it a premonition, a warning, or a sliver of jealousy that made her down her champagne?

'What do you think civilisation is?' she heard Hettie ask Walt.

'Food,' was the instant reply. Both dissolved into laughter.

She hovered. Watched. Turned away from that little grouping which, suddenly, did not include her – and encountered Monsieur Maurice.

Raf.

He was holding a glass of water.

'Don't you drink champagne?' Glancing down at her empty glass.

'Don't like it much.'

'And you a Frenchman.'

He didn't think much of that as a piece of wit. He merely collared a passing waiter and obtained a fresh glass, which he gave to her. 'I probably drank too much too often at one of these events,' he said. 'Didn't care for the consequences.'

She wanted to know why he was at the gallery.

'I had to get in touch with Martin over another matter and he didn't mention you. Which meant only one thing.'

She peered at him over her glass.

'You hadn't broached the subject with him.'

'That's true.' She turned her head. 'Does that surprise you?'

'In my job you see every kind of human response. Your reluctance to press ahead is one of them. It could be termed a little strange. You've paid a lot of money to find your father . . . You've spent your life thinking about him.'

It *was* strange. Very. 'Did you come here to check up on me?'

'Good Lord no. I'm very keen on . . . er . . .' he glanced at the label of the nearest painting, '. . . on the work of Clément Brive.' He drained his water glass. 'Come and have a beer with me. There's a café opposite. We can discuss where you go next.'

Before she knew it, she had agreed.

They sat at a table outside the café. There was an odd spatter of rain, a smell of water on stone. Horns blared. The ice cube in her orange juice clinked against her teeth. She kept a weather eye on the gallery, ready to make the dash back.

Raf concentrated on his beer, which he drank mouthful by thoughtful mouthful. She asked him if he had always lived in the city.

'Not always. The family moved to Provence during the war. After my mother died, my father set up the agency in Paris and I came back to help out a couple of years before my father retired. Now, I can't imagine being anywhere else. My work is here.' He gestured to the street. 'Some say I'm consumed by it.' She wondered who the 'some' might be. 'I've taken up the cross.'

A second beer was ordered.

He leant over the table and she caught an alarming fanatical light in his eye. 'If you wish to find out about your father, you must question Christian Martin. Otherwise you've wasted your time.'

A slight reproof. A suggestion of cowardice.

'Would you like me to talk to him? I occasionally do that for clients.'

'No. I can . . . I must deal with it myself.'

'Of course. It's 1960 and you like to stand on your own two feet.'

She eyed him. To laugh? Or not?

He caught a splash of rain in his hand. 'There's a syndrome. I've seen it at the bureau. Someone is desperate to find someone, let's say a father. It takes a long time, perhaps decades, and during that period, the elements powering the search change. The search itself becomes the imperative and the ending can no longer be desired because the purpose, the mission that has given clarity and meaning, disappears.'

'I understand. But that's not me,' she insisted.

There was a long, sceptical pause.

But it is me, she thought.

She gathered her wits. 'There's a locked room in the gallery.'

'We all have a locked room,' said Raf with an edge to his voice 'Keep things out of sight.'

325

'It seems strange. Odd. As if he's hiding some-thing about the paintings. Something from the war, maybe?'

He glanced down the street. 'The war threw up effluent. Rivers of it. People stole things. Those who fled sold what they could, including paintings, which were bought up very cheaply by the sharper operators who aren't in a hurry to give them back. If there's anyone left to give them back to.'

She looked away. Stealing. Enforced sales. Moral duplicities. Compared to these, Osbert's sins and duplicities seemed straightforward.

'I've checked out Christian Martin further,' he said. 'Facts from that time were and are extremely difficult to verify, but it looks like he *was* instru-mental in the execution of a *collabo* during the liberation. One of many instances of *justice en gros*, popular justice. There was a lot of it at that time and everyone turned a blind eye, including the police.'

'And my father? Could he have been involved?'

'I don't know. I need more time. But I should think it is likely that he was dead by then.'

She stared at Raf, who fingered his empty glass. 'Apart from anything else, murder . . . killing . . . is a corrosive. It's an acid that gets everywhere. Yes, I'm urging you to make yourself known to Martin in order to find out about your father. But, now knowing what I do, I also urge you to keep in touch with me.'

A glance at her folded hands. 'You don't think he would be violent?'

'No. But you should be aware.'

Having delivered his warning, Raf seemed lighter for it.

'If you give me permission, I'll try and track down your mother's relatives who lived in Poitiers.'

A rapid calculation. 'How much would that be?'

'It's included in the fee.' Sophie stared at Raf. Did she sense pity? Or patronage? Kindness? Or a will to protect? Again, that curious, puzzling ripple went through her. As if her body had woken up. Was this being indiscriminate in one's lusts? Base-natured?

'Thank you.'

Raf asked her to tell him about Sussex. She described the village and the crossroads, the wild-flowers, the wetlands, the marsh and the sea. The Rectory. 'I don't belong there, though. The only thing that would have kept me is Johnno, but he's marrying someone else. Johnno, and Dog.'

Evoking Dog's brown eyes and battered body and the way he trusted her made her falter. 'Dog chose me to be with him when he died.'

He allowed her to collect herself before lighting up a cigarette.

'I never thought I could love an animal so fiercely. I miss him.'

'But they live in another way. In your head.' Raf looked very French and serious. 'So you must ask:

what is life? Is it us sitting here? Or the one in our heads?'

That made her want to laugh. It also made her feel dizzy with the delight of it all. Paris, art galleries, baguettes and cheese, serious conversations.

'You've been careful to prepare me for what I might discover. I'm grateful.'

'In my work I get to know things. Some of which are . . . awful. Then and now. Plenty goes on today that makes people want to disappear. We've discussed how the war resulted in confusion and violence. We know the facts of what happened in countries, including fighting and wholesale murder. But it's *how* these facts are interpreted and remembered that causes so much trouble. More often than you might think, the truth is not faced. Competing views of history run alongside one another, causing never-ending trouble.'

She looked at him covertly from under her lids. It struck her that he was . . . She searched for the word. Resigned?

'Do you always warn your clients?'

She knew he would not answer. The rules of office life included discretion. Absolute discretion.

He dug out a card from his pocket. 'This is my phone number. A private one. Use it when you need questions answered – any time.'

'Thank you.' She glanced over her shoulder. Hettie and Walt were standing at the entrance to the gallery, looking up and down the street.

'Raf, do you know the legend of Bluebeard?'

'Charles Perrault? The locked room, like the one in the gallery, hiding the bodies of his previous wives. Why?'

She shuffled to her feet and waved at Hettie and Walt. 'Just a thought.'

He laughed. Loudly but very nicely.

'It was written to illustrate the perils of female curiosity. You *had* better be careful.'

Guide in hand, she shepherded Hettie around the city. 'The boulevard Saint-Germain was one of Baron Haussmann's proudest achievements,' she read out. 'It embodied his concept of the modern city, with wide straight thoroughfares cutting through a network of medieval streets.'

'Pity,' said Hettie. 'Medieval Paris sounds much more interesting.'

Sophie ignored her. 'Traces of the older city can be seen winding in and around the newer boulevards like, as Victor Hugo wrote, "lines of text in an ancient manuscript".' She looked up. 'The baron wanted to bring light and air into the city. The Emperor Louis-Napoléon wanted to ensure that, if revolution was brewing in the alleys, his soldiers could get into the area pronto and break it up.'

'*Definitely* nothing like Dorking, then,' said Hettie.

It was Hettie who spotted the bookshop.

It was in the rue de Savoie, off what the pair of

them had taken to insouciantly referring to as the boul Saint-Mich. It had a sign in English: 'The Treasure House'.

In its main window a witch rode a broomstick, a cackle on her wooden face. *I dare you to defy my power.* In the smaller window there was a moving model of a Ferris wheel with fairy lights, casting a radiance. Then there were the books, masses of them.

'Genius,' said Sophie.

'Never seen a shop window like it,' said Hettie.

That unknown window dresser had magicked enchantment, and they lingered. Look at this. Look at that.

The bookshop's interior was as intriguingly idiosyncratic.

A mother attempted to control her son, who was intent on damaging a copy of *Five Children and It*. A heavily pregnant woman begged for a chair, which was promptly brought. There was a table piled high with popular children's titles: *Warrior Scarlet*, *The House that Jack Built*, *The Story of Holly and Ivy*.

The sales assistant turned out to be English. 'We specialise in children's books,' he said. 'In this bookshop, we believe that children should be put first. Books for adults are in the room at the back.' He shoved his glasses up the bridge of his nose. 'We're dedicated to magic and adventure, to a certain light-heartedness, and to satisfactory endings.'

Sophie wandered the shelves and poked her nose into the room with the adult books. English publications were easy to spot. Their jackets tended to have strong colours and large, blustery typefaces. The French opted for cooler greys, whites and yellows with severe, intellectual type.

Hettie talked to the sales assistant. The old Hettie, that is. Not the new, sad one. The old Hettie obtained the facts in the old manner. 'His name is Harry,' she informed Sophie as they were leaving the shop. 'He's fled from England because of a tragic love affair.'

Sophie squinted at Harry, who did not seem the slightest bit tragic. In fact, he smiled very happily as they said goodbye.

A drink had been spilled on the pavement outside. A steady brown stream rolled towards the gutter, where a discarded paper bag rattled.

'Het, what about you?' Sophie slipped her arm through Hettie's crooked elbow. 'The children thing. What are you going to do?'

They stood close together, staring at the witch and the Ferris wheel. Drinking up the last drop of magic, the last drop of adventure before the promised satisfactory ending.

Hettie sighed. 'It is what it is.'

Walt took them out to Montmartre for dinner. He wished to show Hettie a slice of the wicked Paris world. And Hettie said she wished to see it. Fervently.

It wasn't wicked Paris that Hettie was treated to

so much as Walt's film-star smile, which threatened to become permanent in Hettie's company. Even when he and Hettie argued forcibly over the merits – or not – of garlic in mayonnaise. Woundingly, they were not interested in Sophie's views.

Laugh or cry?

Let Hettie have glorious moments.

332

CHAPTER TWENTY-FOUR

On the train journey to Brindisi (a place of which she had never heard), Sophie analysed Hettie's sigh.

It hurt to consider what it might signify. *That* was the double-edged sword of friendship. You took on friends' burdens and their sufferings and, in turn, were wounded too.

She was travelling First Class. Alongside her, carefully and professionally packed, was *The Skaters*, which she was accompanying on its journey to its new owner.

'You've been watching me again,' Christian Martin informed Sophie.

'I'm learning from you.'

His frown was pronounced. 'Maybe. And, if that's true, it's good to know my money isn't being wasted. But I'm sending you off on a delivery. Then you can stare at something else.'

Christian explained that the painting's new owner preferred his purchases to be personally delivered. (There had been a previous incident where a courier van had been hijacked with its contents.) 'You'll deliver to Kim Athos himself,'

333

Christian instructed, adding disconcertingly, 'If you have to die to do so.'

Christian never revealed personal details about clients: 'It's the first rule of running a successful gallery.' But Walt, who had access to a trove of knowledge from his father's gallery, possessed no such inhibitions. 'Kim Athos is a shrewd guy who knows how to woo *la femme*. His factory makes hairdryers and vacuum cleaners, just what women are crying out for, and he gives them to them in fancy boxes with clear instructions. He's made so much money he can't count it.' Walt's fine skin coloured, one of his endearing traits. 'But he's not so rich that he's careless. Be warned.'

Kim Athos *was* rich. No doubt about that. On arriving in Milan, grubby and tired, Sophie was transported to a breathtakingly luxurious hotel, all white quilts, bouffant pillows and huge mirrors.

The porter wheeled her battered case, plus *The Skaters*, into her room. He spent an age propping it up against the wall, checking over his shoulder to see if Sophie was appreciating his dexterity.

He muttered under his breath.

He dusted off his hands and adopted an expectant pose.

'Thank you,' she said.

The look he threw her suggested that she ranked below the amoeba in the hierarchy of guests. The door closed with an unfriendly click.

She soaked in a glorious hot, scented bath. *Wonderful*. Admired the gold taps, the glass bottles

334

on the shelves, the china soap dish. *So elegant.* It was then that the blush-making omission hit home: she had not tipped the porter.

Walt's Tips for Travelling. (He had been free with these.)

Never carry your own luggage.

Don't assume there's paper in the lavatories.

Always tip the porter. They have more power than monarchs.

Hot and bothered, she leapt out of the bath, dried herself on a towel the size of a small island and ordered room service.

When it arrived, she was sitting on the bed clutching a high denomination note, which was all she had.

The bellhop seemed staggered when she palmed it into his hand, but shot like greased lighting out of the door.

Oh, crap (a recently acquired Walterism). She had forgotten the final rule on Walt's list: *Don't overtip. They will despise you.*

On waking warm, rested and relaxed, she experienced a small but indelible epiphany. Luxury was heavenly. It could soothe the crabbed spirit (much as she feared hers might become) and cleanse and prettify its grubby hems and edges.

And it took only a few minutes to become an addict.

A security man had been detailed to accompany her from Milan to Brindisi. ('Think bandits,' said Walt.) He was not a chatty type – she would have marked him out in an identity parade as a stranger to the word 'cheerful' – but he suited Sophie, who wished to be left to look out of the train window.

Sails furled, a hundred foot or so in length, the sun licking over her bodywork, the yacht *Elizabetta*, a picture of handcrafted elegance, looked as though she was ablaze. Viewing her from the quay, Sophie absorbed her beauty and the panorama of Brindisi's crowded marina. Picturesque buildings. The unfamiliar blue of the sea. Large, sleek yachts, the like of which she had never seen before. Elderly men, paunched and wrinkled, sitting on their respective decks, surrounded by much younger and very beautiful girls.

On board, Sophie was conducted to the state-room by a uniformed member of the crew where, he informed her in a hushed tone, the boss awaited the delivery.

Brass trims, an overstuffed sofa, a couple of upholstered chairs for which a rare animal must have been sacrificed and a crowded drinks stand shackled into the wall . . . These necessities of on-board life assaulted the eye and ran full tilt up the Dubious Taste barometer.

If, she thought, a trifle hysterically, the person who designed them could see the impoverished Knox kitchen, they would faint.

Two Amazonian women in green-and-white livery with matching swept-back blonde hair flanked Kim Athos. Smaller and slighter than Sophie had envisioned, he was dressed in casual clothes so well cut they could have been a formal suit. A sleek man. A confident man? Yes and yes. But her increasingly sharp eye for detail noted that the expensive-looking watch was too big for his wrist.

She handed over the documentation and opened her mouth to deliver Christian's greetings, but the Amazons stepped in front of Sophie and cut her off.

Kim Athos wasn't listening anyway. He had gone very still and rapt. A burly crew member unpeeled the wrappings. Like Venus from the waves, *The Skaters* emerged in all its shock-filled glory and he took up a position of worship in front of it.

Everyone in the stateroom remained reverently silent.

After an interval, he roused himself. Stepping back, he trod on Sophie's foot, failed to mask his surprise at her presence and apologised before asking, 'Do you approve of my choice, Miss . . . er . . . ?'

An Amazon consulted her clipboard. 'Knox.'

'It's an interesting painting.'

'But do you approve?'

All eyes were trained on Sophie and she realised they were waiting to witness her humiliation.

Wash from a passing craft thudded against the *Elizabetta*'s sides.

Kim Athos persisted. 'Some might say this is an ugly painting.'

One of the Amazons gave an anticipatory half-smile, revealing uneven teeth. The sight was reassuring. She would never match Walt in the tooth department.

'Doesn't it depend on what you consider is ugly? The painter wanted to record the moment when the skater, his own mind in turmoil, puts his arm around another human being. To comfort? In solidarity? Human contact of the kind painted here can't be ugly.'

She felt her thoughts falling into place and the elation when the click and shuffle of those conclusions arranged themselves into intelligible speech.

Slap went the diminishing wash against *Elizabetta*'s sides.

'No, it can't be ugly,' said Kim Athos, adding, 'Nicely put.'

The Amazons prepared to escort Sophie off the *Elizabetta* when he said, 'No need. Miss Knox will be staying for lunch.'

The Amazons did not like this. Not one bit. Scooping up the remnants of the packaging from around *The Skaters*, they exited with a synchronised glare intended to kill.

'Now,' said Kim Athos, posed in front of the painting, 'I want to find out about you.'

The hotel close to the marina was not as luxurious as the one in Milan (astonishing how it had only taken putting a toe in the water once to become addicted. Or, rather, critical). However, the muslin

338

curtains billowed agreeably in the late-afternoon breeze when she sat down at the table.

Notebook: *Kim Athos is rich enough not to care if he's liked or not. A sleek fox who knows what he wants.*

No bones at all about being nosy. Very nosy.

Over a lunch of dressed artichokes and grilled fish, Kim Athos had prised out the dossier of her life.

But she learnt something (the epiphanies were arriving thick and fast): if the instruction *always to tell the truth* had been hammered into you from the year dot, the finer skills of lying had had no opportunity to flourish. Thus, she wasn't very good at dodging interrogation.

Your father was a French patriot?

He was something of a hero.

He was killed during the war.

Yes.

You are searching for him.

Yes.

You have always been searching for him.

Yes.

'How troubling.' He refilled her wine glass. 'You should find your answers. Otherwise that sort of not knowing haunts one.' He handed her the glass. 'I've no idea what happened to my parents either. War leaves big gaps which, in my case, I fill with beautiful things. With paintings. Provided, of course, their provenance is clean. That's why I need someone like Christian Martin to check everything for me.'

She wondered how many hairdryers had made it possible to buy the *Elizabetta*.

'What do you think of your employer?'

'He's successful,' she replied.

'Is he selling many paintings?'

'I don't know enough to know what would be considered good rates for sales.'

'The first rule, if you wish to get on in life, is never to admit ignorance. One, you've been working at the gallery and must have picked up some knowledge. Two, it's bad practice. It would be better to say that you never comment on your employer's position.' He raised an eyebrow. 'Was it you who packed up *The Skaters*? It was very professional, if so.'

That was pleasing because it had been a painstaking process. Not least, the minute examination of frame, canvas, paint and labels. Plus the perusal of the documents, which she now had almost by heart.

During the packing, however, she had become aware of an anomaly. A name, 'Joshua Adams', which had been written in black ink on the bottom of the frame at the back. A name missing from the documentation.

He picked at the peach on his plate. 'You have to be careful when buying paintings.'

Astonished at her nerve, she picked up the phone by the bed and asked reception to put her through to Paris. (How she would pay for it, she would work out later.)

'Hello,' said Raf after only a couple of rings.
'It's Sophie. Sophie Morel.'
'I know who you are.' He sounded mellow.
'I shouldn't be ringing.'
'I shouldn't be drinking this beer.'
'I'm staying with a client in Brindisi. He's bought a painting but the name on the back, a Joshua Adams, does not appear in the documentation. Do you think it might have been looted?'
After a moment, Raf said, 'I do.'

In the morning, a taxi waited to take her to the station. To her surprise, it headed for the harbour, where a liveried crew member of the *Elizabetta* waited. She was, he informed her, to return on board.
'Before you say anything,' said Kim Athos when she was ushered into the stateroom. 'I've arranged it with Martin and he's agreed to let you come with me to Corfu to help to hang *The Skaters* in my villa.'
She glanced at her feet, angry at not being consulted, but intrigued all the same.
She heard herself say, 'Of course.' Obligingly. Obediently. (Not the finest hour in the history of the great enterprise.)
'There's everything you might need in the cabin you may use while on board, including your luggage,' he said. 'I'll see you at lunch.'
In the cabin, she touched the towels ranged in the tiny but well-appointed bathroom. They were

341

soft and beautifully laundered, totems of the world she was temporarily inhabiting. Looking into the mirror, she grinned. *Orphan finds herself on luxury yacht.*

Once again, she thought of Alice Knox and pity sent the faintest of tingles down her fingers. The lock-knit underwear. The Sunday blouse. The sad hat. Alice would probably never know the delight of a soft and dazzlingly white towel. Or soap such as this.

The *Elizabetta* got under way. Sophie searched out what she hoped was an unobtrusive spot on the deck and settled down. A white-flannelled Kim briefed the skipper. The Amazons took notes (crossly) on their clipboards. The sea was calm and unthreatening and the glistening water through which the *Elizabetta* was travelling acted as a magnet on her.

Here she was . . . she pictured herself from above, looking down. Hands in lap. Eyes narrowed against the light, the better to absorb the swish and slap of water; the subdued thud of the boat's engines; the cry of a single bird sounding like an outraged child.

Sensations difficult to catalogue. This encounter with sun, air and water made her feel weightless, paper thin. Liberated. She was being lifted out of herself into an experience approaching the ecstatic. Not religious, of course, but an experience that she sensed could change her.

She thought of Johnno.

He would understand about the first encounter with the strange and foreign. He would understand the response: a muddle of nerves and exhilaration.

She glanced at her watch. Possibly, Johnno would be walking the fields. Thinking over the timetable for the summer. Assessing. Ploughing a steady course on and off the tractor.

Perhaps he was holding his baby . . .

In a heartbeat, the glorious transcendental feelings were extinguished.

Love and loss were complicated. The life Johnno offered might not have worked for her. Perhaps *they* would not have worked for each other. But, brooding over what might have been, at this moment it was impossible to deny she yearned for him. For his tender touch. The pleasure of having been chosen. For an undertaking to share.

The *Elizabetta* continued her eastwards course and, presently, lunch was served under an awning to the sound of seabirds and the hiss of water.

The table was small. Even so, it was formally laid up. Dazzling in his whites, Kim Athos sat opposite her.

'Shall we get one subject out of the way? You're wondering if this,' he gestured to the *Elizabetta*, 'is a diversion to get you to sleep with me.'

Wedged under the table, Sophie's legs twitched with incipient cramp. *Hettie, you will never believe how these people go on* . . . Luxury yachts and sex the topic of lunchtime conversation. Unbelievable but fun. She thought of her own experience of sex. How little she knew. How much she knew. (One thought: if Osbert had talked more about sex, maybe he wouldn't have been driven to his dark deeds.)

'Don't most men and women wonder that about each other?'

He did not dismiss the observation. Which was nice of him. 'I believe they do. But I won't be pouncing on you.' He selected a prawn. 'In these and all matters, plain speaking is best.'

She trod with care. 'I'm disappointed, of course. But . . . it would be unprofessional.'

That amused him. 'I'm in a position where I don't have to mind if it's unprofessional or not.' The smile had gone. 'I aired the subject because I did not wish you to feel you had to avoid me. Or to lie awake worrying about it.'

'That's very . . . kind.'

Relief. Plus a spear of cramp in her right calf.

He gave a crack of laughter. 'Doesn't mean to say I don't like congenial companionship.'

The prawns were plump, pink and salty. She ate them with mayonnaise spooned up from an earthenware dish. 'The mayonnaise is wonderful.' He raised an eyebrow. 'You see, in England we have salad cream. It's not like this.'

'That's a relief. I've heard bad things.' When she shot him an alarmed look, he added, 'About salad cream. That's what we're talking about, isn't it?'

Good food, sun and sea must deflect anyone's thoughts to a kinder, most positive slant.

'Mr Athos—' she began.

He interrupted, 'Your first experiences of new foods and travel are magical. Obviously they only happen once, so you must concentrate. Are you a good sailor?'

'I've no idea.'

It turned out she was, which was fortunate. The journey took several hours and the sea grew choppier. When the island of Corfu hoved into sight, the skipper cruised around towards its coastline and set his course to Kalami Bay.

Skirting bays and the beaches on whose rocky outcrops perched houses overlooking an intense blue sea, or half hidden behind olives and scrubby trees, the *Elizabetta* sailed on.

Glued to the unfolding island panorama, Sophie leant on the rail. Kim came and stood beside her. She turned her head to look at him and inhaled musky aftershave. 'Are you Greek?'

'By adoption,' he answered easily enough, but she was aware that he had turned wary. 'The island seduced me. People, the land. History. That's important, you know. If you feel about a place in that way, then it can teach you things. The gods wrap themselves around you.'

Unsure if he was sincere or not, she asked, 'Where did you come from originally?'

She was aware of one of the Amazons hovering behind them.

He was clipped. 'The war displaced people. I was one of those displaced people.'

345

As soon as he moved off, the hovering Amazon pinned her down. 'We don't ask personal questions of Mr Athos,' she said. 'He doesn't like it.'

This Amazon was very slender, controlled-looking and had heavily glossed lips. When she spoke, they almost refused to open.

She supposed that the dictate of forbidding questions was only possible if you had a lot of money. Yes, that must be it. How ridiculous. And how telling. Even in the second half of the twentieth century, the rational century, a sufficiently rich man could behave like a medieval emperor.

The Amazon retreated below deck.

Sophie returned to her contemplations. So Kim Athos had something to hide. Modern potentates – Hitler – had successfully hidden horrors by creating a state apparatus where questions were dangerous. In Russia, Stalin obviously did the same. It made sense that, if you ruled the Kingdom of Hairdryers and Vacuum Cleaners and wished to make money, stacks of it, and to hide the short-cuts, then questions would have to be banned.

How extraordinary was the ocean – spanning a spectrum from the grey-green Sussex sea to the radiantly coloured water at which she now gazed.

She was in danger of becoming a little obsessed by it.

Villa Athos had been built into the hillside over-looking the sea.

It had a wide veranda morphing into a terrace

on the seaward side, and many windows. The cluster of olive trees and cypresses that guarded its north aspect, and its concealed drive meant it was both open to the sea and the elements and also shrouded in privacy.

Sophie was installed in one of the bedrooms with a magnificent sea view by Serafina, the house-keeper. 'You must ask me for anything you want. Anything,' she said. 'I am here to make you comfortable.'

To make *Sophie* comfortable? The notion of someone devoting themselves to her wellbeing was startling.

She circled the bedroom, sniffing.

The soap was scented, the sheets starched. A suggestion of the sea and of plants sifted through the window. The bed was huge and draped in muslin. The bath was heart-shaped. *That* would make Hettie laugh.

Hettie? Hettie had returned to her underworld. With a brave, martyr-like smile on her lips.

Dinner on the terrace was formal. A pot of roses occupied the centre of the table and candles were lit.

Kim did his best to make Sophie relax. He told her about his houses in Greece and Italy. And Paris. 'I've made a lot of money, which you will have observed, and I use it to furnish these houses. I search for the right paintings, the right furniture. It's a form of treasure hunt.' He gave a wry smile. 'Which makes up for many things.'

'Are all your houses as beautiful as this one?'

He didn't seem to mind being asked a question. If anything, he seemed touched. 'I think so.'

They discussed *The Skaters* and where in the villa he planned to hang it. Sophie found herself expressing surprise that he had chosen to bring the painting to Corfu.

'Forgive me, but the painting doesn't feel *southern*. Wouldn't the house in Paris suit it better?'

A long pause.

'I'm sorry,' she said. 'I've been warned not to ask questions of you. But it's difficult not to when I have so many to ask.' She ploughed on. 'But locating where a painting is best hung must be part of the joy of owning it?'

He ignored the last question. 'You think *The Skaters* should be hanging . . . for example . . . in a north-facing room.'

Astonished at her daring, Sophie said, 'Yes, I do.'

'I see.'

'Mr Athos, there's something else. There is a name on the frame that's not mentioned in the papers.'

Serafina arrived with the dessert, a bowl of sliced peaches mixed with grapes and cherries, which she placed on the table. He pushed the bowl towards her. 'Don't worry about that. It's accounted for.'

'But . . .'

He raised a finger. 'It's as I say. Help yourself.'

348

He watched her intently as she ate. 'Mr Athos, is there anything wrong?'

'No. There is much that is right.'

Glancing at her plate, she said, 'Those were delicious.'

She realised then that his smile was a source of his power – insofar as it invited anyone on whom it was bestowed to step into his magic circle. Her initial assessment had been wrong. Kim Athos was not a glossy, clever fox. The monarch of the hairdryer kingdom was a panther.

The grapes were black-skinned and musky and she helped herself to as many as she decently could. 'Which is your main home?'

'Wherever I am.'

Before she said good night, she nerved herself to ask, 'Could I know the arrangements for the return to Paris?'

He placed his napkin carefully beside his plate. 'You'll be here for a week,' he said. The powerfully attractive smile reached his eyes. 'I don't imagine that you'll mind.'

Sophie lay in the luxurious bed, nipped by thoughts and worries. Could she trust this man? Was there something about the set-up of which she should be wary?

What would you think? She addressed the dead Camille.

She thought of Linda. Hefted to Poynsdean like one of the marsh sheep. A girl who knew what she wanted. Willing to take on the traditional tasks.

Sailing pregnantly into the kitchen at Home Farm, then with a baby under her arm. Extracting a sponge cake from the doughty old range and banging it down on the table. *Cake up, everyone.*

Jealous? Yes. But also not. Sophie had been through all that so many times. The Home Farm kitchen was special. Reassuring. But if the choice was between staying in a villa perched on a Corfiot hillside (having sailed across a cerulean sea) and scrubbing cake tins, then there was no choice.

Did Johnno think of her? A little? Did he wish for her company when walking beside the river? Or watching the ducks over the marsh, or searching hedgerows for feathered, muddy eggs? Was there a crumb left over in his heart for her that Linda could not claim and bake into a cake?

Extraordinarily, thoughts of Sussex set a nostalgia trap. For the leafy, semi-putrid wetlands smells, the flights of those ducks, the river sounds where Camille had paced, for damp, tangled grass, for the mud that got everywhere and the piles of autumn leaves.

Yet again, the workings of her mind bewildered Sophie. In truth . . . truthfully? . . . she wanted to be nowhere else but where she was.

CHAPTER TWENTY-FIVE

'Mr Athos,' Serafina reported the following morning, 'has been called away on business. The hanging of the painting will take place when he returns.'

Kim Athos was away for most of the week and Sophie was left to her own devices. The staff were polite and had a trick of merging into the furniture. Anyway, she didn't speak Greek. In the morning, she sat on the beach, loving the strong sun on her skin and hot sand between her toes, thinking about Johnno. And then not.

Then, increasingly tanned and salty, she returned to the villa and the lunch laid out on the terrace, retreating afterwards to the library on the shady side of the house.

The Digbys approach to history had followed a wilfully idiosyncratic path, i.e. the history mistress had striven to omit any reference to Europe unless it was completely unavoidable. 'Europe is Abroad and I prefer to concentrate on the richness of our own island story.'

In Kim Athos's library were history texts written

in English or French, and she spent shaded, sleepy afternoons reading.

One volume predicted the troubled landmass of Europe rising from the ashes of Hitler's destruction. 'A moment of spiritual, moral and economic rebirth.'

Another detailed the post-war vengeance – rape, looting, murder, enslavement – that swept across Europe from east to west. 'Would populations who had experienced six years of organised atrocities and acute privations ever learn to again trust institutions?'

A question that would take years to answer.

She read on. Europe's women . . . now they were something. Scientists, doctors and political activists. Fighters who knocked down prejudice, sometimes violent prejudice, to achieve their ambitions in the public arena. In science. In literature. In medicine. In politics.

Poor Alice, she thought. *Poor* Alice, trapped within the mould-flecked Rectory rooms, dining all her married life off disappointment and unvented rage.

Magically, at four o'clock, Serafina appeared with a tray of cold mint tea and biscuits, returning punctually half an hour later to remove it. The first time, Sophie leapt to her feet and said she would take it to the kitchen. Serafina's cool response was: 'Please, this is my work.'

On his return, Kim Athos announced they were dining in a nearby village.

The evening blue of the sea. The white houses, the setting sun licking over walls, the smell of food cooking in bars and restaurants. The taverna tables running along a wooden pier overlooking the sea. The fairy lights running along the pergola. All enchanting.

'I must remember this,' she said out loud (without intending to). 'I must remember the details.' He glanced at her.

Grilled fish garnished with black olives arrived. It was bony but tasted of the sea and – Sophie entertained the mad idea – of freedom. Kim Athos said the wine was terrible, but it didn't matter.

Afterwards, they wandered for a time along the beach. Sophie did a little dance. 'I can't believe I'm here. *I can't believe it.*'

On the way back to the car, he took her hand. Her trapped fingers stiffened. 'No need to be alarmed. It's just companionship.'

She removed her hand. 'Mr Athos, I'm not your companion.'

That didn't faze him. He patted her arm. 'Quite right.'

That night, she lay in bed puzzling over the provenance of *The Skaters*. The name Joshua Adams did not fit into the official paperwork. An unwelcome question arose: was she dealing with, working for, men who were not quite straight in their dealings? Who might be crooks?

Then, as drowsiness crept in, she thought: no, that is unlikely.

The day before her departure for Paris, Sophie walked up the sloping path behind the villa. It was cloudy and very warm, the vegetation through which she passed cradling the heat.

At the top, the path levelled out beside an abandoned olive farm and she was hit by a crescendo of barking in the distance. Rounding a corner, she came across a compound surrounded by a wire fence where at least forty dogs of every breed, age and condition milled on a stained concrete floor.

At one end, three full-grown pines threw (much-needed) shade. Under one of them, a woman sat on a bench, surrounded by dogs fighting for her attention.

Dogs . . . black, brown, flashes of white, small, large, unkempt, scarred, the clatter of paws on the concrete. *Oh, Dog. You have left a wound. Not yet healed.*

The woman set down the terrier she had been stroking and walked over.

'Can I help you?' She spoke in English. An elderly-looking Alsatian padded over and took up a defensive position beside her. She switched into Greek and talked to him. 'I'm telling him you're not the enemy,' she said. 'You must be the woman at the Athos villa.'

'I suppose I am.'

'Don't look so surprised.' She unlatched the cage door. 'Everyone in the area knows about you. Come in.'

Inside, dogs milled around Sophie's legs, then quickly lost interest except for a black Labrador who stood to attention.

'That's Salome,' said the woman. 'And I'm Talia. I own this place and these are my children.'

'Rescue dogs?'

'They rescued me. You look thirsty.'

A glass of water was pressed into her hand, which she drank gratefully on the shaded bench. Talia sat back against the tree trunk and observed her dogs, occasionally calling one over to inspect their paws or ears. Each time she did so, she washed her hands in a bowl. 'I have to fight infection, day and night.'

'How many do you have?'

'Depends.' She extracted a packet of cigarettes from her pocket and lit up. 'Depends on how bad human behaviour is. Or how good it is in helping me to find them homes. Some are too sick and have to be destroyed.' She blew a kiss at Salome. 'You're not used to dogs?'

'I had one for a short time. I loved him. I would like another.'

Talia said, 'Ah,' as if Sophie had explained everything. Which, in a way, she had.

Talia's hair was unbrushed and her skirt was grubby. So were her feet. But she was beautiful – wildly, unkemptly so.

'It's true,' she said, interpreting Sophie's train of thought. 'I don't care what I look like. Nor should any woman be under that tyranny.'

355

Yes. Yes. Sophie agreed. The tyranny of beauty. But . . .

'Isn't it easy to say,' she said, 'if you're beautiful in the first place?'

Talia looked as though she might argue, but thought better of it. Instead she gave a stiff nod. Stroked the black Labrador.

'Thank you for the water.' Sophie got to her feet.

Talia looked up. 'Get away from the villa.' Sophie frowned. 'You don't understand the set-up. You need someone to give you the picture. Do you know what Kim Athos does? And don't tell me he makes electrical items.'

'He's been generous to me.'

'Of course he has. That's how it's done. 'But he's not a good person to be associated with.' Sophie must have looked bewildered. 'Pleading innocence is useless,' said Talia. 'Innocence is dangerous.'

'I'm leaving tomorrow.'

'Make sure that you do.'

Sophie started back down the path and for a long way she could hear the dogs barking.

Later, she mentioned her meeting with Talia to Kim. 'The mad dog woman,' he said.

'She didn't appear mad.'

Kim shrugged. 'She used to be married to the village mayor on the mainland, but she left him after she found out he was keeping a second family. Because she had influential contacts in Athens, he was forced to pay up after the divorce and she set up that place for dogs. She doesn't have many friends.'

'I don't think she's your friend,' said Sophie.

'Ah. She told you I was a bad person and warned you off me.'

Early the next morning, having packed her bag, Sophie made her way up to the dog compound. Talia was there on the bench, smoking peacefully.

'Your curiosity got the better of you. Or was your employer telling tales about the mad dog woman?'

'He's not my employer.'

'I see,' said Talia.

Sophie settled herself beside her. 'Can I ask some questions?'

Talia invited a white terrier onto her lap and it settled itself with a flurry of moulting white hairs. 'Karisma here will help with the answers. He's wise.'

The concrete floor of the compound was already hot underfoot. 'I gather you're not from here.'

Talia pursed her lips. 'Nor is your Mr Athos. Like me, he's an outsider. With plenty of money, but an outsider. Look and you'll see how carefully he's guarded. Think about it.'

'Forgive me, but how did you learn English?'

'I was lucky. My parents believed in education and had money to make it possible. They believed . . . I believe . . . that knowing how to speak a different language contributes to peace in the world.'

357

Sophie bent over and ran a finger down the back of a shaggy mongrel by her legs.

'You should always ask permission of a dog before you do that,' said Talia. 'You're lucky that Alexis is so good-natured.'

Sophie straightened up.

'You seem smart enough, but you're being slow. But then, men like Athos use the young like you who don't understand how criminals operate.' Her smile was enigmatic. 'You're not a criminal type, and if you associate with him there'll come a point when you'll have to make up your mind if you want to be drawn into his world or not.'

Sophie hastened to say, 'My job is in Paris. Not with him.'

Talia was inspecting Karisma for fleas. 'Don't take everything at face value. Not even his name. It sounds Greek but he's from Kosovo. He'll tell you he doesn't have any designs on you, but he does. Kim Athos doesn't seduce in the obvious way. He'll tell you that his money is made from electrical goods.' She blew out smoke. 'Some is, of course.'

What was she missing? 'I think you must know him well.'

Talia gave a rusty laugh. 'Would you like a story? You look as though you might. Once upon a time, there was a new young wife who loved her husband very, very much. All was well. She ran a good home and there were plenty of family meals and get-togethers and the husband was kind and attentive. Then, she discovered he had another wife in another town. She was so distraught that she fled from her home without ensuring that she could survive. Or taking legal advice. Stupid. A rich man found her, ill and almost starving, and helped her to shame the husband into making provision . . .'

'But he helped.'

'For a price.'

Did Sophie see?

She saw past distress and breakdown. She also saw that, for this woman, survival was conducted on a transactional basis.

'When you're ill and troubled, you're not very clear-sighted,' said Talia. 'After what she'd been through, it didn't matter to this woman very much what happened next.'

She seemed weary. Time to leave Talia to the life she had salvaged. Sophie got to her feet. 'Thank you.'

Talia leant back against the tree trunk and closed her eyes. 'Dogs are so much better than people. More loving and reliable. Remember that.'

On the way back down to the villa, Sophie tried to piece together the moral position of someone offering to help someone in trouble and then demanding to sleep with them.

After all, and after everything, *The Skaters* would be transported back to Paris. Or so Kim Athos informed her. He had taken her point that it was a painting that belonged in the north, but she was not to worry. Transport had already been arranged.

She was astonished. 'Would you like any more information?'

'No. All is as I wish it. I've spoken to Martin, who's expecting you back.'

He spoke with the ease of a man who had matters arranged for him by others every moment of the day. This, of course, did not make him a bad person.

Below them, a gardener moved around with a hose, and the smell of water on the already warm earth was like nothing else.

'About the name on the frame, would you like the gallery to check further?'

Smooth and easy as silk. 'No.'

She inhaled a shuddery breath. 'Are you sure, Mr Athos?'

'Quite sure.' He shoved a hand into his pocket. 'Enough on the subject.'

Just before leaving, she came up to the terrace to say goodbye. Leaning on the balustrade, which had become a favourite thing. Goodbye to the green and lovely island. Goodbye olives and pines. Goodbye extraordinary Mediterranean. Thank you, thank you, for letting me see you.

This place, this house, had been set into its wild, pine-scented context with care and thought. The interior was beautiful, too. To be gifted with that touch, that ability to predict the result of decisions taken on paper, to *wish* to do the best for a landscape suggested a good person was in charge.

Kim joined her and together they looked at the blue quilt of the sea.

'You distrust me,' he said. 'And I'm sorry for it. Not, I'm afraid, that it matters what you think, but I would rather we didn't say goodbye on that basis.'

She stepped away. 'It's not for me to trust or distrust.'

'Maybe you're right about the trust. But I would like to be your friend. I could offer you a sort of protection and you could offer me . . . honesty.' He tapped the coping stone. *De da de dum.* 'Your future. Have you considered it?'

Paris. Her father. Not Poynsdean. Not Johnno. The gallery?

'My future's at the gallery for the time being.'

'Where do you think that will take you? A precarious job in a city that is still picking itself up from the war. Do you know about the shanty town at Ivry? Soup kitchens. The lack of sanitation in the wrecked houses. Let me be blunt. I suspect you've no money and lack powerful connections.'

'People manage. I'll manage.'

'You think I'm rude.'

'Yes.'

'Very rude?' He smiled and his smile was kind. 'No need to answer. Sit down, Sophie. Don't worry, I'll see that you get away in time for the ferry. I've a proposition.' She settled into a chair plump with cushions and made for languor. 'I live all over the place but come to Paris frequently,

361

and I would like someone to accompany me to events. Someone who would look good and take an interest. I don't want you in my bed and I would pay well. It would be something that would fit in well with the gallery.'

A bell sounded faintly in her head.

'Do you think it might have been looted?'

'I do.'

Was this part of a negotiation over *The Skaters* and its incomplete provenance? The endgame being silence on behalf of all parties?

Elderly men sat on their yachts and companion girls sat with them in the sun and drank champagne. That was one kind of transaction.

Osbert Knox preaching that the relationship between a man and woman 'should be conducted along the highest principles'. (Light fracturing through the north window of Poynsdean church. Osbert's words spinning out from the pulpit. Blank expressions in the congregation, who didn't have much idea what he was droning on about.) That was another.

What to think?

Kim Athos crossed a lazy leg over the other and sat further back in his chair. 'Go back to Paris and mull it over.' He accepted a fruit juice from the tray offered by one of the Amazons. 'It's easy to be wary. Easier still to think the worst of people and their motives. So easy that it becomes a habit. You must never be afraid of kindness. Or friendship. It's worth learning. Worth thinking about.'

362

CHAPTER TWENTY-SIX

Paris?

Returning was not as exciting as Sophie had anticipated. It was hot and her shoes pinched. The streets through which she trudged with her suitcase appeared meaner and tougher, less welcoming.

The room at number 66 was covered in dust, and the volume of noise from Weber Métaux seemed particularly intrusive. For a long time, she sat on the bed and thought about money and jobs. Analysing what exactly she was doing.

Just like she had done so many times at the Rectory.

She thought, too, about luxury. How very agreeable it was.

She took herself to a phone booth and rang Raf Maurice at the Bureau. It seemed the natural thing to do. He's away on business, said Mademoiselle Axel. There was no doubting a certain hostility in her manner.

Christian Martin welcomed her back with a nod and several tasks. To be done *vite*. Walt swung into the basement, said 'Hi,' and vanished.

She informed Hettie about Kim Athos's offer. 'What do you think?'

'Are you sure he hasn't got designs on you? Base Nature and all that. Or he wants to make you a captive on his boat and sail around the world without ever docking?'

'I don't *think* so.'

'No sex?'

'No sex.'

There was a pause while both worked out if, based on their (limited) respective experiences, this was a viable prospect.

Hettie sounded far away. 'How's the post office book?'

Sophie grimaced. 'Depleted.'

'Precisely,' said Hettie in her practical voice. 'Don't you think you could earn extra money doing this which would help the search for your father?'

'Het . . .' Small panic. 'He might change his mind about sleeping with me.'

'There are worse things,' said Hettie.

Sophie was not sure that she'd heard correctly. 'Worse things?'

'My life,' confessed Hettie with a catch in her voice.

'Thank the Lord you're back,' said Walt when, eventually, they did catch up. 'Are you the same Sophie that went away?'

'Actually, no. I've been corrupted by the high life.'

They were out at a 'honey of a restaurant' he had discovered in Montmartre. 'I need your fresh, untarnished taste buds,' he said. 'We will be eating *racasse* and I want your best, your most unselfish opinion.' He peered at Sophie. 'You know you should wear your hair back from your face. Stop hiding under those bangs . . .'

Sophie supposed that by 'bangs' he meant her fringe.

The 'honey of a restaurant' did much to restore her spirits and she sounded out Walt on Kim Athos's offer.

Walt examined the fish on his plate. 'I wonder if a little more seasoning would be better?' He ate a mouthful. 'No, this is fine.' Without a pause, he segued, 'I think his offer stinks and I shall have to keep an eye on you. He has designs, Sophie. He's netting you in.'

No designs on her body, Kim Athos had said, and she believed him. Yet, as she roll-called the things with which he surrounded himself – brilliant bathrooms, linen sheets, paintings, wine, food, blonde Amazons in green-and-white uniforms – doubt set in. These were the visible manifestations of a man who understood how to gratify the senses.

Maybe Walt had a point.

'I love you, Walt.' She did too. 'What are you going to do about the food writing and your life?'

'My father's coming over next month. I'm planning a mano a mano. Honest. Direct. Firm.'

'As long as he doesn't have a heart attack after the heart-to-heart.'

'Don't.'

A speck of salt burned on her lip and she removed it. 'In Paris . . .' she found herself whispering the magic mantra, 'in Paris anything is possible. He'll listen to you.'

Walt cast her a look. *Sweet fool.*

Walt became serious. He looked down at his plate. 'Tell me about Hettie.'

'Aha.'

Jealousy was a spear, she realised, expressly fashioned to tear into the softest places. It was clear. Quite clear. Hettie and Walt had instantly discovered something in each other that they had not found in her.

It only took a small shift in focus and she reverted to old childhood habits of calling up the downbeat feelings, the wounding words. *You don't count.*

But. But. She loved Hettie, and Walt should be told about the beautiful mind of her friend. The kindness. The courage. The loyalty. (She would leave out the agonies of the hair that frizzed.) The ambition to live well. How she had saved Sophie from despair, time and time again.

'Tell me every detail,' he commanded. What Hettie said. What made her tick. Her favourite meal (to be answered carefully as the answer would be vital). Who were these ghastly parents of hers?

Had Hettie, by any chance, mentioned him?

366

She had, said Sophie, marvelling that such a small answer should give such grand pleasure.

'And this . . . person she married who shuts her up in a horrible house and insists on brown soup for dinner and has never heard of olive oil . . .' He picked up a toothpick. Snapped it in half. 'Why?'

'It was expected. It's very hard for girls from a certain background to find their independence. It's the way it is.'

Various expressions, most of them incredulous, chased over Walt's face. 'You must rescue her from this horrible fate.'

Dear Walt . . .

A thought slid snakily into her mind. It wasn't a good one. In fact, it was shaming.

Could Walt, who had plans and, almost certainly, money, be an alternative to Johnno? Walt, who was destined to live comfortably (with vacuum cleaner, washing machine, a porch and a car in the drive) in Boston and to become a successful food pundit. Anyone who shared his life would spend time in a kitchen, sharing the secrets of cuisine. Remembering Paris. Understanding that the secret to the luminous brilliance of French food lay in its chameleon qualities. 'Oh yes,' this person would say as they sat down to a cosy dinner of *loup de mer* stuffed with fennel, 'in French cuisine the basic themes can be confected and re-imagined in any number of ways.'

'Walt, would you consider . . . ?'

He put down his knife and fork. 'Are you chatting me up?'

An agreeable, magical even, way of life. 'Yes, I think I am.'

If she gave full reign to this new-found fierce and selfish ambition to survive well and comfortably, she could cut Hettie off at the start.

It would not take account of anyone else, let alone the friend she loved.

It ignored the stated principle of personal independence.

Walt smiled. Fussed with his napkin.

'Actually, Walt, I'm not chatting you up.'

'Not even a little bit?'

She shook her head.

She must think of altruism – and the balance between unleashing desires and servicing them. Think of what she owed Hettie. Her limitless generosity wrapped up into one sweet and funny package. That hair. A yearning for what was true. A contrary yearning to do what was proscribed by her family and by generations of biddable women.

Hettie's dear face held in her mind's eye. A deep breath. 'It's not me who should rescue Hettie.'

Across the table, Walt tried out a warning frown – *go no further* – which failed. Instead, his face lit up.

'It's not me who should rescue Hettie,' she repeated. 'Is it, Walt?'

*　*　*

Kim Athos must have rung Christian Martin and told him that Sophie had discussed the paperwork for *The Skaters*.

Christian cornered Sophie packing up a consignment in the basement. 'You were *the courier*, for God's sake. What were you thinking? These deals are complicated. Loose tongues jeopardise deals.'

'Since the name wasn't listed in the papers, I thought I should say.' She added, 'I think it was a Jewish name.'

'It's all accounted for as everything would be from this gallery. It's not your place to question, certainly not to enter into discussions with a client,' he said. 'You were interfering in matters beyond your remit.'

'But the name was there.'

He beat a shaky hand down on the packing table. 'The name is irrelevant. Understand?'

Irrelevant.

He kept on talking. Mouth opening. Shutting. The slight shudder in the left hand. Still furious.

Listening to him, she searched for the man who had gone to war with her father. Who had – possibly – executed a *collabo*.

In the corridor, Emile belted out an instruction. A crate was dragged towards the lift.

'Understand you do not have the right to discuss a painting with a client. You refer questions back to me. Always.'

'Monsieur . . .'

'Do you want to keep this job or not?'

'Yes . . . I do.'

All true. She did. She wanted to stay in this building which spoke so powerfully to her, to be part of the gallery, study the paintings.

He loomed above her. Impeccably dressed as usual but, in this encounter, she caught extra driven-ness. An iron in the soul – against which she was pitting herself.

It was frightening and she was unsure.

'Monsieur Martin, did you have this gallery during the war?'

An impatient, 'Why?'

'Only . . . that it must have been hard to do business.'

A (very) guarded reply: 'The gallery was owned by someone else then.'

Sophie trembled and did her best to hide it. She was balancing on stepping stones across a marshland – think Poynsdean's treacherous panne and low-lying wetlands – in which was buried hidden and disturbing information.

In every way possible, she ought now to be confronting Christian Maurice. After all, it was her stated quest. *Did you know my father? Who killed him?*

Be careful, said Raf.

To ask would mean leaving the gallery and starting over. To ask would be to finish what had just begun.

Instead, she leapt from marsh onto dry, hard earth.

'Monsieur Martin, would it be better . . .' She took a deep breath. 'Would it not be better if I learnt about the paintings?'

The question appeared to defuse his anger. '*Les femmes. Les jeunes femmes*,' he muttered, without malice but wearily. 'Are you a feminist, mademoiselle?'

'Yes, I am, monsieur.'

'You'd be better off having babies.'

Apparently, this was not a joke.

Once upon a time – if Raf was correct, round about the time that she was born – this man had been a patriotic bandit who'd taken to the streets to defend his occupied city. A street *résistant* who'd fought with men, women and children. Perhaps, then, he had been open to new ideas. Perhaps he had drunk Monacos, a disgusting-sounding mixture of beer and grenadine, on the Left Bank. Perhaps he had been addicted to jazz – *un véritable zazou* – haunting the Café de Cluny or Le Petit Q?

Now? Now he was preoccupied, irritated, weary. Neatly dressed with burnished shoes. Papers all in order and records meticulously kept (except for the Jewish name). Doors locked on secrets. Glass polished. Dust banished.

It occurred to her that war could dull ambition, murder the desire to experiment, trigger a craving to live a boring life. Looking at him, it was hard to see how the flame of liberty and action had once burnt brightly.

His mood changed in a flash when she informed

him of Kim Athos's proposal, and she was back in favour. 'Ah, this could be to our advantage. You could bring in some business. You will accept and you must keep your eyes and ears open for potential clients.'

She tackled Walt. 'The gallery's literature makes a point of its honest-as-the-day-is-long policy. Is that correct?'

'Could be. Could not be.'

They were in the basement, Walt watching Sophie toil – 'Sorry, can't help, *really* useless at that sort of thing' – over packing up the exquisite *Interior at Ramatuelle*, which depicted an open window, a Turkish rug thrown over a table and a vase of peonies.

'Where's that going?'

'Marseilles. It will look at its best there. The light.'

'So, now we're the expert. Do you know Marseilles?'

She grinned. 'You know the answer to that.'

After work, she checked the change in her purse. Not that much. But sufficient. 'Walt, come with me to the Jardin du Luxembourg. I can buy you an ice cream or a coffee.' He hesitated and she slipped an arm around his shoulders. 'Think of all the painters who've painted the gardens.'

'When will you realise,' he said crossly, 'that I don't care about paintings.'

The paths were already summer dry and dusty. It had not rained for some time and leaves were falling in protest.

They paced down one path. Up another. Children ran about in packs. Every so often a parent or a nanny or an au pair called in the high voice that comes with anxiety: 'Don't go out of sight.' A group of musicians in skimpy outfits sang sad *chansons*.

'So, I'm today's sounding board. What are we talking about?'

'*The Skaters.*'

'Thought so,' Walt said. 'Taking long shots here: did the papers given to Athos specify who sold *The Skaters* to the gallery?'

She paged back through her mental notes. Painted in Aachen, sold by a gallery in Munich to the Abrahms family in Paris in 1925. Then nothing. A nothing which, if questioned, was always explained by the war.

As the sun settled over the city, they sat on a cast-iron bench, drank bitter coffee and talked over the war. Paris's war. In the past but still present and everywhere in the city. A vast, dark, radioactive shadow. Hunger and destruction and retribution. The Jewish population taken away. Think of the terrible *Vel d'Hiv* . . . Walt described what had happened in the mass round-up. The result? The Jewish Marais was emptied and an underworld of traitors, liars and murderers emerged to claim their pound of flesh. Then the Resistance formed – communists, socialists, royalists and realists – who hid in the alleys, street labyrinths and double-entry buildings. Fighting back. Furious with the invaders and their country's situation.

373

'It was people like my father who prevailed.'

Walt smiled very sweetly at her. 'If you like.'

They returned to the subject of *The Skaters*.

'There was looting during the war. And afterwards. Particularly of well-to-do Jewish homes. Ask my father, who kept tabs on all this from across the pond,' said Walt darkly.

'So . . . so . . . Christian Martin could be handling looted paintings.'

Long silence. A deep sigh. 'I must be careful what I say. I have no proof. All I can say is that I know the sort of people who work in the art market.'

She gestured with both hands. 'Tell me . . . ?'

'The art world is as it is,' he said. 'Unsentimental. Some in it consider paintings more important than people. They would have noted the Resistance fighting in the streets and occupied houses, quite a few abandoned with all the stuff still inside. The owners weren't likely to return. Rich pickings.'

It's an old story, she would write later in the notebook. *Go to war and return with treasure.*

Sophie continued: 'Walt, I have an idea that Christian might have known my father, during the war. Through the street fighters.'

'Jeez. That's something.'

'But I'm not sure.'

'Is that a creepy coincidence or what?'

Before they parted for the evening, Walt favoured Sophie with his sternest look.

'You believe that Martin knew your father. Right? Possibly fought with him. Have you tackled him?'

Raf had pointed out that the mind placed obstacles in the way of achieving a long-held goal. She shook her head.

'You're as bad, and as weak as I am, Sophie Knox.'

CHAPTER TWENTY-SEVEN

Soon after her return to Paris, Sophie was contacted by a women called Toinette who, she said, had been instructed by Kim Athos to advise.

'On what?'

Toinette was astonished. 'On your clothes, of course. Mr Athos asked that I get you ready.'

Toinette was no beauty, which didn't matter because she presented herself as if she were. Ash blonde, scented and immaculate, she was somehow preserved in the aspic of what was expected of a French woman of a certain age. No explanations were offered as to her relationship with Kim. Mistress, friend, employee? Sophie didn't ask.

What Toinette did make clear was her programme of shopping and fittings. A military operation, as Sophie described it to Walt, who looked disapproving.

Whether she wanted them or not, Sophie ended up with hats, high-heeled shoes and three dresses reminiscent of the ones worn by the betoqued gazelles at Dior. Pink, blue and what Toinette called *dernier cri nu* (which was, in fact, beige).

376

They were sleeveless and narrow-waisted with bell-shaped skirts. She felt at least thirty-five wearing them.

A glorious green duster coat was the only thing that found favour.

Parked in front of many mirrors (Alice would have had a fit at their size and number) and subject to the attention of the fitters, Sophie was recruited into a world of deep-pile carpets, ruffles, expensive scent, and the hushed worship of cut and material that acted as the gatekeepers to corseted, controlled female beauty.

She thought of the Left Bank girls in their drainpipe trousers and red lipstick. Longingly. Hungrily. Then she thought of Simone de Beauvoir's distinction between the biographical sex a woman is born with and the instant social and historical construction of herself from that moment onwards.

Toinette gave her lengthy tuition on how to wear these clothes. *Stomach in. Hunch a little.* At the beautician's, her face was massaged and her eyebrows shaped. Thence to the hairdresser, who said, 'That fringe is a disaster.'

Sophie was also instructed by Toinette never to eat lunch.

There was nowhere in the bedsit to put the new clothes. No problem, declared Walt and whisked Sophie to the nearest flea market. 'Buy this.' 'This' being an iron rail which he slung between the chest of drawers and the bedhead. It's good to know I have some uses, he said, and she wasn't sure if he was joking or not.

Sophie took time to examine her new face. What had emerged? The eyebrows appeared to enlarge her eyes, which was very welcome. The swept-back hair chiselled away the semi-finished aspect from her schoolgirl countenance. To what did it all add up?

She had no idea.

She did protest at one thing. Whatever Toinette's strictures, the beautician's coral lipstick was ageing. 'No way. It makes me look haggard,' she said, pressing it onto Toinette. The plucked eyebrows climbed up. 'No buts,' said Sophie and dropped it into Toinette's handbag.

'As you will,' said Toinette, anxious to return to her apartment which, she informed Sophie, was furnished entirely in chartreuse. '*Bonne continuation.*'

The first outing.

Put on torture underwear. Slide into dress. Paint face.

Stroke on foundation. A smoothed layer, hardening into the glossy patina of a puppet's face.

Was this Sophie Morel?

The event was a champagne *vernissage* at a rival art gallery – all plate glass and white paint – held for an artist who painted seascapes in a Cubist style. They were brightly coloured, attractive and popular.

'What do you think of them?' asked Kim, who was wearing a white linen suit.

378

He had his hand under her elbow and was doing a skilful steering job.

Rockpooling, le Lavandou, 1955. An out-of-proportion seashell reposed on a sandy beach. In the distance, two squarish females trawled rockpools with nets. The colours were eye-watering.

Finisterre, 1952. Square rocks, a bright green sea, a rectangular rock-strewn beach. A yellow sun.

A woman squealed, '*Chérie!*'; a glass was dropped; expensive scent wafted around Sophie.

'They're decorative,' she said. 'And nostalgic if you love those places. And fun.'

'I think there may be a "but".'

'Not really. They are what they are.'

'Never a truer word,' said Kim. 'But I think what you mean is that they don't go that deep. Luckily our dear artist has plenty of rich friends.'

He steered her through the crowd, introducing her here and there, and it pleased her that her French was now up to speed. Kim had asked her to converse agreeably – and that she must do.

'They're not interested in me,' she said eventually. 'Why should they be?'

'Make them be.'

They were interested in Kim. Of course.

He read her thoughts. 'I have money,' he explained – as if it needed explaining. 'But you might well turn into a beauty, which has almost as much power attached to it.'

After a moment, she said, 'I don't think it does, and I will never be beautiful.'

379

He gave one of his smiles. 'Depends on what you consider beautiful. And it also depends if you *wish* to be beautiful. Then you will understand power.'

Walt was also at the *vernissage*. If you have a father in the business, it's easy to wangle invitations, he said. Every so often, he came up behind her and hissed into her ear that he was keeping watch.

'Does he ever leave your side?' asked Kim, irritated.

'He's my friend.'

She returned to the bedsit in the Marais still tasting the champagne and smoked salmon canapés and smelling of the heavenly soap from the ladies' powder room.

The second outing with Kim was to a dinner given by the Duchesse of Auvergne, to which Sophie wore the pink dress and swept up her hair. 'It was more of a banquet,' she recounted to Hettie on the phone. 'It had *ten* courses.'

'*Nor!*'

Ten courses, candelabra the size of a cathedral, silver, crystal and staggering flower arrangements. Afterwards there was a *musicale*, from which, Sophie noticed, many of the male guests fled. 'Probably,' said Hector de la Crochais, '*une cocotte* awaits.'

Thank God for Hector and his mixture of scandal and philosophy. And for his matter-of-fact take on sex. 'Now that the brothels have been closed, the women operate differently. In the old days, you visited establishments like la Maison des Nations, whose rooms were rigged up to be different countries. Austria one night, Italy the next. If you were a railway buff, there was a room mocked up like a railway carriage and, in between exertions, you could watch the countryside flash past. These days one must make different arrangements.'

He was both pensive and expansive. 'It's just luck which side of the blanket you land on. Some of those *grandes cocottes* would have made excellent queens, and vice versa.' His sigh exuded nostalgia in waves. 'Have I told you about la Belle Otero? Daughter of a gypsy. Made millions lying on her back, but gambled them away. Her German lover used to summon her to bed with a substantial jewel. But . . .' he shrugged, 'she died in poverty not so long ago.'

'So, diamonds are not always a girl's best friend,' said Kim.

'If she had held on to them,' said Sophie, discovering that she could be wry, 'they would have been.'

Hector giggled. 'Quite right, *ma chère*. I like your sensible approach.' When Kim moved away, he bent over and said into her ear, 'Is he your lover yet?'

Sophie took a step back. Sharpish. 'No. That's not our relationship at all.'

'The dress suggests otherwise.'

381

She felt desperately uncomfortable. 'Please don't.'

He was too habituated to this life, and knew so little of her, to truly care. 'Then you must make your way by other means. And ignore what will be said about you.'

The flicker of massed candles caught her eye as he moved off.

Kim's hand was under her elbow, guiding her to the coffee tray. 'A lot of people want to meet you.'

They did. Smart and, this time, curious. They asked questions. The women's manicured nails clicked on their frosted glasses. The men exuded drifts of aftershave and cigarettes.

At the end of the evening, Kim gave her a lift and instructed the chauffeur to stop by the river. 'We must walk. Walk off all the grubbiness of money and champagne.'

'But you like money.'

'I do. Very much. But once you have it, you must be careful that life does not become dull. And you don't become dulled by it.'

She couldn't imagine this, and his switch to melancholia surprised her.

'Are you not satisfied? You have so much.'

'Yes, I have much. Some want family, some power and some want money, as I did, so I could have the things that I do have.'

'Well, then,' she said.

She thought of Alice and Osbert. They had never

had anything except privation with which to make do. They had to build on having nothing. Insanely, cleverly, they turned the necessity for eating Spam rather than an excellent Fray Bentos beef pie into a philosophy of willing sacrifice to God. (Or, at least, Osbert had.)

Kim stood close to the river. 'It never does to outlive your own optimism. Or to run out of will to succeed,' he said. 'One day I'll do so. Then it's time for the end.'

'That's ridiculous,' she said, unable to agree. A little outraged that he was so careless of life. 'If you have everything, you have a duty to love what you have. Even if you are in a wheelchair.'

'A child speaks.'

Again, he placed a hand under her elbow, pushing her towards the water.

'Take a look.'

She was forced to look down to the water, which was punctuated by the reflections from a car headlight or a building.

'It wouldn't be so bad,' he said in her ear. 'Just jump in; a few minutes of discomfort and then it's over.'

She raised her head. 'I don't chose to do so and I don't wish to do so.'

'I agree. If you have most things in life, you have a duty to relish being alive. All those things I talked to you about. Remember? But when you no longer have them, then it is different.'

The melancholy deepened.

383

This was stupid. 'What *do* you want from me?'

There was a faint hiss and bubble of water, murmured exchanges from people passing by.

He didn't answer but, in a flash, she got it. He craved her youth and the luxury of the years that lay ahead – which he no longer had.

She understood. And she also understood that the rich man could weep out of sight.

'Don't look so alarmed, Sophie.' He touched her cheek. 'You're safe with me.'

He was more complicated, less straightforward than she had reckoned. He didn't want sex, or so he said. But he seemed to want *her. For God's sake*, said Walt, *what did I tell you? The man's a pervert. And a good thirty years older than you.*

Two days later, Kim took her to the opera where they sat in a box, ate lobster sandwiches in the intervals and listened to Violetta dying spectacularly in the arms of her lover.

The chauffeur picked them up and Kim ordered him to head for the Marais. 'I shall be out of Paris for a while.' He placed an envelope between them on the seat.

The envelope was white, oblong and stuffed. It appeared to stare up at her and she averted her gaze to look out of the window.

'Till I'm back,' he said. 'I shall ask what you've spent it on.'

The money was a down payment to buy her soul. A transaction Alice would recognise, as someone who had also agreed to be bought –

although for far less. No money for Alice. Only Spam and Osbert.

It was an arrangement that put her into boxy silk dresses and hats that made her look thirty-five. An arrangement that dictated how she voiced her opinions. How she made her way through the cutlery of ten courses.

Whereas she craved the flat pumps and black trousers of the not yet twenty-year-old. She wanted her ponytail to swing unimpeded to the music in the streets and her jumper to be tight. She wanted her mind to spark, to challenge and to reject. She wanted to eat *frites* from a rolled-up newspaper.

'Mr Athos . . .' With effort, she looked directly at him. 'This arrangement is not right for me. I'm sorry.'

He rolled his eyes. 'I thought this might happen.'

'There must be hundreds of women who would like to be your companion.'

'Yes, but I asked you.'

They drove along the Quai des Tuileries.

To live ambitiously. To have independence of mind and body. Those were the ideas hammered out during the miserable Digbys and Rectory years.

Was there always a gap between principle, considered and settled on, and its actual application? She supposed there must be.

The car purred through the streets. Silence inside it. The chauffeur braked at junctions and shifted gears with professional ease.

385

The Paris streetscape through which they were travelling was now familiar to her. Money? It was easy to stick to principles if you had it.

The contents of the envelope would probably pay her rent. Calmness and boldness were necessary: *Mr Athos, this is an unhealthy partnership*. 'You need someone far more *au fait*.'

She had bottled it. Her cowardice made her angry.

'I agree,' he said.

'Then, thank you for the very excellent evenings and I hope your trip goes well.'

At that, he smiled. Very nicely. Very kindly. Very understandingly. Very cunningly. 'But I asked *you* to accompany me, not someone more *au fait*. I like that you are an ingenue. That your opinions are not yet formed. I look forward to having an input into them.'

This time she was quite clear. 'I would have listened. Of course. But I wouldn't have let you influence what I believed in.'

'Inform your opinions, then.' He smiled. 'You have much to learn, Sophie.' He was very gentle. 'Is your change of heart anything to do with the problem of *The Skaters*?'

'Yes and no.'

'Then we must certainly see each other again to discuss it.'

'You might not like what I think about it.'

He turned his head to look at her, bestowing that beneficent, inclusive smile. 'We would probably agree. I find people do. Reconsider while I'm away . . . despite what I said the other night, life is so interesting, you know. There's music, colour, wine and sensation. I'm offering you a chance to keep yourself in rent, to learn, to find out what you want to find out and, yes, to have some fun.'

She wasn't sure, but she thought the tip of the chauffeur's ear had turned pink.

Music, colour, wine and sensation. Sticking to her guns would cost her in regrets. 'Thank you but I won't change my mind.'

Kim leant back in his seat. 'Then I must let you go.'

The car halted outside 66 rue de Turenne. 'Goodbye, Mr Athos.' She got out of the car. 'Thank you.'

He leant forward to speak to her. 'Ask Martin to get in touch. About the painting.' The final rider. 'You're being foolish,' he said.

The car picked up speed and was soon out of sight. Clutching her bag, she looked up into the Parisian evening sky and took a calming breath.

The great enterprise was back under her control.

Notebook: *To sell a soul for a pair of high heels and a crumpled pink sleeveless dress. (Not forgetting the money for her rent) To be enticed, via deep-carpeted, scented boutiques, into a milieu where the talk was of money and* cocottes. *Where the art mattered and millionaires were kings.*

'So that's that,' she informed Walt. 'I'm sorry but not.'

'Good. You were in danger of becoming a kept clothes horse.' He gave a wintry smile. 'One thing always leads to another.'

'You're too young to be so cynical.'

'Trust me, I'm not. You were a project. Just like a hairdryer.'

Sophie laughed uproariously.

To celebrate her release from the harem, Walt and Sophie took a trip to the Left Bank to Chez Francis. Now savvier in dealing with different Parisian milieux, Sophie donned her old skirt and Hettie's (far too warm for the summer) jumper over the cone-shaped brassiere. This was to baptise it anew. Even with her startlingly pointy bosom, she felt able to breathe deeply. Differently. With a lighter spirit.

Walt was invariably late, and she was there first and chose a table towards the back. Regretted it because of the cigarette smoke but didn't quite have the nerve to move. Instead, she asked for a *citron pressé*.

'This is fun,' said Walt when he arrived, placing a white camellia in front of Sophie. 'They were being sold by a woman in the street who looked ill. Very Traviata.'

'That's the opera I saw.'

Walt explained the camellia was associated with Marie Duplessis, a beautiful courtesan (the opera was based on her life) who succumbed to tuberculosis aged twenty-three. He gestured expansively. 'It sums up Paris. Or the French, because

388

she died with her husband and her lover holding her hands. But they are also Paris . . .' Walt pointed to a couple of men. 'Hot intellectuals.'

Sophie peered at them. One of them was small, the other rangy. Neither wore a tie (of course) and both had nicotine-stained forefingers. Both were holding forth to a circle of girls who were dressed in a uniform of black trousers and flat shoes.

Was there any difference in intent between the 'hot' intellectuals (who didn't look that appetising) and their ponytailed coteries, and the elderly men surrounded by the swimming-costumed beauties she had seen on their yachts?

She stroked a camellia leaf. It was smooth and glossy. How short life had been for Marie Duplessis. 'Twenty-three is so young to die. At least my mother got to thirty.' She pinched the leaf. 'Don't know what age my father was.'

'Yet,' said Walt.

They talked about the Gallery Martin and Walt's future. 'Big confession, Sophie.' He sounded anguished and uncharacteristically awkward. 'The old man's kicking up. The meeting did not go well and I may be leaving Paris.'

'Walt, *No.*'

He shrugged. 'The reckoning arrives.' He ordered absinthe. 'It always does.'

She imagined the deadly liquorice liquid sweeping though his system. 'It's too early to get drunk.'

'This is Paris, Sophie, and I'm about to be

deported and to grow up. I know, I know, at long last.'

Her bra strap dug into her shoulder. 'You won't give up?'

Gusty sigh. 'My father holds the purse strings.'

'*Walt* . . .' She stared at him. Men were supposed to be go-getters. The ones who always had resources to take things in hand. Having money from an early age was also supposed to be a good thing, a lucky thing. It bought you the space to nourish ambitions. But, perhaps, it weakened and diluted them?

'My turn to lecture.'

He ducked his head.

'Get a job. Ring a newspaper editor and tell him you'll write a food column. Write for all the papers if you must. If it means you're doing what you wish. If it means you can stay here.'

'Maybe.'

'*Not* maybe.'

A lesson? The divide between doers and non-doers did not split neatly between the sexes.

'I'm no hero.'

'You *could* be.'

'Tell that to my father.' Half-smile, half-grimace. 'Don't worry, Sophie. We'll keep in touch.'

She wanted to say: *you must promise me*. But the old habits learnt through childhood dammed up the words. All part and parcel of the *never show you're hurt, lonely, frayed of spirit*.

She should say that she wanted to know Walt

for the rest of her life (as she wanted to know Hettie). That her childhood dreams had contained friends like him. That the luck of encountering kindness and lack of pretence conjured into flesh from the ether was a magic, magic thing.

Instead she said: 'Anyway, you have to do some rescuing. I'll write and tell Hettie that you might be going.'

He dodged that one. 'Will *you* stay at the gallery?'

'Yes. I came here to find out about my father. So I will.'

'Not only your father,' said Walt.

She frowned. Then it clicked. 'You mean I'm finding out about myself.'

'You could say that.'

That made her feel better.

CHAPTER TWENTY-EIGHT

Christian Martin did not like it when she informed him of her decision about Kim Athos. 'Not helpful.' His tone was acid. 'What were you thinking? It would have been useful to the gallery.'

'It was difficult.'

'Most things are difficult.' He gestured irritably. 'Are you serious about your work here?'

That stung. 'That name . . . Joshua Adams? Was it cleared up?'

He was silent for a long moment. 'Have you learnt nothing since our last conversation? This kind of work is about keeping your mouth shut. About discretion. They're very important elements if you wish to make your way in the art world. However, as you're not much use to me now, it's irrelevant.'

He vanished into the packing area.

She followed him.

'You must teach me, Monsieur Martin.'

Fingernail pressed hard into her palm.

'It's in your interests, monsieur. Only you can tell me. Use me and what I know. Think of not having to start again with someone else.'

He picked up a pen and set it down on the bench. 'I have enough worries.'

She stood her ground. 'Why waste me?'

The pen twirled to the right . . . considering thrift and expediency, she reckoned . . . it moved to the left . . . considering if she knew too much to ignore.

'All right.'

Decision taken, he led Sophie up into the gallery and positioned her in front of the picture to the right of the door. 'Listen, and listen carefully.'

Here began a lesson in scholarly enchantment and commercial realities. Paint. Brushstrokes. Vision. Interpretation. The vanities of art buyers. The (many) vanities and (the many more) miseries of artists.

They moved from painting to painting. This one is good but won't sell so easily. This one is not so good but will sell long before the other one.

'Why, monsieur?'

'For God's sake, call me Christian. It will sell because at its heart is sentimentality. Never fails.'

The thrum of new knowledge rippled through her brain. She wrote in the notebook: *It's like drinking clear cold water after having been thirsty.*

And Christian Martin?

Over and over, she endeavoured to marry the image of the Resistance fighter with the contained, neatly dressed, buttoned-up man for whom she worked. Most of the time she failed. Except for the moments when there was a flash of anger, an edge revealed.

'Were you always interested in painting?' she asked over a mid-morning coffee.

There was a palpable hesitation before the answer. 'I suppose not. I wanted to be a lawyer.'

'But the war got in the way?'

He evaded a direct answer. 'In July 1942, the Germans rounded up the Jews in the winter velodrome before shipping them off to the camps.'

'Walt told me a bit about it.'

'Buildings were cleared of people who were forced to leave everything behind. The temptation to help yourself if you were starving, or even if you weren't, was huge. Objects appeared all over the place. The black market thrived. Furniture. Jewellery. Clocks. Paintings.' He avoided looking at Sophie. 'Stuff which went for a song.'

'I believe the Marais was emptied.'

'Not entirely. It had become run-down, but there were quite a few better-off families.' He avoided looking at Sophie. 'But it's true, those of us left behind had the run of the area.'

'Including the gallery?'

He didn't like the question. 'Not your business.'

She said to Walt: 'I reckon that when the war ended, Christian Martin saw his chance, occupied the gallery and filled it with paintings that had been "going for a song".'

'Close enough, I imagine,' said Walt. 'Either he knew the owner was dead or he did a cheap deal.'

394

He added. 'He's savvy and works out how to take advantage.'

'Don't we all. Particularly in bad times?'

'There's a limit.'

She understood. It was important, though, to reflect on where that limit was.

She took to staying late in the gallery, working her way through the shelf of reference books in the basement. It was no hardship. She and the stones that had built the gallery had come to an agreement. They had settled down to like each other. Or rather, they had invited her to feel at home. There was peace in the gallery's silences. Space. Plus a strong (inexplicable) sense, which she drank in, that the gallery already *knew* her.

It was ridiculous, really. Anyway, she read about painter's tricks, their visions and techniques – the well-placed dot of red, the use of perspective, the baroque line, the rococo flourish. She read about art markets, the drama of auctions. The crises.

Packing up her bag in the basement one evening, mulling over the choice between a slice of elderly Brie or a slice of ham to eat with her baguette. Thinking, too, about Poynsdean and her brief stay in London but viewing them, so to speak, from the wrong end of a telescope. Poynsdean and London had now been reshaped into the distant and miniature.

Thinking, too, about Madame Marie and the agency. The clients' urgent dash to get married. Claudine filing furiously in her overcoat while airing scurrilous opinions of men in general and de Gaulle in particular.

Down the passage, the door to the locked room banged shut.

She froze in the act of fastening her bag.

The gallery was empty. Christian, Walt, Emile had all said their good nights and vanished into the evening.

She crept down the passage. Not exactly frightened. More curious than anything. Conscious, though, that her experience of dealing with break-ins was nil.

Adrenaline surged, its spiky sensations burning up common sense.

She positioned herself outside the locked door. Listened.

Nothing.

Who did she think she was – the heroine of the Bluebeard story? The one who forced her way into the barred chamber to be confronted by the decaying bodies of his wives?

With the utmost care, she depressed the door handle. The door nudged open.

For a room around which the gallery's myths had settled, it was disappointing, being small and in need of repainting. The window had been left open which, presumably, had caused the door (normally locked) to snap shut.

Deeply disappointing, she would report to Hettie and Walt. *Not a body in sight*.

The room was stacked with books and ring files.

Shelving ranging along one wall and a dozen or so paintings were propped up against the opposite one.

She gravitated first to the bookshelves. Ran her fingers along the spines. A couple of language dictionaries in Italian and German. An impressive tome on the impressionists. Another on expressionism. Two on pre-war art collections in Vienna.

An open box file lay beside the latter, stacked with papers. The top one was an invoice, dated August 1946, for repairs made on a window.

She rifled further and disinterred more invoices for the maintenance of the gallery which, clearly, was expensive to run. Then, a list. Stained and dusty.

Still Life with Vegetables (rue Pavée)
The Seine at Neuilly (rue de Poitou)
Landscape with Satyr (rue de Sévigné)
The Skaters (rue de Turenne)
Etc.

She checked it against the paintings against the wall. Sure enough . . . Vegetables laid out on a table . . . Fred would have approved. The Seine cluttered with boats. A melting landscape. Colour, beauty, artistry. Some of the paintings were exquisite, others bolder and more experimental. Even to her half-tutored eye, these were the work of substantial artists. In his landscape the capering satyr (bearing a resemblance to Osbert) pointed to a daisy growing by a rock. The sun in the water slid under a river boat moored at Neuilly. The still life was anything but frozen. Its leeks, tomatoes and the melon almost breathed.

One painting on the list was missing: *The Skaters*. But then, she knew where it was.

Possibly . . . probably . . . all of them had been looted all those years ago. The years when the crackle of gunfire could be heard in the streets.

The *Landscape with Satyr* frame was ornate and carved with acorns and flowers. When she touched it, a speck of gilt transferred itself to her fingertip. Or guilt? Men and women had been driven from their homes. Children snatched up. Pets abandoned. The rooms in which these paintings hung emptied and gradually accumulating dust. Their silence entombing cries of grief and fear.

She returned to the box file. Bills, lists, a legal document at the bottom. Maybe . . . maybe all was above board and the paintings had been acquired in bona fide transactions?

The document ran to eleven densely typed pages. Much of the language and terms were too difficult to understand but the gist was clear. Dated January 1945, it granted Christian Martin a leasehold term for the gallery of fifty years. Leafing through to the page with signatures, she skimmed over the penultimate paragraph.

This she read.

And re-read. Twice.

Stumbling from shock, she made for the door. Shut it hard behind her.

* * *

'Have you come across the French proverb: culture remains when all else is forgotten?' asked Raf.

Sophie had always considered 'books', 'theatre', 'film' under their separate headings. Feeling out of her depth, she smiled uncertainly at Raf.

'Culture being the thing that defines a society,' he said. 'The French love ideas, the British love comedy.'

'Actually, the British are defined by their drama. Much of it dark and dangerous.'

'Touché.'

They were in Le Discothèque in Saint-Germain-des-Prés. Dim lights. Small tables. Raf sipped at a whisky. Sidney Bechet was playing. 'He lives in Paris full time,' said Raf. Afterwards a youth in a striped jumper sang songs in fractured English. Then a group got up onto the dance floor and danced *les slows* and *le lindy*.

She couldn't make out what Raf was thinking. 'This is fun, but why have you brought me here?'

'Look around. Many here are communist supporters. But they are also passionate about American jazz. The communist leaders worry about that. They don't want their supporters admiring the US.'

'That's not the reason.'

He finished the whisky, set the glass down on the table and held out a hand. 'Shall we dance?'

Claude Luter and his clarinet took over. The music dropped to a smooch. The noise to a murmur.

Raf held her lightly.

'I don't know how to dance.'

'Doesn't matter. Just hang onto me.'

It took a moment or two. Then, her nerves crackled into full play. *This is life*. Music. Dancing. Being held. Paris. A hint of whisky. More than a hint.

'It's nice to forget about everything,' she said. 'Is this what you do after a tricky case?'

'Sometimes. No, let's be honest. Frequently. I like to sit here, watching, thinking, drinking whisky.'

She wanted to ask: *but don't you have a family to go home to?*

'What is a hero, Raf? I can't make up my mind.'

'You are,' he said. 'Coming to Paris in the first place. Coming to this place with me.'

'You like teasing.'

'It's true. The hero usually embarks on a journey to become the hero.'

'And lays down his – or her – life?'

'Not always. And some might argue it's more heroic to survive.' His hand lay comfortably on her waist. 'I brought you here because you're worrying about something. I don't know what it is but I thought a night out might divert.'

'Do you always take care of your clients like this?'

'Always.'

'It's about the gallery and Christian.'

'Can I help?

'I have to think about it.'

'I see.'

He probably didn't. All the same, he had warned Sophie how war could turn men and women, nice good people, into killers and liars.

'Raf, I'm sure my fee has been used up. I'm sure you have many other cases.'

'That's possible. I must check. I'm not a charity. And, yes, there's much else to do . . . Many are clamouring for my attention . . .' A hint of unwanted jealousy sneaked through her. 'But if you have come across something that's really disturbing, it's probably a good idea to discuss it.' He stopped dancing and faced Sophie. 'In my experience.'

'Which is extensive,' she said.

'Yes. I think it is.' Her eyes flew to his face. 'My reason for existing, my work, is to be asked questions.'

'Seriously?'

He shrugged. 'Seriously.'

Being on a dance floor and not dancing seemed odd. Emblematic of her confusion. 'You're right, there are many questions. I'm only just beginning to see. Only beginning to sort them.'

He led her back to the table. 'Don't wait too long before asking them.'

Notebook: *Suspicion is an octopus. It coils its suckers around the mind and grips. How it grips.*

With Osbert there had been a vague uneasiness

401

about his intentions. What exactly did he want? (She found out, of course.) But her current suspicions of Christian Martin had taken on a sharper, more shocking edge.

CHAPTER TWENTY-NINE

The following day Raf turned up at the Gallery Martin.

Sophie was checking a list at the front desk. He smiled down at her and she smiled back. 'Have you come to complain about your bruised feet?'

'The bruises are huge. But I've ignored them.'

'So you want to buy a painting?'

'Do you think I should?'

'The agency could do with smartening.'

'The cruelty of the critical eye.' He pointed to a ravishing still life with fruit. 'That one.' He peered at the price tag. 'Jesus wept. If I bought this the agency would go bankrupt.

He placed both hands on the desk and leant over. 'I didn't say anything last night, but I have something for you. Information about your family that will take you to Poitiers if you wish to follow it up.'

'Well . . . yes. Of course I want to take it up.'

'I have some business in Poitiers, and I could drive you there.'

Family. The moment having arrived, it was hard to absorb.

'When?'

'Tomorrow.'

Assuming a potential client had come in, Christian emerged from his office. The two men exchanged greetings. The dapper, pressed, stiff Christian. Raf in perfectly decent clothes but – somehow – unpressed, watchful but knowing exactly how to disarm.

Raf had an unfair advantage, she thought. He knew who Christian was. Had studied his photograph. Knew his record and had probably come to conclusions. Whereas Christian had no idea how much information Raf had on him.

He listened politely as Raf talked, smiled and persuaded him that Sophie needed to have a day off to pursue a legal matter. Christian agreed, 'On the condition that you courier a couple of pictures to Tours.'

Raf insisted that they should drive. 'I have a car. You haven't seen France yet. Trust me, I'll be an excellent guide.'

They drove out of Paris through the porte d'Orléans. 'This was where the French armoured division came through in August '44 to retake the city. An important moment for the nation.'

Raf was taking his duties seriously.

They stopped at Orléans for lunch and he showed her the house where Joan of Arc had slept before riding out to help lift the famous siege of the city. 'How did she do it?' In her passion to know, Sophie grabbed Raf's arm. 'A girl from the

404

fields who was probably illiterate. She had never ridden a warhorse. Never worn armour. Never been taught military strategy . . . but somehow, there she was. How?'

'The power of belief.' Raf touched the hand on his arm.

On the road to Tours, he said, 'During the First World War, up to 25,000 Americans were garrisoned in the city and set up textile factories to mend uniforms and a military hospital. And, God help them, munition dumps.'

'Raf, you're the most excellent guide.'

'Objective achieved. Now you know France.'

He didn't mean it. Knowing a country took years of being bedded in. Of observation. Of breathing the air. It was ironic that she *was* French but the neural networks knitting together her thoughts and behaviour were still, she had to acknowledge, English.

That would change. Of course it would. She was now uprooted, her mind and future fluid. She could remake herself. She *would* remake herself.

At Tours, they managed to find the gallery in the city centre – not without tension. 'Have you never read a map before?' snapped Raf as they made a second wrong turning.

'You don't listen to instructions,' she pointed out.

He frowned, then sent a wry smile in her direction. 'That's what my sisters tell me.'

Once the Loire and the Cher had been crossed,

the grey roof tiles of the north gave way to red terracotta. Peering out of the window, Sophie observed, 'France is so much larger than I thought.'

'During the war,' said Raf, 'my sisters and I were sent to live in Provence with my grandparents on their olive farm. It was magical for children. Goats, dogs, cats, plus the odd snake or two. I think about it often.'

He shifted into a higher gear. 'We have a way to go. So tell me again about your village.'

Marsh, river, village, the church, Fred. Digbys. The WI hut, the terrible bus service, Winchelford library. The enigmatic sea. She shaped her story into coherence, taking delight in its form, all the better for its second telling. Experiencing a curious peace in that shaping and telling.

'I stole chocolate from the school bully. Twice.'

'And why was that?'

'I was permanently ravenous. But I also felt she had so much, and I had so little. I felt I was owed it. Of course, I wasn't. I suppose I was fabricating a justification for filling my empty stomach.'

'Many a political philosophy has been based on less.' Raf paid her the compliment of treating it seriously.

Then there were Osbert and Alice.

A familiar disgust sidled in and, as Raf listened, she opened up some more and told the unvarnished version of a childhood containing dark feelings that were never aired. Of dread and

406

sadness. Of terrible novels and murdered piano pieces. Of a beautiful house eaten up by decay.

'You see, when I was young and still lived there, I thought Osbert was normal. And good, even though I disliked him. It was a shock to discover he wasn't. After he assaulted me, I ran away to London and made my way to Paris.'

'*Brute.*' Raf's frown was of a different calibre – much, much steelier – to the one that had greeted her map reading.

'I was helped . . . I had Johnno, who I told you about.' Closeted in the intimacy of the car, seduced by the careful listening and by her wish to be honest and open, she went further. 'I asked him to take my virginity. It was a business arrangement because I wanted to find out about . . . about what people do.'

Raf grinned broadly. It was not the response she expected, but it nudged her into seeing the funny side of it too.

Raf said, 'I would expect nothing less of you.'

'The business part didn't work out. I fell in love and decided to marry him. Then he found out his previous girlfriend was having a baby, and that was that.'

Raf drove for a while in silence. 'When these things happen, we often feel we will never get over them.'

'I thought I wouldn't but if I'm honest I don't think I wanted that life. Even though . . . it still hurts thinking about it.' She folded her hands into her lap. 'It's in the past.'

407

'I agree in principle. But the past can be toxic.'
He glanced at her. 'As we discussed at our first
meeting, it can bite.'

Without thinking, she asked, 'Has it bitten you?'

Raf was silent for a good long time. 'Since you
ask. Yes, it has.'

'I'm sorry. That was a question too far.'

Raf, however, was not offended. 'In my work,
I'm rarely a subject of interest. It has novelty
value.'

She wished to justify her question. It seemed
important. 'So much in our everyday dealings is
unspoken or hidden, don't you think, because we
feel we should be polite?'

Raf concentrated on the road while he considered. 'Politeness is a form of evolution. Being too
honest can have consequences.'

Sophie looked out of the passenger window and
a flush rose up her cheeks. 'Sorry. Sorry. Forgive
me.'

Raf changed gear as the car slowed at a crossroads. 'Don't be. I'll tell you about the past that
bit me. I married very young. Far too young.
Twenty. Unsurprisingly, it did not work. That was
the reason I left Provence and came to work with
my father.' He was mouth-puckeringly dry.
'Nothing like divorce to sharpen ambition.'

He accelerated and the car kicked up white dust.

After a while, he said, 'Still sense you're worried
about something.'

'Yes, I am.'

There was no effort to probe. Or to dismiss.

'All I will say is, don't let it overwhelm you.'

She glanced at Raf. He was concentrating on the road. 'Thank you.' It was growing warmer. The roads were emptier. Flanked by fields filled with maize and vines, they sped along. Raf sang under his breath.

Suddenly, a lurch. A bang. A noisy skid. Raf hanging onto the wheel, fighting to steer the car onto the verge and to avoid the ditch. Fighting to bring it to a standstill.

Slumped over the wheel, he said, 'My turn for the apologies. I should have changed the tyre. I thought it was a bit dodgy.'

'We're alive.' Sophie sounded steadier than she felt. 'Do you have a spare tyre?'

He breathed out audibly. 'Never without one.'

They heaved the overnight bags onto the verge and extracted the heavy spare tyre from the boot. Raf jacked up the car and tackled the wheel nuts. That took some doing and he sat down to catch his breath. Sophie eased the tyre off and replaced it with the new one.

'You've done this before,' said Raf.

'I helped Johnno on the farm. Tyres were always getting punctured.'

He watched as she reaffixed the wheel nuts, only scrambling upright to allow Raf to do the final tightening.

She wiped her hands on the grass, then held them up. 'Still filthy.'

Raf handed over his handkerchief. 'Be my guest.'

It was made of beautiful cotton and hand hemmed. A mother? A sister? An ex-wife? 'I'll ruin it.'

'Let me see. I've nearly killed you, but I begrudge you using my handkerchief.'

Somehow, they were facing each other. Over Raf's shoulders, the vines stretched out as far as she could see. The sky was clear and, above them, birds called.

She handed back the handkerchief. 'Will you tell me who I'm going to see in Poitiers?'

'I had thought it best to wait until we arrive. But I've found a member of your mother's family. Your mother's cousin.'

In Poitiers they checked into a hotel which had seen better days. Or perhaps had never had them. The towel in her room was the size of a postage stamp and the mattress needed replacing. But the journey had tired her and, after a modest dinner at a nearby bistro, she slept like a log.

Raf was finishing his breakfast when she joined him the following morning. He pushed the coffee pot in her direction. 'Thought you'd be an early riser.'

'I am.'

'We need to get a move on.'

The dining room had a deer's head mounted on the wall which kept catching her eye while she ate baguette and jam as fast as she could manage.

Raf placed both hands on the table. 'Ready?'

'As much as I can be.'

'Your mother's cousin, a Madame Boilly, lives at Quinçay, just outside the city. We've exchanged letters and I've talked to her on the phone. In the end she agreed to see you.'

'In the end?'

'You'll understand that it was a shock.'

A constellation of baguette crumbs was scattered on her plate and over the table. Under her blurred gaze, the separate crumbs configured and reconfigured. Could it be that, after all, she had a place in a family tree? Or had been discussed? Could it be that she was known about in theory?

She looked over to Raf. 'You've gone out of your way to help me.'

He got to his feet. Was he frowning? Or smiling? 'You paid me, remember? And this is my business.'

Quinçay wasn't far and, a short while later, Raf drove down a muddy lane to a square house flanked by a couple of outbuildings.

Sophie stared through the car window.

Built of white stone which shone extra white in the sun. White shutters. A small tourelle set into an encircling wall, complete with a sloping roof and arrow apertures. Bent over by the wall, a woman with a basket searched the undergrowth.

A dog barked and hens scratched in the dust. Raf parked and got out, followed by Sophie.

'Madame Boilly?' The woman straightened up. She was perhaps in her mid-forties or so with greying hair. She scrutinised Sophie. Transferred the basket from one hand to another. Then back again. 'Sophie Morel?'

'Yes.'

Raf reached over. 'Shall I take the basket?'

Her eyes never left Sophie's face but she seemed confused. Almost overpowered. 'There's a few more that need collecting . . .' She indicated the long grass at the base of the tourelle. 'Could you? You must gather them quickly. There're sharp fingers around here who steal eggs.'

'Leave it to me,' said Raf and took the basket from Madame Boilly.

'Mademoiselle, come with me.'

She led Sophie into the shuttered house, stepping from bright morning light into the dimness of a flagged hallway, and then into a sizeable kitchen where pots and pans, alternating with bunches of herbs, hung from crossbeams.

'Please sit down, Sophie Morel.' The woman pushed back the hair from her face. 'We must take a moment.'

A moment passed. An important one. Sophie wanted, needed, to give it the focus it deserved. Infuriatingly, her body had its own agenda and all she could do was to concentrate on her rumbling stomach.

'My name is Barbette.'

Barbette . . . Barbette? The naughty, charming cousin of her mother's reminiscences.

'I know about you from the stories. You stole *tartines*.'

412

'Perhaps I did.'

The two women assessed each other across a scrubbed kitchen table. Did Barbette have her mother's eyes? Sophie couldn't remember that well. Or her hair? Scrolling through the litany of questions, it was impossible for her to answer. All she could remember for sure was leaning against Camille's warm flank, her smell. Her cries of pain.

'How did Monsieur Maurice find me?'

Sophie explained she had commissioned him to find out about her father, and his profession was to search for those who were lost.

'Your accent is a little odd.'

'I know.'

The hands spread on the table were swollen-knuckled, the skin dry. 'How do I know you are who you say you are?'

Sophie extracted her birth certificate from her bag and unfolded it on the table.

Sophie had imagined – when she allowed herself to picture this moment arriving – being greeted with cries of joy. Being enfolded into an embrace which said: *you are one of us.*

Cousin Barbette's forefinger travelled from word to word. Transcribing a world. Sophie's world. *Mother. Father. Date of birth.* Sophie tried to point out *Place of birth* and was rebuked. 'I will work it out.'

'My mother died . . .' As was often the case, the words were hard to say. She produced Camille's death certificate. 'You can see here.'

413

Again, Barbette enacted the same careful tracing of dates and places. This time, it was the trajectory of her mother's life.

Barbette pushed back her chair. Hesitated. What was holding her back? Saying nothing, she got up. She filled the kettle. She lit the gas. Still she was silent. Sophie's thoughts went haywire: *Barbette didn't believe the evidence*. Surely that wasn't possible? *Barbette didn't want her*? That was possible.

Eventually, her back still turned, Barbette said: 'I'm the last one, you know. My brothers were killed in 1943. My parents died soon afterwards. They couldn't cope . . .' The information sounded rusty. Information and grief that she kept deeply buried. . 'Marie-Thérèse, your grandmother, never recovered. Her family had been destroyed. I know she longed to see your mother. Camille was her only child.' She stared at the mantlepiece cluttered with papers and pieces of string. 'She died on Christmas Day, the day when the family used to gather. But there was only me left.'

The kettle whined.

'Camille was in Paris when the Germans arrived. She had met your father. After that, it was difficult to remain in touch.'

Rusty information. Long-ago partings. Death that had come too early. All her life, Sophie had wanted to know the substance. The details. *Family* details.

'My mother talked about you and the adventures

414

you had as children. She said she came to stay with you and your brothers in the holidays.'

'Ah, yes. Camille was very wicked. *Very*.' Barbette switched off the kettle. 'We had a magic childhood. I never knew your father. He lived in Paris and during the war it was impossible to see each other. Travel was difficult.' She turned around. 'You English prefer tea, don't you?'

'I'm not English.'

'Ah.'

A nervy silence.

It was broken when Raf came into the kitchen. 'Madame Boilly, I congratulate you. You have champion hens.'

He placed the basket, now filled with eggs, on the table.

Sophie stared at the tumble of brown and pearl-white shelled eggs. Smudged with dirt. An odd feather or two.

Home Farm, Johnno, the bitter and the sweet. All gone.

She told herself: that was good. That was how it should be.

Raf said: 'We should not start for Paris too late. Madame Boilly, I must take Mademoiselle Morel back as she must return to work.'

Sophie sent him a look.

Raf had been here before, she thought. He knew about these meetings. Knew that time was required to adjust.

'No, you must eat before you leave,' said Barbette.

Later, after a meal of hard-boiled eggs, tomatoes, cheese and bread, where not much was said but much was felt – certainly by Sophie – she folded up the certificates, stowing them with great care in her bag. 'Cousin Barbette, may I keep in touch?'

'I'm not sure,' was the reply. 'I must think about it. I need to get used to the idea of you.'

Sophie swallowed. This was hard. This was not kind. She wanted to cry out: *Accept me.* Please.

'All that war business,' said Barbette. 'It's hard to get over. I don't want reminders.'

Back in Raf's car and heading north, Sophie was silent.

'I'm not going to ask if you're all right because you're not,' said Raf. 'But it might help to know it's not unusual.'

He began to talk about nothing much. The weather. The traffic. The presidency of Charles de Gaulle, the problem for the French in Algeria, slipping in a few questions here and there. Where should they stop? Was there anyone she could confide in on arrival back in Paris?

'Not really.' Walt, for instance, having too much family, might not understand having too little of it. 'I'm on my own.'

'War has a long reach.' He sent her a look. 'It left you in another country. My family was disrupted and so were many others. The sadness can't be dodged and can last a long time. Years, in fact. It can be complicated and it has to be

416

carried somehow. But, if it has a purpose, it's to remind us that we are alive.' He paused. 'We should never put too much trust in the dead. They're not trustworthy.'

Trauma was being acknowledged. Raf was showing her the delicate connecting strands between it and the present, and how to spin it into substance.

'Yes,' said Sophie. 'That must be right.'

'When there are problems, I walk. All over the place. It helps.'

Instinctively she knew that this was a confession which was not often made.

'I have stories . . .' She struggled because the words were, not exactly lame, but not as precise as she wished. 'They seem to need writing down.'

'They probably do.'

Driving on towards Paris, the afternoon wore on into evening and she began to formulate the story of Peter, a seven-year-old boy, and his dog.

'Peter will be a hero.'

'Ah,' said Raf.

'He and Dog go in search of adventure and rescue many other animals. They fight demons. Perhaps they will have a run-in with the Pirate King.'

'Definitely, they should. You must have obstacles in a story.'

She inhaled the smell she had come to associate with him. A touch of cologne. Tobacco. Coffee (sometimes). Mouthwash. 'They find treasure.'

'And what exactly is the treasure?'

She glanced at him, smiling. 'That depends.'

'You know,' he remarked, 'when you look like that it tells me you can be happy.' A tiny pause. 'And also rather wicked.'

Late, late evening, the car turned into the rue de Turenne, and headed north past the Fontaine de Joyeuse. Past the bakery where she bought her baguettes.

The car traced her evening route back from work. At Merlot's she stopped to buy milk and more bread. At the street corner, she often narrowly avoided putting her foot in dog mess. Almost daily, she debated treating herself to an aperitif at Chez Voltaire, the corner bar. She always decided against. Once she indulged herself, she would wish to repeat it every night, and it was too expensive.

Past the statue of the Madonna on the corner of rue Villehardouin. Wondering once again what the 'S' and 'D' carved into the stones signified.

This was a small parcel of Paris. Hers. Her Paris, chiselled out of a larger, still-unknown city. Its streets and crossings were now installed in her head. She thought, she believed, that she already understood it better than she had Poynsdean. The smells, the topography, the colour of the stone, the shape of the buildings and the spirit that animated them.

How might she fit in? This French-English hybrid?

Raf brought the car to a halt alongside the passageway leading into number 66. Clasping the wheel, he looked over to her. 'Mission done. You found your family and you didn't.'

'Thank you, Raf.'

He must have registered the tiny inflection of sadness. Almost, almost in the hunch of his shoulders there was a suggestion of *I warned you*. Of course, that would be so. His experience in this work had been too extensive for him to peddle optimism.

'You must not be miserable.'

No point in denying it.

His eyes did not leave her face.

'In cases like this, it's tempting to imagine that there's instant connection. Sometimes, there is. Sometimes, it takes time. Of course, it might never work, but being patient helps.' He smiled. 'Not that I know about being particularly patient, but I've seen patience bear fruit.'

The chrome handle of the passenger door was cool to the touch. 'Cousin Barbette hasn't much family left. Why wouldn't she welcome me?'

'People are mysterious. You're mysterious.' He grinned. 'I am too.'

It was her turn to look at him.

'Raf, you've been so good to me. I cannot really repay you. *And* you never got to your business appointment in Poitiers.

'Couldn't be helped.' He switched to being serious. 'Remember you are almost certainly

419

capable of happiness but . . . it takes a bit of work. It takes an act of will.'

'You make it sound simple.'

'Simple and complicated.' He slotted the gear into first. 'And deal with Martin. I think it is time.'

Clear vision and courage was required. 'Yes. It is.'

She watched the car move off, then walked down the passageway past the Weber Métaux offices towards the house tucked into the left where her room was.

A figure, surrounded by luggage, sat on the stone step. Worryingly thin, blonde hair escaping a head-scarf. *Sans* gloves. Ringless?

'Het . . . what on earth?'

'Thank God. I was just about to go in search of a hotel.'

Sophie counted the suitcases. Five. *Five!* Hettie was incapable of travelling light. Even so. 'You've left William?'

'Yes.'

'I thought you said there's never been a divorce in your family.'

'There will be now.'

'Are you sure, darling Het?'

'Never more so. I want to be drenched in pearls like Coco Chanel, drink red wine and eat baguettes. I want to choose to do what I want to do.'

'I should warn you Walt might be going home.'

Hettie breathed hot tears and defiance. 'I don't think so, Sophs.'

The two women clung together until the breath was driven from Sophie's body.

Sophie made a phone call. In fact, two. The first was to secure the empty rooms upstairs from the landlady to install Hettie and her five suitcases in them. (During the night, Sophie heard her pacing up and down. Up and down. She recognised the up and down. The feelings of astonishment and disbelief that a choice had been made. *And acted on*.)

The second phone call had been to Walt.

'What's she doing in Paris?'

'You must ask her.'

'Has she left that man?'

'Yes.'

The intake of breath was audible down the phone.

'And Walt . . . she might forget to tell you this, but she took a cookery course back in London.'

Actually – and she very nearly didn't do so – she made a third phone call.

When it was answered, she said, 'I just wanted to tell you that I think *you* should acknowledge that *you* too are capable of happiness. Not stuck in the mental bog with the divorce.'

'Oh,' said Raf. 'On what basis do you make that judgement?'

'You sang "La Mer" when we approached Paris.'

'Rather badly.'

'Yes, it wasn't great. But I could tell when you sang the bit which goes *La mer a bercé mon coeur*

421

pour la vie, you were smiling. You were happy. Something about the sea made you happy.'

'Thank you. That was very thoughtful of you to tell me. One forgets to register one's own feelings.' Pause. 'It's true. At that moment I was happy. It was kind of you to remind me.'

'I wanted you to know.'

A longer pause.

'And, Raf . . .'

'Sophie?'

'Even if Cousin Barbette never gets in touch, thank you.'

CHAPTER THIRTY

'**P**aris,' Sophie read in *La Nouvelle Paris*, 'is a city through whose veins runs resistance. The alleyways, the churches, the dark streets have inbuilt subversion structured into them. You have only to think of the first French Revolution.

'In June 1940, the country was occupied. Paris was occupied. It was a shocking, depressing *fait accompli*. The question was: where would be the push back? And when? The answer: in school-rooms and lecture rooms where pupils and students openly invited the exiled General de Gaulle to return to save the country. (This put them at odds with communists, who supported a socialist form of government to take over after a Nazi defeat.)

'Resistance in schools was a clever strategy. For fear of being called child-killers, the occupiers held back from launching playground reprisals.

'It wasn't enough. More was needed. Guns. Bullets. Planning. Any resistance in Paris would have to be led by the secret fighters. The sniper, *le franc tireur*. From balconies. The street ambush. From behind street blockades. From moving cars.

It needed those willing to kill without question. Slowly, groups began to form. Réseau Saint-Jacques, Réseau Nemrod, the Musée de l'Homme group. It was hard.

'There were vendettas and betrayals. And murders.'

This was the journeys's end she had anticipated through the long years of helplessness. Had thought about with the deep need to know – a typical *cri de coeur* of the child left alone. Then, growing older and the dissonance and pain having retreated a little, arming herself with practical plans. Earn money. Go to Paris. Etc.

Predictably perhaps, at this point, the actual moment when she was about to make the move, the *what ifs* went on the attack. What if her father had been violent or traitorous or stupid or weak? What then would she do with the shiny image she had enshrined in her mind?

What if Christian Martin was dangerous?

What if he had done the unthinkable?

Thought and care went into the preparations. No baguette. No coffee. The body empty of everything except resolve.

Hettie clattered downstairs, hair mussed, old jumper over her nightdress. 'Go forth,' she said. 'Conquer.'

Evoking the spirit of Juliette Gréco, Sophie pulled back her hair and put on a black polo-neck sweater.

'Do I look like Juliette Gréco?'

Hettie kissed her. 'Doesn't matter if you look like Old King Cole.'

At the gallery, she knocked on Christian's office door.

'Christian, may I speak to you?'

Christian was busy and the request was clearly an irritant. With a sigh, he gestured for her to step into the office. 'Five minutes.'

Constructed at the back of the original building, the office was a slap in the face for the purist. It was bold. It was bright. It had a large plate-glass window, ultra-modern furniture and made no concessions to fit in architecturally.

Christian instructed Sophie to sit down, and scrutinised her from across the desk, on which sat a single buff file.

'And so . . . ?'

Falling in love with Johnno had not been part of the plan.

Osbert's assault had rocked her.

The enchantment of glorious, undaunted, war-wounded Paris had taken her by surprise.

But this encounter, its anticipated cut and thrust, had been precision-planned by her, even to the point of working out its running order.

Hours had been rolled out during the writing and the rewriting of a script. The rehearsal in front of the small mirror (which only reflected one half of her at a time) had been tough and demanding of her reserves.

Stage directions were included: her expression should be confident. Her body stance non-aggressive. Her tone firm but neutral.

'Monsieur Martin. I have a confession. And a question.'

Polite interest? Deepening irritation? In the months she had been working at the gallery, she had never been able to read him.

'I should have talked to you sooner. It has weighed on my conscience.'

An unexpected flash of humour. 'Not that heavily. Otherwise you might have done something about it.'

'I've learnt much being here.'

He sat back in the chair. 'Sophie, why don't you get on with it.'

'It's true.'

He gestured as if to say: *If you insist.*

She had the sense that she had launched herself into a wilderness of space and time. 'Christian, I'm not who I say I am.'

Merde – as Emile had taught her on the packing desk. She had sounded neither confident, nor in control.

She folded her hands into her lap and waited for the response.

When it arrived, the aggression took her aback. 'My God. You're working for *le beau chasseur.*'

'Who?'

'You've been infiltrated into the gallery.'

'What?'

'Ex-detective Suchet.' There was a heavy emphasis on 'ex'. 'Retired but still used by the police. Infiltration is one of his tactics but because he's a holier-than-thou type and he misses sorting out black-market deals, he's kept on the books.'

The file was pushed around the desktop. This way. That way. Those unnecessary, nervy actions mirroring her own agitation.

Joshua Adams. The private clients. The contents of the locked room.

'I don't work for anyone except you.' Again, a nervous trip over her words. 'I've no idea who he is.'

'Then you haven't learnt that much. Everyone who has the slightest knowledge of the art market in Paris knows about Suchet.' There was a slight contempt. 'You should, too. If you're serious about this work.'

The script? She scrambled to bring it into play. 'My real name is Sophie Morel, not Knox.' In the moments that followed, she made two discoveries. The smell of paint and varnish endemic in the gallery nudged her to the edge of queasiness, and the way the light fell on her knees exposed the weave of her cheap skirt.

He placed the folder in the drawer and shut it. 'Why are you telling me this? I don't care who you are if you do your job. It's a waste of my morning.' He looked at the window. 'Names mean nothing. Anyone can take a name.'

Her nerve faltered; threatened to fail; but she

forged on. 'My father was Pierre Morel. You fought with him. In Les Loups.'

He pushed back his chair hard. Leapt to his feet. Went over to the window and repeated in a barely audible tone: 'Les Loups.' The tremor returned noticeably to his left hand. 'Pierre's . . . *daughter*?'

So. Her father had been real. It was a wonderful affirmation to counter the times she had doubted his existence. The light spilling through the window turned radiant.

Silence. The seconds ticked on. Swivelling around, he was quiet for some time before asking, 'Why the deception? I could be very angry.' He returned to his chair. 'Perhaps I am.'

'I want to find out about my father.'

'Then why didn't you ask?'

Being honest was as much a weapon as anything else. She understood that now. With honesty one derived a power. 'I was frightened. And I wanted to work in the gallery and I thought you'd tell me to go if I asked you earlier.' She watched his reactions. 'I didn't know how to handle it.'

'Why frightened?'

'My mother told me he had fallen out with someone over a painting before the war . . .'

She needed her wits, those sharpened, tempered wits, as much as she needed the adrenaline streaming through her limbs.

'If you knew my father, did you know my mother?'

'Pierre and Camille. Of course.'

428

She bit her lip. 'Could you . . . please . . . tell me about my father? I want to know how he lived. How he died.'

He frowned. As if to say: *Be careful what you ask.*

'You were friends.' Still no reply. 'You fought together because you were friends.'

'Yes, Pierre was my friend.' He stirred himself. 'We knew each other most of our lives and it was natural that we saw the war out together.'

She sat forward on her seat, ravenous to put a shape to him.

'It was a time when we lived with intensity and purpose, a time never to be repeated. Part of you burns away. War can alienate, but it binds friends more closely. It was a long war. Full of misery, death and . . . betrayals. Constant danger. Les Loups was our outfit. Pierre was older than most of the others and we looked up to him. Some of us didn't survive. Or had to escape. Like your mother.'

His voice was tender. 'She was beautiful, you know. Special. Your father was obsessed. War did that, I think. It sharpened emotions. Enlarged them. Love. Fear . . . and . . . jealousy. Emotions that drove you to extremes.'

The words seemed to burn in her mouth, but she got them out.

'This was his gallery, wasn't it?'

Christian clasped his left arm. '*What* did you say?'

Her voice was steady. 'I found evidence in the room downstairs. You left it unlocked one night. I read the lease in the file. It stated my father was the previous leaseholder.'

It took an ashen-faced Christian a good minute to bring himself under control.

From a distance . . . from a long distance, she heard herself persist. 'You wanted to be a lawyer. The war put paid to that and you needed something to replace it.'

'You know nothing about it.'

'I want to know how my father died. If it was the enemy who killed him. Or . . . someone else.'

The words encompassed a world of speculation.

It was as if she had hit him. 'Good God, you think I had something to do with your father's death because I wanted the gallery?'

The urge to turn tail and flee almost mastered her.

'When I found out about it, I thought . . . I thought it possible.'

He stood stock still.

'You will come with me. *Now*.'

He pushed her downstairs, past the packing area to the locked room.

She watched his pale fingers turn the key.

A rush of stale air washed over them as they stepped inside.

'I can't deny you have shocked me.' He shut the door and leant back against it. 'But I suppose I knew that one day it was possible that Pierre's child might turn up. You searching me out suggests that you have your father's spirit. He could be difficult. Stubborn. Very. You look as though you're the same. He was practical; a realist, and clever. Loved his paintings. Loved your mother. Loved me. He made me laugh, we forgave each other much and looked out for each other.' A slight pause. 'Even after he met your mother.'

She looked away.

'I'm aware you don't know whether to trust me or not, but your mother managed to phone here after she found out that your father had been killed. She told me the baby had been born safely but nothing else. We discussed the gallery.'

She imagined her mother's pain.

'Your mother instructed me to take on the lease because she knew her situation was difficult. We were coping with chaos and trying to get back to normal. You don't understand. How can you?'

True . . . but . . .

'These paintings. *Landscape with Satyr, Still Life with Vegetables?*'

'You looked at them, then?' A pause. 'Yes, of course you did. You're a willing pupil. Almost excellent.' He pointed to *Still Life with Vegetables*. 'Taken from a house in the rue Pavée in 1942. The family had either been rounded up or fled. Your father loved this one.'

'I knew he would.'

Christian raised a sceptical eyebrow. 'Did you?'

No, no, she thought. No. Of course she could not know what her father loved – or hated.

'It's always a temptation to ascribe thoughts and feelings to the dead.' With careful, professional expertise, he extracted *Landscape with Satyr* from the pile. 'Rue de Sévigné. One of the older houses where the family had either fled or been killed. The looters had been there first, but they missed this.'

'That was theft. My father was stealing. You . . .' she pushed out the words, '. . . both of you were stealing.'

His shrug encompassed all manner of realities. 'The Germans were taking what they could lay their hands on. You had to be quick. I relied on your father. He knew what was good. He knew a lot.'

'The paintings didn't belong to you.'

'The owners were never going to come back.'

'He could not know that.' Out of all those hundreds and thousands of people, there must be some remaining who could claim the paintings. 'There are, there must be, survivors.'

'Have you ever seen a *rafle* . . . a round-up? No, you were too young and in a different country. You don't know the ways of war or occupation. Have you ever listened to the cries of parents trying to protect their children?'

'No.'

'Have you ever seen the elderly being flogged through the streets? No.'

432

Images formed. 'Horrible, horrible . . .' she said.

'We didn't know for sure where they were being taken, only that it was likely that the death rate would be excessive.'

All the same, she persisted, 'He . . . you . . . couldn't be sure.'

A couple of paces took him to the end of the room. 'We were alive. They had almost certainly gone to their deaths. We needed all we could lay our hands on.'

'I have to sit down.'

Christian stuck his head out of the door and called to Emile to bring two chairs.

Once upon a time, long ago and far away, she had stolen chocolate. *Liddy doesn't need it. She has too much.*

My God.

My hero father stole paintings.

'Shall I tell you how we got *Landscape with Satyr*?'

'Yes.'

'I'm going to try and tell you as it happened. As he told me. As I witnessed it.'

'To survive in occupied Paris meant coming to terms with German authority. Police. City politics. The curfew, which was 9 p.m. to 5 a.m. We had to live with it. We had to outwit it. My career was finished, and your father struggled to keep his gallery going.

'Word had come in that Vermeer's *Astronomer*

had been lifted from the Rothschild house and taken to Hitler's retreat – clearly only the first of a massive art heist to Germany.

'Les Loups was in its infancy and its activities had to be secret. Very, very secret. Meetings were held in out-of-the-way places. Requests went out for arms and for someone to train *résistants* in their use.

'Pierre had forbidden Camille to be involved, but she didn't listen. She never did. Having already taken one risk too many, she'd had to disappear from the job at the Jeu de Paume, but that wasn't going to stop her. "We're a team," she said. "Warriors. We are free to give our lives if we wish."

'We hid and we learnt to fight. We studied how to read the enemy. Especially Camille, because she was our messenger. She disguised herself by cutting short and dyeing her hair, wearing shoes with thick cork soles to make her appear taller than she was, and she got herself a bicycle.

'The gallery, this gallery, Pierre's gallery, turned into a nerve centre for the resisters. We had to be careful. So careful. So tight in our security. Stashing guns and ammunition, training, planning operations.

'Buying and selling paintings was our cover. Actually, a good proportion of our stock had been brought in by people before they fled the city in *l'exode* of 1940; offered for sale in sadness and terror, and purchased by Pierre in honourable transactions. Less honourably, sold to German officers, many of whom liked the fine arts.

'He also sold to the *collabos* who hobnobbed with the enemy and had an eye for investment. "I'll take their money," he said. "Use it to buy arms."

'Then Camille snaked her arms around his neck and breathed into his ear that they were having a baby.

'A few days later, she was waiting for a contact in the Café des Arts and got pulled in for questioning by the French police who were, of course, supervised by the Germans.

'Pierre was incandescent when she was released. "What did they do to you?" he raged. "*Tell me.*"

'Your mother never elaborated. Except for: "They hit me, but it was only once." The rest he could never get out of her. But, from that day, she lost something. I couldn't place a finger on it. But something. Optimism? A belief in a better world? In its place was an anger that pushed her to extremes.

'Your father saw it too. He took note, and the decision was made. "They've got your number. You must leave," he said. "Get out of France and wait until the war is over. You cannot risk our baby's life."

'Camille said, "I'm not abandoning you, Pierre."

'"You must."

'"I have to fight."

'Holding her close, he said, "Yes, you must fight to keep this baby safe. If you love me, you will go."

'Eventually, she said, "I love you, Pierre."

435

'Money was needed to pay for the passage and for the *passeurs* who would lead Camille over the Pyrenees. Once she was over and into Spain, she would need funds to survive wherever she ended up.

'Then intelligence came in from street scouts: the Famille Daumier, who lived in a house stuffed with art in the rue de Sévigné, had been rounded up a day earlier. Later that afternoon, Pierre drove a van into the Daumier courtyard and stole three of the paintings. A Renoir portrait, a Berthe Morisot domestic scene and *Landscape with Satyr*.

'The sale of the Renoir and the Morisot was easy, bringing in more than enough money to fund Camille. *Landscape with a Satyr* was kept with the others we had picked off from other empty houses. They were there in reserve to fund operations, to help escapes. And, if necessary, as aids to negotiation.

'"Tainted money," said Camille, sewing the notes into her chemise. "*Tainted.*"

'"It doesn't matter," said Pierre. "Get to a bank as soon as you get out of France and change it for dollars or pounds."'

'That was more or less how he told it to me,' Christian finished.

'So that's how it was done,' Sophie said, brushing an angry finger over a wet cheek. 'It means . . . it means I was brought up on the proceeds of looted paintings.'

436

'If you wish to put it that way. It's a hard fact, but not the worst you will hear. Getting your mother out of France consumed your father. He was not going to stop at anything. Stolen paintings versus two lives.'

She looked down at her hands. 'It was a love story.'

'A great love story.'

'I'm here in Paris using the money from those paintings. I should make reparations.'

'Perhaps.'

'And you kept the paintings in order to sell them off to people like Kim Athos.'

'Those tricky facts again.' He eyed the box file on the shelf. 'The war ended fifteen years ago, and no one has come to claim them. It's time they were hung somewhere.'

'Why the locked room?'

'You should know by now we have competitors who would like to get their hands on them. Buyers demand privacy.'

It was airless in the small room and sweat prickled under her arms.

'Does your conscience bother you?'

He got up. Held out his left arm. 'I have nerve damage here. The aftermath from a bullet wound. It serves as my conscience.'

'I'm sorry.'

'It was war. You do what you can. Cross lines. Steal. Die.' He got up and replaced *Landscape with Satyr*. 'And kill.' The word slid between them.

'Most of us crave a clean conscience but that's a luxury. You were lucky. Your parents saw to it that you had a chance.'

He clasped his arm and brought it under control. 'You should be grateful. Everything was done for you.'

She tried to grab the certainties slithering away.

She looked up at him. 'But you haven't denied you had anything to do with his death.'

He reached towards her.

She braced herself. She would take any blow that came, for her father.

It never came.

CHAPTER THIRTY-ONE

The taxi deposited Christian and Sophie at the junction of the rue Danton and the boulevard Saint-Michel.

Traffic bore down from all directions. The air was thick with fumes and the majority of the buildings were covered in soot. (The current *on dit* had it that post-war Paris was due a facelift, but no one had instructed the surgeon.)

'Why are we here?' she asked.

'You'll see.' He steered her down the rue Danton. 'You know, you owe me an explanation for your dishonesty.'

'My sources—' she began.

He cut her short. 'You mean your mother.'

'There was someone else.'

'A source suggests authority. In a war, sources are questionable and require following up. Who is it and have you checked it out?'

'I can't say.'

'If you can't produce or verify sources then, like provenance, they're useless.' He was at his most sceptical. 'In any situation, it's dangerous to throw out accusations without evidence. You

439

should know that by now. Have you not learnt anything?'

'But, surely, it's not wrong to ask questions.'

'But you didn't ask them. Not once during the time you've worked for me. Merely snooped.'

'I'm asking them now.'

He stared at her. Anger warring with an emotion she could not pin down. An old sorrow?

'I'll ask again. Do you suspect it was me who might have killed your father?'

What to think? What to trust? The information Raf had given her? Her own instincts?

'I did.'

She waited for the onslaught.

'I did because . . . because of the gallery. But I didn't want to believe it. I knew I could be wrong.'

'Honesty at last.' Astonishingly, his anger appeared to fall away and he spoke almost affectionately. 'You're young and you know so little to arrive at such a terrible conclusion.'

His answer caught her on the raw. Through dry lips, she managed: 'Of course, mistakes can be made during a war. Awful ones. Also, I know it changes people. Nice people who become something else. That's what many say. There are vendettas. Politics.'

'And you speak from experience?'

'No. No . . . but I've listened.'

'If I had killed my friend and blood brother, would I have admitted it to you? An employee whom I barely knew? Did you ever consider that

440

if I was this depraved war criminal, I might have killed you as well?'

She remembered an Osbert sermon in which he'd observed that truth and lies grew in the same thicket. At the time, she'd thought it ridiculous imagery.

Christian placed a hand on her arm, forcing her to stop in her tracks. 'What happened to us in Paris, all of us, was not a fairy story or something out of a novel.'

She thought of the times she had sunk into stories of battles, of love affairs, abductions and noble sacrifice – which had served their purpose and released her for an hour or two from everything she hated.

'Words are fine things,' said Christian. 'We cannot live without them. But they won't prepare you for holding a gun that must be used. Or for the moment you place your finger on the trigger. Although by 1944 we were hardened to the violence, I never got used to it. I don't think Pierre did either.'

Hand under her elbow, he propelled her into a street leading off the rue Danton.

'Have you any idea, *any* sort of idea of what it is like to fight against an occupier? With no training and insufficient weapons? In the early days, the best . . .' he spoke with a deep bitterness, 'if you can call it the best . . . the best we could do was to organise arranging discarded Métro tickets into the shape of a "V" on a platform.'

441

Passers-by pushed past them. Traffic kept up a steady stream. She had to strain to catch everything he said.

'You want to know what happened? It's a story of war and retribution, which is never simple. Imagine that it's August 1944. Bands of us had been fighting as best we could in the streets for a long time. We, your father and I and others, as you know operated in the Marais area. Sometimes successfully. More often not. We had to survive until the Allies landed. We had to believe they would come.'

Sophie's knees were by now cotton wool. Her nose ran.

'We lived in greyness. Think of a landscape painting with every trace of blue washed out of the sky. We never slept in one place for more than a couple of days. We had no time to grieve our comrades. We kept away from our families. Your father never even visited his dying father.'

They had reached a junction. 'What do you see?'

She glanced at the street name. 'The rue Danton. Side streets. Cafés. People.'

'It didn't look so different then, but it was. Things could turn nasty in a heartbeat. Trust was in short supply.'

They passed a newspaper kiosk. Two Frenchmen Killed in Algeria in the War for Independence, spat the headlines. A thought slid through her mind: nothing changes.

'First off, we had word the Red Cross had moved

into Paris, which was a signal that the Allies were making progress. Then we got news they had reached the outskirts of Paris. The wait was over. It had been almost the worst bit of the war, thinking the Allies might not make it.'

Christian's gesture embraced the scene around them. 'Death and ambush for the enemy was being plotted from balconies. In houses. In churches. Everywhere. There were homemade Molotov cocktails. Stolen guns, secret arms stashes. Communists and Gaullists uniting. Politically, that was almost unheard of.' He glanced at Sophie. 'I can't describe the mixture of dread and elation.'

She thought she understood.

'We made our way down here to find ambushed German tanks and cars in the place Saint-Michel, some of them still ablaze. We took what arms we could scavenge and left them to burn.'

Do not *think about the men trapped in the tank infernos.*

'Up went the barricades. Trees were felled, cobblestones dug up. The women came out to help.' The details appeared to be still vivid and fresh. 'Many of them had got themselves up in frocks and lipstick in honour of the moment.'

Adrenaline. Fear. Hope. Frocks.

But for her pregnancy, it would have been her mother on the street in a bright-coloured cotton dress, beautiful mouth stained scarlet, pulling up cobblestones and dragging felled trees across the road. But for Sophie, Camille would have been there, sharp-shooting from a balcony or manning a barricade.

'Your father and I were there . . . and there . . . and there.' His finger searched out points. 'If you looked down the boulevard Saint-Mich, tell me what you would see.'

'A more or less straight street?'

'Exactly. The Germans could have taken a clear run down it. So we set up a field hospital in the rue Saint-André des Arts, which runs east-west off the rue Danton. We chose it because the enemy would find it difficult to penetrate, and it would give the wounded a chance.' He shoved his left hand into his pocket. 'We knew both of us might end up there.'

The light slanted onto Christian's face, tracing the lines of harsh experience.

'Listen well. Don't make up your mind until the end.'

She looked into his eyes, her heart contorting in an unfamiliar way. 'Agreed.'

'Right from the beginning, your father was always going to fight. So was I. But, as you know, France fell early in the war . . . which meant the fighting was left to the *résistants*. We waited. We plotted. We helped underground presses produce their stuff. In the beginning we wanted to take out traitors, the *collabos*, or assassinate German officers. But the reprisals were too great. We had to make do with nobbling enemy cars or the goods trains

444

that were taking our produce to Germany. In that way, the years passed. The gallery survived.'

Cars and a lorry roared past, almost drowning him out.

'Such a strange time. We had longed for it. Planned for it. Yet, when it arrived, it was chaos.'

He signalled that they should cross the street.

'The communists wanted to be in there first because they were after full-blooded revolution. The Gaullists hated that they weren't first, but they had been ordered by the General to hold back. All of them were searching for extra arms and ammo. And all of them were beaten to it by the police, who took to the streets ahead of us.' He sounded grim. 'They wanted . . . and how they needed . . . to rescue their honour, because some of them had cooperated with the occupier.'

He led her down the rue Danton and turned right into the rue Saint-André des Arts.

Did buildings talk? She supposed they did. New mortar here, a blocked-up window there. Bullet holes. Look hard at any masonry, and the history, written into its construction, revealed itself.

Halfway down the street, Christian halted by a shop with an arched doorway. 'Pierre was carried here.'

'Was he suffering?'

He made no attempt to spare her. 'Yes. He had been hit in the back and the bullet had exited his chest. I propped him up against the wall to ease his breath. The morphine had run out and the runners hadn't returned with supplies, but I got some brandy down him.'

'Did he say anything?'

'No. But he didn't want to die.' He fanned his fingers over the pockmarked wall. A reverent gesture. 'His dying was hard.'

Was this, this recounting of his death at the place where he had died, to be close to Pierre? At last. At long last.

She stared down at the pavement where he had taken his last breaths. A coffee stain. Cigarette butts. A paper bag.

Trembling a little, she pressed the palm of her hand against the wall where Christian's had been. Willing it to render back to her its memory of her father.

He was here.

'What did he look like?'

'He was of medium height. Brown hair like yours. Fine-boned. Like you.' He stared at Sophie. 'There's much in you of him. I should have seen it. He was a serious person who loved paintings.'

Did it make it easier, knowing you were giving your life for your country? She had to believe it was so, because she could not bear to contemplate her father meeting his end with bitterness and regret.

Flights of angels singing him to his rest. The ultimate sacrifice. Dying so that others might live. It wasn't up to her to decide his state of mind when Pierre choked on his own blood. Or to garnish it with

446

consoling nostrums. If she wished to create fiction to give comfort – if indeed fiction *could* give comfort – then she must find another way.

The street was busy. People pushed past. Some hissing they should move, and fast. Others barging through.

'Who shot him?'

'Not me,' said Christian. 'Not me.' He stood aside to allow a girl in a beige mac to pass. 'I know now why you were watching me. I thought it was because I was the boss.'

'I didn't know what I was looking for.'

He gave a wry laugh.

Her gaze was glued to the messy pavement, the field hospital of only fifteen years ago. Politics was no tame thing then. No soft-boiled egg of belief to be eaten off a tray covered with a lace doily, as Alice so yearned to do. Political conviction was hard-boiled by the hatred and by the killing.

She stood foursquare in front of Christian, moved and troubled.

'You say he was shot in the back,' she said. 'You must have some idea.'

But Christian replied, 'We must have a coffee,' before picking his way along the street.

She turned for a final lingering appraisal before following him.

At a brasserie favoured by Christian in the place Saint-André, they faced each other across the table.

Sophie's cup was of thick, white china, trimmed

with a red line. She cherished it in her hands. 'In the village where I grew up, a cup like this would be considered too foreign.'

'The English are an enigma.'

'Maybe.' She swallowed a mouthful of coffee. 'Would he have known who shot him?'

'You're asking the impossible. Nothing was clear. Nobody knew what was really happening. All we knew was that we must fight.'

'I have to ask,' she said. 'I must. Did he know my mother was safe?'

He shrugged. 'He knew your mother had made it from Ariège over the Pyrenees and on to Lisbon, where she managed to get a message back to him. There was nothing after that. But he told me that he sensed, he *felt*, that she had made it to England.'

'I haven't worked out how she knew my father had been killed. And why she would ring you.'

'He'd thought of that.' Christian was matter-of-fact. 'He left instructions among his papers. "To whom it may concern", etc, which turned out to be me. He and your mother had agreed she would make for Sussex. Don't ask me why Sussex. If he didn't make it through the war a message was to be placed in the personal column of the *Sussex Daily News* on the first of every month for six months after the war ended. He said she could probably find it in the local library.'

Yes.

A memory.

A dim memory.

Yes.

Riding with Camille to Winchelford on the bus. The hurried passage to the nabob's library. Being made to sit with the Rupert Bear annual while her mother paged through newspapers.

'Camille phoned after she read the message.'

The next question was freighted with her long-standing grief. 'What did it say?'

'It said: "*La vie en rose est finie*".' His voice dropped. 'And the date.'

Her cup had found its way back into the saucer,

She turned her head and caught a whiff of petrol fumes. With astonishment, she suddenly felt homesick for Poynsdean. Worse, she felt a longing for Johnno. Johnno's normality. His tenderness.

'People still talk about your father. Your mother, too. They were both brave, resourceful people. In the early days, they were not supposed to meet. Security, you know. But . . .' he gestured at Sophie, 'clearly, they managed.'

The table adjacent to theirs was a merry one. Four students toasted each other. 'To *nos chers confrères et amis*, and to our heroic stomachs.'

She watched them. '*Was* my father shot by a Frenchman?'

'Your father was clever, committed and he had your mother. His politics made him enemies, his love affair someone to envy. The war had ground us down. All that shame and frustration, the black market and racketeering. The boredom. The constant watchfulness. Pierre wasn't a saint. No,

449

not at all. Does that bother you? He got his butter and brandy on the black market and he sold looted paintings.'

'Yes . . . it does.' She edged across the moral stepping stones and her image of the hero dissolved and remade itself. 'And no, it doesn't.'

He spoke carefully, seemingly taking time to choose each word. 'Your father was involved in the taking out of Jean Vertigan. A *collabo* in the Marais who sold information to the Boches. Vertigan's brother ran an underground gang and a black-market operation from the Place des Vosges. After Jean Vertigan's death, the gang targeted Pierre.'

'Were they here in the rue Danton? That day?'

His shrug said it all. 'Of course. The Allies were coming. They needed to save their skins. They saw to it they were on the streets, fighting.'

The adjacent table was now ordering: '*Les hamburgers*', '*Un baby Scotch on the rocks*'. The calls were riotous, good-natured, energetic.

'We had waited so long for liberation and we fought like there was no tomorrow. But ammunition was limited. There was a dead Wehrmacht soldier in the road and your father volunteered to salvage the gun and ammunition. I watched him run over to the body. At the same time, a Boche tank drove into the street and the shooting started. There were bullets everywhere. Pierre fell, but managed to take cover under a tree. *C'est tout.*' Christian looked away. 'We got him to the field hospital.'

'I know you're reluctant to say, but was it Jean Vertigan's brother?'

His answer was brief. 'It was.'

She felt a mix of hot hatred and helplessness. 'What happened to him?'

He looked past her shoulder into an arena in which she had no place.

'I never speak about it. I hate to speak about it. Because it shows what I turned into . . . but I shot him,' said Christian. 'After it was all over. Pierre was my brother. I would not let it pass. I stalked his killer. There was a shoot-out and that's when I got my bullet wound.'

'An eye for an eye.' Those biblical phrases that had dropped from Osbert's lips – they had a use after all. 'Vengeance is mine.'

'How is it possible to live with all this?' she wondered aloud.

Christian signalled to the waiter for more coffee. 'There's a very sensible philosophy, a French one, which says one must accept what is and move forward. I follow it . . .' He glanced down at his arm. 'Carrying my guilt.'

She shook her head. 'Even so.'

'But you who have come after us will never have to do so.'

'*Plus de hamburgers!*' went the shout from the adjacent table.

'I'm sorry,' she said, the words disobedient on her tongue. 'Sorry for . . .' Of all moments, this was the one where she needed to be what she

451

aspired to be: direct and brave. She took a breath. 'For . . . for suspecting you might have killed my father.'

Still she couldn't read his response until he looked directly at her over the table.

Hard-earned memories. Grief. Acceptance. A certain pride. They were all there.

He said: 'You are Pierre's daughter, and I forgive you.'

CHAPTER THIRTY-TWO

Hettie had been shopping – apparently William had not got his hands on all her savings.

'Oh, the joy!' she cried, clutching a copy of *Elle* featuring Brigitte Bardot on the front cover and a stuffed carrier bag. 'Walt came too.'

She had clattered down the stairs to Sophie's bedsit, which was so cramped they had to sit close together. Neither minded. The proximity only echoed their closeness.

'The plan is . . .' Hettie was light-hearted, giggly. 'The plan is for me to start divorce proceedings.'

'Great. But I hope it won't be too awful, Het.'

That new look settled over Hettie. Less innocent, more world-weary than usual. 'He'll cooperate because he knows I'll let it be known that he didn't tell me about his . . . war wound.' She rustled around in the carrier bag. 'Walt and I will live together in Paris until it's all over. I've persuaded Walt to stay. If it works, we might get married.' She pulled out a pair of checked Capri pants. 'Who knows if it will. Or if it won't.'

'Don't get married, Hettie. Not yet.'

held up the Capris. 'I know you don't
e in it.'
believe in *us*. We should stand by ourselves.'
'I agree. Now. All the same, I had a go at it and
you were tempted.' She smiled joyously. 'It's not
always straightforward.'

Sophie thought of Juliette Gréco and Simone de
Beauvoir. Of the men at soirées nipping out of the
musicale to meet a *cocotte*.

Of love and death.

Of the darkness inherent in sex. Its drives, its
force.

Its beauty.

Of the seduction of possessing a mind that was
free to think what it wished. The freedom, too,
to read what one wished. To argue how one
wished.

Of being a woman in 1960.

Hettie made another dive into a second bag
which, this time, produced a light-coloured trench
coat. 'Isn't this bliss?'

It was. They tried it on in turn and paraded two
steps up and two steps down. Sophie turned the
collar up and cinched the belt in tightly.

Walking down the rue de Turenne. Easy, uncon-
strained, chic. Free-thinking. The *new* woman on
the great enterprise.

The image found, a shared one.

Did it bring resolution? Composure? Serenity?

'We'll take turns to wear it,' said Hettie. She
turned her hands up in a votive gesture. 'To the

gods, I say: who would have thought life could be like this.' Sophie was silent. 'Sophs, are you all right?'

She found herself clutching Hettie. 'I'm going to phone Johnno.'

Hettie took time out from her own happiness. 'Unwise.'

'Yes. Unwise. But something's unfinished. I don't know what it is.'

'Stirring the pot, Sophs. It'll make you miserable. Don't.'

'I need to do it.'

Later on, in a telephone booth smelling of urine, she pushed a *jeton* into the slot with trembling fingers and requested a trunk call to Home Farm.

By luck, Johnno answered and his sharp intake of breath when he realised who it was contained multitudes.

'Are you all right?'

'Yes. I wanted to know if you were. If the baby was born safely?'

'Yes.' Tiny pause. 'It's worked out fine. We have a son, Robin. Linda wants another one. The farm is doing OK. The parents will be moving out soon. To a cottage.'

A shadow fell across the conversation, and which, despite all her efforts, was dissonant and disturbing. Still capable of engendering panic.

'Osbert Knox?'

'I warned him that I was watching him. He suffers from bad headaches.'

She bit her lip. 'From you hitting him, do you think?'

He was brisk. 'Possibly.' He cleared his throat. 'Alice Knox is ill. Mum visited her and said it didn't look good.'

To her surprise, she heard herself say, 'So unfair on Alice.'

'If life was fair, we'd be married,' he retorted. Harshly.

'It's hard to escape the way we're brought up. Almost impossible.'

'But you've done it.'

True. 'But often I'm still the little girl with no future except to help out in the parish, yearning for my mother.'

Precious, empty seconds ticked by.

'Johnno, I wanted . . . I wanted to say how important you were to me. I never told you.'

The words constructed a castle into which they could retreat and haul up the drawbridge.

A love affair. Parting. And grief, which does not obey orders.

'I reckon that means you're staying in Paris.'

'Yes.' It hit her then that she really was. 'Yes.'

'I'm glad you rang.'

There was no doubting the emotion.

'What's Paris like?'

She looked up and out of the telephone booth to where pigeons clustered on the roof of the block of apartments opposite.

'Filled with stories. Histories. It's beautiful. And,

456

sometimes, there's foulness. I got lost a lot. Still do. Did you know there wasn't a map of Paris until the end of the eighteenth century? In the old days, people who lived here had no idea about the rest of the city.'

There were voices in the background. One of them called out, 'Johnno!'

'I must go.'

The words appeared to clutter up her throat. 'I wanted to tell you everything was all right and I'm fine. I wanted to know that you were fine and that your life suits you. And your . . . son gives you happiness.'

'I want . . .' he began. Faltered.

Johnno wanted the winter sky louring over the marsh. The sound of the river and the wind coursing over the tussocky grass and the reeds. He had chosen to hear the high, sweet screech of swifts and feel the warm sun impregnated with the sea a couple of miles away. He wanted the sweep of his fields, the fragrance of the hay, the sound of a door shutting him into the farmhouse for the winter.

'I know,' she said. 'I understand.'

The pips sounded. 'Sophie, I won't forget you.'

'Nor I you, Johnno. But we're at peace with each other?'

'That's it,' he said.

Later, Hettie scolded Sophie in a way that she had never done before.

457

'You were trying to find out if he still thought about you. I call that selfish.'

Sophie thought it over. 'You're right. But it was useful.'

'To you, Sophie. Not to him. He's stuck. You're just at the beginning of your life.'

Hector had said something like that.

'Like you, Het,' she countered.

Hettie twisted a lock of blonde hair around her finger. 'I know what it's like to feel stuck. To yearn.'

Hettie was spot on. She *had* needed to know if Johnno had thought about her.

It *had* been selfish.

'I couldn't begin again without knowing that it had meant something,' she said. 'And it was good that we spoke.'

'But wrong,' said Hettie.

'Maybe one day one won't care about leaving a love affair. Will that be any better?'

'Still wrong,' said Hettie.

Sophie sent her a look. It was returned. 'All right, I shouldn't have done it,' said Sophie. 'You can help me with a penance.'

Fifteen minutes later, they were picking over the soaps in the pharmacy.

Inhaling the rose one. The sweet, musty odour of crushed petals that meant early summer. A meal spread on a table under a tree.

Inhaling the lavender one. Evergreen woodiness. Hot sun. The *terroir* of the dry south.

She held out the lavender bar for Hettie to smell. 'I think this is best.'

But she also bought the rose bar.

Quite an outlay. But necessary.

Afterwards, they settled themselves at a café close to a post office and Sophie packed up the lavender soap.

The new, sharper Hettie observed. 'Washing your conscience clean?'

Sophie wrote the address. 'Mrs Osbert Knox, The Rectory . . .'

'I was right,' said Hettie, satisfied.

Sophie imagined its arrival. Being carried up to Alice in the bed she had so triumphantly occupied solo. The unwrapping. Lifting the bar to her nose. Smelling its reputedly healing scent. Perhaps she would think of lavender growing in the fields. Of sun bearing down. Perhaps she would think: *I have never had soap this luxurious. Anything so luxurious.*

In the note, Sophie had written, 'This is for you, Alice, and not for the parish. I hope you enjoy it.'

She pushed the bar of rose soap over to Hettie. 'But this one's for you.'

Very early the following day, Sophie headed down the rue de Turenne. Unsure where she was going. Nerves jangling. Thoughts muddled.

Distress saw her gravitating towards Notre-Dame and its astonishing Gothic certainties, to gaze up at her favourite rose window. The earliest of them. To think that it had witnessed the roster of human life since the first mason had placed his chisel on the stone and raised a hammer.

Fellow early risers speckled the square, a number filing into the cathedral.

She observed them carefully.

The mysteries they would seek out and their worship were not for her. Yet, she envied them.

She felt . . . she felt what?

Despite what she now knew, despite everything, the raggedy, motley pieces of her spirit were refusing to knit together over the hollow, bereaved spaces that she carried.

You're just at the beginning of your life, said Hettie. (And Hector.)

Turning away, she walked in no particular direction. Or, rather, without conscious decision.

Perhaps it was unsurprising, then, that she ended up in rue Danton.

This was where her father had taken up arms for the last time. But the present street scene, so busy and indifferent, could never properly enshrine the sacrifice. Or the violence.

What a business death was.

She imagined . . . she imagined holding his hand, oh so tenderly, as he lay wounded on the pavement. Feeling the once strong, capable fingers, the soon-to-be-extinguished pulse of the father she had never known.

'So is life a business.' He managed a smile. 'Forget this war and go and see.'

Led by an instinct that she couldn't name, she found herself in the street where the children's bookshop was situated.

She halted in front of the window, dazzled and enchanted. A dragon breathing fire occupied the centre of the display. Facing it was a model of St George, shield aloft. At his feet played a rabbit and a duck whose stuffing was spilling out of his tail. A magical light played over the tableau. Behind was ranged a selection of books.

The Children Who Lived in a Barn
The Princess and the Pea
Melissa Ann
Five Children and It

She looked. She digested. Swallowed tears. She also laughed at the duck and his outraged expression.

It was of no matter that she was solitary. That she had learnt the lessons of autonomy early. That she was in a country that was strange, but not. That she might never have family. That she might never marry. Probably out of choice.

Or she might.

But here was magic. Enchantment. The promise of escape. Dreams. Discoveries.

And a source of the power to create them.

She reached out to take it.

A while later, she walked across the Place des Vosges towards the gallery. On the way she had

461

stopped for a coffee and a croissant. These were settled happily in her stomach.

Fresh energy. Fresh thoughts, which she would bring to her work. She was late and was counting on Christian giving her a little leeway. But she couldn't be sure.

'If you want to continue to work for me,' he said, 'you must put your heart and soul into it. You must put your conscience on hold while I consider what to do with the paintings. It doesn't matter who your father was, because if you let me down, then . . .'

She came to a halt.

Occupying the bench nearest to Gallery Martin was a now familiar figure.

Raf.

Beside him was a dog. Large-ish. Brown fur. Big paws. Raf had his arm around it and was talking into his ear. The dog was listening.

She moved towards him.

'Raf, I didn't know you had a dog. You never said.'

He looked up.

The notes of *Les Barricades Mystérieuses* spilled through her head. Her spirits lifted, almost soared. She heard the fanfare of new emotion, felt the shudder of desire and the sense that she – almost – belonged.

Raf smiled. '*Bonjour*, Sophie.'

EPILOGUE
THIRTY YEARS LATER

'The Peter and Dog series have sold in huge numbers around the world,' said the interviewer. He had done his homework and named a figure. 'What do you think is the secret of their success?'

'Perhaps,' replied the author, 'because telling a story is my main consideration. We so badly need stories. In mine there's usually a battle between the underdog and his or her oppressor. But it's never quite clear until the end who will win.'

'In Book Five, Peter and Dog rescue a swarm of bees . . . In Book Six, they save a minke whale trapped in fishing nets and in Book Seven, they mount an assault on a lorry transporting sheep in vile conditions. Are these subjects for children?'

'Children are funny, demanding, miniature Neros,' the author replied. 'Vulnerable but also brave. They tell me exactly what I should write and what they want. They crave adventure and deep affection. They love secrets and riding to the rescue. They want their minds to be filled with magic and the promise that all will be well.'

'Do you have a favourite?'

'Maybe . . . maybe the first book where Peter and Dog go off to find treasure.'

'And who are Peter and Dog?'

She took her time to answer. 'They're me.'

ACKNOWLEDGEMENTS

I would like to thank my editor, Sarah Hodgson, and the team at Corvus Books. They are amazing, totally supportive and extremely generous with their time and expertise. I am privileged to be published by them. Plus huge tribute to Amber Burlinson, who so nobly and professionally wrestled the manuscript into shape.

Especial thanks to Isabelle Grey, who held the faith, and to my agent, Judith Murray, and all at Greene & Heaton.

Especial thanks are also owed also to Penrose Halson, author of *Marriages Are Made in Bond Street* (Macmillan, 2016), Anne Sebba, author of *Les Parisiennes* (Weidenfeld & Nicholson, 2016) and Karen Webb, author of *A Stranger in Paris* (Impress Books, 2018), who generously allowed me to make use of material from their excellent and inspiring books.

Other books which proved invaluable are: *Paris in the Fifties* by Stanley Karnow (Three Rivers Press, 1997), *Walks Through Lost Paris* by Leonard Pitt (Shoemaker & Hoard, 2006), *Parisians: An Adventure History of Paris* by Graham Robb

(Picador, 2010) and *Bad Blood* by Lorna Sage (Fourth Estate, 2001). I have taken details and scenarios from all the above and acknowledge my debt. Any mistakes are mine.

My beloved friends have done their customary hand-holding bit and I send them much gratitude. To Benjamin, Adam, Lucinda, Alexia, Flora, Eleanor, Henry, Fin and Arto, I send my love.